## About the Author

Eve Seymour is the author of nine novels and has had a number of short stories broadcast on BBC Radio Devon. Educated in Malvern at an girls' boarding school, which she detested, she spectacularly underachieved. Sixth form in Cheltenham proved a lot more interesting, enjoyable and productive.

After a short and successful career in PR in London and Birmingham, she married and disappeared to Devon. Five children later, she returned and began to write seriously. In a bid to make her work as authentic as possible, she has bent the ears of numerous police officers, firearms officers, scenes of crime, the odd lawyer and United Nations personnel. She also works by day as a freelance editorial consultant, specialising in crime fiction.

Eve lives with her second husband and often has a houseful of offspring, sons-in-law, partners, and a growing tribe of little ones. Nomadic by nature, she is planning another move very soon.

🐦@EveSeymour

www.

# VIXENHEAD

## EVE SEYMOUR

**harper impulse**

A division of HarperCollins*Publishers*

www.harpercollins.co.uk

Harper*Impulse* an imprint of
HarperCollins*Publishers*
1 London Bridge Street
London SE1 9GF

www.harpercollins.co.uk

A Paperback Original 2017

First published in Great Britain in ebook format by Harper*Impulse* 2017

A catalogue record for this book
is available from the British Library

ISBN:9780008240868

Set in Birka by Palimpsest Book Production Limited,
Falkirk, Stirlingshire

Printed and bound in Great Britain

For John
The father of our children.

*In the beginning*

*D*awn breaks and the body of the boy is almost imperceptible in its still-grey light. There are no obvious marks upon him, no apparent cause of death. His eyes are closed, lids tinged Delphic blue. His body, which is small for his age, curls in the way it once did in his mother's womb. Safe and warm. Now dreams he once dreamt lie smashed around him like falling stars. Not for him a future of bright city lights or rural anonymity. No rough and tumble with the lads. No jibes thrown or hurled in boozy pumped-up heat of the moment. No lover awaits him. No marriage or hope of becoming a good old boy and passing on a legacy through his children and their children. For him there is no tomorrow. From this moment on he will be forever in the dark.

# Chapter 1

*Present Day*

It kicks off the moment Tom spots his photograph in our county magazine.

"For God's sake, how the hell did that happen?"

It all began with a party at Lily Gin's, a popular cocktail bar off the Promenade. Free booze. Ear-bleeding beat. Everyone hollering. The local newspaper I work for has a sister magazine that held a joint bash there for advertisers and the great and good of Cheltenham. Their way of saying 'thank you'. A roaming rookie photographer snapping folk glad-handing is the source of Tom's ire. It's strange because he isn't confrontational or quick to anger. Not chilled, like me, but quiet and mostly silent with an undertow of edge that I find a bit Darcy-like and dead exciting. Tom blowing his stack isn't a thrill at all; it's worrying.

Personally, I think how nice he looks. "It's a great snap." It really is. The picture isn't posed. We are deep in conversation. Slightly turned away from the camera, the scar at his temple that makes him look dangerous and sexy is more prominent than usual; dark-blonde beard neatly trimmed; his nose with a slight kink at the bridge, full kissable lips close to my cheek. For once we are captured together, which makes a change. Anyone viewing my photo album for the past few years could be forgiven for thinking I'm single.

"Fuck's sake, you *know* I hate having my photograph taken."

To the point of phobia, but as it was clicked, with Tom unawares, by some newbie photographer, I can't see what the problem is. Sleek, monumentally happy and relaxed, Tom is whispering something in my ear that makes me smile, although I can't for the life of me think what it was, mostly because I'm now half into my dress, trying to get ready for work.

"It's only the county mag," I point out, finally zipping myself up.

"*Yours*," he says, fury in his eyes, as if I am personally liable. I don't bother to point out the inaccuracy of his accusation.

"For goodness' sake, I'm not the editor, Tom. You know very well I don't write a thing for the magazine these days." Still, he glowers. "Look, I'm sorry," I say, spreading my hands, thinking that I really should be heading out. It was all right for Tom to chunter on. He'd got a day off from the restaurant where he works as a chef.

"I told that bloody photographer to go away."

"She's only a kid." Which explained why the celebrity especially invited didn't get so much as a look-in, to the embarrassment of all.

"I never wanted to go to the launch in the first place," he growls, prowling around our tiny sitting room.

Didn't you? I can't recall any protest at the time, but think it best not to say so. "Well, you did. It's done now," I say, softening my tone. In my experience with men, it's never a good idea to get arsey. Not really in my nature in any case. Others remark that I'm laid-back to the point of horizontal, a family trait, care of my mother. Somehow my chalk-and-cheese relationship with Tom works. Classic attraction of opposites.

"In a week's time it will be in the recycling bin," I add. "Forget about it."

"How can I forget when it's online for the world to see?" His normal deep tone is high and tight. How someone raised in South London can sound as if they have Welsh vocal cords remains a conundrum.

"Jesus, if you looked like the Elephant Man, I could understand it but..."

"It's an invasion of my privacy."

I don't know whether to laugh or cry. I appreciate that Tom is a private person. He's not into social media like all my friends. He's more of a low-profile, right-under-the-radar kind of guy. I get all that, but this is an extreme reaction by any standard. Time to shake him out of it. "For goodness' sake, lighten up."

"Don't you dare fucking speak to me like that."

My cheeks never flush because I have a sallow complexion. Heat fills my face as if I'd been plunged head first into hot water. "Will you please keep your voice down," I hiss. "You'll wake Reg." Reg is my younger brother. He's actually called Max; more suitable for his rock god, shag everything that moves, image, but I christened him Reg years ago because I thought it would annoy him. Somehow, it stuck.

Tom's expression is one part grimace, two parts hauteur. "I don't think that's very likely, do you?"

He has a point. Reg, who has the lifestyle of a bat, stumbled in around four in the morning and is dead to the world. But I could do without Tom's sarcasm.

I try to outstare him and fail. The stubble on his cheeks, the set of his jaw, the rawness and slightly lost expression in his eyes, which are the colour of dark rum make him despite myself, maddeningly attractive.

"Bloody hell, Tom. Are there to be no photographs at our wedding?"

He blanches. "What wedding?"

He was joking, wasn't he? He means no photographs, no twenty thousand quid down the toilet matrimony? Stupidly, I burble on. "And family snaps with kids—"

Now he looks as if I plunged *his* head into hot water. "Kids?"

"The ones we're going to have." I practically screech, thinking the row has taken a surprising and horribly revealing turn. Didn't we discuss this? I'm sure we did.

Lines set into his forehead contract. "I don't want them." His brutal words pound into me, smacking the air out of my lungs. Dear God, he means it.

Had I been kicked in the gut by a mule while drinking ten double Stollys in quick succession, I couldn't feel more wounded. At thirty-seven years of age, my biological clock, unlike some of my friends' timepieces, ticked, tocked and apparently stalled. I have many ambitions but, as much as I have a life plan, I envisage children being part of them. My mum gave birth to my brother when she was forty-three. Everyone says she looks younger than her years and that she passed that same 'youth' gene on to me. In my head I reckon I'm roughly thirty, same age as my kid brother. Surely state of mind and disposition count for something when it comes to reproduction? Besides, Tom is younger and in his prime. Even if my fertility is jeopardised by age, there is always adoption or fostering. To know that the man I love simply does not want children leaves me stunned. Bereft. Desolate.

"Besides," he continues quietly, "it's not really on the cards, is it?"

Words that threaten to tumble out of my open mouth halt in the back of my throat, retreat and expire. Had they lived, they would have gone something like: "YOU BASTARD. WHAT ABOUT ME? YOU NEVER SAID YOU DIDN'T WANT KIDS." So much for my horizontal 'hey man' and chilled disposition.

I gawp at him, trying to contain the hurt in my expression. Denial dribbles out of me. "You don't mean that."

He stares stony-eyed – so much worse than saying something.

"You're being daft, Tom." My voice is dead shaky.

"Am I?" This is not said with rhetorical intonation, but bone-shaking affirmation. Doesn't he realise what his words are doing to me? Doesn't he see that he is not only trampling on but also destroying my dreams?

"Tom," I say, nervously, trying to dislodge the unexpected

shard of fear stuck fast in my soul. "We really should talk it through."

"This," he says, rustling the shiny pages and thrusting the magazine in my face, "is what we need to discuss."

Something in his expression, unnerving and creepy, alarms me. Dumbfounded, I realise what it is.

*Tom is afraid.*

I swallow, glance at my watch, dance from one foot to the other. "Look, I've really got to go. Elliott will have me spit-roasted if I'm late again. Can we talk this evening?"

He doesn't answer. Standing there, bare-chested, abs rippling impressively, he seems outwardly inviolate yet also vulnerable, reminding me of myself when we first met. When he runs his fingers through his thick mane of hair as if he single-handedly carries the weight of the world's problems, I have a sudden, urgent desire to dump my bag, take off my clothes and fuck him right there and then. Instead, I ask him what he is doing for the day.

He shrugs, the anger dissipating from his voice. "This and that. Might go for a swim."

I brighten up. Displacement activity, I think. "Will you sort dinner?"

At the mention of the word 'dinner', his field of expertise, he relaxes. "I'll pick up something, a bottle of wine too."

I read contrition in his eyes. "Fine," I say, smiling with relief, as I make for the door.

"But what about Reg? Will he be joining us?" Tom's inflexion is arid. Why does he have to spoil what I assumed is a truce? Admittedly, things between us have not been easy since Reg pitched up. My thirty-year-old 'baby brother' came to stay for a few days that turned into three weeks. Since our old hippie mum moved to Australia with her new husband ten years earlier, and our dad, a retired dentist, lives in the States and has done for many years, I feel responsibility for him. In my head, I'm sort of in loco parentis. If I tell Reg this, he'll laugh in my face. I love him, yet can't help count the days before he flies to LA with his band Robberdog. He plans to pay Dad a visit while he's there, to 'reconnect,' he maintains. I don't know what I feel about that, other than the fact that our father will throw a fit when he sees the state of Reg's buckled teeth.

I assure Tom I'll sort it with Reg. Once more, I turn to escape.

"Roz," he calls after me.

"Yeah?"

Tom moves like a ghost. One moment on the opposite side of the room, the next right up close, hypnotic eyes melting into mine. When he reaches out I drop my bag, the intoxicating smell of warm, naked skin and man enveloping me.

His mouth finds mine. Lust radiates from my brain, through my chest to my groin. He doesn't ask me to stay. He has no need. He simply hitches up my dress, slides down my knickers and takes me there and then in the sitting room, up against the wall. Fool that I am, pulsing with desire, I'm willing.

# Chapter 2

Praying the darkening late-January sky doesn't unleash its payload, I run all the way from my rental in All Saints Road to a drab seventies-style office block in the centre of town. It usually takes under fifteen minutes at a good walking pace. Today, I bomb it in ten, which is impressive considering my mind is blown with disappointment and my legs feel vaguely sticky and tremble from instant and urgent sex. Tom's behaviour is counter-intuitive for someone who professes never to want children. On my race to work, this thought consumes me.

Elliott takes one look at my shiny, perspiring face and hikes a hairy eyebrow. "Miss Outlaw, so glad you can join us."

"Erm... sorry, I got held..."

He raises one pudgy hand, the thin band of his wedding ring almost buried in his fleshy finger. My boss doesn't believe in excuses, no more than he believes in God, or accidents. Suspicion, the single most important attribute for a journalist, or so he tells me, is as firmly enmeshed into his corpulent physique as his DNA. I believe curiosity is a pretty good attribute too. Elliott also maintains that this is why he gets to do all the juicy investigative stuff instead of me. When I once argued the point, he left me in no doubt about where I stood.

"I don't want you landing me in court."

"Thanks for the vote of confidence."

"You're simply not ready, Rosamund. Didn't your mother ever tell you that you have to walk before you can run?"

My mother told me a lot of things, mainly about auras, finding my bliss and the necessity of being centred, but walking before running was not one of them. A product of the hippie generation, she spent her youth in a commune in Totnes, Devon, where she met my dad. Frankly, I count myself lucky not to be born with a name like Zoflora Moonstone, particularly as I have weird-coloured eyes that are a similar hue to the gem. Put it this way, my parents were free spirits until the spliffy glow wore off and they decided to rejoin the real world. Safe to say, she believes in us kids 'going for it', as she puts it, which is why she never smashes Reg's dreams and tells him to find a proper career. To be fair, she never warned me of the perils of aimlessly flitting from one dead-end job to the next well into my thirties either. When I finally decided to settle down and get a degree in journalism, admittedly from a little-known college that punched above its weight to obtain uni status, it wasn't due to any parental guidance.

With our faraway parents, my brother and I have a strange, more complex, relationship. Physically absent for much of our adult lives, in the past five, our dad is displaying more interest than during the previous twenty. Age and impending mortality does that, but it's hellish confusing for offspring.

I glance over to Helen's desk. Our sports correspondent, she is one of the few full-time staff. Most of our crew are contributors who write columns in return for a by-line. God only knows what the National Union of Journalists would make of that. I can be writing about counterfeit items one day and interviewing a local publican about his plans for a new venture the next. Book and theatre reviews sometimes fall into my lap and that's great because it means I have a constant delivery of brand-new releases and get to see all the best plays fresh from the West End. For a couple of days a week, I basically go where Elliott, the editor, and hulk of a man, sends me. Jack-of-all-trades, I also knock out blogs for any company that will pay; the odd bit of copywriting when I can lay my hands on it. I'm not a workaholic. By nature, I'm lazy. Financial needs drive me. In short, I'm a woman trying to make up for decades of drifting and earning a pittance. Not good. Unlike when my parents belatedly decided to make waves, you're now considered over the hill in the career stakes after the age of thirty-five.

Helen grins and winks. Goodness, is my mascara smudged? Surely, my knickers aren't caught in my dress? I surreptitiously smooth down the creases and run an index finger under each eye. I badly want to talk to her about Tom but, judging from the predatory light in Elliott's eye, he has my day already mapped out.

"Get yourself down to the train station," he says.

Fabulous. London beckons, or could it be Oxford, Birmingham, perhaps? "Where am I going?"

"Nowhere. You're going to interview train users about the travelling experience at Cheltenham Spa."

"Is this a wind-up?" Purleese, surely we have more important issues to report than this?

"Spend what remains of the morning there and, this afternoon, two o'clock sharpish, you're interviewing Detective Sergeant Mike Shenton."

At this I brighten, dare I say. My nosy gene kicks in good and proper. "Terrific. About what exactly?"

"The force are—"

"Can't call it that any more. It's a police service."

"Whatever," Elliott says, "although it's pleasing to see that you're paying attention to detail at long last." Why is it that Elliott always manages to turn my desire to impress into an insult? "The police are running a big initiative to target sexual crime and crime against the person. You are covering it."

"It's such a wide subject, wouldn't it be better as a rolling news story? We could expand it over several weeks?"

Elliott briefly closes his thick-lidded eyes. "Did they teach you nothing at that college of yours?" *College?* Before I can respond he taps his watch and thrusts me a dirty look. I get it. Scarper.

Train stations are hubs enabling travellers to get from A to B. That is their sole purpose in life. They are not supposed to be entertainment centres or the hippest place in which to meet your best mate for coffee. It's stating the obvious and why, whether coming or going, nobody wants to be rail-stepped by someone like me and especially on a day when the wind is howling and the rain is sheeting. The only good news is the cafeteria on the platform, from where I purchase several cartons of coffee. Variations on a similar theme emerge. Frankly, I could have written them myself from the comfort of my own kitchen table: '*For what they charge for the rail fare they could fly us to the moon*'; '*The service to London is crap.*' One glossily dressed woman complained: '*You should see the state of the toilets*,' although which toilets she is referring to I have no clue because she pings off her impossibly high heels and leaps into a taxi, speeding off before I can ask her to be more explicit.

Fed up and freezing, I decide to slope back home. Tom's outburst and white anger bother me. Correction, it undermines and concerns me. His challenge to my worldview makes me question the entire nature of our relationship. I think I get him and now realise I don't. I think I understand myself, too, and that, also, seems elusive. To my mind, I'm a strong resourceful individual. In my heart, I'm a mushy mess. If Tom doesn't want marriage and kids, really doesn't want them, where does that leave us? Is it an emotional deal-breaker? Honest answer: I don't know.

Nabbing a cab, I turn up with an hour to kill before my appointment later at the police station in Hesters Way. I don't want sex and I don't think I can iron things out, hey presto, but checking in might, at least, help me to appreciate my lover's point of view. Maybe he's plain scared of being a dad. Lots of blokes are like that. His parents died in a boat accident when he was eleven and an elderly godmother brought him up, a lady I never had the chance to meet because she passed away not long after we met. Despite the tragedy of his childhood Tom never gives the impression of having a messed up life, and he rarely talks about his past, although it would be fairly impossible to emerge from that sort of thing unscathed. And true, I occasionally catch him with a lost look in his eyes. My upbringing, punctured by divorce, seems like a saunter in the sunlight by comparison. When Tom walked into my life he seemed such a good fit because he was so different. We certainly clicked on a sexual level. Naively, I never factored in his apparent lack of commitment when it came to kids.

I open the door and almost trip over Tom's sturdy sports bag. About to call out, I hear his low voice humming from the kitchen. Probably talking to Reg, although one o'clock in the afternoon counts as dawn in my brother's eyes.

Intrigued, I creep towards the kitchen door, which is ajar. I hope to surprise him, in a good way, of course, but instinctively I hold back and, as sneaky as it is, find myself listening. It becomes clear that Tom is on a mobile, a fairly rare event. Do I imagine a thread of panic in Tom's low and urgent tone?

"Don't you understand? Anyone could see it... What do you mean, hang loose?... It's all right for you, but what if there's another cock-up?... She doesn't suspect... No way... Well, you'd better find out." I blink. Was *she* me? My head spins. Gripped with nerves, I'm only thinly able to process that the person on the other end of the line is delivering a lecture. Eventually, Tom says, "Yes, I think that's best... When?... No sooner?... All right, if you say so, the usual place... Wednesday." He hangs up.

Now I was in a bind. Burst in and shout "Honey, I'm home," better still, "What the hell was that all about?" Or should I hightail it back to the front door and pretend I never set foot in the house? Crushed with indecision for all of two seconds, I blunder in at the very point the landline rings.

"No worries, I'll get it," I say, retreating and glad of the diversion.

"Is Tom there?" I recognise the voice immediately. It's the sour-faced manager of the hotel and restaurant where Tom works. A call like this spells trouble. At once, I see my rare evening alone with Tom vanishing into next week.

"I'll get him."

Tom pops his head around the door. "For me?" He is unflustered and not remotely guilty. He is back to his default position: calm as a secluded reservoir in high summer.

"Work." I hand him the phone.

I leave him to it and stroll into the kitchen. Surprisingly, Reg's laptop is open on the kitchen table. My naturally inquisitive nature kicks in. At a glance I see that it's open on Facebook. Tom is one of those people who 'lurk' but don't post. *What's he up to?*

I look. Compute. Stare. A strange buzzing sound rattles through my brain, only half of which absorbs what I'm viewing.

A good-looking brunette called Stephanie Charteris looks back at me. Casually dressed. Smiling. Pleased with life. A more detailed inspection reveals an oval-shaped face, olive skin and bone structure. Only her eyes, brown like Tom's, are different to mine. Her hair would be similar too, except mine is currently dyed deep magenta. Other than that, she's a dead ringer for me.

Unable to take it in, the other part of my brain jots down the setting. A castle with a cannon in the foreground. Park with benches. People sitting, cartons of coffee clutched, some eating sandwiches. My eyes scroll down to the message: 'Happy times. I miss you so much.' Instantly, I recoil and my blood sprints. What is Tom doing viewing a woman who looks so similar to me?

"There was a mix-up over a game order," Tom says, striding in. I jump aside, desperate to quiz him, yet not keen to be caught snooping. A pulse flutters above my top lip that I can't control as Tom, with a cool half-smile and without a word, reaches over, closes down the page and switches off the laptop. He doesn't explain that he borrowed it from Reg, although I know this is not unusual and that Reg doesn't mind.

I nod rapidly. My skin feels raw, irritated, physically reflecting my state of mind. Jealousy is an alien emotion to me, yet following on from the morning's revelation, I register something dark, bitter and corrosive, which is how I imagine it to feel.

"A potential crisis averted," he says. "Didn't expect you to be home," he adds with a loose grin, as if we might have an action replay of sex in the sitting room.

I force a smile that hurts my face. "Forgot something." Improvising, I swipe an apple from the fruit bowl. "Gotta go. Appointment at the police station," I say, with as much throw-away style as I can manage. Colour instantly drains from Tom's face.

"What?"

"For work," I say uneasily, making a fast exit. Inside, my heart is thumping.

# Chapter 3

"Are you getting this all down?"

Detective Sergeant Mike Shenton seems like a no-nonsense copper. After making a wisecrack about my unusual surname, we get down to business. Except I don't.

Tom's phone conversation spins around inside my head, each damning sentence equal to the combination numbers of a safe. However I rotate, slice and dice them, I cannot open the contents.

"Mmm? Yes, of course, you said that violence was nothing like the media presented." I recite like teacher's pet, the statement an own-goal seeing as I am part of the 'meedja', but I can't give a rat's arse. "We're more likely to be the victim of someone we know than be attacked by a stranger."

Detective Sergeant Mike Shenton's Air Force-blue blue eyes smile back, my reward for giving him the impression I'm keeping up. He's nice looking, clean-shaven and with even features, but I'm too ensnared in analysis of Tom's phone call to pay much attention.

"That's not to say you can't take simple measures," Shenton reminds me. "And of course if you suspect..."

I tune out. *She doesn't suspect…* Suspect what? If the alarm in Tom's voice is anything to go by, I don't think a nice surprise is on Tom's agenda. And who the hell was on the other end of the line? Could it be 'that' woman – the pretty brunette on Facebook? If so, oh my God. Was that why he doesn't want a child? Does he ever plan to marry me? Is he cheating?

Attempting to shut Tom off and look interested, I gaze at Shenton, who is still talking. Elliott is a dinosaur for detail and I worry I missed something important. I nod and grin as Shenton runs through a list of bog-standard safety precautions that any sensible person past the age of twenty should automatically know. Two stand out from the crowd: walk with confidence and, if suspecting trouble, notify the police. Hmmm. A mate of mine once alerted the police when a brawl broke out in the street. He got arrested.

Thirty minutes later, I wrap up the session with my tame copper and head back to the newspaper office. Helen is out and Elliott, thank the deities, is tucked away in his office engaged in a high-level meeting with the publisher of our newspaper and sister magazine. Rumour has it that both are in trouble. This should bother me more than it does, but I'm a glass-half-full merchant. Or I was until Tom took a dirty great gulp out of it.

Sneaking a quick glance over my shoulder, I slip my laptop from my bag, log on to Facebook and check out the brunette. I gawp again at the pile of ruins in the background and wonder where exactly it is.

Stephanie Charteris's profile tells me that she lives in Shropshire, not a part of the world with which I'm familiar.

My face clouds when I see how old she is: twenty-sodding-nine, nearly a decade younger than me. It turns out that she is a sales advisor for Argo Homes, a national property developer. Clearly, she has friends, both male and female. She also has a fat black cat called 'Theo'. She makes no political statements. She doesn't push what she does for a living. She doesn't get into rants or scrapes.

My eyes strain so tight they feel as if they are about to eject from my eye-sockets. I squint again, but there is no mistake. In one photograph, Stephanie holds a baby of indeterminate sex. I shoot through the rest of her details but there is no other reference, pictorial or otherwise. Could be anybody's child, yet from her wide-hipped stance, the evident pride in her eyes, I don't think so. Not every mother plasters their profile with their offspring, especially if they are uber-private about their personal life. More common ground with Tom, I think, jolting with alarm from a ton of mashed-up feelings. The only saving grace is that Tom does not appear in any of her photographs. My relief lasts less than a nano-second. Why would he? Tom doesn't allow a digital or pictorial record of his existence.

With the beginnings of a headache, I check out new development sites in Shropshire. Not one belongs to Argo Homes. Click and tap, a scroll through the website reveals two developments in the neighbouring county of Herefordshire. Shared with two other developers, the first site encompasses six hundred houses that include starter, town house, and three-, four- and five-bedroom properties geared for working people and families. Another smaller development in which Argo is the sole developer seems more appropriate for the retired. My eyes graze through the spiel and cut to the chase. I write down the telephone number of the sales office at which there are three advisors, including Stephanie Charteris, her name seared into my psyche with the equivalent of a branding iron.

I get rid of the page and wonder how to talk to Tom later. Should I confront him and reveal what I overheard, and entirely ruin the evening? Perhaps it would be best if I wait and see if he speaks first. There could be a simple explanation, surely, one I'm missing? I remind myself that I rarely flare up at everyday inconveniences and that I'm a slow-burner in a crisis. Yet this has the makings of a catastrophe and one I'm not sure I can handle. Honestly, I feel impossibly jumpy – an alien emotion. Truth is I love Tom. I envisage spending the rest of my life with him. I planned a family and...

In a dilemma, I do what all women do in this predicament: phone a friend. My best mate, Victoria Braiche, is an actor, code for she works in a call centre. I'm a little unfair. She used to have a top London agent, did a couple of commercials and took small parts in Rep and, according to her, had a walk-on part in a gangster movie nobody's heard of. When she isn't 'resting', she acts in local amateur productions held at the Playhouse at the end of the Bath Road. Last time I saw her, she played a 'weeping woman'.

"Vick, it's me, Roz." All my friends shorten my name.

"Hiya. Luckily, you caught me on a toilet break."

I squirm at the very idea. These call centres work their staff like dogs. "Are you free straight after work for a quick chat? I'm having dinner with Tom, but if I could pop in first..." My voice peters out. Vick knows me well. She'll fathom that something's up.

"You okay?"

"Yes." No.

"Half-past five?"

"Fabulous, see you then."

Elliott's door swings open and burly men's voices bloat the dry office air. I put my cell phone away and get busy looking busy. A stout man glides past and throws me a disdainful glance. Probably my hair, although it's not as striking as the peacock blue I sported last month, my way of paying homage to Picasso's Blue period. Not really – Vick made the facetious remark and it remains a kind of private joke between us. Thank God he can't see my latest tattoo – a humming bird – discreetly positioned on my left shoulder blade and covered by my warm winter dress. Two other men follow. They are dressed in suits with ties. Official. Elliott fills the doorframe of his office, hulking and broody. I can tell that things are bad, but don't say a word. I've my own shit to deal with.

"All right?" Elliott finally says when they are gone.

I nod.

Anything but.

# Chapter 4

Vick lives in a terraced home that makes an IKEA interior look sterile. Muted Cream. Muted Blue. Scandi-Mute. In person, she is not in the least washed out. Big-boned, she has a wide, open and honest-looking face, great skin and generous figure. Her nose is straight. Her eyes are hazel, flecked with green. Unlike me, her hair is short, curly and blonde. She wears jeans with a cerise-coloured shrug over a French-grey shirt. She is the kind of person who engenders trust. Anyone would talk to her freely and reveal his or her secrets. Obviously in the wrong career, she'd make a great investigative journalist.

"Coffee?"

"Lovely," I say. "How's it going?"

We sit at her scrubbed-pine kitchen table. Nothing on the work surfaces bar essentials: a toaster, kettle and coffee-making machine. Makes my kitchen look like a hoarder's paradise.

"Not bad. Work is shit."

I watch as she spoons coffee beans into a grinder. Serious stuff. Me, I reach for the nearest jar of instant.

"But I had a call from my new agent today." She says it with a flourish, a 'ta-da' in her tone.

"Really?"

Vick offers a toothy grin. "Don't look so surprised."

"Didn't mean it like that. You know I've always been your biggest fan."

"I couldn't have kept the faith without you."

"Nonsense. So what's she got planned?"

I don't hear the answer because it's blasted out by the sound of beans pulverised to dust. The smell is better than the blare.

"Sorry," she says, screwing up her eyes in apology.

"You were saying?"

"Only a role in some Agatha Christie number." She finishes with a glorious smile.

"Wow, when did you find out?"

"Message on my answerphone when I got back. I phoned her straight away and bingo!"

"God, tell me more."

"Later," she says, a stern expression in her eyes. "What gives?"

I take a breath and tell her everything about my morning with Tom, bar the sex, and then motor through the overheard conversation and my find on Facebook in the afternoon. Vick fiddles with the coffee-making contraption.

"He went absolutely schiz," I say, miserable at the memory.

She puffs out through her cheeks. "Blimey, that's a lot to take in. So are you suggesting Tom is cheating on you?"

"I don't know, but after his revelations about no children and, frankly, no wedding, not that this bothers me so much," I add hastily, thinking that I'm a liar, "it seems a distinct possibility." Now that I say it aloud, the full force of its implications shrivels me.

"Sugar and cream?" she says, pouring out a thick stream of strong dark liquid into two white mugs, no adornment.

"Cream, please."

She pushes my drink towards me; sits down opposite. "The kid in the Facebook photograph could be someone else's."

I agree without conviction.

"Repeat the conversation you overheard again."

I do, word for horrible word.

"So, he's going to meet someone, maybe this woman, on Wednesday," Vick suggests. Less than a week's time, I think anxiously. "Simple. Follow him."

"Wednesday's our busiest day at the newspaper. I can't take off."

"But I could."

"You can't. He'll recognise you."

Vick arches an eyebrow and flashes a smile. "I'm an actor, mistress of disguise."

I have a sudden vision of my best friend dressed in a raincoat with a false moustache and spectacles with milk-bottle lenses. Scrub that thought. "You won't be allowed to take time off work."

"Who said anything about asking? I'll throw a sickie."

"They'll fire you."

"So what? If this role comes off, I'm packing my job in anyway."

"Goodness," I stutter. This really is a dream come true and I'm pleased for her. I'm less thrilled by her next piece of news.

"Could be away for several months. It's a touring theatre company."

I make all the right noises despite the sense of impending abandonment.

"Anyway, this isn't really helping. Why don't you check Tom's phone?"

I baulk at the prospect. It displays such a blatant lack of trust. If Tom did that to me, I'd be furious. I burble the same.

"Desperate measures," Vick says, as if Tom's behaviour hands me carte blanche to do as I please. Truth is, part of me doesn't want to know. If I find a string of texts or calls to an unknown number, I'm sunk.

"Pity he isn't more active online," Vick muses. "A quick search could yield all manner of results."

Simply because Tom appears to have no digital footprint does not rule out that somewhere, some place he is as busy as hell online. There's the Dark Net that people keep banging on about, usually with heavy associations with child sexual exploitation. Hell, what am I thinking? Thankfully, Vick interrupts my more wild-card thoughts. "What about the castle?"

"What about it? A pile of ruins isn't that identifiable."

Vick flicks a smile, tips her head to one side. Her earrings catch the light and jangle. "You know, there could be a rational explanation. I mean the woman could be ancient history. A hanger-on. She could be nobody at all."

I wish I could believe my friend. She peers at me over the rim of her coffee cup. "Is there something you're not saying?"

My mouth tightens in dismay. "She looks like me."

"What?"

"Here, I'll show you."

I drag out my laptop, fire it up and point out Stephanie Charteris. Vick's strained expression, the way her cheekbones tug, tells me that she's as astonished as me. She looks again. "The child definitely looks like the mother."

My head snaps up. "Oh God, do you really think so?"

"I didn't say the child looks like Tom," Vick says in reproof.

"What about the rest of the stuff," I say, shutting the laptop down, "the phone call?"

"Only way to find out – ask him."

I sip my coffee. I know this.

"Or you could ask her."

"God, Vick, I don't think I have the nerve."

Her expression infers that I'm not normally lacking when it comes to courage. I might be horizontal – admittedly not at this very moment – but I don't lack fire when the need arises. I haven't managed this long without a shred of steel in my adult backbone.

"Do you really think Tom means what he says?" Vick says after a pause. "You know, about kids."

"Vick, if you'd seen him this morning, you'd understand he meant every single word." I look her in the eye. Honest people find it difficult to be dishonest. Something about the way in which Vick fails to hold my gaze, the way in which she cradles her drink, the slight hunch in her shoulders, reveals there is something she isn't saying.

"What?" I push her.

She returns the mug of coffee to the table, untouched. I hold my breath so tight I feel dizzy. Her eyes remain fixed on the scrubbed wood. "I like Tom. I like him a lot. I know he makes you happy, Roz."

"You think he's a player, don't you?" I blurt out.

She looks back up. Straightens. Gathers herself. She doesn't take her eyes off me. "Seems to be a popular pastime." There's a cynical, bitter, cheated-upon twist to her voice. I get it. Vick's love life was, and is, a mess. "I've known a few chefs in my time. Some prone to alcoholism and, occasionally, pathologically hostile, and every one of them is highly strung and angst-ridden."

"But that's not Tom at all."

"He's no drunk." She speaks in a tone that leaves open the possibility of other unappealing traits. "I know you both seem loved-up." *Seem.* Oh my God, what is Vick driving at? That I'm deluded, that my heart rules my head, that I'm bonkers to pin so much on Tom as prospective father material? Even as I think it, I recognise it for what it is: the truth. I'm so distraught I barely catch hold of what she says next. "I don't know. Little things start to make sense."

"What little things?" I repeat. My voice is dull, no energy, no shine. Aged. I think immediately of Tom's fear of the dark, of his aversion to confined spaces, his rabid hatred of any record by Frank Sinatra. In the realm of 'peculiar things I detest', this is one of the strangest, surely. And then there's the other thing, the big thing, the bloody elephant in the room thing that is not standing idly in the corner but running amuck.

"The packed rucksack under the bed," Vick declares.

Why did I mention it, I silently wail, but how else to explain my discovery not long after me and Tom moved in together? When I delved inside I found a change of clothes, money in a separate wallet and a brand-new phone. I teased Tom about it at first until he explained it away as an adult-sized comforter, the residue of a damaged childhood and a sense of never feeling quite secure. Afterwards, he closed down every conversation when I brought up the subject.

"Maybe he's about to make a run for it," Vick said at the time, only half joking now, it seems. I remember dismissing it.

She scratches her temple, struggling. "He can be quite nervy."

"Tom? Come off it, Vick." And yet I know exactly what she means. Underneath the composed exterior, there is a definite edge.

*And that lost look.*

She seems suddenly as nervous as me, blinking, snatching at her coffee as if it's medication for pain control. I don't push it. I want to, but hope Vick will fill in the gap in her own good time. I can tell she finds the subject awkward and sensitive, and dread drips sweet nothings in my ear. The wait is almost intolerable and I nearly botch it, but then she takes a breath and shifts her weight in the chair.

"For a man who doesn't socialise, he was well out of his comfort zone at the magazine bash. Every time the photographer got within sniffing distance, he literally slid off into a corner."

Into the shadows. Feeling his way through the darkness or crouching in it? Goodness, where did that come from? I remember he made a deal about wanting to leave early, complaining of a headache. But that's not what Vick is trying to tell me.

An anxious, face-saving smile breaks out, lighting her eyes. "Remember, we used to joke that he was the 'doesn't do' man." Another frown of bewilderment from me ensues. "Doesn't have a passport. Doesn't socialise. Doesn't use social media in the accepted sense," she explains.

"Mildly strange." I force myself to sound relaxed, no sweat.

"Doesn't have a driving licence either." Her pupils suddenly dilate.

"It's not a hanging offence." She thrusts me a startled look and I realise that my volume control is switched to full. I dial it back. "Aren't we speculating too much?"

"Yeah," she says, pushing a smile, eager to roll the conversation to a less- contentious footing. "Probably," she adds in a soothing tone that is usually mine to dispense.

I glance at my watch and stand up, my coffee unfinished. "Better fly. Dinner with Tom," I remind Vick. In the past it would have elicited pleasure and thrill and anticipation. Now, I regard it with trepidation and fear. "Oh shit," I burst out.

"What?"

"I forgot to ask Reg to make himself scarce."

"No problem, I'm more than happy to feed him." I catch the slow smile on her face. Vick doesn't admit it but, in common with many women, she has the hots for Reg. I'd like to let on that offering to mother him is not the way into my brother's heart, let alone his pants, but it would be too cruel.

"You make him sound like he's five."

Vick hoists an eyebrow. "In his head, he is." But to your mind, he's all man, I think.

We both grin at shared anarchic memories of my Peter Pan-like brother. Vick instantly relaxes. She sees me to the door, slides her arms around me and gives me a hug that would crush stone. "You know where I am if you need me."

Hot and shiny with sudden tears, I wonder if my body is kick-starting into action and I'm about to have a period. "Thanks," I say thickly, clinging on as if Vick is *my* surrogate mother.

"Don't forget to tell Reg that I'm cooking pasta tonight."

"I won't." Still I cling.

"Go," she says, loosening my grasp with a firm smile. "Have a lovely lovely time. It will sort itself out, you'll see."

Weakly, I smile back. Why don't I believe her?

# Chapter 5

I pause and catch the wary expression on my face in the hall mirror. Little Miss Horizontal is no more. Little Miss Vertical took her place.

No welcoming smell of spice, or meat cooking, or sweet aroma from onions caramelising in butter, the air feels dead. Inert. There is no sound, not even from the spare room inhabited by Reg. I glance at my watch. It's past six-thirty. He can't still be asleep. Everything is silent. Then it dawns on me. Tom is at work. Emergency cover for a chef calling in sick, possibly, or perhaps the crisis that morning was not averted.

I briefly consider driving to the hotel restaurant and pleading for his return. The thought shakes me. I'm not needy and yet events of the day and Tom's atypical behaviour make me so.

Numb with disappointment, I wander through to the kitchen, expecting a note scrawled on the shopping pad we keep by the fridge-freezer. It's blank. This is how our home feels. Vacant. Gone. Something missing. A bubble of panic floats up from my tummy, pings off my heart and pops the moment I hear movement from upstairs. Tom, I think, yet the tread is not his. Tom's is soft, like a panther stalking prey. This is clunky and shouty and 'I've got enormous gonads.' Has to be Reg. Dim of me, but it doesn't occur that it might be a burglar.

Reg bursts in. I don't fancy my brother but, with his slim, snake-hipped physique and his angular looks and dangerous eyes framed by jet-black hair, I admit that he is breathlessly good-looking. The facial ironmongery – nose and tongue stud – and cross hanging from one ear and tattoos on his arms – do nothing to detract from his film-star features. Even his tangled teeth look sexy.

"Hiya," I say. "Vick says you can eat at hers tonight, not that it looks as if I need you out of the way." My eyes drift around the empty-looking kitchen.

Reg doesn't speak, but draws up a chair, twists it around and sits on it astride. Poser, I think. Then I catch his troubled expression.

"You may need to sit down, Roz."

I follow his eye-line to the comfy chair squashed in the corner, and spike with alarm. "It's not mum or dad, is it?"

He snatches a smile and his thick eyelashes flicker. "No worries. They're fine."

"Well, what then?"

"It's Tom."

"Has something happened? Has there been an accident?" Tom travels everywhere by bicycle. I permanently worry that a reckless lorry-driver or motorist will knock him off and splatter him across the road.

Reg clears his throat. His musician hands, with their impossibly lithe and dexterous fingers, grasp the top bar of the chair and the knuckles show white. Christ. "He's gone," Reg says bluntly, which is Reg all over.

"Gone where?"

He shakes his head. "Cleared out. Scrammed. Vamoosed."

"What?" I don't gasp. I pull a face and smile at the sheer preposterousness of Reg's words. "No," I say, "that can't be right. We only had a minor disagreement, nothing serious. Nothing..." I run out of negatives.

Reg awkwardly pushes a box of tissues in my direction, as if he thinks it's the done thing to do. Too shocked for tears, I shake my head. Stubborn. Resistant.

"I don't believe it." Searching his face for a positive sign, I find none.

"It's true, Roz."

"You've misunderstood. You've got it all wrong." My voice is hoarse and shaky and vulnerable, something that Reg detests almost as much as I do.

"I haven't."

"You have."

Reg issues a sharp, uncompromising look.

"All right, where did he say he was going?"

"He didn't."

"Well, what the fuck *did* he say?"

My brother's jaw flexes. Like Tom, he hates argument and why, I guess, Tom fled without a goodbye instead of manning up and telling me to my face. "Don't take it out on me, Roz."

"The fucking coward," I burst out. To which, Reg frowns and raises his palms.

"It's not nice, but it happens. Circle of life," he drawls, settling back into his default 'no shit' speaking pattern, louche meets stoned.

"For God's sake, spare me the meditational crap. You sound like Mum."

"Only saying. It might actually help."

"It doesn't." Shamefully, I have an urge to rearrange my brother's good looks.

Springing to my feet, I scope the kitchen. Tom's cookery books remain, squat and scowling on the designated shelf near the cooker, as if pissed off that he abandoned them in the same way he abandoned me. I have a sudden urgent desire to destroy them, page by bloody page.

I rush into the sitting room. Tom's a keen gamer yet his DVD's are exactly in the same place. 'Muse' CD's remain too. Might it mean that he'll come back, if only to reclaim the lot?

Upstairs, my shoes pound the treads. Tearing open the wardrobe. Most of his clothes are there, but not all.

Pulling out drawers in the bedroom. Similar.

Raking though stuff in the bathroom. Gone.

I don't bother to check whether or not Tom's go-to bag is missing. Instinctively, I know that it would be the first thing he laid his hands on.

Stumbling back to the kitchen, I collapse into the squashy chair before my legs give way. "Sorry, Reg," I mumble, "Shouldn't have a go at you."

"No worries." He means it. Very little affects Reg. I only see him get antsy if he runs out of tobacco and booze.

Unspeakably cold, I hunch my shoulders, trying to generate warmth into my bones. I'm upset but I'm damned angry too. "I need to know exactly what happened. Was he agitated, distressed?"

Reg gives it to me straight up. "There was a phone call."

"When?"

"About half-three."

Another after I left. "How did he seem?"

Reg slow-blinks, glances away. I push for an answer.

"Scared," he says with a level look.

Tension grabs my shoulders, gives them a nasty twist. "Of what?"

"I'd say if I knew."

Anything for an easy life, he wouldn't, but I don't pursue it. "Any idea who was on the other end?"

Reg shakes his head.

"Did you hear what was said?"

"Not really. Something about a licence, I think."

I puzzle over this. "For what?"

"Search me. Anyways, it didn't last long."

"Then what happened?"

"You know Tom, Mr Controlled. Packed up his kit and asked me to break the news to you that it's over."

"Is that all?"

"Yes."

"What did you say?"

His impossibly long lashes flutter. "Nothing."

"Nothing?" I'm outraged.

"Never cross a man whose mind is made up." His gaze

36

darts around the kitchen and homes in on the cupboard where we keep alcohol. "Drink?" he says.

I grunt 'yes' to mask my irritation at my brother's cowardice and failure to fight my corner.

"Whisky or wine?"

"Wine," I say. "The whisky belongs to Tom."

"Belonged." Reg corrects me in a 'shame to waste it' tone. He gets up, pours himself a large measure after fixing me a glass of Picpoul from the fridge. Chinking his glass with mine, he takes a swallow and looks at me as if I'm on the run from prison. Will I lash out, or come quietly?

"Whatever happened this morning," he says, "it's not about that. The row is only a symptom of impending breakdown."

My brother sounds so uncharacteristically pompous that I almost burst out laughing. "Who made you an expert on relationships?"

"I've only been here a few weeks and even I could pick up tensions."

"Damn right, emanating from you, and can you stop nicking my razors, please?"

"Jeez, it was only once."

"Well, once is too much." I glower. Silence, slithering and snake-like, encircles the pair of us. My brother would not be my first choice of confidante. We are poles apart in values and opinions. Mr Treat them Mean, Keep them Keen lives by a different code of ethics. Horribly similar to those adopted by my erstwhile lover, it seems.

Reg is still giving me the look, like he is older and, by default, wiser. "You know very well that Tom can be sparky."

"So what? He'd be dull as hell if he were quiet all the time. It's what fuels our relationship."

"Fuelled," he points out, not in a mean-spirited way but because he really wants me to understand that Tom's departure is final.

"All right," I say, taking a big breath. "Explain these tensions you noticed."

He meets my gaze with candour. "Tom's exterior doesn't meet match the interior."

At this, I laugh. "You mean that underneath he's cool, calm and collected?"

"Nope. What I mean is that the silent shit is a cover for something else. Underneath, he's a fiery, agitated and miserable mess."

*Miserable?* I badly want to tell Reg that he's talking garbage, but then I remember Tom's peculiarities, his phobias, the way he reacted this morning and what Vick said about him. "Hardly surprising, bearing in mind his upbringing."

"Oh yeah, the man with the tragic past." There is an ugly note in my brother's voice that I don't much care for. He picks up on my disdain as only a sibling can. "Have you noticed that when a writer wants to ramp up a character in a film, their parents are always dead? Death by road accident is almost a cliché."

"Tom's parents died in a boating accident."

"So he says. Funny thing is, I believe him."

"Funny?" I explode.

"Not funny ha-ha. Nothing fake about that; unlike other aspects of his life."

"What other aspects?" I sound as incredulous and defensive as I feel.

"Education. Friends. Places he's been to. He's flaky, Roz. Secretive." His voice is sibilant, tongue and teeth chewing on the words before spitting them out.

"Private," I thrust back.

"Yeah, right."

"What exactly are you driving at?"

"Okay, okay, a minor indiscretion, granted, but he smokes." I snort derision. "He's a chef. His taste-buds would be ruined."

"God, Roz, where have you been all your life? All the top chefs smoke."

Sensing I'm on shaky ground, I don't know how to reply. I wonder whether this is why Tom's voice sounds seasoned. Seems irrelevant now. "Anyway, how do *you* know?"

"He bums cigarettes off me."

"You're winding me up."

Reg's full lips puff out, like he's blowing smoke rings. "Why would I?"

"All right," I concede, trying to remain dignified in defeat, "So what if he does?"

He flashes a grin. First point to Reg. "Extracting information from Tom is like nailing jelly. The thing about secrets, they take a huge amount of energy to conceal. No wonder he's screwed up."

A strange sensation fizzes behind my eyes. "You swan in here for five minutes and claim you know more than me about the man I've been living with for the past three years."

"Why are you defending him? The guy just walked out on you?" Reg's voice rises and I get the weird impression that he wants me to get a whole lot angrier than I appear. 'Appear' is the operative word. Inside, I'm hurt beyond belief; in equal measure I'm also bloody furious. Were I in a better frame of mind, and seeing my little brother so exasperated, I'd ask how the 'circle of life' fitted now.

As if he hasn't already said enough, Reg persists, "Remember the weekend I dropped in to see you before I moved here?"

"Yeah, Tom wasn't around." A one-off event in London, Tom cooked dinner for a wealthy entrepreneur. I moaned at the time because I thought it would be fun to go with him and spend an afternoon mooching in the West End. Tom talked me out of it.

"Where was he?" Reg demands.

"You know where he was. Hampstead."

"He wasn't."

"He was." I take a big glug of wine, the liquid equivalent of a mighty full stop.

Reg breathes in tight and lets out a sigh. "He went to Wales."

I jitter with nervous laughter. "Wales? I don't believe you." From his skewering expression, I see that he has the drop on me although, to be fair, he isn't parading it.

"I wasn't going to show you but, well, in the circumstances..." Like a magician pulling a bunny from a hat with a flourish, Reg produces a card and pushes it under my nose. It's for a taxi firm based in Conwy. The date written by hand coincides with the timeframe Tom was allegedly in London. I take and handle it as if it's an ancient relic.

40

"Where did you get this?" Planting it face down with deliberation, I just about mask the icy note in my voice.

"Found it on the floor inside your wardrobe."

"You went into our room to snoop? You went through my stuff?"

"*His* stuff, and only after Tom split today. Jesus Christ, Roz. Don't have a go at me. I'm only the fucking messenger."

"You had no right." My voice cracks. My chest expands and contracts, and a dry sob catches at the back of my throat. Tears that I'd held in check for all of today erupt and I stagger out of the room, down the hall and into the night. Reg calls after me but I don't look back.

# Chapter 6

The fucking bastard, I rail to the cold night air. Unable to take it in, I stumble through dark wet streets. Planning to berate him with obscenities, I phone Tom's cell phone mobile but nothing happens. Must be switched off. I can't even let him have it and tell him exactly what I think of his lousy behaviour.

Torturing myself, I obsess about the recent past. Were there signs I failed to spot? Like the night he was exhausted and didn't want to be intimate and made me feel a fool for trying to initiate sex? Did I really put him under pressure to go to the magazine party? I'm full of things I'd like to say and do to him. I'm not a violent person. It's against everything I believe in, yet for his cruelty and his cowardice, at this precise moment I'd like to beat the living crap out of him.

To think that only this morning we made love in the sitting room, or would it be more appropriate to say that we 'had sex'? Thundering with alcohol, rage and confusion, and without any recollection of where I'm heading, I plunge down to the centre of town, past shops and restaurants at full tilt and feel such an overwhelming sensation of desertion that it mangles me. With sharp and penetrating focus, my minds reels back to how we met.

It was Vick's idea to use an internet dating site. With hindsight, and given Tom's general avoidance of social media, it seems paradoxical. Did it for a laugh, I remember without mirth. Most of Vick's dates were either fully functioning alcoholics or gym-mad narcissists. One looked nothing like his photograph, another had dog's breath. According to Vick, every male expected her to perform a sex act on him on a first date. Meanwhile, I land Tom Loxley. Burning at the memory, I press my hand to my lips to force down the dry cry that threatens to escape.

*He looked so gorgeous and rock-solid dependable and all I could dream of in a guy.*

Smothering my distress, I consider going to Vick's. Except Reg is probably already there, feeding his face. The thought of both of them dispensing tissues and sympathy is more than I can bear, but I can't go back home. Instead, I take a minor diversion and head to Bayshill, with its white-stuccoed houses, and beyond to leafy residential Overton Park. The hotel and restaurant where Tom works is tucked away, its short forecourt crammed with cars screened from the road by laurel. I weave a path around them to the back entrance.

Sure enough, there are two sous-chefs working at a manic pace, and a lad, no more than eighteen, pot-washing. I don't hang around. "Is Tom here?" I ask.

Three men stop what they are doing and swivel their gaze to me. I feel as if Tom's name is the equivalent of uttering a profanity.

The eldest of the three by at least fifteen years, a man with a greasy complexion and eyes the colour of pebbles, steps forward. He doesn't look friendly. "Handed in his notice."

"Well at least he wasn't scheduled to work tonight," the lad chips in, eliciting a dirty look from Grease-face. "It's true," he bites back, giving the impression that he can be subjugated in a kitchen environment but not outside it. I briefly wonder how long he'll last.

"Do you know where he might have gone?"

"What's it to you?"

I turn to the second chef. Silent until now, he stands, watching me like I'm the dish of the day. "I'm his girlfriend," I say with a pleasant smile, even though it near kills me. It isn't reciprocated.

"Left you in the lurch, has he?" He runs his hands down his apron in a suggestive manner. Creepy sod.

Grease-face intervenes, the self-elected spokesman. "Tom isn't here. That's all we have to say."

My eyes scope the kitchen. Food piled high. Unwashed plates. Hobs and workstations all in need of a good clean. Nothing like the glam disorganisation of TV cookery shows.

"Could be on a bender. It happens. Maybe he'll come back."

I look at the young guy who spoke and is doing his best to make me feel better. The second chef is still stripping me with his gaze. The tip of his tongue touches the corner of his mouth, as if he imagining what I might taste like.

I force a smile. "Sorry to have bothered you." My shoulders round. My hands plunge into my pockets as I back out and exit.

Fuming, I walk slowly, head down. A fast footfall behind me, I twist around into a fug of cigarette smoke that darts straight into my eyes. It's the young guy. "Fag break," he grins, jabbing the air with a lit cigarette. "My name's Stevie, by the way."

"Thanks, Stevie, I really appreciate what you did in there." I look furtively in the direction of the kitchen. "I don't want you getting into trouble on my account."

"Fuck 'em. They don't own me."

Telling the world to screw itself is the luxury of naïve youth. How much I miss it. Being dumped makes me feel spectacularly middle-aged. "Mind me asking why they are so defensive?"

"Easy." He takes another drag. "Chef runs a little business on the side. Not that I'm knocking it. Cooking is a high-pressure game." I ignore the pun because I'm staggered by what Stevie, so like my brother, infers.

"Drugs?"

"Blow, uppers, downers, you name it. For the right price he can get you anything."

My thoughts spiral. I remember Vick's perception of Tom as a nervy guy. I recall Reg's declaration that Tom bummed smokes off him. "Was Tom taking anything?"

"Reddys."

"Speed?" I splutter.

"Red capsules, amphetamines," he expands.

How could I miss something like this? "Did he take them often?"

"All the time. Good for your confidence, although the headaches can be a bit of a fucker." He blows out another cloud of smoke, narrows his eyes, reading me. "You really his girl-friend, then?"

Angry tears brim to the surface of my eyes in response.

"Harsh," he says. "Might have been a bit contained, private like, but I reckon he was fond of you." Fond, but not *in love with*. "He hated working really late because it meant you were on your own, see?"

I'm puzzled. "That worried him?"

"Proper mind-fuck."

"Was he jealous?"

"Tom?" He snorts with a loose grin. "No way. Cared. You on your own and that." He says it with emphasis as if I am dim as well as deaf. Again, I feel all of my thirty-seven years.

"Ever thought he was about to flit?"

"Not really." Which is not the same as no.

I hike an eyebrow. "Another woman?"

Stevie pauses. "If there was, he never said."

"So?"

Stevie looks left and right as if he expects Tom to stride out of the darkness. "He wanted me to do something for him, couple of weeks ago."

"Yeah?"

"Asked me to buy contact lenses off the net."

My mouth screws into a frown. "Tom never mentioned a problem with his eyesight."

"Nah, you know, the ones that change your eye colour."

Disguise, I think with a thud. 'For what?', I say.

"He wanted blue. Tom had—"

"Brown eyes, I know." I baulk. By chucking simple details in the air, the bigger picture is about to come crashing down, gashing open my scalp badly enough to require ten stitches.

"Did Tom have enemies?" I'm scrabbling for something tangible to grab hold of, something that makes sense and provides a lead.

Stevie hitches a shoulder. "Never said."

"Anyone he had a problem with, someone he disliked?"

Stevie considers, his face serious, and then breaks into a stupendous smile. "Yeah, actually."

"Who?" I catch my breath. Could this be the breakthrough I'm looking for?

"Frank Sinatra. Couldn't fucking stand him. Shit," he says, dropping the cigarette to the ground and stubbing it out with the heel of his trainer. "Gotta get back."

"Thanks," I call after him, dazed. Like quicksilver, he's already gone.

# Chapter 7

Tom smokes. Tom takes drugs. Tom cares about me, but isn't in love with me. Tom is a jabbering heap underneath a spiky hostile exterior, or so Reg would have me believe. And what's with the contact lenses? I gulp, for if, as Stevie claims, Tom requested them a couple of weeks ago, Tom's exit was premeditated. The utter shit *planned* his getaway. How does any of this fit into the image of Tom, the quiet, solicitous, dependable boyfriend?

Screaming inside, I cut down an alley, something I would never usually do. God help anyone who attempts to mug me.

The rain abates. The wind drops. The pavement is slick with surface water and I splash my way back home.

This time the silence is welcome. I dump my sopping-wet coat, rub a towel through my hair and kick off my shoes. My appetite is non-existent and I put on the kettle and make coffee. No beans. No machine. When I'm done I sit and try to calm down and reduce my anger to a lower level. I should take Reg's advice. Forget about Tom. Move on. No point seething.

If only it were that easy.

I glance across at the cabinet where we keep our CD's. One is out, next to the CD player. Paul Weller. My all-time favourite track, 'You Do Something To Me.'

Our song.

So I thought.

My eyes swim with misery.

For all Tom's occasional moodiness, his edge and fire, I cannot imagine my life without him. I love the way he talks, how he touches me, his intensity, so much a part of his personality, thrills me. Is it possible to recover from such desolation? Hot tears seep out of the corners of my eyes. Unlike previous encounters, ours was a 'safe' relationship that I was sure would run the distance. Certain that this was the man I would have children with, and grow old with. Even my mum liked him, which was a first. I go through it all again and again. I'm not normally obsessive, but I can't help it.

*Damn him.*

Relaxed, Tom could be funny and quick-witted. Composed, he could be aspirational with dreams of one day running a restaurant of his own. Calm, he made me feel secure. I *thought* I did the same for him. I *thought* I smoothed out his occasional edginess and lightened his life. Racked with misery, I see now that although he lit me up inside, I failed to do the same for him. *Fond*, Stevie said, like Tom was my elderly aunt and I his niece.

I see now that Tom always had the drop on me.

When will I stop hurting?

*When will I quit raging?*

Tempted to phone Mum, I change my mind. Currently

trogging through Vietnam with Al, she's probably out of reach of a signal and the last thing I need is a lecture on the grief cycle following another failed love affair, or her views on karma, which, actually, I share.

Fractious, I set the mug down on the table. The magazine and apparent source of all my problems, lies open at the very page in question. But what if it represented a tipping point, what if something else was going on? What might it be? Instantly, I remember the colour draining from Tom's features at my innocent remark about my visit to the police station.

Maybe, it's my curious gene kicking in, but I'd rather put my investigative powers to good use than either dissolve in self-pity or self-combust with anger, as tempting as the latter is.

Feeling a little bit more sorted, I reach for, and look at, our picture, really look this time, not through the lens of my own absurd imagining, but with 20-20 hindsight. Sadness washes over me at how happy I appear. My dark hair, natural for once, is swept back from my face, neat chin tilted, smiling lips parted, as if I am about to burst into laughter. Vital and alive, I am the personification of joy.

But it's Tom I zero in on.

Several inches taller than me, his build is lean and rangy. His short hair seems much darker in a way I hadn't noticed before, and it's suspiciously at odds with the distinctive blonde stubble that obscures the lower half of his face. He wears a castaway smile, out of synch with his otherwise strong features. Although his mouth does the talking, the words don't reach his watchful eyes. There is nothing off-centre about his pose and yet the way he holds himself, shoulders rounded, drop-ping one knee to disguise his height, suggests a man unhappy with the body he inhabits. This is not a man at ease with himself. My conversation with Reg darts through my mind.

*"How did he seem?"*

*"Scared."*

# Chapter 8

"God, I'm sorry, Roz."

Vick calls first thing. I imagine Reg beating his Tom-Tom drums the previous evening while relieving Vick of half a ton of spaghetti. For a slim guy, he packs away a lot of food – another source of conflict between Tom and me, due to the strain on the household budget. All the time, I remember with a thud, Tom was funding a drug habit and possibly preparing to run. What else is hidden?

"Yeah," I say, masking the effect of the previous twenty-four hours. Every room, stick of furniture in the house yells cold and empty.

"Think Tom's gone off with that woman on Facebook?"

"Who knows?" Who cares? Who am I kidding? If I don't give a damn, why did I phone him first thing this morning? Same result: Not switched on. Not listening. Not answering. God, I hate being ignored, but this is intolerable. I'm *owed* answers.

"What are you going to do about it?"

"Nothing." I squeak not a word about the Welsh connection, drugs or smoking.

"Roz, do you—"

"Sorry, Vick, I need to get moving. Don't want to be late for work."

I'm never short or moody with Vick, or anyone for that matter. In reality I have bags of time, but if I don't get up and soon I'll draw the covers over my head and stay there. Obsessively, I trawl the past. Again.

Surely, he wouldn't leave without a goodbye? Surely, he will come back at some point if only to reclaim his things? Or am I wildly optimistic, some might say delusional?

When I told Vick that I would not act, I was dishonest. That phone call Tom took after I left for the second time yesterday proved a game-changer. This thought bugs me.

One moment, I seethe with anger. Another, I want to howl. I have no desire to make Tom change his mind (I do, but don't admit it aloud). I certainly won't stalk him but I need to understand his reasons for leaving. Living together as we have for so long, I demand an explanation, even if it means that he loves someone else – the bloody cheat.

I shower and dress, skip breakfast and beat Elliott to the office, which rates as a first. He lumbers in and I expect to see, at the least, a flicker of surprise and pleasure in his eyes. He doesn't even ask for coffee. He utters five words and they don't start with 'Good morning.'

"Meeting at nine. Tell Helen."

He avoids my gaze and his face is a shambles of shadows, creases and lines. His clothes are rumpled and I suspect he had a bad a night, like me, but for very different reasons. I think back to the meeting yesterday. Perhaps the rumours are true.

I'm right. It takes Elliott two minutes to deliver the news, eighteen to justify the publisher's decision. Straight away, I deduce that Elliott secured a deal for himself that allows his only members of salaried staff, bar the girl who answers the phones, to be shoved out into the cold. Helen's field of expertise is narrower than mine and she recently took out a mortgage. Her face falls into a portrait of stunned disbelief. Normally, I'd sigh, accept it for what it is and resign myself to looking for gainful employment. It might even trigger a panicky phone call to Mum. I have stockpiled a little money, but my big savings plan is now officially screwed. If Reg weren't off to LA I could charge him rent. On a monetary level, it's a bummer, yet with a spring in my stride I embrace the freedom to get to the bottom of Tom's vanishing act. I'm determined he is not going to get away with it, as if what we had meant nothing.

Helen flings herself out through the door, muttering about tribunals and back pay, leaving me with Elliott. I say nothing. Elliott fidgets. Sweat sheens his brow and moistens his eyebrows. He seems fleshier than ever. To be honest, he doesn't look healthy.

"I'm sorry, Rosamund. I'll give you a great reference, of course."

"Thank you."

"What will you do?"

I respond with a dry smile. "You know, Elliott, you're the second person to ask me that this morning."

I don't reveal that I have a plan that does not include a job search, catching up on domestic chores or hacking through the wilderness that passes for my garden. Shock and anger is replaced with a demand for truth. I do not fess up that the thought of never seeing Tom again cripples me. No man should hold that power.

I pack up my stuff and head back home to where my car, a clapped-out Ford Fiesta is parked on the street, the only advantage being it's re-sprayed canary yellow. You'd be blind not to see me coming.

According to the blurb, the Argo Homes sales office opens at 10.30 a.m., giving me plenty of time to get there. Setting my sat nav, I follow A roads all the way to Ledbury, through and on to Holmer, a residential suburb that also plays host to an ugly-looking steel stockyard.

Banners flying in the chill breeze denote the development and I hang a left off a roundabout, following signs for the site and sales office, before finally pulling off another round-about and swinging into a visitor car park. With diggers, cranes, dumper-trucks and forklifts, it's a swarm of rattle and hum and bone-jarring activity.

Climbing out of the car, new homes in varying states of assembly eyeball me and convey a sense of how massive the development actually is. There are literally hundreds of shiny rooftops.

The sales office is set at the end of a row of three show homes with majestic- sounding names that infer, as a home-owner, you too will scale the social ladder of life should you be smart enough to purchase a 'Kingston', for example. Fat chance.

Inside, a large desk around which three women, wearing

simple navy shift dresses, discuss business of the day. An entire wall is dedicated to an artist's impression of each house model, together with descriptions and floor plans. A large site diagram sits astride another wall, under which lounges a large squashy sofa. One section of the room is reserved for floor coverings and kitchen finishes, the choice so dazzling it would make most would-be buyers giddy, if not downright confused. By contrast, sensible yellow hard hats, boots and high-viz jackets hang on hooks near the entrance, a stark reminder that this is about dirt and bricks, pipes and drains and the labour required to amalgamate the lot.

The squeak and bubble of conversation comes to a halt. Three smiles greet me as I stride through a blizzard of dry, oxygen-sapping heat. I have no problem in identifying Stephanie Charteris. We could pass for each other in the right light. If Stephanie spots a similarity in our looks, she keeps it to herself. The youngest and possibly most junior of the three, she is first to engage me with a pleasant "Can I help you?" The others scatter to another part of the office that sits behind a dome of glass, in which there's a desk, a water filter and drinks machine.

I return the smile. "Could I view the show homes?" I slide my eyes towards the door on the other side, beyond which a paved path leads to three houses.

"'Course you can." She's sprightly and 'can do'. I hesitate, thinking that she will take me on a guided tour, but this isn't the way it works, apparently. "Through there." She indicates with a hand that wears a single wedding band.

My chest expands and contracts. Lightheaded, I fake a smile

and wander through. How to engage Stephanie in conversation without involving the others?

I go through the motions and enter the first house, slip on a pair of overshoes, and pad around inside. My first impression is one of space. It smells squeaky-clean fresh and new. Carpet springs beneath my shoes and the kitchen diner, with its shiny laminate floor, is a triumph of modern design. Most of all, there is no damp, no suggestion of mould; a little-discussed, if common, problem with many older houses in Cheltenham. Having always rated the average new-build as a thin-skinned sterile excuse for a home, I'm prepared to modify my opinion. Throughout the viewing, I reason and observe as if in stereo, the other track in my head fastened on the wedding ring, the fact that Stephanie seems perfectly nice and without guile.

The second house, a four-bedroom design has a glorious landing. I don't bother with the five-bedroom. I suck up enough information to help me ask intelligent questions and pass myself off as a potential buyer.

The sales office is one woman short by the time I return. Stephanie pecks away on a computer while the remaining sales advisor, a middle-aged woman with super-greased, tightly braided hair so that the skin on her scalp shines through thin and white, sits inside her glass dome like a scientist in a laboratory. She is talking to a couple with a young child, who'd rather be climbing the furniture. I get the impression that braided woman is leader of the pack. The upright way she sits and sweeps from one sheaf of papers to another, using the desk like a pianist playing a piano; she's definitely in charge, the domed office her personal fiefdom. I bet there isn't anything she doesn't know about the job or the people who buy and view, me included. Worrying.

Stephanie looks up. Unlike me, she has a dimple in each cheek when she smiles, which is a lot – me before my life crashed and burned.

"What did you think?" she says.

"Very nice."

"What stage are you at?" Her eyes flicker with hope. She indicates a seat and I sit down.

"We have plenty of good deals on at this time of year. Between you and me..." She drops her smoky voice, so similar to mine, and leans in with another wide beam, "...we're about to start a new phase so, if you're in a position to buy, now's the time to clinch a bargain. On the larger models we'll pay your stamp duty, turf the garden, and carpets all thrown in."

"I see." I give her a sage look, giving the impression that it's worthy of proper consideration. "Actually, I'm scouting for my mother." I curb the fake ring in my voice. "She's travelling right now. Renting at the moment." My whopping lie plays well with Stephanie, who leaps on it as if I had handed her combined power of attorney and access to my bank account.

"The perfect position in which to purchase." Her smile travels from her face, skips around and lights up the entire room. The woman is liquid sunshine.

Feeling as if I'm deceiving a toddler, I step in before she gets carried away. "I'm afraid it's slightly complicated."

"It usually is." She trills a good-natured laugh.

Extemporising like crazy, I say, "Like I said, Mum is travelling through South-East Asia, Australia and Vietnam. She's currently having a high old time in Thailand, so it would be some time before..."

I stop, not because I run out of steam, but because sunny Stephanie looks as if I've produced a crowbar and am about to smash her teeth in with it. Recoiling, she lets out a low moan. A hand shoots to her mouth. Eyes film with tears, one pounds down her cheek and carves a thin white line through her foundation. Visceral. Agonised. How can such an innocuous remark yield such a raw reaction?

Her chair screeches back, "Excuse me." She scrabbles to her feet, the hand still clamped to her mouth, the other spread-eagled against her stomach after the vicious verbal punch I threw. Streaming with tears, she flies out of the room, to a back office, I presume.

I sit rigid, conscious that three pairs of eyes are fixed on me, the cause of Stephanie's distress. In a way, I am. Except I have no idea why.

The woman with the braids marches out of her office and advances. She is taller than I thought, a good three inches on me and I'm five feet six. A badge on her dress says her name is Anita. She glances from me to the closed door. Everybody hears the painful sound of someone sobbing.

"What happened?" Anita's pale features are etched with anger. Word for word, I report what I said. Eyes half-closed, she shoots the palm of one hand to her high forehead, lets out a sigh and disappears to the back room from where I hear 'there there' noises.

I sit bewildered. The couple in the next-door dome continue

to eye me with condemnation while failing to disapprove of their only offspring, who leaps from one sofa to another with muddy shoes. At last, and thank God, Anita returns.

"You weren't to know," she says, sympathetic now that she realises I'm not a bitch and didn't deliberately set out to create mayhem. "Steffi's husband died in a car accident in Thailand."

A nasty taste floods my mouth. I want to say I'm sorry. Stephanie's reference on Facebook was to this man. Not Tom. Someone else. Her husband. What a plank I am, yet despite feeling bad that I unwittingly upset a woman I don't know, I almost buckle with relief that Stephanie Charteris has no connection to Tom.

I repeat it silently and slavishly, as if weaving one of my mother's cosmic, supernatural charms. Consoled, I forget to ask myself why Tom was looking at her in the first place.

Anita calls to the abandoned couple, inviting them to help themselves to coffee from the machine. "Shan't be a moment," she says, her sympathetic gaze directed to the closed door.

"Tell her I'm very sorry." Feeling small, I get up to leave.

"There's no need to go," Anita assures me with forced over-the-top jollity. "I can deal with your enquiry, if you don't mind waiting."

"It's fine. I'll come back another day."

She looks pained and reluctant, the sales person in her disappointed at not closing a deal. "Let me give you some literature," she says, briskly assembling a home pack while I stand there awkward, eager to escape the suddenly stuffy office. She thrusts a brochure into my hands. "My phone number is on there." And then, as if remembering her manners or feeling that she hasn't done enough already, she picks up a framed photograph that hides discreetly behind a plant on the desk, and waves it in front of my face.

"That's him," she says, "with Stephanie and their little girl, Zoe. What a lovely little family."

Feigning interest, I look. At once, the air punches out of me. I stare. Don't move. The walls shrink, compressing the room, so that I find it hard to breathe in or exhale. Dazed, I try to speak, but the words won't come. Not at first. Run, I think. Run and never come back. "His name?" I mutter.

"Adam," she says. "Adam Charteris."

Or the man I know as Tom Loxley.

# Chapter 9

I sit in my car and let the wind scream around me. The sky, an unrelenting grey, hisses rain.

Like someone with locked-in syndrome, I think but can't move. Not at all. I'm paralysed.

*Tom Loxley is Adam Charteris.*

My mind sprints: the dead parents who I found so credible; the extinct godmother I now think implausible. Through a fierce blur of stunned confusion I remind myself that Tom was married with a child and this is why he cannot marry me and refuses to father our children. It all falls into place and yet so much remains a mystery, not least why Tom would fake his own death? A spark of rage catches hold and lights me up inside.

*How fucking dare he.*

For if Tom had been living a lie for the past three years then, by living with him, so did I. And how could I be so easily and comprehensively deceived? Betrayed? What does that make me other than cheap, used, tawdry and second-best? God alone knows where this leaves poor Stephanie Charteris and her child. Should Tom appear at this very moment, I'd slap his face so hard his teeth would drop out.

Anger writhing inside me, I see that, in the light of my discovery, his behaviour stacks. The photograph signalled the ending of our relationship because, should someone who remembered him as Adam spot it, his deception would be exposed. No wonder he was worried. I was too close to finding out and paid the price. As motivation went, it felt solid. Knowable. Concrete.

*But who the hell is Adam Charteris?*

The sales office door swings open, startling me out of inactivity. Stephanie Charteris, scarf and coat pulled tight around her, runs toward the car park. Her eyes fix blindly on uneven tarmac and puddles, which she doesn't bother to avoid. I doubt she will notice, but I slide down from view in case.

Listening.

Footsteps close by.

Cheep-cheep sound of a car unlocking.

Door swinging open and the dull tin thud of it closing.

An engine turns over. Tyres grip gravel at such speed, it spits sharp-edged bits exuberantly, machine-gun style, against the mudguards. I edge back up in my seat and watch a white Fiat 500 travel towards the exit and indicate to turn onto the main road. Quickly, I start my car and follow, dropping in two cars behind, and wish that my vehicle wasn't quite so conspicuous.

At the end of the road the Fiat bears left at the first round-about and picks up the A49 heading back over the border to Shropshire. Speed drops, its trajectory less erratic. Stephanie is calmer now, the upset of the morning wearing off. More than can be said for me. I shiver, despite banging the heater on full blast. Fractured thoughts swirl, collide and bruise. Instinctively, I rub my temple.

*Stephanie believes her husband is dead.*

*How would she react if she found out that the father of her child lived somewhere else with someone else?*

The thought makes me giddy. In a few words, I have the power to break down walls and destroy. God alone knows the fury I might unleash in Stephanie. But it would do nothing to expose Tom and, more than ever, I want him nailed; I don't want him getting away with it.

A sign for Leominster appears. We travel in tandem for several miles. A car in front turns off. A tractor towing a trailer piled high with swedes slips in front of the Fiat. Although the journey is painfully slow and tortuous, it gives me time to survey this snapshot of unfamiliar scenery. Rolling countryside. Messy unkempt hedges. Muddy roads splattered with dirt and manure and debris. A beautifully tended estate that runs for miles behind black metal railings stands out from the rural crowd. Alongside twisty, turny roads, the landscape is alien and far from what I know in Cheltenham with its chic streets, wealth and café culture vibe. Far from what Tom aka Adam knew too.

At last, the tractor with its load pulls over, allowing the traffic to free-flow. The little Fiat speeds up, careering around bends in a way that suggests the driver is intimately familiar with these roads. I urge my old Fiesta on, pushing the engine to destruction, tearing up a fast stretch towards the market town and entrance to the Welsh Marches, Ludlow. Here, the Fiat veers left, heading for the centre, it seems. I follow too, over a narrow bridge, and straight up a hill, through a medieval stone arch and wide street flanked with cars on either side. The Fiat glides into a parking slot, leaving me with no alternative but to continue and funnel into the one-way system, where a narrow street packed with shoppers and pedestrians hem me in. People spill from tiny pavements onto the main thoroughfare. One guy puts the flat of his hand on the Fiesta's bonnet to indicate that he is crossing the street, car or no car. I feel as if, expecting a Harrods experience, I wind up in Primark. Alien to Cheltenham, for sure, but alien to my groovy Totnes, Devon roots too.

I crawl past a square with an outdoor market in full swing despite the sodden weather, search for somewhere to stop when, right in front of me, I spy Ludlow castle. There's a car park nearby in a street between a chocolatier and a slick-looking Pizza Express. I park in the pay and display, grab a ticket for two hours for the simple reason I don't have the right change, and head back out to the square, but not before I walk past the castle entrance. To my left, as I cast a glance at the ancient stone, there is a small grass area with benches. In front, a cannon squats. A tiny piece of a bigger picture fits. This is where Stephanie stood, thinking of her beloved husband. This is the shot that appears on her Facebook page. Perhaps Tom/Adam even took the photograph. Madness almost attacks my mind, propelling me back to my car, but more primeval instincts kick in – survival and a blind desire for knowledge and certainty and, *hell,* payback – and I dart away and head towards the centre, past a group of middle-aged women who chatter away in Welsh, all hard consonants and upward inflexions. The street narrows and I turn right, down the hill, to where Stephanie's Fiat is parked.

It's absolutely bitter. Further west, and bordering Wales, the climate seems to have its own weather system: frigging cold and several degrees down on the rest of the country.

"Hey," a voice calls behind. I twist around. "Thought it was you," Stephanie says, pink-cheeked with embarrassment. "Look, about earlier, I hope I haven't put you off."

I smack a fake smile on my lips. "Not a chance, as you can see. Why else check out the surrounding territory?"

"Unfortunately, there isn't much in the way of new-builds here. Not yet, at least."

"Pity."

"It's a lovely place to live." She casts around, her gaze resting on the ancient building, a half-smile on her face. With pride.

"Your home town?"

She nods.

I stand clumsily. Frozen inside and out. There is so much I want to ask but daren't for fear of messing up. Stephanie looks awkward too, her face tense with strain. "I was having a particularly bad day, I'm afraid. So sorry about what..."

"Absolutely no need to apologise. It's me that's sorry. Anita explained."

"Did she?" She flinches and her eyebrows draw apart. Sensitive. It's one thing to endure tragedy in your life, another to have someone talk about it to a complete nobody. I touch her sleeve lightly. Make a connection. It's not hard. I like Stephanie on sight and it's not because she looks like me, or sounds a bit like me, or that we share the same lover, but because I sense that she is a better person, somehow. More grown up. More sorted. Perhaps motherhood does that to a woman. Inside, I squirm with longing.

"It's all right. I understand." I feel no fraud in the loss department. We both forfeited the same man. We were both duped. God alone knows why.

She studies me for a second. Thoughtful. Weighing me up.

People tell me I have a listening face. At this moment Stephanie is wondering whether she can trust me and, perhaps, tell a perfect stranger things she won't tell anyone else. Except I'm not a stranger. We are more alike than she could ever imagine.

A great burst of cold air surges past, vandalising an A-frame sign, almost knocking us off our feet. Fearful the opportunity passed, I blunder in.

"Look, is there anywhere we could grab a coffee? Of course, if you have other plans," I add in a 'no problem' manner.

She glances at her watch, frowns. "I'll overstay my parking space."

"Doesn't matter," I say, thinking it matters enormously. Pushing my luck, I blurt, "I just don't want to be on my own."

"Oh?"

"Must seem pathetic by comparison to you, but, well..." Breaking off is not part of my act. I'm straying into deeply dangerous territory, from which retreat may be completely cut off.

"Yes?" she says, eyebrows drawn together in concern.

I swallow. "I lost my job this morning. My boyfriend dumped me yesterday. Been living together for years. Thought he was the real deal." There is a catch in my voice. A tear creeps into my eye. I'm not faking either. Saying it aloud to Stephanie makes me so exquisitely and maddeningly sad.

"You poor thing," she says, resting her fingers lightly on my arm.

"I'm okay." My smile is shaky. The tear now trickles down my cheek and plops onto the pavement. Oh God.

I hate the way my emotions hijack me. I need to stay angry. I *must*. If I do, I'll be all right. Cry later, and only if I have to, but not until I get to the bottom of Tom's massive Houdini-like vanishing trick.

Fired up again inside, I stand a little straighter. A decent woman, Stephanie raises her chin, freshly determined, strangely mirroring my moves, "If you don't mind jumping into my car, we could get something to drink at my place. I live on the other side of town."

She's so trusting and open and, although I feel bad for me, I feel worse exploiting her. "Are you sure? I really wouldn't want to put you to any trouble."

"What else will I do until my daughter comes home? Sit around and mope? Come on," she says. "You need cheering up."

I snap a smile, thinking that Stephanie was a pushover for someone as manipulative as Tom Loxley.

# Chapter 10

We head for the Fiat and I jump in beside her. Stephanie expertly reverses out and drives back the way we came, taking a left along a narrow street and left again up a hill that finally drops down, past an ancient-looking hotel called The Feathers. I stare up at the exterior, a triumph of Medieval and Tudor architecture.

We don't speak and already I'm regretting my decision to inveigle my way into her life. What started out as a mission to find out why Tom upped and dumped me changed to something sinister and inexplicable. I remain in a dilemma. Stephanie exists under the illusion her husband and father of her child is dead. How can I shatter that? Should I even try? Surely, it would be too cruel.

Medieval quaintness left behind, we travel over a bridge and underneath a railway arch, up an unprepossessing hill, past a hospital and dental surgery, until we finally turn off into a street of artisan terraced houses, Victorian by the look of them.

Stephanie drops me out while she parks tight along a wall.

"I'm here," she says, indicating a forest-green-painted front door with an empty hanging basket attached to the red brick by an ornate metal bracket. Having lived in a tepee for the first six years of my life, I tend to notice nice surroundings more than most.

I follow her through a gate, and garden the size of a wardrobe. The front door leads straight into a sitting room with a wood-burner, and two battered sofas, a bookcase along one wall, a dresser against the other, on which there are several photographs in silver frames of a cute-looking big-eyed child, whom I assume is theirs. Only one rare pic with Tom solo graces the family collection. Recalling the photograph of him in the magazine, I'm in no doubt that he is the same man, despite the change in hair colour. I want to linger and snap a copy on my mobile, but Stephanie propels me through to the kitchen

"Sorry about the mess," she says, although, to my eyes, it's tidy. She sweeps off her coat with a shiver, dumps it on a chair, on which a fat black cat snoozes. "Sorry, Theo," she says, although he doesn't appear to mind. "I'll put on the heating. Not normally here at this time. Take a pew."

It's no figure of speech. A settle in the kitchen looks as if it's been reclaimed from an old church. I sit and watch as she makes coffee, instant, the way I like it. Mugs apiece, Stephanie stands with her back to a fancy-looking range cooker. I can't help but notice that she is slimmer than me, her body more toned and supple. I'm not overweight but feel chubby by comparison.

She starts the conversational ball rolling.

"What did you do before you lost your job?"

I tell her. A lot of people react to journalists, or hacks, with hostility. They assume that even lowly reporters are synonymous with gutter journalism, hounding folk to get a story and dig the dirt. Uncomfortably, this is not far off the truth. I *am* here to dig the dirt.

A smile blossoms on her face.

"Is that funny?" I say, intrigued.

"I meet a lot of people in my line of work. All shapes and sizes. With serious buyers, you usually find out what they do for a living."

"I suppose you need to know whether they can afford the house they are buying."

"Not only that – because people love talking about themselves," she says with a laugh. "Sometimes somebody will spring a surprise, but I'm right ninety per cent of the time."

"So what did you have me down for?"

She inclines her head. "I didn't, but now you tell me, it makes sense."

"Really?" I exclaim, not a little unsettled.

"Journalism is a career I contemplated once but, as a young single mum, it went out of the window."

I salt the reference to single parenthood away and sip my coffee.

"Can you get another job?" she asks thoughtfully.

I shrug. "Only if I move from Cheltenham." I don't enjoy revealing where I live. Makes me jumpy.

"Nice place," she says. "I see your dilemma."

I agree with a smile.

"So this man in your life," Stephanie gently probes.

"Oh, let's not talk about him." All I want to talk about is him, but not in the way Stephanie suggests.

Endeavouring to introduce a more personal dynamic to the conversation before I tramped all over it with my big feet, she averts her gaze. Maybe Stephanie regrets inviting a stranger into her home. Eyes now fixed on the quarry-tiled floor, she asks, "What did Anita tell you, exactly?"

"That you have a daughter. That your husband was killed in Thailand in a road accident."

She looks up with candour, sorrow in her eyes. "Four years ago." I clamp my teeth together. Barely a year afterwards, Tom shacked up with me. "One of those soft, warm July days when the sun glows and makes promises it never intended to keep." Her voice cracks with longing, as if a shard of pain penetrated her heart years ago and stayed there. "I'd been so looking forward to having him back."

Her voice is plaintive and I want to reach out and put an arm around her shoulder. Tell her I'm sorry. For her. For me. Towards Tom, I feel nothing but venom.

"It doesn't get any easier," she murmurs.

Not daring to contemplate the difficulty of my own emotional journey, I focus on what I came for: answers.

"How come Adam was in Thailand?"

She shakes her head, grips the handle of the mug until her knuckles almost crack. "His stupid pointless brother." What might be a plain statement coming from anyone else sounds like a curse from Stephanie's lips. I am rapt because this doesn't compute with Tom. Is this why Tom had such a downer on Reg?

"You didn't know Adam, but he had a wandering spirit. Part of the reason, I loved him." She snatches a breath, as though it physically hurts her to recollect. "Mikey, Adam's younger brother, got into a scrape in Thailand. God alone knows what he was doing there, but I can imagine." There's a bitter tang to her voice. Mikey sounds like a pain in the rear. "Anyway, Mikey got into trouble with some locals. Had his money stolen and, when he complained to the Thai police, they weren't interested. So there he is, stuck in a foreign land, destitute, according to him."

"And Adam went to help?" I don't mistakenly say 'Tom' because already it feels as if I'm talking about a totally different person.

She chews her bottom lip and nods.

"Couldn't Adam have simply wired funds?"

"There was a problem with it, again according to Mikey."

"You didn't believe him?"

She shrugs. "It's hard to know what I believe any more." Now is my moment to tell her the truth. I take a breath. A lick of fear travels up my spine. No, I can't.

"So Adam dropped everything?" I say in a piercing voice that doesn't sound real.

"Yes," she says quietly. "He was a chef. Had quite a good job but the pay was rubbish. It's pretty typical here. The classier the restaurant, the lower the wages. You're supposed to work for the love of it, the prestige and status it confers." She says it with another rare note of cynicism that doesn't sit easy with her personality demeanour. But this isn't what reso-nates with me. Tom used his occupation for both identities. I wonder about the significance of this, but not for too long because Stephanie is still talking. "And he was having to drive quite a way, all right in the day, not so good at two a.m." I force a sympathetic smile to cover my surprise. Tom, who doesn't drive, doesn't have a licence. Another stupid, pointless lie. Then I remember Reg's comment about Tom's conversation. Is the license significant? Consumed by the thought, I almost miss what Stephanie says next. "In a way I think he was looking for an excuse to hand his notice in.

"And, as Mikey's only brother, he felt a responsibility. Their parents died when they were children," she explains, taking a drink. "Brought up by an elderly aunt."

I take another scalding sip of coffee to mute a reaction. With subtle variations, same story. Same lie? I'm tempted to ask whether Tom took drugs, yet I can't think of an easy way to slip it in. Maybe he only started when he was living with me. "The aunt?" I force the question, already suspecting the answer.

"She died before I met Adam."

Pain seizes the muscles in my shoulders. My jaw grinds with anger. "How did you two meet?" When I talk I feel as if I'm speaking in tongues.

Beaming at the recollection, she says, "At a pub I was working in at the time. My mum had Zoe while I did evening shifts. Helped to keep the money flowing.

"We found each other really. Adam was such a gentle, private, enigmatic man." She pronounces 'enigmatic' slowly as if she's heard the word on television and thinks the description fits him best. Not a man who was edgy and unpredictable, then. Not a man who was miserable. Part of me wants to meet this paragon of a husband. It occurs to me that Stephanie had the best of him while I had the worst.

"Couldn't stand having his photograph taken," she recollects fondly. "I think in all the time we were together, I managed to get two shots of him."

"The one you have on your desk," I say.

"Anita showed you?" She frowns at the liberty taken.

"Sorry."

She leans over and briefly touches my hand. "Not your fault. It's my favourite because it summed him up. Little bit clueless about how the world worked, if you know what I mean, but he was such a smiler. Smiled all the time."

*Smiled?* No, I don't know what she means. I have no idea at all. "So brave," Stephanie continues with admiration, "because, underneath it, I recognised he was a lost soul."

I have no need to assume a troubled expression. This is for real. "In what way?" Perhaps living with Stephanie rescued him in a way that I could not. The Adam she talks of sounds like a new, improved version of Tom. After he faked his own death did his dual life screw him over?

"Wasn't very worldly. Didn't seem to know where he was heading. Innocent, really. And, oh my God," she rolls her eyes and beams, "hopeless with money. As soon as he earned it, he'd blow it." My mind seizes hotly upon the arguments I had with Tom about his propensity to spend. "Naïve about life, or maybe that's because I'd had to grow up, what with having a child on my own."

"Young for his age?" I chip in.

"Twenty-one going on fifteen," she laughs. "We married two years after we met, on his twenty-third birthday. We only had four years together." With a jolt, I factor this in with what Anita said and realise that it doesn't compute. If I have this right, Tom is now thirty-one not thirty-five, as he led me to believe.

"And Zoe's dad?"

Stephanie shakes her head. "Off the scene. Never should have happened, but I'm glad it did." She flicks a shy smile. "Adam was lovely with Zoe. Very calm," she says proudly. "Sorry, I'm droning on."

"No, it's fine." And it was because every piece of information was going into my mental database.

"As you probably gather, I could talk for both of us." Like me, I think numbly.

Her face relaxes. Happy. Sorted. She needs to talk about her man. It provides solace for her.

My coffee tastes bitter on my tongue. I allow Stephanie her memory of the husband she still clearly loves, while mine lingers ailing, sickly and not breathing terribly well.

"Did you consider travelling with Adam to Thailand?"

"What would I do with a small child in the middle of Phuket?"

I shoot a smile. "I can think of worse places."

Stephanie shakes her head vehemently. "My family and friends are here. Mum, who isn't very well now, lives over the border. My part of the world," she says, looking around her, "not Adam's."

"Where was that?" I believe I know, but I could be mistaken; so very wrong about many things.

"Torquay, Devon."

Seaside resort. Palm trees. Tourists wanting affordable low-end breaks. Not city. Not rattle and hum. Not South London.

"And the accident?" I shouldn't press her emotional wound, but cannot help myself. Besides, after her initial response, she doesn't appear to mind. It seems almost a relief.

"On the way from the airport. A cab collided with a tanker. Mikey was with him."

"They both died?"

Her look is raw, bleeding at the edges. "First I knew was when I received a knock at the door from a couple of police officers."

My eyes blink with confusion to prevent them from shooting wide. Coppers? How the hell did that work? "I'm so sorry," I mumble, although my apology is for something else entirely. "And your poor little girl."

She pushes a feeble smile. "Adam might not have been Zoe's dad, but she loved him like he was."

"I don't know what to say." True.

"I thought, with my family and friends, I'd be okay." Her expression is one of great sadness and loss.

I tiptoe up to what I say next. "But you're not?"

She lets out a breath. "It's worse. Nobody tells you how much grief hurts. It's almost physical." She thumps her chest to emphasise the point. "Anti-depressants take the edge off it, but they don't really help. There's no medicine to mend a broken heart, is there?"

I can't bear to meet her bleak expression. I stumble a platitude.

77

"And there's only so much your family can take," she continues. "It's as if there is a set time of mourning, after which you're supposed to pick yourself up and get on with life."

Oh God, should I tell her the truth? How can I reveal that we've both been deceived and betrayed? How can I rip the ground from underneath her feet? "Rarely works like that."

"No," she agrees with a lonely smile. "You understand, don't you?"

It isn't said to trap me. She speaks simply like one woman reaching out to another. Crucified, I look away, fix on a stain on the wall, and listen to the kitchen clock pounding a beat. I should go and never ever return. "Grief is the price we pay for love," I murmur. Placing my mug on the table and pulling my coat tight around my shoulders, I make a move to leave.

And then she floors me.

"I know this is really really stupid, but I keep imagining that he's still here. That he hasn't died at all. That there's been a terrible mistake."

Unseen hands with grimy fingers close around my throat. I grip the table, as if by steadying my body I will also compose my mind. "Unsurprising in the circumstances."

"But I believe it, do you see?"

"Part of the grieving process," I say in a trite voice that jars.

She shakes her head. "I understand what you're getting at. I've read all the books about bereavement and grief, but what I feel, what I *experience*," she insists, eyes raking mine, "is stronger than that."

Despite fear tripping through me, I check any physical

response that might give the game away. Mentally, I run and keep on running. It strikes me then that this is what I do often.

"I'm not a religious person," Stephanie says. "No time for church, but what I feel," she says, her fingers wrapping around a pretty necklace that I suspect Tom gave her, mainly because he never gave me jewellery, "is that his spirit is here, not in my heart, but *here*, maybe not in this town, but somewhere. Maybe, it's because there was nothing left to bury."

"No?" This time, I'm unable to muzzle my shock.

"The crash obliterated everyone involved. It was literally an inferno." Her eyes fill with utter sadness, "Thailand isn't like England when it comes to taking care of people's remains. Perhaps that's why I still can't grasp it." She looks at me with such fervour that, although I understand that her feelings for Tom take a dissimilar shape to mine, I know deep inside how much this woman loved the man. It humbles me. "We had a funeral of sorts, so that should be the end of it." Her voice tails off. I have no idea what to say. I'm too busy trying to stop myself from ranting and spilling all I know.

Stephanie fills the gap. "Is that so stupid of me, do you think?" Voice cracking again, she turns and swipes a box of tissues from off the work surface, snatches one out and stems a tear seeping from the corner of her eye. It takes everything I have not to do the same, if for rather different reasons.

"Hark at me go on," she says, blowing her nose. "You have your own troubles."

She deserves better than this. How I long to tell her the truth because, out of all of my friends, including Vick, and my brother, Stephanie alone would share my burden. It's selfish of me, yet I'm torn. She has more right than she'll ever know to be told that the bond she feels has not been broken, that Adam, or Tom, is alive somewhere and out there in the real world. I stumble a reply, despite a sensation of stone-cold panic that she might read the blatant struggle going on inside me. What's worse, her face breaks out in a wide expression of warmth and reassurance.

I feel a heel. Morally bankrupt. A dissembler. Just like the man called Adam who changed his name to Tom.

# Chapter 11

"Will you be able to find your own way back?"

"Down here, straight over at the roundabout and keep on walking, didn't you say?"

"I could run you in the car? Oh, goodness," Stephanie breaks off, glancing over my shoulder. "I hadn't realised the time." I turn, step aside and follow her gaze to a young woman with two children, a boy and girl in primary-school uniform. The woman smiles and walks toward us. The little girl bobs along, fizzing with energy. She carries a pink lunchbox decorated with unicorns. A sparkly slide glitters in her soft dark hair and, Vick was right, she has the same oval-shaped face as her mother, although her eyes are different, green, not brown, and the lids heavier, probably taking after the man who fathered her.

Stephanie opens her arms wide and the little girl skips towards her, beaming from ear to ear. "Mummy, can I go and play at Wilf's house? Jess says it's all right."

"Steady," Stephanie laughs, tousling her daughter's hair.

"Don't, Mummy," she scolds, pulling away. Stern.

"Roz, this is Zoe," Stephanie says.

"Hi, Zoe," I say. The little girl glances up, pays the least attention, mumbles 'Hi' and then dismisses me. After all, I'm a grown-up, a strange species. Who can blame her?

"And this, Roz, is Jess, and Wilf, Zoe's best pal."

Jess nods hello with a friendly expression. Wilf tugs on Zoe's arm, indicating that playing at his house is a done deal.

"Can I?" Zoe wheedles, "Please say yes, Mummy." To impress the point, she tilts toward Stephanie, reminding me of a loyal dog leaning hard against his owner's legs in a gesture of affection. Stephanie grins and throws a questioning look at Jess.

"Fine by me," Wilf's mum says. "I'll bring Zoe back after tea, if you like."

"Yes," Wilf bursts out, punching the air with a fist. His cheeky face splits into a wide grin.

"Looks like I don't have a choice," Stephanie says with a wry laugh.

Zoe pushes her bag and lunch box into her mother's hands. "And look after Sealy for me," she commands, before belting off down the street with Wilf in tow. "I will. Be good, poppet," Stephanie calls after her. "Sealy is Zoe's favourite toy," she lets on. "Adam gave it to her when she was tiny. They're inseparable."

"Better go," Jess says, trotting after them.

Observing a small slice of family life, I'm gripped with envy and sadness. Any hope I have of motherhood, or being in a secure financial position that allows me to adopt, disappeared less than twenty-four hours ago. I'm seized with the idea that my life will be forever bleak and empty. Irrational, perhaps, yet my heart aches for imaginary and random misfortunes as well as the more obvious one of being betrayed by Tom. Stephanie slices into my sudden melancholy.

"I know I'm biased, but she's glorious, isn't she? So full of life."

I agree, my fingers digging deep into the palms of my hands. "I'm glad for you."

"Right," Stephanie says, switching from Mummy-mode to professional. "I'll grab my keys and run you back."

"Honestly, it's no bother." I want to walk. I need to. I think better that way. How else do I process that the man for whom I still have strong feelings, confused and bad, acted a role in which I played no part in the production?

She sketches a frown. "Are you sure? I don't mind."

"Enjoy your moment of freedom." I itch to escape into anonymous, alien streets.

"Come and see me when your mum gets back," Stephanie says, hovering on the doorstep. "Better still—" She breaks off, disappears for seconds, returns and presses a card into my hand. "My direct number. I'll come up with a good deal for her, promise."

"That's kind." I push another smile. "Thanks for the coffee," I add, plunging my hands deep into my jacket pockets. The wind, if anything, is stronger now, boisterous too. Good.

"Thank you for listening," she says, touching my sleeve.

"Likewise."

I feel Stephanie's gaze bore into my back as I trudge away. Turning left, like she said, I cross over past a one-stop shop and head straight towards town. My gait is leaden. My mind is a grubby and disorganised mess, a cheap sale of bric-a- brac in a tatty village hall. Tom and Adam Charteris are one and the same. No doubt about it. While there are consistencies in his story, only his occupation is verifiable.

One thought jabs at me more than the rest: why is Tom on the run again?

Something makes me shiver and I hitch a fast look behind, yet there is nobody there. Bound to be jumpy after what happened, after what I was told.

I pick up pace and cut down a narrow cobbled alley, past a French restaurant and deli on my left, and old-fashioned sweetie shop on my right, and cross over the road at the brow of a hill as the lights switch from red to green. Keep walking. Keep moving.

I consider the dead brother and the Devon connection and whether or not I can trace Adam's trajectory. Surely, there will be archived information about what allegedly happened to them both?

Inserting myself into a shoal of shoppers keen to bag a bargain in one of the gift shops that line the street, I take a furtive look back to check again whether I'm being followed. Perhaps it's Tom lurking in the shadows, or Tom seeking sanctuary with the woman he once deceived so badly. Somehow, I don't think he's there, but you never know. My grand idea that Tom is a serial cheater who has a problem with commitment rings hollow in time with my fading footsteps.

It's way bigger than this.

I continue towards the market square and finally the car park. With relief, I open up, climb inside, lock the doors and let out a long, perplexed breath. Slumping across the steering wheel, I grind my brow into the plastic.

Adam smiles, is nice, caring and quiet, 'enigmatic,' she said. Life histories are similar in most aspects and dissimilar in a few. A brother is in the mix with Adam and absent with Tom. With a taste for the dramatic, multiple personality disorder floats across my mind, but I sense that this is not what I'm dealing with. It isn't a medical issue. It's criminal.

*I am tainted by it.*

To my way of thinking, Tom has a lot in common with arms dealers and gangland figures. They, too, are averse to leaving digital footprints. They, too, shack up with multiple partners. They, too, live a lie. I briefly wonder how many identities Tom actually has and give up because it makes my brain expand and bang against my skull.

And do I feel rage? You bet.

A shudder passes through me at the recollection I very nearly weakened and confessed to Stephanie who I was. With a couple of sentences I could proclaim that her belief in Adam's existence is warranted, that he is alive and has been for the past four years. As cruel as it is to withhold, it feels crueller still to be the messenger. Leave that to others.

Oh God.

With a tight chest, I realise that I have absolutely no choice but to report my findings to the police. How I'm going to disclose the information without destruction following in its wake, I don't know. Revenge is not my motivation. And, after what I was told, I wouldn't have him back if he begged me. It's the search for truth that spurs me on. If Tom's intention was only to deceive Stephanie into believing he was dead, why did two police officers pay her a visit? Were they duped too? Or, I breathe heavily; does corruption lie at the heart of it?

I briefly wonder what Vick will say. Itching to tell her, I decide to go to the law first. Immediately, I think of D.S. Michael Shenton. With the contact already made, it would be easier talking to him about what is essentially a delicate matter. Before losing my nerve, I pull out my mobile and phone the police station. It takes what seems an age to connect the call.

"Yes?" It's a brisk response, as if I caught him in the middle of something.

"Can I come and talk to you?"

"Could you drop me an email? Be easier."

"It's not about the article. I have information that I think you'll want to hear."

"Like what?" His voice sharpens.

"I'd rather not say on the phone."

"Has a crime been committed?"

"I don't honestly know."

"Only there are avenues for—"

"Please. I believe it's a police matter and I badly need to talk to someone." I hate sounding flaky. "Would you be free at three this afternoon?"

I hear him exhale.

"I'll come to you," I insist before bursting into a chorus of appreciation and gratitude.

"I'm at Gloucester," he says, "HQ.'

Headquarters is good for this is certainly an HQ matter. "Fine."

I start the car, pull out of the car park, and wish I didn't feel in ruins. Of the potential consequences, I don't spare a single thought.

# Chapter 12

Tom felt the cold as keenly as a knife embedded in his chest. It was preferable. At least now he felt something other than numb, crushing remorse for what he'd done to Roz. He made no excuses.

Jacket drawn tight around him, hood up to mask his profile, he cursed the way in which his life had changed again.

The second he saw the photographer at the party, he'd known the way it would roll. Earthquake, plague, destruction and fire. Should have got out then. Should have known better. Should have disappeared to a place where the police and anyone else would never find him. Should. Should. Should.

A puddle of dirt and filthy rainwater shot up in a thin stream, soaking the back of his jeans. Fuck's sake. If only he were gas-guzzling miles away.

Trudging on, he wondered if he dared risk a night in a cheap motel. He had the money. He'd planned for that. Somewhere he could hide, think, straighten out his head, *calm down*.

Without breaking step, he reached inside his jacket, pulled out a 'Reddy,' popped the capsule into his mouth. Better.

Needed to stay practical, grounded, to drown out the bedlam that threatened to demolish his mental architecture and bring it crashing down. Never meant to use Roz, mislead or dupe her. Never meant to break her heart. Jesus Christ, he missed her, needed her. *Craved* her.

Shame flamed his cheeks at the memory of her face, the crushed look in her free-spirit eyes. He remembered them fucking each other in every room in the house, including the sitting room, the very morning he deserted her, the smell of her skin, her hair, and the way she'd given herself to him so freely. With abandon and joy.

What a bastard. And she'd be right to think so. The thought dismantled him.

Roz was lovable and funny, light and offbeat, all things he wasn't. That was the big attraction. Roz looked so much like Steph and yet was so different in countless wayward ways. She didn't deserve to be treated badly and didn't deserve him. Roz never knew to what extent he was damaged, that long-ago events had irrevocably changed him. And he could never say anything, because to do so would put her life in danger. Abandoning her now was the best way he knew to protect her.

Naturally, he'd always known of her grand plan for marriage and children. He'd wanted it too, truth be told, but it was impossible for a man like him. How could he bring a child into *this*? Guilt flowed through him. Every time she touched on the subject he fed the lie because it was easier, yet the biggest lie of all: he wasn't who she thought he was. For the past three years he'd been a man who'd grabbed hold of someone else's life and struggled to cling to it. Fear shattered inside and splintered into a trillion jagged pieces.

And there was anger. It almost lifted him off his feet. How could he confess that people were dead because of him? The last guy's name, Jack Prior, was inscribed on his heart. Weirdly, Jack had also provided him with salvation.

At first.

Hadn't lasted. Nothing did. He had the cops to thank for that, double-dealing, treacherous bastards. Mads included. So composed and confident. So reassuring. So understanding. Christ, he'd listened and bought it when she told him he'd be protected. Done exactly as she said. Taken the rap for everything. He'd trusted her, not once but twice. Put his life in her hands and she'd let this happen to him. *Again.* The first cock-up was served up to him as an administrative error, someone accidentally leaking information. Yeah, right. He'd pushed Mads hard, but she never flickered, never deviated from her story. *As a precaution*, Tom was moved on. Scrubbing at his scalp, a fresh burst of chill rain shot over the planes of his face and dripped down his stubbled chin.

This time, after Mads called him back, he'd cleared out of town like a man with a one hundred-metre world record to break. Good sense dictated that you don't cut and run, but he'd no choice. The trick was not to get caught. He'd gone off-grid immediately, ripped the SIM from his phone and thrown both away, so that he couldn't be traced, hit the nearest main road, where he blagged a lift from a lorry driver heading towards the M5. The guy was Polish. Didn't speak a word of English. Suited him. They'd listened to a radio station playing country music. Broken hearts, twanging strings and good old boys. Meanwhile, the soundtrack in his brain played a different tune. Clashing guitar riffs. Drums with a syncopated beat. Crazy rhythm. Offered a smoke, he'd gladly accepted. It felt good to light up in an act of solidarity, to draw the heat and tar deep into his lungs. Made him feel alive, all those blood vessels and capillaries straining and exploding in preparation for a carcinogenic showdown. Now he could smoke his head off if he chose to. God knew he'd missed fully indulging his habit.

Traffic whizzed past. Blare and noise and wet light. Didn't flinch. Kept right on moving. This was him. *The real skin-crawling him.* Always on the run. Always hiding. Bloody sick of minding what he said. How he said it. Tired of his chameleon ways. Exhausted by the subterfuge of perpetually changing his appearance. This time, he'd taken the precaution of acquiring contact lenses, blue the new brown. Last time it had been easier. Summer. Shades. Shorts. Flip-flops. Everyone the same. Job done – and he'd had help back then. In winter, you're screwed.

A sign for Wolverhampton glared down at him. Jesus, he needed to be anywhere but here, a place he would never blend in, yet to go west risked having his heart ripped out. More importantly, it threatened the lives of others he loved.

Spun out, a low moan jettisoned from the back of his throat and disappeared into the moist, claggy air. He'd lost too much, more than was conceivable in such a short lifetime. Perhaps he could finish it now. Show them what he was really made of, have the last laugh on the lot of them. Anger in his despair. Despair in his anger. Surrender too.

Step off the kerb and into the road.

Arms wide.

Tossed off his feet.

Bones crushed beneath rubber and metal.

*Splat.*

Did he have the balls?

Rooted at the edge of the pavement, roar and whoosh of traffic clattered against his ears. Rain bled over him. Indecision gripped him.

*Are you a quitter or survivor?*

Think, for fuck's sake. Mustn't look back. He'd tried so hard to forget and to contain the past in a box marked 'trash', where it belonged. Exerting every mental sinew, he'd done his best to move forward, inhabit someone else. Embrace a brand-new start, he was told, and he'd snatched hold gladly, with courage and faith. It had seemed like fate smiling down on him, bathing him in warmth and love and colour. A smile scampered across his lips in bliss at the memory and as quickly expired.

Joke.

They told him the past gets easier, that time heals. Liars. Acute, sharp-edged, his past was catching up with him faster and with the same relentlessness as a drone strike. Vacant smiles and passive attitude to conceal the truth and the lies didn't cut it any more. Never really had, now he came to think about it. Amped, rage coiled inside him at the injustice of it all. He had been so massively failed by a system supposed to protect him.

He pushed back a smudge strand of hair from his face; adjusted the weight of the rucksack on his back; hands plunged into his pockets. One night in a back-street doss house, then he'd move on.

Should never have got close to anyone, least of all darling Roz. And yes, he mourned the loss of her in his life. Should never have let things escalate and get out of hand. They always did. And that was fucking scary.

# Chapter 13

"Right," Mike Shenton says.

Pacing for twenty minutes while waiting to see him, I rehearse what I will say and how I will say it, but it doesn't come out the way I intend. To any sane person, it's a bewildering story.

I convince myself that Shenton is a police officer and has heard it all before, except that his facial expressions change like the seasons. Just when he settles for a warm padded jacket, beanie hat and sturdy boots, he discards them and reaches for shorts, Tropical shirt and flip-flops. After exploring the possibility of a 'domestic', he moves on to 'missing persons', which, he assures me doesn't apply because, "Tom passed on a message to your brother," and finally fetches up on 'fraud'. Next, he fires a host of questions about Tom's finances and whether or not he has debts or life insurance.

"I don't know the extent of any liabilities, except to say that Tom was rubbish with money. Aren't you missing something?" At this, Shenton flares his nostrils. "Police officers went to Stephanie Charteris's house to deliver the bad news. Doesn't that indicate that they were also deceived?" Or in on it, I infer, taming the mutinous note in my voice. I always fancied being a crime correspondent. Perhaps I missed my calling.

Shenton shoots me a contemptuous glare, which from his fair features assumes grave significance. He takes notes, backtracks, corroborates certain points and blows out heavily through pursed lips. I suggest he logs into the nearest computer and combs through records. Clearly not copperly policy, he views me as if I'm bonkers. My problem is that I never had close dealings with police, unless you count a speeding fine when I was twenty-four that banged up my insurance; and my little sortie into police public relations on behalf of the now defunct local newspaper.

"Wait there," he says in an authoritative voice.

I do and examine the small room with its dun-coloured walls and minimal beaten-up looking furniture. I roll the pad of my index finger against the surface of the table, examine the sticky imprint and wish I hadn't. After a nerve-grinding wait, the door sweeps open. I don't get Shenton. I get a man who looks as if he has no eyes.

"I'm Detective Inspector Falconer," he announces. From underneath a thick greasy fringe, strong features emerge, coarse in the pallid light of the interview room. His thick lips inhabit the lower part of his face, as if they are specially designed to frame questions that demand the truth, the whole truth and nothing but the truth. And God help you if you don't.

The epitome of controlled professionalism, he stands while I continue to sit, ultimate power play in motion and a classic way of asserting authority and ensuring the dynamics work in his favour. I sense the mood music change from easy listening to punk.

"You have information, I understand." He speaks rapidly, cutting to the chase, no mention of Shenton.

"About Tom Loxley."

"Your boyfriend." When he talks the right side of his upper lip curls, confirming his generally surly appearance. It's really difficult to imagine this man sharing a joke, having a laugh, let alone engaging in a romantic relationship with either sex.

"Four years ago, he was someone else."

If it's at all possible, his eyes recede further, as though someone rubbed fresh rock salt into them. "You mean he went under another name?"

"Adam Charteris."

"How did you come by this?"

I have made it clear already, but start over again. The moment I mention Facebook, Falconer's lips twitch, implying he derides all forms of social media. My meeting with Stephanie Charteris sounds so blatantly contrived, my cheeks burn. I get the feeling that Falconer thinks I'm one crazy bitch, and this is a replay of 'Play Misty.'

"How do you know this Adam character is Tom?" He speaks quietly so that I strain to hear, but there is no mistaking the tetchiness in his voice.

"I saw a photograph of him. He had a different hair colour, but that's irrelevant." Falconer flashes a look that tells me we are simpatico on the subject. Forlornly, I continue, "Both Tom and Adam's stories match."

"Stories?"

"Like I said, I spoke to Stephanie Charteris."

"Did you now?" Still quiet, but his lean and boringly gym-fit body looks tight, springy and fit to snap.

"I didn't tell her about Tom being Adam," I add quickly, hoping to defuse his unreasonable anger.

"Thank heavens for small mercies." Snippy with it.

"Don't you believe me? Don't you think there is something fishy about it?"

I try to keep the frustration out of my voice. Not sure I succeed.

He waits several beats. My chest is dry and rattley. My throat is parched and I can barely speak. This is a bad idea, a very bad idea.

"You're mistaken."

"No, I—"

"Fancy yourself as an amateur detective?" Why doesn't he go the whole way and suggest that I watch too much TV?

"No, I simply—"

"Want to help." He adopts a singsong voice. Taking the piss. "If you *really* want to help," he says, "you'll keep your private fantasies to yourself."

"They aren't fantasies."

"And that includes Tom Loxley," he adds, railroading.

"Aren't you interested in him?" I erupt. "Don't you realise he's wormed his way into the affections of two different women, spinning them lies? He has a wife. He was like a father to Stephanie Charteris's little girl and faked his own death in a road accident in Thailand. He deceived two police officers, for God's sake, unless they were part of the plot," I throw in recklessly.

His upper lip doesn't curl. It's one blunt line. Oh God, I realise that by inferring something dodgy I went too far. Defensiveness doesn't really cover his reaction. "Those are very serious allegations."

"It *is* very serious."

"How do you know that this Adam character and Tom Loxley are one and the same?"

He sounds like a broken record, but I don't dare point this out. "I don't know for certain of course, but—"

"What makes you think that we haven't spoken to Mr Loxley?"

My jaw almost hits the deck. "You've spoken to him?" Was that why Falconer took so long to talk to me? Was he phoning around the country looking for, and locating, Tom? Fuck. "How the hell? Where is he?"

Falconer issues a nasty smile. All over me now. He'd make even the Pope seem degenerate. If it's possible, I feel worse than when I started.

"Tom Loxley was rather surprised to hear from us following your allegation. On the back of our enquiry, we can assure you that this is a simple case of mistaken identity. Moreover, Mr Loxley does not want to be contacted by you again. Ever."

"Right," I mumble, desperate to escape the chair, the room, the stuffy temperature, this blasted man.

After crushing me to dust, Falconer's expression softens from granite to soapstone. "My best advice is to put your broken heart behind you and get on with your life. I don't need to spell out the necessity of leaving a grieving widow to recover from her loss."

"I understand." I am the very picture of meekness. Not enough, judging by Falconer's edgy body language: crossed arms, ramrod spine, straight set of his muscular, pumped-up iron shoulders.

"You'll do more than that, Miss Outlaw," he says, advancing again, with a black look. "If you persist in harassing a perfectly innocent and vulnerable young woman with your wild ideas, the full weight of the law will come crashing down and ensure the swift termination of your career."

Sledgehammered, I reel. "I have no career." Which is true, but this does not deter Falconer.

"Do I make myself plain?" he glowers.

Am I affronted? Yes. Am I fearful? Absolutely. But it does not prevent a big shiny light pinging on in my brain. Considering the *crime* I committed, Falconer selects a hefty weapon with which to pulverise me into submission and, let's face it, the dirt. Good. He not only shows his hand, he over-plays it.

I glare at him, thinking he needs to learn the benefit of taking a more nuanced approach. He'd be better at dealing with organised crime. Perhaps counter-terrorism has an opening for him.

Anger surges so hard through my veins, I fear it will explode out of my chest *Alien*-style. "Thank you for your time," I say stiffly.

"You're welcome," he says, eyeing me.

I get up and slink out.

# Chapter 14

Stumped for answers that make sense, I call Vick.

"Are you in?"

"Ready and waiting."

"See you in fifteen."

On arrival, the fire is lit and two glasses sit beside an open bottle of red wine. I subside into the nearest comfy chair. Vick hands me a drink, we clink, and I take a deep swig.

"That bad?" Vick curls her legs up underneath her.

Where to start? "The police spoke to Tom."

Vick unfurls and her body bolts forward. "The police? Is he in trouble?"

"Not according to them. I'm the one who needs watching."

She rubs the side of her nose and her eyes narrow. "Who told you that?"

"A policeman called Falconer."

"You're joking."

"I'm not."

"I don't get it. What the hell has he got to say for himself?"

"Falconer?"

"Tom bloody Loxley, you idiot."

"That he doesn't want to speak to me." *Ever.* "But that's not all."

I launch in and, sooner than you can say Victoria, she interrupts.

"Whoa, hold it right there. You're saying that Tom lived with another woman for years and faked his own death?"

"Not another woman, his wife."

"Christ on a crutch, are you sure?"

"I know it sounds outlandish, but it's true."

"Hey, you don't think he's one of those undercover coppers who shack up with women in order to access information about anti-establishment groups?"

"Stephanie Charteris is a sales advisor for a construction company, Vick. Taylor Wimpey is hardly some kind of subversive organisation, is it?"

Wildly, I remember a stink about police officers stealing the identities of dead children to prop up their covers. Using the dead to give fake life to the living. Did Tom use a similar device? I shiver at the prospect.

"Yeah, you're right," Vick says ruminatively, in a *glad we got that one nailed* tone.

She tops up our drinks. Her hand is as shaky as my voice and she spills some on the chair she's sitting in. "Doesn't matter," she says, which is odd for Vick because it usually matters a great deal. "Run through it again, slowly, this time."

I do. She lets out little gasps of disbelief, each one louder than the one previous, and her eyes flare with shock as she takes it all in. By the time I finish, the colour in her cheeks is high; thread veins imminent.

"But that's preposterous."

"Which bit?"

"All of it," she says. "You're really certain this Adam is Tom?"

"I'm not losing my mind, Vick."

"I appreciate that." She talks with a dulcet, fair-minded intonation parents adopt with delinquent offspring who maintain that they tried their best to behave but don't really give a flying fuck. "Obviously, you're quite stressed and when people are upset they—"

"I know what I saw and I'm not deaf." My voice is deadweight. "How do you explain the similarity in stories?"

Pensive, she blows out through her mouth, hot cheeks puffing like a set of old bellows. "I see your point."

"Thank you."

"I guess it's easier to sham a car accident in Thailand."

"An obliterating car crash," I remind her. "Not so much rigorous record-taking and officialdom in that part of the world." In a dismal moment I wonder exactly what Stephanie buried at the funeral.

Vick glances away, momentarily lost in thought. "How would that compute with Stephanie receiving the bad news from the police?"

"That's the part that most concerns me." Why else would Falconer use such a needlessly aggressive tone if not to carry out a spectacular amount of whitewashing and rear-covering? That little voice in my head whispers *corruption*.

"Maybe Tom fooled them too."

"Bit of a stretch."

"But not impossible."

I tell Vick about Falconer's threat.

Vick's eyes crinkle with strain. "He said what?"

I repeat Falconer's uncompromising words.

Silence waltzes into Vick's pint-sized sitting room. Vick twizzles it around and throws it, *Strictly Come Dancing*-style, to the other side of the room, where it smacks against the wall. "Does Tom have any vices?"

"Apart from practising deception on a grand scale?"

"You know what I mean."

"Not that I know of, other than he's not great with money."

"Join the club."

"Worse than you."

"A gambler?"

I smile ruefully. "Nothing like that, but honestly, Vick, would I know?"

Vick hitches one shoulder. "What I don't get is why the police would lie to you. I mean they wouldn't, would they?"

My jaw stiffens. "I'm not imagining this. I'm not making it up." I snatch at my drink to emphasise the point. Tom's edginess, it seems, has transferred and squirreled its way into my personality.

"No, of course," she says, adopting a soothing tone again.

"And there's Tom's mystery trip to Wales when he should have been in London," I point out.

"Reg said. Does Tom have relatives or friends there, do you think?"

"How would I know?"

We sit in clumsy silent communication. She drinks. I drink. She fiddles with a button on her sleeve. I twiddle a lock of hair. I get that horrible impression again for the second time in as many days that she is holding something back. I stay quiet and watch as she moves her fingers and anxiously rubs the grain of the leather on the armchair.

"There is something," she says, snatching at the words before they run away from her. "Tom never struck me as a man who settled. Do you know what I mean? Always seemed to be looking over his shoulder."

It stings. How could I be so stupid? She glances up at a single minor crack in the ceiling above my head, as if lost in some private thought about when to have it fixed, re-plastered and re-painted. I stalk the silence until it's too uncomfortable for her to stay schtum. "He was a man who seemed to be waiting for something horrible to happen." She speaks softly then tears her glance from the fabric of the building to me. "Suppose Tom is involved in something criminal."

Oh God, it's one thing to entertain the thought, quite another to have your best pal thinking along the same lines. I don't know how to respond. Comprehensively cornered, fear whips through my veins. Shaken, I say, "Gangland connections?" Before the afternoon, it was pretend. Now it could be real. Precisely what did I inadvertently stray into? Except, I remind myself, I walked into it the day I met Tom Loxley, damn him.

"Goodness, I wouldn't put it that strongly." Vick leans so far back in the chair she's in danger of flipping over the top.

"Well, criminal connections then."

She reaches for the bottle, splashing more wine into our glasses. "You're a journalist, can't you find out?"

"Vick, I'm a Z-level reporter, not some investigative bod working for *Panorama*.'

"Don't you have contacts?"

"Not the kind you're suggesting." I wonder about Elliott, my old editor. Might he be able to help? I'd need to couch any questions carefully.

"You could talk to Stephanie again."

"Not without bringing down all sorts of shit on my head and, worse still, hers." I run my fingers through my hair and encounter a knot – a metaphor for my current circumstances, it would seem.

Vick tacitly agrees. "I wish I could help, but I really think you have to do as the cops say and let it go."

"Let it go? Are you kidding? Tom is answerable, not only to me but to Stephanie Charteris and her child. As for the police, how dare they push me around."

"Do what's best for you," Vick says softly, yet with such firm authority I know she means what she says. "Tom's gone, Roz. Falconer was right. You need to move on."

Very slowly, I put down my drink, stand up and reach for my coat.

"Aww, don't be like that."

"I'm not." My voice is metallic and my smile short. "You're probably right."

"Then stay and have a bite to eat with me."

"Honest, Vick, I need to get back. Busy day tomorrow." Entirely true. Vick registers my excuse and, from the embarrassed light in her eyes, knows I'm pissed off. I give her a hug to show there are no hard feelings. How can I blame her?

Some things in life are too peculiar to process. And this is one of them.

"Take care," she says from the safety of her doorstep.

I walk quickly down Naunton Park Road and cut into the crescent that will eventually lead back home. Rain batters the street and sticks my hair to my face, tangles and all. Not even a dog or cat would venture out on a night like this. The plane trees dotting the road creak and moan in unison. They had enough, too.

For the second time in a few hours, a creepy sensation assails me. It starts at the base of my head, bores into my shoulder blades and trips with creepy fingers down my back. A pulse flickers in my neck and my foe-detector switches on. Casting a furtive glance backwards reveals that nobody is there and yet I sense that someone is. Tom, I think, whipping round, properly this time, hoping to catch him out. But it's simply me and empty street and...

Ghosts of old failed relationships rattle their chains so loudly that I turn and break into a trot, bordering on a run. Head down, my chin practically touching my chest, I don't detour into the pub on the corner on the way home, despite the lure of bright lights, noise and company.

Helplessly, my mind zeroes in on Tom. Which bits are true and which are false? If he were orphaned in childhood it would have a profound and traumatising effect. His ability to overcome it would depend on the kind of life he experienced afterwards. Was the elderly aunt, if she existed, sympathetic, content to take on a parental role? Did she resent it? I read somewhere that children who lose parents can become highly motivated adults. If they fail to resolve the tragedy, however, they can also be consumed by unspecified rage that will leak out at inopportune moments. Tom could as easily become a high achiever, seeking excellence in the kitchen, or a misfit more likely to lash out and bash the nearest sous-chef or kitchen porter over the head with a copper-bottomed saucepan. And gangland connections? I shudder.

Truth is if 'Smiley Tom' can hold down a job, engender friendship, love even, with a woman who looks so like another and fake his own death, it points in a direction that I don't want to think about. Is Stephanie somehow part of the ruse and not so mysterious at all? Husbands will often desert wives to hook up with a younger version that often appear very similar to the abandoned older model. But the reverse is true in my case. Adrift and floundering, I long for terra firma, certainty and knowledge.

Back in the safety of my own environment, I speed to the fridge, open it and select a bottle of sparkling water, popping it open. Pouring a big glass, my mind spans ranges across Tom Loxley and Adam Charteris. By the time I'm halfway down the glass, Tom wins hands down. Safer terrain.

A packet of crisps extracted from the cupboard to still the growl in my stomach, I grab a notepad from the workspace next to the kettle, sit down at the kitchen table and list Tom's known haunts. I jot notes of the similarities in his story. I write down his character traits, according to Reg, Vick and Stephanie, paying close attention to what his wife said. Not that being married to someone ensures transparency. In a sense, we all play roles. We all have agendas, some hidden even to ourselves. It's how two people can witness the same event and yet remember it in different detail. Somehow I need to nail two competing narratives and discover the truth. I think about timeframes and work out that Tom met Stephanie and hooked up roughly a decade previously. Two years later they marry, four years afterwards, something cataclysmic happens, and it isn't a road accident.

*We found each other really.*

*Didn't seem to know where he was heading. Young for his age.*

I take another swig and consider Tom's Welsh burr, that distinctive lilt in his voice. Stands to reason if you spend any amount of time in Ludlow. But then there's that cab card from a taxi firm in Conwy. Perhaps Tom's roots are genuinely Celtic. Could have moved from Wales to Ludlow and capital of the Welsh Marches. Why would he do that? How come he seemed young for his age when forced to grow up so very fast following the death of his parents? A life-changing event like that usually engenders maturity. I think about Stephanie's insight into Tom feeling a responsibility for his brother, Michael (if he exists). What happened to the two of them?

But on which we could all agree; something we could all agree on, during the past ten years Tom spent a disproportionate amount of his time on the run and continues to do so. He is not simply nomadic, like people who buy a house, stay there for a few years, and then sell and move on, often to different parts of the country. Tom is something quite other.

Steeling myself, I call Elliott.

"Miss Outlaw," he says, as if unsurprised to receive a call

from yours truly. "Actually, I'm glad you phoned because, keeping my ear close to the wire as I do, there's an opening in the *Gloucester Echo*."

Normally, I'd leap at the chance but, overtaken by events, I feel singularly lacklustre about the prospect. I hear Elliott out about whom to approach and how to make my pitch. I don't enquire politely about what he's up to because I can only focus on Tom and why he cut loose, not once but twice.

"You don't sound enthused. Are you already in gainful employment?"

I skip his question. "Thing is, Elliott, I need your advice." I expect him to make a flippant remark but he doesn't. Evidently, I sound as serious as I feel.

"I'm following a story that concerns someone who faked his own death."

"You mean like that couple who pretended the husband died in a canoeing accident in order to claim life insurance?"

"Sort of."

"Sounds interesting. Which rag are you working for?"

"I'm not." My heart rate stutters. "This is strictly in confidence, Elliott."

"Of course."

I take a big breath. "I'm investigating Tom."

"Your Tom?" He sounds as flabbergasted as if I'd proclaimed I was entering a nunnery.

"Believe me, he's not mine any more."

"I see." Except he doesn't. How could he?

I reveal the grand highlights, including the reception I received at the police station.

"That *is* curious. Who did you speak to?"

"Two police officers, a DS and a DI."

"Names?"

"Shenton and Falconer, respectively."

"Nobody more senior?"

"No."

Elliott appears to consider this. "What exactly do you want to find out?"

"Isn't it obvious? Why Tom did what he did? Why the police are protecting him?"

"Did they say that?"

"Of course not but…"

"Rosamund, never make wild claims about the police."

"Yes, of course, I…"

"And you're coming at this from a personal angle. Never good."

"So if I were looking at it from a news perspective, what would you say then?"

Elliott lets out a slow breath, suggesting that I have much to learn. "But, my dear, you're not. Understandably, you're upset, but all you have is circumstantial evidence and wild speculation."

I want to yell at him. I don't. "So what should I do? How do I proceed?"

"Honest answer?"

"Yes."

"Drop it."

"You don't believe me?"

"I didn't say that."

"Well, what are you saying?"

Elliott goes very quiet. "Hello?" I say.

"Okay," he says with the greatest reluctance, "as a favour to you, I'll put out some feelers."

"I'm grateful." I really mean it.

"Do not get your hopes up," he counters, leaving me in no doubt that his one desire is to prove that I am reading the wrong chapter in the wrong book. "I'm on good terms with the superintendent. We regularly play golf together. I'll see what I can find out."

My heart catches. "You'll need to be discreet."

"I'm aware of that," Elliott says stonily. "Perhaps if you hadn't barged in with all guns blazing, you'd be more in the know than you are now."

Dispirited and rather worried, I call it a day and stagger upstairs to an empty bed, in which I'm destined not to sleep for more than twenty minutes at a stretch.

# Chapter 15

Tom looked around the room in the nastiest-looking doss-house in town. It would have to do. Bed linen was stained; walls the colour of stale turmeric. Queasy illumination care of an energy-saving bulb that had run out of juice. A mirror over a cracked sink loitered in the corner – about as en suite as it got. When the man once called someone else enquired about basic things like a lavatory and shower, he was told that these were down the corridor. Next to the room into which he'd seen an elderly fat man propel an underage girl with laddered tights and gaunt expression.

He crossed the threadbare carpet and glanced out of a dirt-rimmed window. It yielded a perfect view of a broken-down car park, in which an overflowing skip of builder's rubble stared back malevolently. The railway line, a few feet beyond, assured him he would be kept awake all night.

"I'll take it." He thrust three tens into the man's palm. Grooved and shrunken fingers closed over the loot. Tall and skinny, the B&B owner had deep-set eyes and pockmarked skin.

"No food in the room. No guests," he warned, releasing a

cloud of bad breath. Tom was tempted to ask whether booze and fags would be okay, but didn't want to spend any more time than was strictly necessary in the man's company, so he nodded deadpan agreement.

The sound of slapped flesh followed by the familiar screech of someone in pain ricocheted from the room along the corridor.

Alone, and glad of it, he chucked down his bag, removed his soaking jacket and hung it up in the wardrobe. Peeling off his shirt, jumper and jeans, he threw them across a chair that looked as if it had been reclaimed from the skip outside his window.

Fuck, without the pills he craved, his head hurt and he was dead to his bones with fatigue. Depression was normal for him, so he had no idea whether what he was experiencing was more extreme than usual. He didn't yet have the balls to top himself. If that changed, he guessed it displayed some kind of progression. Hey, by then, it wouldn't matter.

Both taps on, nicotine-coloured cold water ran into a sink rimmed with scum. Sliding out both contact lenses, he took a deep breath and, screwing up his eyes, plunged his head underneath the filmy surface then; with a great swoosh, stood up straight. Erect. Water dripped off his ears, nose and chin. His reflection peered back from a mirror spotted with black marks. One question battered his brain.

*Who am I?*

Am I Tom Loxley, thirty-five-year-old dark-haired male, with a scar at the temple following a prank, an only child of two dead parents, brought up by an elderly godmother in

Southwark, who intermittently bunked off school, trained as a chef at catering college, who hates travel, doesn't drive, is anti-social, enjoys heavy metal and Muse, has an allergy to cats and strong sexual chemistry with a woman called Roz?

Or am I Adam Charteris, thirty-one-year-old blonde-haired husband, with a scar at the temple following an accident, child of two dead parents, who has a brother called Michael, brought up by an elderly aunt in Torquay, who ensured he had a great education at private school, learnt his trade as a chef by working in a Michelin-starred restaurant, starting at the bottom, who likes to travel, drives, is happy, a little bit quiet but not anti-social, who enjoys classical music, has no allergy to cats, a woman he loves unconditionally, a child he adores?

Or am I none of the above and someone quite other? And who will I be tomorrow, or will that choice be ripped from me like all the other choices in my life?

It seemed to him that he'd spent his entire existence living like some crook, pretty ironic in the circumstances, but without the money or power and material success.

Always watching and waiting.

For the bullet.

For the fade to black.

For the ending.

Fear, like a crush in a crowd, pressed hard against him, encircled his bare chest, smothered his face, squeezed and choked his lungs. There was only one thing worse than being disavowed and that's disavowing others.

*Those you loved.*

He gaped at his body. From any visual inspection, he looked toned and solid for a man with a rangy build like his. Both arms revealed numerous marks that both women in his life mistook for culinary mishaps. The mental scars, thin and badly healed, were far worse. Without warning, vicious words expanded inside his head, filling his mind, screaming, as real to him as the clapped-out furniture in the room.

Reaching for a towel, rough and brutal from too many washes, he rubbed his hair and face dry, decided that if he were to stand a chance of survival, the hair had to go, completely this time. Bound to be a backstreet barber in these parts. That was as far as he'd got. A small step forward, yet an important one. Meant he was still in the game, intent on staying alive. If he weren't, what the hell had the last decade been about?

The bed was like a marble tomb. Hard. Cold. Unforgiving. He'd slept in worse. Wriggling below the grimy sheets, his hands linked behind his head, resting against thin pillows that smelt of stale hair cream, sebum and dandruff. One thought carved into his brain with the precision of a laser-guided scalpel.

I'm alone now, impossibly so.

I'm sorry for all that I've done, to Roz, and to Steph and Zoe. What he'd give to spend one more day with each of them.

He did not switch off the light.

# Chapter 16

Without a job, I lie low for two days. Scrap that. I give the *appearance* of going to ground. In reality, I'm on it. The criminal connection assumes fresh life and colour. It gains momentum during a conversation with Reg, who sits cross-legged on the floor of the spare room, rolling a cigarette, surrounded by his belongings, a guitar and two packed bags, plus three bin-liners full of rubbish that he expects me to dispose of. His flight is the following afternoon. Unlike Vick, his facial expression doesn't alter. King of Cool my brother.

I finish revealing all. He lights up. Part of the rental agreement is that my home is a non-smoking establishment. With so much going on, Reg having a smoke doesn't raise a flicker of complaint from me. In fact, I'm in two minds whether to bum a ciggie off him. Eventually, he pronounces.

"No shit."

"Is that all you have to say?"

"Always thought he was a control freak," he drawls, "but no idea he was such a fucking dark horse." His cheeks hollow, lending definition to his impossibly high cheekbones, and he blows a perfect smoke ring.

Reg's unconditional acceptance of what I say lifts my spirits. I practically hug him, although I resist because Reg wouldn't like it. Takes after our dad. Our mum, on the other hand, is as tactile as a masseuse.

Swelling with gratitude, I squat down, swoop the cigarette from his hand, take a puff, feel a bit dizzy, hack and hand it back. "Why do *you* think the police would lie?"

Reg glances at me with an easy smile. "'Cos they do."

I'm not an ingénue, but my brother's anti-establishment and anti any kind of authority position can be a royal pain in the bottom. "I need informed opinion, not dogma."

"Chill," he says. "I'm getting to the point."

"Well, can you step on it?"

He chucks me an easy smile, offers me another smoke, which I decline. "It's ludicrous, but there's only one scenario that makes sense."

Will Reg concur with Vick's assessment? Will he flag up a criminal connection? Does he believe that Tom is a spook, an arms dealer? Trust me, I considered them all and can barely contain myself. As usual, Reg takes his own sweet time.

"See, with cops – I'm talking the good guys here, not bent bastards on the take – they operate with two things in mind. One: protection of the public and two: protection of their sorry arses." I have no idea where Reg is going with this, but uncharacteristically, I don't break his momentum. "Ergo," he says, in the way Archimedes declared 'Eureka', "I reckon Tom is their bitch." In response to my bewildered frown, Reg explains, "An informer."

*Informer?* My breath comes in fits and starts. "And that's

the reason the police are protecting him?" This is so far outside my experience I have no handle on what I'm dealing with.

"He gives them what they need. They protect him. I've read a lot about this shit."

"You? Read?" I don't think I ever saw Reg read so much as the back of cereal packet, never mind a newspaper.

"True crime. Got loads of books at the London pad. You should dip in some time, especially if you're thinking of becoming a crime reporter."

"I'm not." I'm right off the idea, particularly after my sortie with Elliott.

Reg shrugs, drops the remains of his cigarette into a cold mug of coffee in which it fizzes and sinks. He jumps to his feet. "Have we plenty of hot water? I need a shower."

"Switch on the immersion."

Reg doesn't walk. He glides towards the stairs. Before he disappears, I call after him, "If Tom is an informer, how would I find out?"

Reg doesn't break step. "Chat up a bent copper."

I sigh. With pretend handcuffs on, my mouth gagged, I ditch the idea of making either verbal enquiries or paying another visit to D.S. Mike Shenton. Tom is like a hateful tune that lodges itself inside your brain. All I can think about is HIM, who he is, what he did, and why he decided on me for his particular form of displacement therapy. Questions, like multiple viruses, assail me. Was he monosyllabic in conversation by choice, or because it's enforced? What were the dynamics that governed his early life? Where did he go to school? Did he have friends? How much of his existence with both Stephanie and me was a lie? When building a legend or falsehood, it's useful to hang on to elements of the truth because they feel right. They're easy to remember.

Among the mayhem, I make a terrible admission to myself. Once crazy about the man I only know as Tom, I don't like him at all.

# Chapter 17

"We're having the most marvellous time," Mum announces. "Yesterday, we explored Paradise Cave in Dong Hoi."

We are on Skype. It is evening and I'm pleased to hear from her and listen to someone loving life in the here and now.

"It's absolutely beautiful," she enthuses. "Very few travellers bother to stop off, too intent on getting to Hanoi, but I'm so glad we did. Fifty-five metres long and unfathomable in depth, it's a marvel," she rattles on, oblivious to my less- than-sparky responses. "And Al booked us into the most wonderful little hotel, more of a farmhouse, really. The people are charming and helpful, so full of insight," she gushes.

I don a smile. "I'm pleased you're having a smashing time. Where to next?"

"Back on the train to Hue. I gather there's a lot of war memorabilia to look at. Then on to Da Nang."

She gives me a rundown of classic dishes eaten, enquires about my health, which I assure her is fine, and then she asks about Tom.

"We're not together any more." I pretend to be breezy, relaxed and grown up about it.

"But that's terrible news."

"I'm all right," I insist.

"Roz, darling, whatever happened?"

"Long story." How true.

"So strange," she says, lowering her voice in a way that I know she's about to go all mystical on me, "But I had the most intense, instinctive feeling that things weren't right between you. I read it in the stars." That's not how I refer to Mum's sixth sense, but I don't call her on it. "Do you think you'll patch it up?"

"Mum, can we not talk about it?"

"But you must, Rosamund. It's imperative you let it all out. Is this a sexual matter?"

"Mum, for goodness..."

"There's a man I know in London. Harley Street, actually. He has a clinic for sexual therapy based on reading one's runes."

"Runes?" I sputter. "We're not living in the Middle Ages."

"Modern version, darling. Bit expensive, but he's saved thousands of relationships. I could put it in a word."

"NO."

"I'll send healing crystals right away."

I groan. "You're on holiday."

"Well, make sure you get hold of some. Agate is best for encouraging emotional strength. There's that shop we visited together."

I remember. Top floor in Regent's Arcade.

"And are you eating plenty of tinned fish?"

"What?"

"Omega 3 for depression."

"I'm not depressed."

"You are. I can see it in your eyes."

"It's the picture quality, Mum."

"I tell you, I can sense it from thousands of miles away. St John's Wort is an essential supplement at times like this." She jabbers about positive energy, herbs and voodoo, and healing thoughts that are, as we speak, magically winging their way from deepest Vietnam to glossy Cheltenham, about as likely as a combine harvester driving along the promenade. Desperate to find an amulet that wards off lovelorn spirits, she signs off.

I love my mum. I'm accustomed to her witchy way of thinking. I even buy into a lot of it, but sometimes I wish she'd wrap up and keep her sorcery and psychic powers to herself.

After a night of pouring rain and jangled sleep, the clouds clear, the sun bleeds golden light across the town and I say goodbye to Reg first thing.

"You'll soon get your mojo back," he says, giving me an uncharacteristically warm hug that makes me sad.

"Let me know when you arrive. Give my love to Dad."

"Will do." Reg doesn't mention Tom. I don't blame him. Probably sick of me banging on.

"Take care of yourself," he says, climbing into a taxi, heading for the train station and the first leg of his journey to Heathrow.

In danger of succumbing to self-pity, I decide to venture

out. Grabbing a scarf and jacket, I hurl through the front door and down the path. Reaching the gate and out onto the pavement, I bash straight into Mike Shenton. I can tell from his clothes and the tense way he looks that he's on official business. Awkward.

A horrible thought assails me. Has Elliott opened his mouth and put his size tens in it? I want to pitch in with a defence. I want to impress that I did nothing wrong, that since my pep talk, I stopped poking my nose in. "If this is about my conversation with Falconer, I fully accept that it was a blatant case of mistaken identity. I haven't contacted Tom, spoken to or approached anyone," I say, cursing that I sound cowardly, lame and unconvincing.

He flashes a short smile that tells me he doesn't believe a word of it. It strikes me then that Shenton is smoothly handsome and quite different to Tom, who could be described as ruggedly good looking. "If you say so," he says, looking over my shoulder to the end of the street.

Inwardly cursing, I stand tall in a *things to do, places to see* manner. He should simply walk on and yet he looks at me squarely. His eyes, if at all possible, are bluer and more intense. His jaw is firm. Authoritative. Despite this, he doesn't move and it makes me think he took a hard decision and isn't sure it was the right one. The air feels electric. It pulses through me. I'm afraid but also edgy.

"I'm sorry about what happened."

"Do you mean about my boyfriend doing a bunk or the way your chum, Falconer, threatened that I would never work again?" I conclude with more than a bitch in my voice.

He frowns, obviously insulted. "He's no chum of mine."

I suspect petty police politics, of which I have no desire to become embroiled, and say so.

The frown deepens to an angry crease. "You think that's what this is about?"

"I've no idea." Perhaps he's baffled by the behaviour of his superiors. Maybe he is caught in an internecine conflict between departments. How should I know and, anyway, this has nothing to do with me.

"Roz..."

"Miss Outlaw," I say. Rattled, I don't trust him. I don't trust anyone.

"Miss Outlaw," he repeats solemnly, "I'm taking a huge risk by speaking to you."

Why? And then I catch the way he looks at me, like he gives a damn. He seems sincere. My eyes are in danger of dissolving into his. Flustered, I'm entirely wrong-footed by what he says next.

"You need to forget Tom Loxley, walk right away and keep on walking." He pauses, waiting to see if it sinks in.

"Don't you people communicate with each other? As you well know, you're not the first to say so."

His expression flashes with disappointment. "And I won't be the last unless you pack it in." When he speaks, there's a warning glint in his eye.

"Noted."

"Please," he says, more gently, resting his warm hand on my sleeve. "Take care." And with that, he breaks away and heads back into the busy street.

Elliott told me never to speculate, but I can't help it: Mike Shenton asked questions in the wrong place and received a reprimand for his troubles. Rather than curbing his natural enthusiasm, I sense it sparked it. Seems my 'tame copper' is a maverick.

# Chapter 18

I sleep badly and wake early. Spread-eagled across Tom's side, Tom fills my every thought. Lodged in my brain, I wonder where he is, what he's done and where he's heading. Ludicrous when I no longer have any stake in his future.

Turning over and wrapping the duvet around me, I make a conscious decision to *not* think. Immediately, I zoom in on Shenton.

Isn't he a bit too nice, too good to be true? His social skills are excellent, the polar opposite to Tom's. Apparently, he has noble intentions; although the way I caught him looking at me suggested something other. I don't quite know what I think about that. Did nobody ever tell him that it's never a good idea to mix business with pleasure? Frankly, I need a man in my life like I need a head transplant. Actually, the latter would be preferable.

On this sour note, I stumble through the darkness, make tea and throw myself into a shower before I can change my mind. Dressed, I toast two slices of bread, eat one, chuck one and attempt to plan my day when my mobile rings. My nerves shredded, I almost knock the mug over. It's

Elliott. He doesn't announce. He doesn't pull his punches.

"If you know what's good for you, you'll take my advice and keep out of police business."

"Is this the official line or because you missed a hole-in-one?"

"This is no joking matter."

"I know." Obviously his chat with the Super wasn't so super.

"We won't ever speak of this again."

Before I can acquiesce, Elliott hangs up. I wonder whether to call Mike Shenton and warn him that those higher up had their cages rattled too. Bang on cue with the noisy imagery, the doorbell rings. It's a few minutes after nine. A glance through the spy-hole reveals a woman standing, side-on. She wears dark- blue jeans and a soft, expensive-looking brown-leather jacket. Expecting that she's trying to flog me something, I select a pre-prepared 'not interested' speech from my personal selection, and open the door with a wide, *about to go out* smile.

It's hard to resist warmth from a potential customer. Even the most basic salesperson and charity collector understands this. Yet this woman manages to resist with finesse. She is not peddling anything. My eyes are immediately drawn to her lips. They are painted brick-red, startling against porcelain-fine skin that I would kill for. Her natural ash-blonde hair is swept back into a pleat in a way that I could never manage to perfect. She stands very straight, shoulders back, as if she studied deportment at some posh finishing school. I feel a weird sense of role reversal, as if she should be standing on the threshold of my home and I am the suitor for the content of her wallet, or whatever it is she wants.

"Rosamund Outlaw?" She arches a professionally threaded eyebrow.

"Yes." I instantly place her as one of Vick's actressy friends. Right bearing. Correct air of poised sophistication. Spot-on perfume with hints of jasmine, neroli and rose. Sometimes you can simply tell with people that they enjoyed a cultured upbringing. A couple of sentences are all she uttered and yet I glimpse this. She wears black Convex trainers, but I reckon she'd be tons happier in stilettoes.

"And you are?"

Her lips briefly stretch wide. "Call me, Jane. I'm a police officer."

My eyes flare with dismay. My stomach feels weighed down by rocks. That explains the peremptory manner. Jane represents a step up the pay-grade. Bloody hell, which rank tops a superintendent? Is she here because of Elliott's faux pas, or because a lowly sergeant told me yesterday to watch out? Could Shenton be heading for a disciplinary? The thought alarms me. "You'd best come in," I say dully, stepping aside.

I close the door and follow her down the hall. "This way," I say, with as much composure as I can marshal, pushing past her and flinging open the door to the kitchen. I offer her a seat, which she takes. I stand.

Everything about her shrieks that she has a job to do and doesn't mess about. My eyes are drawn to her leather gloves that are the same colour as her lips. I reckon she'd be good in a fist fight. She has 'graduate' written all over her. Fast-tracked. A big gun. Disturbing.

She flicks another brick-red smile and manages it without showing her teeth. "Why don't you sit down?"

I sit. I suppose I should ask for a warrant card, but fear that it will make me seem pissy.

"Tom Loxley," she says, as if he is the Holy Grail and meaning of life all wrapped up in one. "It's vital he's found."

I fail to contain either my shock or confusion. It's scary because I know I must act as though Shenton and I never had a conversation. I stare blindly at her.

"Something has arisen."

"What kind of something?"

She doesn't answer or explain and I am in no mood for being mucked about. "Let me get this straight: you want my help?"

"And why I'm here."

"I don't wish to be rude, but I still don't follow."

She leans back, in no hurry to explain. I feel vaguely like the schoolgirl hanging around outside the head's study, waiting to be expelled.

"Do you have any idea where Tom is?" she says.

"I can't tell you."

"Can't, or won't?" Her gaze is as penetrating as an ice pick.

"As in *I wish I knew*."

"Are you certain?"

"Absolutely."

"He left no clues, no note?"

I lean back, cross my arms in indignation for the second time in forty-eight hours. I dislike the idea of being jerked around by anyone, let alone this woman. My mouth shortens to one tight uncompromising line. What was that I said about laid-back?

"Mind if I take a look around?" Her eyes briefly comb the room, no doubt sussing out Tom's cookery books before she starts raking through his taste in computer games in the sitting room, and his personal belongings upstairs.

I do mind and wonder about important things, like search warrants, but I nod. It will either be now or later. "Be my guest." I don't really mean this but think I need to rein in my exasperation. If she's hoping to find Tom hiding in a cupboard, she's going to be disappointed.

She gives a bland smile, stands up slowly, moves forward with poise, and strolls out of the sitting room, owning it. I watch her disappear, sit and wait while she takes an unfeasibly long time to cover 900 square feet. Creaks and the swishing noise of drawers dragged open and shut drift down through the floorboards. As invasions of privacy go, this is one grade up from burglary.

When she reappears she twitches a cool smile and sits down. I have no idea whether or not she stumbled across anything of significance.

"Does he have a computer?"

"No."

"Does he use yours?"

"No."

"Does Tom have close friends? People he would rely on?"

"No."

"Think."

"I said no."

"Can you supply information about his known haunts, places he feels comfortable, a friend he might go to, somebody he might confide in, lifestyle factors that might reveal his where... "

"Hold on, what is this?"

Jane glances away. When she looks back she locks on and I can tell from the purposeful expression in her eyes that she has reached a decision based on Plan B. Because Plan A: me shedding clues like a shorthaired terrier in full moult, is officially screwed.

"What I'm about to tell you must be handled in the strictest confidence, do you understand?" Her baby-blue eyes, so different to Shenton's, search mine. I rub the side of my face. Part of me is desperate to find out. The rest: not keen at all. Whereas Shenton probably has his own ideas, this woman has knowledge. This woman is the real deal. Shit.

"I think so."

"*Think* won't cut it," she says with an abrasive smile. "Do I have your word?"

What on earth are you supposed to say in a situation like this? I do the obvious. She has my word. Even that isn't good enough.

"You must not speak to anyone about what I'm going to tell you."

"Not even D.S. Shenton and D.I Falconer?"

Her eyes flicker. "Not even them."

I swallow. Is this a way to string me along only to charge me with interfering in police business? Is this what they call entrapment? With each question, my inner voice climbs. "I don't understand." Not only do I not get it, dread locks me in its slimy and repellent embrace. "I'm not good at keeping secrets," I blurt out, hoping that this will put her right off. It also happens to be entirely true.

Her gaze manacles itself to mine. "You must not breathe a word either about those involved or about me," she reiterates. "If you break my trust you will endanger not only my life but the lives of others and, quite possibly, your own."

My pulse jitters. I feel like a person stirring from a deep sleep, waking up serene and calm, only to recall soul-destroying loss. It's not a nice feeling. My body tightens. My breath hisses. Walk away, everyone warned. Nothing more guaranteed to make me do the exact opposite. Yet now, on the cusp of finding out, I suddenly don't want to know. I'm too afraid.

I stand up. "I don't want to hear it. I don't want the responsibility. In fact, I'd like you to leave. Now."

Her lips curve, nice and easy, still no flash of teeth. Not because she doesn't have any, but because she doesn't want to be that pally. "Please, sit down." She turns her palm over, gesturing at a chair. "I wouldn't be here if I didn't require your assistance."

"Assistance?" Too worried to be argumentative, I say it like it's a statement of fact and it appears to pay off. This really is unknown territory, one I don't wish to traverse. I'm not feisty now. She ensnares me with what seems like a genuine smile this time. A weak flicker of light invades and catches the right side of her smooth cheek. I try to think, to concentrate and block out a blizzard of emotions. With Tom, I moved from love, love, love to hate, hate, hate and now I don't know what I feel, other than my future fucked off and showed no sign of ever coming back. "Please," she presses, indicating for a second time I take a seat. She smiles again and it's mesmerising. This woman has such charisma it's hard not to look away. Reluctantly, I obey and sit, or rather, perch.

"Good," she says, in a way that I can only think the opposite will happen.

"Some years ago, there was a road-rage incident in which a man died."

What does it mean? Where does that leave me? I blink. Uncomprehending. "His murderer was a known criminal with a vicious pedigree," Jane continues. "There were no other witnesses to the crime other than a man whom you know as Tom Loxley."

# Chapter 19

Tom could still picture him nearly thirteen years on. At any moment, and more so lately, he would see Swain's dead-eyed face framed by insanely bleached blonde hair.

At the time he was taking a leak in a field the other side of a hedge. He'd heard everything from the sound of screeching brakes on wet road, the exchange of curses and abuse, to the noise of tearing metal and the screams of a man in shock and pain.

And he'd seen it. Hidden, barely drawing breath, he'd seen it all. In slow motion. In Blu-Ray. At top volume. Swain's spare body coiled like a lightweight boxer, his black leather-gloved hand in a fist, the way the screwdriver was plunged repeatedly first into Jack Prior's chest and then up to the hilt into Jack Prior's temple, blood and tissue spattering the grass, oozing onto the road. And the smell. Of ordure and piss. Of death and dying. Every time Tom recalled it, fear and panic shot right through him.

Giving evidence, even behind a screen, was one of the most terrifying experiences of his life and, of these, he'd had many. Swain was banged up, but Tom always knew it wouldn't be forever. He had mates. He had pals, rough men prepared to carry out brutal acts.

"Is that all right?" the barber said.

"Fine," he replied, jolted back into the present. If only changing yourself was as easy as transforming your appearance, he thought, admiring his newly shaved reflection.

Paying up, he gathered his jacket and rucksack and stepped back onto the street. One more night in Dumpsville and he'd be back on the road, although where to next, he had no idea.

More alone and lonely than ever, he felt irresistibly drawn back to Roz, while perversely yearning to return to his ordered, secure and blissful life with Steph and Zoe.

Was it even possible to love two women?

How to explain the inexplicable, he thought, pulling up his hoodie, his scalp super-sensitive to the elements. Another man with a wife and mistress in tow would declare it a perfectly feasible state of affairs. But it wasn't simple.

He thought of Steph, his first love.

*I'll kiss you better.*

*Make it all better.*

*I'll love you forever.*

Shaken by the memory, fresh shame burnt holes in his cheeks. His relationship with super ultra-smart Roz, (to avoid repetition) the chemistry between them, was entirely different. Roz quenched the hunger in him. At times he couldn't get enough of her. She was more adventurous. More challenging. More demanding. Just *more*.

Something dark and unforgiving twisted inside. He prayed to God she wouldn't try to find him.

Christ, anything could happen if Swain got out. The possi-bility of his release on licence made his guts boil and disintegrate burn inside him. Surely, it would be ruled against?

Obsessively, he went over his last conversation with Mads.

"He cannot, must not, be released on licence."

"It's unlikely, but he has the right to go before a parole board."

"What about my rights?" Wouldn't matter that Swain would be under so-called supervision. Those out on bail or deemed ready for release into the community had committed plenty of murders in recent years. He said as much.

"I appreciate where you're coming from."

His jaw ground with irritation. Sometimes Mads came out with the most asinine remarks. "Thing is, Swain has a heart condition," she continued. "Theoretically, it could result in a move to an open prison."

"Theoretically?" He growled.

"Again, I'm looking at worst-case scenarios."

"Like you did last time?" he said sourly.

"Can we please stick to the here and now? Swain has proved himself to be a model prisoner, a reformed character."

"And I'm the President of the United States."

"I hear what you say, but you really did take an unholy risk by...'

He never heard the rest. He cut the call.

Glancing up at clouds swollen with winter rain, he thought about the odds of survival – not good. Swain was out to get him, according to Mads's intelligence. He'd known it from the get-go. So had Mads. To cap it off, Tom, as he now called himself, didn't think she ever entirely bought his background story.

He remembered the first time they met, how she'd told him that his life, as he knew it, was over. And thank Christ for that. It had been hard not to react, to say 'Thank you for saving me.' Except that it wasn't Mads who'd saved him, but two men, one a killer, the other a victim and a man he never knew, who had paid with a beating and a howling and six pints of his blood on the road. So much blood, he recalled with a shudder.

Afterwards, the police had taken him to a crappy room in a modest hotel and offered him a deal. He recalled sitting on a cheaply upholstered chair at a table smeared with cold coffee, plastic cartons and a packet of cigarettes waiting to be opened if he said the right words. Mads, his soon-to-be witness protection officer, stood over him with what felt like dragon's breath in his face. They would protect him by putting him on a protection programme if he played ball. He would need to leave friends and family and everything he'd known behind. Any funny stuff, any time he went off the reservation or felt like coming out into the open, he was on his own. Over and out. And there was nothing they could do to save him from Swain and his cronies.

After establishing his identity and receiving confirmation that his parents were dead, the terms of his disappearance were explained. They told him that he had a week to make up his mind. He didn't need a week, an hour or a single minute. Yes, I'll do anything you say. Anything. I belong to you now. Just get me out of this hell I'm in.

*This.*

To be as convincing as possible, he'd hidden like a fugitive for seven whole days, hardly daring to breathe. Every time the wind blew he thought his time was up, that he'd be marched back to where it all began, that his incarceration and punishment would be even worse, if that were humanly possible. He knew he'd be hunted the second he failed to show up at Vixenhead, the place that was supposed to be his home, but, somehow, he evaded recapture. When he returned a week later to the hotel, he was given a phone. Two days after that, he received the call that would change his life. From that moment he had learnt fast and proved himself to be an excellent student. Voracious in his quest to learn how to behave, to interact, to appear 'normal', he had surprised himself. The laugh was that the police wanted him to act a part, while not realising that he was doing it the second they offered him a way out.

And he'd been acting out different roles ever since.

# Chapter 20

"He testified?"

"He did."

Astounded, I stare, blink and nod to disguise the relief trickling over me. Tom is a good man, a hero, no less. He is not a criminal, as Vick suggested. He is not an informer, as Reg suspected. He left Stephanie and her daughter to *protect* them. Why else would he leave? Shame snatches a lump out of my heart and I smart at the memory of how I cursed, listened, entertained and then bought into other possible scenarios. I was not only standing on the wrong rung, I was on the ladder with a broken set of steps.

Whoever Tom really is, he must have been given a new identity, not once, but it now seems, twice. I picture a scenario in which, hell-bent on revenge, the road-rage killer picks up Tom's scent, endangering the lives of Tom's wife and Stephanie's daughter. The only way in which to safeguard all of them was for Tom as Adam to fake his own death. Undoubtedly, the police played their part to make it as credible as possible, which now explains why I received a warning to back off. In the light of this revelation, Falconer's aggression now makes perfect sense.

But where does this leave me?

"Something you need to grasp, Miss Outlaw. We offered Tom protection in return for him testifying. We gave him a new identity." She looks at me in an 'are you with me so far?' kind of way.

I nod again blindly. I'm not an authority on the subject – who is? – yet even a simple soul like me knows that witness protection programmes, the most secretive of police activities, are fraught with danger for anyone involved.

A big part of me wants to run and hide and I'm not encouraged that Jane's account is a blatantly potted version of the truth. She makes no mention of Stephanie Charteris. In other words, she is releasing only what she sees fit, to get what she needs from me. I'm only a pawn in a much bigger game, a game over which I have no control. What I can't comprehend is why she is telling me anything at all. Isn't that the whole point of protection, that it's secret? At the realisation, fear crawls belly-down along my spine at the thought of my stupid meddling and how it might turn a spotlight in Stephanie's direction. And there's something else.

"Why did nobody, nobody," I repeat, "think to inform me that my life might be in danger?" I recognise that my logic is flawed. Shaken to my core, I'm in shoot- the-messenger mode.

"I'm perfectly satisfied that a risk assessment was carried out with regard to yourself."

"Are you? I'm not some bloody building in danger of collapse. If Tom is running from bad men, so am I."

Jane's gaze sharpens. "Have you been threatened?"

"No, but I believe I'm being followed." I catch my breath.

Is Vick right? I am stressed. Who wouldn't be? But if Jane is right, surely it's not so outlandish? I tell her when and where.

"We can guarantee your safety."

In this particular enterprise, there are no guarantees. She knows it. I know it. "What are you going to do?" I say mutinously, not keen to be ejected from my life.

I wonder blindly how she'll sell the requirement for my protection to those higher up the food chain.

"We *can* protect you."

"I don't want to be protected. I want my life back. I want closure. I want the freedom to grieve for the man I loved. I want answers and I want space." I'm gabbling and my voice is ripe and thick. A maddening tear trickles down my cheek. It feels like acid. Unexpectedly, Jane pulls out a clean handkerchief and hands it to me, her expression one of concern. I wipe my eyes, blow my nose, go to hand the handkerchief back, think better of it, and stuff it in the pocket of my jeans.

Perhaps Reg's distrust of authority in general, and the police in particular, rubbed off on me. I don't know. Perhaps it's shock, but I don't want to co-operate. I will be like the rogue spy who spills his guts to the other side, is schmoozed with promises, drained of information and then, isolated, left to manage as best he can. Screw any duty of care and responsibility to people who gab.

"I was nothing more than a smokescreen to help him maintain his cover, to lend it credence and authenticity, and you, as his witness protection officer, knew all along." I imagine Tom calling her from time to time, reporting in and discussing me. "Now you want my help," I finish. Seething.

"You're upset. Perfectly understandable." She flashes a cool, contained smile that reminds me so much of Tom on a good day. "The point is, you had a recent relationship with him. You know him better than most."

My laugh comes out dry. "Clearly, I don't." The evidence of the last few days demonstrates this. I'm not sure I ever knew the real Tom. "Can't you put a trace on his phone, check any cash withdrawals he makes?" Then I think about the 'new' phone in his bag, the wallet filled with twenties.

"I can assure you that all necessary steps are being taken, but Tom is adept at covering his tracks."

No wonder. "What's his name, his real name, I mean?"

A smile crackles behind her eyes. "That's classified information."

I scrub my face with my hands. "I'm no use to you. He never said anything. Don't you get it? Tom was as secretive as an MI5 spook. You trained him well."

She uncrosses her legs and re-crosses them in one practised, perfectly choreographed, movement. "He must have mentioned places to you."

North Wales. For a second I consider telling her before I change my mind.

Not for one moment do I believe her name is Jane. Perhaps that's the point. She's supposed to be anonymous.

"No."

"Did he take much with him?"

"When he ditched me for good?"

She nods. I get a whiff of perfume, or hair spray or both. I shake my head. "He was a low-maintenance kind of guy.

Kept a bag underneath the bed for three years." I should have known he was a man primed to run. A wave of exhaustion rippling through me, I want to sleep and sleep. I want Jane to clear off and never come back.

She reaches over and squeezes my arm, as if I'm being very brave. I don't welcome the physical attention. Holding her gaze for a fraction, I stand up. "That's it."

She looks up and I look down. A stalemate silence inhabits the room. She ought to get up and leave. She doesn't move a muscle. Again, I get the feeling that she is deliberating whether to hand me another morsel of information in the mistaken belief that I will suddenly dredge an arcane clue from my memory that will lead her straight to Tom.

Eventually, she speaks. "What you must understand is that if Tom blows his cover, he's a dead man walking."

My eyes prick with tears. I spread my hands. My voice cracks with distress and frustration. "I get that but, I already told you, I don't know a thing."

Jane's eyes are slow. She doesn't speak. A cloak of fear envelops me. Suffocating. I sense a revelation and I'm frightened.

"There is another reason why we cannot simply let him go."

"Yes?" I brace myself.

"Tom Loxley has blood on his hands," she says in a flat tone. "He killed a child. Now will you do your best to help me?"

# Chapter 21

Back in his room, Tom fuelled up with a smuggled take-away pizza washed down with a can of Coke. Ravenous, a side effect of coming off speed, he wolfed it down and dropped the carton into the bin – he'd be long gone before evidence of his illicit meal was discovered. Rolling a cigarette, he lit up. The next day, he intended to board a National Express bus to London and lose himself in the capital. There, he could get a job, working in any number of kitchens.

Stretching out on the bed, he flexed his toes, thought about Garry Swain, a terrifying individual with a force field of hostility surrounding him so strong you could taste it.

Often, after a few too many drinks, he imagined stalking Swain on his release, discovering his routine, pouncing when he was alone in the dark and taking him out of the game. Booze talking. Swagger and bluff. Except it wouldn't be such a momentous act for a man like him, a child-killer, no less. Isn't that what they all said?

A smoke ring floated up into the air, followed by another. When told of Swain's impending release he felt that same degree of fear he'd encountered when he'd been forced to move the first time, except it was amplified a thousand-fold. Minced up and spat out, he was unable to go back to Steph and unable to move on. Even if Swain snuffed it in prison, Tom feared that he was still in danger from men loyal to him, the bounty on Tom for testifying in perpetuity and akin to having a fatwa on his head.

Mads disagreed with his assessment but went crazy when he confessed to his rare trip to where it all began. Not that she understood. He'd never told anyone about Joshua. It's why he returned: to find closure. Standing there by his grave, wind whistling through the trees like forgotten ghosts, it struck him that there was a lot of sadness in a graveyard, a lot of lives not lived.

He took another deep drag of the cigarette. Police had done fuck-all to protect him and Swain was as faceless, determined and ruthless as he ever was. God alone knew from where the next danger would come.

If he were an optimist – he wasn't – the cops were already turning Swain's crew over and preparing to watch the man who had stated openly that he would kill him.

But Mads was right about one thing. Even without the photograph, he'd signed his own death warrant by revisiting the place where it all began. No point in denying it. Shame assailed him at the way he'd blamed Roz so vocally, a cop-out for his own stupidity.

Roz, he thought, how much I miss your sunny personality, your warmth, your smile, your smooth, naked skin against mine.

The best he could hope for was that Swain would put a

foot wrong, get charged and taken down for good this time. Sometimes he'd fantasise that Swain's dirty dealings would catch up with him, that someone of his own ilk would remove him from the scene altogether, either inside prison or outside. Then Tom could come out of the shadows, show his real face to the world and pick up the threads of his old life, although which one that would be continued to plague him.

Not that the cops would subscribe to that. What was it they said? You blow your cover and you're on your own.

He exhaled another smoke ring into the air, watched it rise, drift and loop. With an idea forming in his mind, it seemed like he had nothing left to lose.

# Chapter 22

"Tom killed a child?"

"He did."

I jump to my feet so fast she starts. "You're a bloody liar. I lived with him. I would know." I realise the contradictory nature of my words, too late. Tom duped me to survive. Could he deceive me over something as grotesque as this?

*Wouldn't I notice some predilection in his personality? Wouldn't I spot something like that?*

"I'm sorry," she says, looking up into my eyes, certainty drawn all over her face.

My head spins. Blood rushes through my veins, with heat and fire and fury. Rendered speechless, I cannot think with any degree of logic, let alone clarity or self-possession.

*Tom a child-killer.*

Extraordinary.

Obscene.

Horrific.

This is why Tom didn't want kids, a nasty little voice whines inside my head.

The only way I can hold things together is to verbally lash

out and shatter Jane's serenity. If I have to inhale defiled air. Let her do so too.

"Aren't there laws to prevent police from aiding and abetting murderers?" This woman sitting in my living room might be a witness protection officer. She also looks after informers, orchestrates deals with grasses, consorts with murderers, fraternises with paedophiles and other undesirables. My home feels contaminated by her. *I* feel contaminated by her.

"I understand your ire, why you're angry, but—"

"You don't." Anger lets rip through every cell in my body. "I guess you're about to tell me that it was worth looking after Tom in order to hook a bigger fish. What about collateral damage and innocent lives ruined?" Something disconnects in my brain. Would the police knowingly allow a child-killer, in circumstances such as these, to strike up a relationship with a single mother? Is this what falls into a perpetrator's protection of human rights, Tom's that is? In my mind, Tom boomerangs from lover to cheat, from bad guy to hero, and back to the worst criminal ever. With so many mental hoops to jump through, I feel sick and giddy.

"We fell short." The dull light in her eyes reveals a gross lack of conviction. She might as well add it to the mantra of 'lessons have been learned,' the standard defence from those who lack accountability and are never forced to live with the consequences of 'falling short'. And then, I realise, something else doesn't compute. When in Tom's busy and itinerant life does he find the time to target and kill a child? I ask Jane this.

"At the time of the murder, he was a child himself."

Lurid newspaper stories with sensationalist headlines rear up and batter me. I fail to suppress a spasm of fear. "I still don't believe it." Just how much worse can things get? "And his victim?"

Jane tenses. I know nothing about this woman, whether she's married, or has children of her own, but I understand. It's easy to demonise. Children who kill are unknowable. Unfathomable. Chilling. It definitely thumps a nerve.

She scratches the side of her mouth. "You'll appreciate that I have a duty to protect the family of the boy who died."

I give her a hard-nosed look. "I'm accustomed to handling confidential information." A bit of a stretch. I'm not an investigative journalist with sources to protect.

Makes no difference.

"Did Tom know the child?"

"I'm sorry, that's all I can tell you."

"How old was Tom at the time?"

"Eleven."

I barely take it in. "But why did he do it?"

Jane shrugs her shoulders. All she was prepared to say.

"How did he do it?"

"Irrelevant."

"Not to me." It's the one question over which I know I will obsess and imagine and drive myself demented, the one that demands an answer.

She lets out a long sigh, spreads her palms in apology.

"Please."

"I already told you, it's out of the question."

I collapse back down. "If you want me to search my memory

149

bank for some offbeat remark he made, it's critical I have the facts."

"Then you'll have to rely on me." Jane remains implacable and resistant.

I'm not keen on a second-rate version of Chinese whispers. In reality, I need his file, the case notes, records, and I can't even pry into basic information. Shenton flashes into my mind and streaks back out again. It's no use. I can't involve him and I can tell Jane won't budge.

I go silent. An unfeasibly long time passes. I think she'll weaken. She doesn't.

"I can't help you trace a ghost."

She shrugs.

I don't speak but consider Tom's criminal trajectory from killer to pin-up boy to rogue witness. I return to my earlier jibe. "Tom must be an embarrassment to you." The real reason for needing to track him down, I suspect. What would the public think about it if this got out or, God forbid, Tom kills again?

She shrugs once more, the leather of her jacket complaining. Another light bings on in my brain – I know too much.

She leans forward. For a horrible moment, I think she will touch my knee again, but she doesn't. "So will you think carefully? We need you."

*Need* rather than *want*. The oldest trick in the manipulative manual, a plea for help is more likely to yield a positive response. We all desire to be needed. I experience a terrible tug on my heartstrings. Isn't this why I really want a child, someone to love and love me without conditions? Someone who will be constant when the men in my life are not?

*I thought Tom needed me.*
*He neither needed nor wanted me.*
*I never even knew his real name.*

"Any little detail that might reveal where he would go to ground would be extremely useful." She dons a reassuringly elastic smile.

"Hello?" I say wearily. "I've already told you: I. DON'T. KNOW."

Why on earth don't they use one of those shrinks with a bent for reading the minds of criminals, a profiler? I look suitably blank because that's how I feel.

"Come on, you're an intelligent woman, Miss Outlaw. You've already proved that."

I have to hand it to her: she's persistent. "Stephanie knows him better than anyone, certainly better than me, probably even better than you. She was his wife, after all." I attempt to dilute the bitterness that runs through my veins like acid.

"Awkward," she says, hitching a dry smile.

"Very," I say tartly. To seek help from Stephanie, the police would be forced to explain that her husband's death was fabrication and sanctioned at the highest level.

I stare her down. The chair creaks as she gets up. We stand eyeball to eyeball. She's openly railroading me. "I have nothing more to say. If you want to find Tom, talk to Mrs Charteris, and now I'd like you to get out." The bullish note in my voice elicits a stern and physical response this time. The reassuring expression long faded and died. I can practically hear the woman grinding her teeth.

I see her to the door, where she fakes another smile while

slipping a notepad and pen from her pocket. She scrawls a number, rips off the sheet and hands it to me. Ink smudges her long fingers, which pleases me no end.

"Call me." She speaks with authoritativeness, reminding me of Falconer. Learned cop behaviour. They're more similar than I gave them credit.

After she's gone I sit in the silence for what feels like a long long time.

# Chapter 23

*Back to where it all began...*

*R*unning *through the woods. Joshy dragging along behind;*
*Linus, fleet and sure-footed, closing in.*

"*Just because your mummy and daddy are in a watery grave,*
*you want us to feel sorry for you.*"

*Eyes glassy with tears, the boy stumbled on despite the rock*
*of grief crushing his chest, ripping his lungs apart. What hurt*
*most was that Joshy joined in, his reedy voice tight and taunting.*
"*Poor little rich boy, poor little rich boy.*"

*Except, as everyone made plain, he wasn't.*

*He'd tried to talk to Uncle Geoff about them bullying him,*
*to explain what was going on, but couldn't find the right words*
*and his uncle was too nice to see what was erupting in front of*
*him. Hand resting on his thin shoulder, he'd said, "I know it's*
*hard for you, lad, what with your mum and dad, but all things*
*pass. Things will get better, trust me. They always do. I vowed*
*I'd look after you and I intend to keep my promise. Now run*
*along and see what Joshua is up to." How could he tell his uncle*
*that he'd really be better off somewhere else? Couldn't he send*

him away? Anywhere but here. Except where could he go? This was home now, whether he liked it or not.

He tore off into the undergrowth, hoping the brambles that tore at his clothes would deter the others.

The trouble with Uncle Geoff was that he saw the good in everyone, especially his own children. That's why his parents had liked him. It was never because of Aunt Ursula, who was cold, stuck-up, a 'bitch'. Others said that she'd only married Uncle Geoff for his money. He'd sometimes heard them quarrel. Grown-ups fighting seemed strange to him because his parents had never fought. They seemed made for each other, unlike his auntie and uncle, who really didn't go together. They were like cabbage, which he hated, and ice cream, which he loved. Couldn't put those two together on a plate, although he wouldn't put it past Linus for trying.

They lived in a huge house, but it wasn't nice or even very comfortable. Formerly a school, it was creepy and draughty and, if you weren't careful you could get lost in it. Once Linus had locked him in the boot room. Nobody came looking for him and, by the time they did, he'd wet himself. For days Linus and Joshy had mocked him about that and told him he stunk of wee. Aunt Ursula (who was not his real aunt) did nothing to stop them. She thought it funny.

He slowed down, drew the back of his hand across his face, wiping away snot and tears, tried to muffle his heavy breathing and the snap of bracken and twig cracking underneath his plimsolls. If he waited long enough, they'd lose interest. Joshy would tire and Linus would take him back to the house. He'd wait until after dark, if he had to. Only here and on the water *did he feel safe, although those times out to sea were less often. Uncle Geoff thought it would distress him, remind him of the accident. It didn't. It awakened lovely memories of his parents, of happy times when all was good and safe in his world. It made him believe that once his life was normal, not the screaming chaos it had become.*

*Without thinking, he'd overshot and breached a clearing. A sharp pain shot through his temple. He touched where it stung. When he drew his fingers away they were smeared in blood.*

*Twisting around, he saw he'd been outflanked. Linus stood, solid and proud, his patrician features stretched into a lazy grin. A catapult hung loose in his hand.*

*"Little twat," he cursed, reaching into his pocket for a stone, preparing his next salvo.*

*"My turn," Joshy wheezed. Small for his age, his pigeon chest never seemed to have the capacity for running, or even walking quickly. In build, he was quite different to Linus, who at fourteen, was already tall, muscular and strong. Caro, by contrast, had a slim, wiry build. Her muscularity lay in her tongue, which was poisonous. Girls for you. Due to the physical differences, Aunt Ursula made out that Josh was special. The boy later known as Adam and then Tom had heard the word 'delicate' applied, although there was nothing delicate about Josh's intention to hurt him.*

*"Stop it, Joshy. What's got into you? I thought you were my friend."*

*"You haven't got any friends," Linus said. "Mr No-Mates, that's what we call you."*

*"Mr No-Mates, Mr No-Mates," Joshy trilled. Tom recognised*

*that he was showing off to impress Linus, but it didn't prevent the anguish rising like a flash flood inside him.*

*"Shut up, you prick."*

*Joshy stood square next to his brother, puffed out his cheeks, his normal pallor flecked with pink, like candy. "Shut up yourself. I'm not a prick. You are."*

*"And it's tiny," Linus joined in, with a smirk. "Caro says it's the size of a raisin."*

*Tom flushed crimson. "She was talking about him," he said, gesturing at the smaller boy with his chin.*

*"Don't let him talk to you like that, Joshy. Here." Linus stood behind him and placed the catapult in his small hands. Without taking his eyes from his quarry, Linus palmed a sharp-edged stone from his pocket. Cornered, Tom's legs turned to stone, anchoring him to the ground. Breath inside him came in short, desperate bursts. A week before, Linus had smacked him in the face, cutting his cheek, the pebble missing his eye by a fraction. Looked like he was lining up for an encore and, at this distance, he could really hurt him this time.*

*Survival kicking in, Tom took to his heels, heard the whoop of the pack animals at full tilt behind. He wished with all his being that they would do him a favour and drop down dead.*

# Chapter 24

Children who kill children.

I don't move. I am rooted yet rootless. Out of sorts. Spaced-out. Sluggish. Spooked.

Aside from in fiction, child-killers exist but they are rare in the real world. More exceptional still, the murder Tom committed when he was, himself, a child. What on earth could trigger such a tragic event? Was Tom or Adam, as he was once known, one of those little boys who got a kick, sexual or otherwise, by persecuting others? Did he taunt and bully? Was he the kind of kid who pulled the legs off insects? Did he carry a bad gene that predisposed him to violence? I lived with the man for three years and had no idea.

*No idea.*

Aware that Tom would be granted anonymity, I cruise the internet for information about child-killers in the UK. I drill the stats and discover that four hundred children were convicted in the UK in the past two decades, the youngest ten years of age. Names synonymous in the public eye with evil pop up. Adults are mostly responsible for killing kids and, it appears that when a child kills, they are as likely to bump off family members.

Would Stephanie talk of the man she still loves in such ardent terms if Tom committed such an act when he was a boy?

There must be an alternative version with mitigating factors: a game that got out of hand, some gang element in play, or an accident.

*He was a man who seemed to be waiting for something bad to happen.* Isn't that what Vick said?

Chill blows right through me. I struggle to find purchase in a mind-jam packed with criminal acts, each worse in my imagination than the one that preceded it.

Surely, a child who kills can change, with careful guidance, in the same way that an adult rehabilitates? Tom's later involvement in crime, on the side of the angels second time around, suggests that he made that transition. Doesn't it?

Or did he? How easy is it to change, to be redeemed?

Cold to my bones and abandoning all thought of going out, I get up, light a fire, watch as fresh paper and wood flare with life. Stretching my stiffened limbs, I sling on a fleece to warm myself up. Mentally, I take a step back, disentangle my feelings of revulsion, and try to regard Tom as though he were the next breaking news story. What's the angle and how do I incorporate narratives fairly on both sides of the crime?

For a child to be attacked by another is emotionally traumatising, but what separates a child who kills from a grown-up is the extreme emotional trauma experienced by the perpetrator, in a way that doesn't always occur with an adult.

Tom was a screwed-up, messed-up kid. Ergo Tom is a screwed-up, messed-up adult. I don't believe it's possible to be unaffected by such an act unless you happen to be a psychopath.

*He isn't one of those, is he?*

Encouraged and praised and loved by both my parents, I grew up to be confident and self-assured. Divorce didn't embitter or taint me. As a result I'm fairly resourceful and able to deal with the world. I suspect, for Tom, that the reverse is true. I admit that he is emotionally distant. Does the root cause lie in his past? And how would Tom, as a young boy, fare with the police in the aftermath? It would be hard for officers to conceal contempt or anger. Was Tom referred to as Child A, or B, or some other letter from the alphabet, concealing his identity but also reducing him to nothing more than a cipher? It strikes me then that Tom was destined for manufactured anonymity from an early age.

I wonder whether he cried when caught. And if he did was it with or without tears? Did he lie? Was he sullen in his defence? Did he affect boredom? Was there contrition and remorse, and how long did he spend in a children's unit? Without answers I can't put together a picture. Jane gave so little away. In truth, I'm flying by wire and hurtling blind into something vast and deadly and dark beyond.

And yes, I'm scared because I can't discuss it with anyone, not Shenton or Falconer, not Reg, not Vick.

Nobody.

Except Jane.

I study the card she gave me. In black and white, with a traditional font, it shrieks officialdom. I don't contact her. Instead I phone the direct number to the sales office for Argo Homes. It's engaged. Cutting the call, I go to my bag, filching fishing out Stephanie's card, and punch in her number. Straight away, I get an unobtainable sound and a voice message that tells me the number is no longer in use. Puzzled, I try the sales office again, this time it rings out and is answered by a voice I recognise, Anita, the woman who gave me the lowdown on Stephanie. I ask to speak to her.

"Sorry, Mrs Charteris isn't here. Family emergency, I gather."

I feel as if I swallowed a ton of coffee beans whole. To check I'm not misunderstanding or going deaf, I ask her to repeat what she said. She does. No change in the story. I remind the woman who I am, the drama surrounding my visit resonating with her immediately.

"Oh, hello," she says, familiar now. "Yes, it came completely out of the blue. Most unlike Stephanie. She's usually so reliable."

"Did she phone herself, or did someone call on her behalf?"

"No, she at least had the decency to phone in personally."

"Was she specific?"

From the frozen pause, I realise I overstepped the line. "No," Anita says bluntly.

I remember Stephanie's remark about her sick mother. Perhaps this is the reason for her sudden departure. I want to ask Anita whether she sounded stressed, whether it was possible that someone else was in the room with her when she phoned, whether she was under duress or whether, God save me, she sounded happy and light and as if the love of her life had returned from the dead. To ask any of those questions would make me sound very strange indeed. Oh Christ, and what about Zoe? Needs must. I ask.

"What on earth are you suggesting?" Anita shoots back in alarm.

That was the point. I don't know. So I hang up.

Howling inside with anxiety, I check that the front door is locked and slip the chain across.

# Chapter 25

On his way to London, Tom gazed out of the train window at the countryside rushing by. How he longed to go back and come clean, tell Roz everything. She'd get it. But that would mean she'd discover the truth. She'd find out that, although he believed they were good together, that he loved her, that she would always be special to him, deep inside his heart beat stronger for Stephanie and Zoe. *He thought.*

It was only with them that he'd discovered true and unconditional love.

*Love.*

A strange phenomenon and one that he'd treated with misgiving at first. Each act of kindness worried him. Each kiss made him flinch. Where was the hitch? When did a smile turn to sly entrapment? Even the ultimate physical connection with Steph reminded him of other acts, when he'd been forced into doing things he never wanted to, laughed at, ridiculed and humiliated afterwards. Having a mind overthrown on a regular basis creates a child full of doubt and despair. He was mangled long before he became an adult. A shrink had told him this when he'd first escaped and thrown himself on the mercy of the police, but the shrink didn't know the half of it. Only thought he did.

There could be no going back because he couldn't guarantee either Roz or Steph and Zoe's safety and there was no sense in him thinking otherwise. More practically, Steph would be reluctant to leave her home, the place she'd grown up, her family – her mum had never been too clever health-wise – for a liar like him. The thought of her rejection stripped his insides raw, reducing his marrow to jelly. Better to hang on to the hope that she still thought well of him, maybe even loved him.

Suddenly, a monstrous thought entered his head: when Swain found out that Tom's death was rigged, it would only be a simple process of elimination to rumble the connection to his wife and Zoe.

Knee jackhammering, he glanced around the crowded railway carriage. Should have thought it through. Should have stopped to think, yet how to change the habit of a lifetime? His whole existence involved thinking on his feet, taking risks, waiting for the next blow to strike him down. Fleeing from Cheltenham and Roz had been an act of sheer instinct, but what if he'd made the wrong call? Every time his mind allowed him to think, he wanted to shut down and throw up. All that blood. The way Jack Prior had died with a 'fuck you' message scribbled all over his dead body. If they got their filthy hands on little Zoe, sons of bitches...

In an agony of indecision, he gawped out of the window. Protection, that's all he'd ever wanted in life, the stuff you take for granted. He'd had it once with his mum and dad, both fine people, caring of him and caring of others. His dad, especially, had a soft spot for Joshua, he remembered. He had witnessed it in his eyes. Didn't make him jealous. Only added to his belief that he was lucky to have a father like that. Dad promised that when Joshy was bigger he'd take them both out sailing together despite Aunt Ursula swearing that it would never happen. The promise died with the accident.

Scenery was slowing. A sign for Rugby appeared. Without another thought, he got up, pushed his way through the carriage and, when the train juddered to a halt, followed the crush out onto the platform and headed for the ticket office. After he'd fled, he'd thrown away his burner (US expression) pre-paid phone and only communication to Mads. Besides, if he got in touch now and announced his return from the cold, she'd be more focused on picking him up than ensuring Steph and Zoe's safety. Only one option left: he had to break cover and check up on them himself.

Head down, collar rolled up, he took his turn in the queue. Eyes sliding from one bland face to another, in every space he looked he felt that someone was out to get him. But nobody pounced. Not yet.

The next available train to Ludlow left in sixty minutes. After a three-and-half- hour journey, he'd reach his final desti-nation after five 'clock, by which time it would be dark. He didn't think beyond getting there. He didn't plan what he would do or how he could warn Steph without giving the game away and throwing her life into anarchy. Driven by fear and love, he only knew that he had to do something. That he couldn't keep running, not from the law or Swain's mates, or from demons that roared in his ear. Sometimes you had to stand up and be counted. And that time was now.

With dread, he plodded from the station up Gravel Hill. Avoiding streetlights, checking for tails, he slid from one shadow to another. It took him ten minutes to reach the one-stop shop on the corner, another to cross the road by the Chinese takeaway, the damp night air thick with Five Spice and garlic.

Standing at the end, heart pumping wildly in his chest, he peered down the street as though it were a sniper's alley. Outside his old home would make a perfect killing ground for Swain and his men. With room to single-park opposite, it was possible that cops were on a stakeout in case he should be foolish or reckless enough to return. Those were the two worse-case scenarios. He gambled on a third.

Drawing the hood of his jacket up, he dropped his head to his chin and, with a slow but steady tread, veered to the right past a row of small Victorian terraced houses, the place he'd once called home. A mixture of tenanted and owned properties, perfect for the first-time buyer or downsizing elderly couple, places changed hands in the street with regularity. Chinks of light peeped out from behind closed curtains. In some, he spotted the flickering blue rays of a television. He scoped the street, alert to anyone loitering, or a car occupied yet with its lights off. How many times had he faced danger? How many times had some sick supernatural fuck decided to hand him another helping of twisted fate? Was this going to be another of those occasions?

So far, so good, his luck, if he could call it that, held.

Most people appeared to be hunkered (US again) 'bunkered' down for the evening. From an upstairs window, he heard the sound of rock music. From another: the noise of a trumpet murdering a solo. He didn't doubt that behind closed doors there would be as many rows and heavy atmospheres in motion as there were people sitting comfortably. Domestic life was messy, yet it triggered an emotion that he hadn't felt for so long he doubted its existence: pure love, without expectations. Love for his little family and for what others sometimes took for granted. With it, swept over him a terrible emptiness and longing for the peace he had once found there. Back in the best days with Steph and Zoe he had smiled, really smiled, and meant it. With the raw realisation came guilt. He had not found that same sense of peace with Roz, although he'd tried. Wasn't her fault. It was all his.

Two paces and, nearly there, he cast around nervously a final time. The street remained normal, a cat stalking past, king of all it surveyed, the only movement.

With a deep breath, he turned and stopped.

Curtains open upstairs and down, each window presented a chasm of darkness. This was not what frightened him. The open gate that was always shut for fear of Zoe escaping into the street was like an alarm clanging inside his head.

An unseen hand beckoned him close. Repelled and captivated, he drew near, body tensed, expecting trouble. Depressing the handle on the front door got him nowhere. Locked. He took a step sideways, stumbled into something on the ground.

Crouching down, he touched whatever it was, grimy fingers playing through soft damp and matted hair. Startled, he peered more closely, picked it up and instantly recognised the toy, an irresistibly fluffy seal that he'd given to Zoe for when she was bigger. He'd imagined that it went everywhere with her and the fact that it lay discarded was an omen. Hastily, he scooped up its soggy remains and pushed it into his bag.

Nerves twisting, he strained to look inside the downstairs window, seeing nothing. The rational part of his mind told him that they could be out for the night, perhaps at a friend's or maybe Stephanie had gone to Joy's, her mum. The irrational part said that they'd left by force. When a front door swung open next to him he nearly leapt over the wall.

"Sorry, mate, didn't mean to make you jump," a man's voice said. This followed by the sound of empty bottles and cans clattering into a recycling bin. "If you're looking for my neighbour, you're out of luck."

Against instinct, Tom turned to face the man – fortunately, a newcomer. Exceptionally tall, he must have had at least four inches on Tom. Built, too, by the look of the muscles bulging from his plain black t-shirt.

"Any idea where they've gone?"

"Search me. Left with a woman, official-looking." Mads, Tom thought, fear subsiding. "My Mrs thinks it could be the social."

*Social services?* Confusion swamped him. "You mean the little girl was taken somewhere else?"

"No, they went together."

"When was this?"

"Earlier today." The man had a ragged expression. Tom knew he was firing too many questions and the guy was getting jumpy, but he had to know.

"Can you describe the woman?"

The man blew out through his teeth. "Tricky," he said. "It was raining."

"Please, can you try?"

The guy stiffened. "All I can tell you is that they left in a hurry. Got into a four-by-four, one of those Jeep things," he added unnecessarily.

"Did you—"

"That's it, pal. See you around," he said, retreating to the house, the door shut firmly behind him.

Fear swelled until he thought it would burst out through his ribs. Without a description, he couldn't be sure it was Mads. What if Swain's men had sent a woman to pick up Stephanie? What if they were kidnapped already? What if Roz were next on their criminal playlist? Should he return to Cheltenham, warn her? He dug his nails into the soft palms of his hands. Had to get a grip. Hadn't come this far to lose it now. Needing a smoke, he took a pack of cigarettes from his pocket, shook one out with trembling fingers, dropped one, cursed, plucked another and plugged it between his lips. Match struck. Deep inhale. Bliss.

Turning on his heel, he headed back the way he'd come. An advantage of living there once, he knew exactly where to find the nearest pay phone – back at the train station.

Mads gave him a number to use only in emergency, if he

couldn't get through, for whatever reason on his burner. He'd never used it, but it was part of his DNA.

Glancing around and satisfied that he hadn't been followed, he fished out the right coins and punched in the number. Mads answered after two rings.

"Tom?"

"Don't speak, listen. Are Steph and Zoe safe?"

"Yes."

"And Roz?"

"There's no cause for alarm."

Thank Christ.

"Where are you?"

"Doesn't matter, that's all I need to know."

"Tom, wait. I can help you but—"

"You were right about me, Mads. I'm better off on my own. Watch Swain's every move...'

"Tom, relax."

"How can I after what happened last time?"

"I understand and I'm sorry, but we have your back."

"I wish I could believe it."

"Look, I apologise if I panicked you, but Swain isn't going anywhere."

"That's not what you implied."

"I have a duty to tell you about any moves his lawyers make."

"What about his crew? What about the threat?"

"We're on it, Tom. Some are dead, banged up, or abroad."

"Then there's still a problem."

"Which is why I'll say it again, you need to come in. We

have to talk. I don't think you've been quite straight with us, have you?" A vile taste flooded his mouth, like he'd chewed soap.

"Tom, do you know a man by the name of Linus Verdi?"

He retched, dropped the phone, and ran.

# Chapter 26

Frustrated and tetchy, I log into my laptop, and check out road-rage incidents in the UK. There are a ton of them, but not many in which people are killed. One catches my eye. It happened outside Llandudno. Grabbing my bag, I fish out the card Reg found for the cab service Tom used during his illicit stint in Wales. Furlongs of Conwy, it reads, the distance between the two places a little over four miles. I jot down details, scrawl two names: Garry Swain, a nasty piece of work with a string of violent offences to his name, and Jack Prior, council official, cyclist and victim. I look at the date. It's almost three years prior to when Tom – for me he will always be Tom – meets Stephanie.

I rock back on the chair. The timing fits. Tom would be roughly eighteen years of age and it corroborates what Stephanie and Jane told me. I'm the dummy, the one he deliberately misled. There is no joy in the discovery.

My mind flips to who was following me. What if it's one of Swain's crew? Will Jane offer the kind of protection I need? I toy with picking up the phone, until another heading throws me right off-balance. The lawyers for Swain the road-rage killer are arguing for his release on licence. So that's what the phone call to Tom was about. That's what made him run. Why didn't Jane simply tell me? Why spin me a line? Was she the person responsible for calling Tom and pushing him over the edge? A darker thought formulates inside my brain. *Is she who she says she is?* I punch in her number. Engaged at first, it then switches to voicemail. After the tone, I leave a short message. In the meantime, I do some digging into the process of witness protection and, not unexpectedly, discover very little aside from the fact that officers working within protection use different computer systems to avoid corrupt police accessing highly confidential data. So that backs up Jane's story about the need for confidentiality.

It's late evening by the time she returns my call. "Things to do," she declares, all business. "So what have you got for me?"

Nothing. I come straight to the point. "Why didn't you tell me you'd already spirited away Stephanie and her daughter?"

"I'm not entirely certain why you think I'm answerable to you. As importantly, how the hell did you find out?"

"I phoned her office." Meanly, I wonder how Jane's little scenario played out. *Excuse me, your husband is alive, in witness protection, and your life and Zoe's is in danger.*

"Let me be quite clear," she says. "You do not involve yourself at any level."

"Okay."

"And I do not trade information with you."

My eyes feel like grit. My cheeks burn with passion, but I'm not out of control – far from it. In any case, one uppity woman getting exercised won't make much of a dent on Jane's emotional spectrum. Although I don't doubt that, if I rattle her cage loudly enough, she'll react in kind. Jane might have a plain fake name, but I have her notched for a pitbull dressed as a poodle, possibly called Delilah. Perhaps these are all essential attributes for the average witness protection officer. How should I know?

"Now can we move on?" She speaks gently, a polite way of asking me to dig the dirt and spread it.

I take a moment. Actually, several. Call it recalibrating the dynamics. "I'm assuming you didn't see Tom when you removed Stephanie and her daughter to a place of safety?"

"Would I be talking to you if that were the case?"

"Is a full-scale manhunt in play?"

She clicks her tongue at my apparent stupidity. "Behind the scenes." I get the impression that she thinks me a tiresome but necessary encumbrance. "Tom is an especially sensitive case and there's a news blackout."

What she means is that something like this wouldn't look good on the rap sheet. "What did Stephanie have to say when you picked her up?"

"Nothing that would lead us to Tom," she says with finality, in a bid to close down that particular avenue of exploration. I'm having none of it. Besides, I'm sick of being on send while she's on receive. I visualise her shoulders hitching, her spine tensing.

"Presumably he had strong feelings for the woman he made his wife?" It fairly kills me to utter this, but I recognise it to be the truth.

"A fair assessment."

"So how did he react when a plan was hatched to fake his death?" I demand.

"Hated it."

"He put up a fight?"

"Tom always put up a fight." She says this in such a knowing manner I'm inclined to believe her. "Kicked and fought all the way," she adds. Seems he loved Stephanie as much as she loved him.

"Yet he went through with it."

"Didn't have a choice."

"You persuaded him?"

"Not only me. The team." There's a wary note in her voice. I hear her breathing hard and wonder what 'the team' are up to now. Is Stephanie being subjected to similarly intrusive treatment? Is it part of a joined-up strategy?

"Miss Outlaw, you seem to be muddled about what is required of you. I'm the one asking the questions."

My turn to fall silent.

Jane clears her throat. I stay silent and, this time, she doesn't push it but asks about Tom's routines and lifestyle. Other than stating that he cycled every day to work and liked to keep fit by swimming a couple of times a week, I give bland responses. I do not mention his penchant for drugs. While I talk, I walk and check the door is double-locked and that the downstairs windows are secure.

"His state of mind prior to him leaving; how was that?"

"How would I know? He kept me in the dark."

She waits a beat. Cool. Persistent. In charge. I have no

problem with authority, but I have a problem with her particular brand. I'll go further: I dislike her for her incessant badgering. I don't trust her. My mind is hooked on suspicion and won't dislodge. "Did he upset easily?" There's a hitch in her voice.

"No." Tom's cool approach to life in general was faked, whether he ever reconciled himself to the crime he committed as a child is debatable. Then another thought occurs. When Tom left he was terrified, yet not terrified enough to warn me that I, too, could be at risk, I recollect with bitterness.

"You're not really playing the game with me, are you?"

I could protest, but I'd only sound false. My mood, previously strewn in tatters at my feet, improves.

"You need to trust me, Roz."

"Works both ways. Which establishment was Tom sent to after he killed the child?"

"Nice try. That's confidential too."

Thought it would be. With a name, I could find out quite a bit.

"Tell you what, I say, choking off any further discussion. "If I think of anything, I'll let you know."

"Do that. Thank you for your time. Appreciate it. About your protection..."

"It's fine," I say, levelling with her. "I can look after myself."

# Chapter 27

At least the barn was dry, if not warm, and offered basic protection against wind and pulsing rain. Tom burrowed a nest out of bales of straw, sunk into it and became his very own baby Jesus – without harbouring thoughts that could pass for Christian.

After the call to Mads, he'd hurried to Whitcliffe Common, a popular place for walkers and dog-owners by day. He and Stephanie used to regularly walk there on Sunday mornings, Zoe tucked up, snuggled in her buggy. But this was no trip down memory lane for him.

He knew of a farm close by. There, he planned to spend the night and think.

He believed Mads when she told him that the police were checking out Swain's crew, men who were either dead, in prison or sunning their arses in foreign, more criminally hospitable, climes. He had to trust her on that.

"Someone saw you," Mads had told him the second time she called him in Cheltenham. "Swain knows you're alive." And so, it seemed, did Linus.

The energy that fired his anger and despair turned him in

only one other possible direction. Deep down, he'd known all along. He was a fool for not acknowledging it before. If only he'd paid more attention to his instincts. As surely as he was responsible for Joshua's death, he was to blame now. He should never have gone back to visit Joshua's grave. Guilt, its closest of cousins, raged through him with the uncontrollability of a fire started by arsonists. He'd put his own needs above the safety of others. God alone knew what that would do to Stephanie and Zoe, to Roz.

Without warning, he was back in the woods and the last time he'd seen Joshua alive; half term, a February day and a blue sky etched with frost and ice.

It was Uncle Geoff's madcap idea that the boys should camp in the woodland adjoining the house. Aunt Ursula kicked up a terrific fuss, saying that it was too cold and dangerous. She'd been right about that. He'd no idea how she'd been persuaded to agree, but she had, worse luck. The prospect of spending the night in the open alone with Linus created raw panic inside him still. After all these years, bright terror bit deeply into him at the recollection.

He couldn't bear to remember the sequence of events, let alone the detail. By the time the adults found out, it was already too late. Linus and Aunt Ursula never forgave him and, in the wake of Joshua's death, his life took a catastrophic turn of events that became the pattern of his existence from then on.

Which was why he believed that Linus, with his twisted mind, had tracked him down and forced him to abandon his new life, the women in it, and child he loved.

# Chapter 28

Pouring myself a glass of wine, I piece together the scraps of knowledge that Jane unwittingly, or more likely wittingly, supplied. My problem is sifting the truth from the cobbled-together story of Tom Loxley, aka Adam Charteris, aka someone else entirely.

Tom is the equivalent of a sleeper, an individual whose legend is indistinguishable from his real life. To make a legend or falsehood stick, it's a good idea to prop it up with truth. So much easier to be convincing if the liar believes the lie spun. I'm no shrink, but it makes sense that Mikey, Tom's imaginary younger brother, is a stand-in for the boy Tom allegedly killed. Is the aunt for real or dead? Whatever her corporeal state she figures in his psyche. His parents are dead, I'm sure of that, boating accident, or not. This is something I intend to pursue. I wonder for how long Tom will run, how long before he flakes out and emerges from the shadows.

Letting the alcohol spin through my brain, I consider Tom's choice in women. I can't help but think that he deliberately selected me because I was older, reflecting an unconscious desire to be mothered. My stomach clenches in despair at my mistaken belief that the spontaneous combustibility of our sexual relationship was fuelled by a desire to have children when, in fact, he probably chose me because I couldn't.

Tom isn't simply running from Swain. All his life he was running. It started the moment he lost his mum and dad.

I return to the Swain case on my laptop. Before, I looked at players and geography. Now, I look at choreography. Tom might not have passed his driving test until later. If he were on a bike, unless he was a prototype Bradley Wiggins, his then-home could not be far away, twenty miles' radius maximum of Llandudno.

My mobile suddenly rings. One glance tells me who it is. "Hi Vick," I say. It seems a lifetime ago since we last spoke.

"Are you okay? Haven't heard a squeak from you."

I tell her about losing my job and make out that this is the reason for going off- grid.

"That's harsh. Do you think you'll find another?"

"Hope so." Who am I kidding? The local free weekly was the pinnacle of my journalistic career. Closer to forty than thirty, I suddenly feel as if a large chunk of my life passed me by, a bleak and depressing thought.

"Could always get temporary work at the call centre," she says with a chuckle. "With me handing in my notice, there's bound to be a vacancy."

I don't dignify her suggestion with a response. "So you're off to play Miss Marple?" How bloody ironic.

"Cheek. Vera Claythorne, I'll have you know."

"Who?"

"The love interest in *And Then There Were None*. The BBC did an adaptation."

I remember. "Let's hope your Philip Lombard is as good looking."

"No link, but have you heard from Tom?"

I badly want to spill my guts to Vick, but daren't. Too risky and it wouldn't be fair. This is too big for me and definitely too big for her. I lie that I'm doing my utmost to forget him.

"Unlike you to take my advice, but I'm relieved. It's for the best, trust me."

I smile at the wall and make meaningless neutral remarks, Tom's talent for deception rubbing off on me. After she wraps up the call, I take a long, hot, steamy bath, and my mind drifts. I think of Tom and what he did and how I hate him for it. I think of Jane and what she said and...

I sit bolt upright with a great big sploosh. Tom was a teenager when he witnessed a crime. I can't think of many teens keen to do civic duty at such a young age, but Tom was no ordinary person, far from it. He committed murder and would not long be out of a specialist unit. In fact, he would have absolutely no intention of tangling with the law again. For him, the police would be scary entities, people to fear and run a mile from. He would be extremely reluctant to engage with authority of any kind, let alone testify. In fact, Tom would do what he always does. He'd run. It's such a big anomaly I'm having trouble getting past it.

I draw on all my hack resources and soldier on while briskly towelling myself dry. What made him change his mind? Why was he so eager? Fresh start? Redemption?

Genuinely afraid that if he didn't report what happened, he'd be at greater risk?

It's generally understood that Swain, the man Tom crossed, is formidable; out of fires and into blazing infernos. Then another quite random thought crosses my mind, one that turns everything upside down.

I pack an overnight bag and choose appropriately warm clothes for the next day. I take money out of my emergency tin and stuff it in my purse. I'll need to top the car up with petrol in the morning. A quick scoot through the best route and I'm done. I know exactly where I'm going. What I don't know is what I'll find when I get there.

# Chapter 29

First thing, Jane drops me a text, asking me to call her. I drive to a main petrol station at one of the big supermarkets on the way out of town. I'm filling up when I feel a pair of eyes bore into the side of my head. Twisting round, I spot Mike Shenton. He raises a hand and smiles. I smile back, put the nozzle back on the rest, flip the petrol cap back in place and make for the kiosk to pay. Shenton falls in step beside me.

"All right?" he says. Friendly, a tad nervous. Maybe he's embarrassed. I know I am.

I want to say 'fine.' I also want to ask him about a protection officer called Jane who told me that the man I lived with is a killer. Like I said, I'm not good at keeping secrets. Admirably, I don't say a word other than to mutter, "Yes. You?"

"Yeah, day off."

"Gotta be good, then."

He laughs freely. It's nice. Wild and carefree. Something inside me withers because I wonder if I will ever be like this again. Tom, it seems, was primed for self-destruction, but he didn't have to drag me with him.

Shenton and me are level when we reach the entrance. He hangs back, allowing me to step in first. I mumble thanks, wishing I'd left home fifteen minutes sooner. "Pleasure," he says. There is genuine warmth in his voice. Is he flirting, buttering me up, or what?

I go one way. He goes the other. Locked in some strange petroleum-themed tango, we pay simultaneously and wind up side by side, shimmying down the aisle between sweets and newspapers.

"You really okay?" he repeats, pushing open the door.

The kindness in his eyes makes me want to melt. It feels like a long time since someone was solicitous towards me. I assure him I'm fine. "Roz?" He reaches for my hand. His touch is as warm and reassuring as the first time. "Please." He speaks as if asking a huge favour, a smart tactical move on Shenton's part, guaranteed to make me weaken.

I stop, turn and look at him straight. The expression in his eyes suggests that he knows I jettisoned the advice he gave.

"Roz…"

"Sorry, I really am in a tearing…"

"Listen carefully. I want you to know that I believe you."

Stunned, my heart misses a beat.

He glances down. Colour flashes across his cheeks. He's breaking a code, the one he signed up for, yet I sense that Shenton, the maverick, has a code of his own, that he plays by different rules. Does that mean he's not on the level, or the reverse?

"When you came to the police station," he says in a low

voice, clarifying what he means, so that there is no mistake. "What you told me."

Oh my goodness. What will they do if I breathe one word about witness protection? "Mike, I, really don't...'

"You're not the only one being closed down, Roz."

He looks at me with such directness I swallow hard and cover my mouth with my hand. "I'm sorry," I mumble, "I..."

"You don't have a clue who Tom really is, or what he might have done. You don't even know his name." Shenton speaks softly. I don't think he's trying to score points. Irritatingly, my eyes fill with tears because what he says hits home. All I have are stories told by others. What does Shenton think Tom did?

I open my mouth to say things that should not be said, then remember the risks, not simply for me, but for others.

I shake my head, shrug and walk away.

"Roz," he calls after me, followed by "Miss Outlaw." There's a touch of desperation in his voice. My heart swells in my chest. I don't want to walk away, but I must. Perhaps it's because his admission hands me immense power. One word from me, and his career could be finished.

I'm by the car now. Cheeping it open, I wrench open the door, climb inside and shut myself in. Sliding the window down, I poke my head out and say, "It's okay. This conversation never took place." Next, I start the engine, clutch in, brake off and drive away. One look in the rear-view mirror tells me that D.S. Mike Shenton, goggle-eyed and stock-still, is out on a limb and doesn't much care for it. Ditto.

An hour and a half later, I stop trembling, reach Ludlow and cruise slowly down New Street, where Stephanie Charteris lives, and park alongside a wall in a street beyond. Grabbing an umbrella against the rain, keeping it low to obscure my face, I double back and saunter past. Mail hangs half in and half out of the letterbox. Curtains are open upstairs and down. The brickwork doesn't look clever. The window frame needs a lick of paint. Why didn't I spot this the first time? Without doubt, the house now has the neglected, lonely appearance of the recently separated prior to divorce.

I glance down the road to where a red postal van is parked together with half a dozen other vehicles. Most people at work, there are plenty of gaps and no cars with occupants, either undercover police officers or villains. Satisfied that I'm not being watched, I push open the gate and peer into the downstairs room. The sideboard is as I remember it. Aside from silver-framed photographs, a mug sits randomly next to a plate on which a lone biscuit sits. Scattered laundry litters the rug in front of the wood-burning stove, as if a poltergeist went to work. Other than this, there is nothing that suggests anyone is coming back any time soon. About to leave, I spy a single cigarette on the front step to the door. Fallen out of a pack, by the look of it. Protected by the gable overhang, it isn't soggy or damaged. Could be anyone's.

Stooping down, I pick it up, roll it between my fingers, and put it in my pocket. Standing again, I look both ways, combing the street for signs of Tom before heading back to the car in sheeting rain.

Out of Ludlow, I pick up the A49 and head towards Wales. Driving conditions are atrocious, visibility poor. I virtually drench some poor soul dragging along on a pushbike on the way out of town. A long time ago, I would stop and offer a lift. After what happened, I'm not certain I will trust anyone again, and drive past, mourning the unwelcome change in my personality. The rhythmic swish of the windscreen wipers fails to calm or make me feel better. Only Mike Shenton, with his warm eyes and caring expression, briefly penetrates my gloomy mood. I so nearly reached out to him before I bottled.

Driving on, I don't know what I think of my new unfamiliar and alien surroundings. Even the most beautiful places seem grim in heavy weather. Having rejected the place where I was brought up in search of a more exciting city life, I sense that this is another one of those places in which I would not be happy.

Armed with the magazine, I plan to visit the taxi company first, and, afterwards, carry out good old-fashioned legwork. It's a risk because I could run into Jane or Falconer, worse still the man or men allegedly chasing Tom. Or even Tom himself, the child-killer, the liar and cheat. But run into him I must.

I want answers. I want truth and I want justice.

# Chapter 30

I turn the radio on, catch a sad refrain from Adele and switch it off.

With so many people after him, I wonder how Tom stayed hidden. The common consensus is that it's more difficult than ever to escape the attention of the law in our technological universe. It is if you're a fully signed up, engaged and socially active member. But Tom sneaks under the radar. Deliberately so and now I understand that he always has. Easier for him to blend in to our homogenised world in which everyone dresses similarly, follows trends, eats international imports, adopts a herd mentality in which celebrity culture and money trump intellectual rigour, values and individualism. Or maybe, I think, changing up a gear, at the ripe old age of thirty-seven, I got old. Or grew up.

Driving is slow going and, desperate for a pee, I pull into Chester, a well-heeled walled city with black-and-white architecture, some of it medieval, a lot of it Victorian. The car park leads onto Bridge Street and there I belt into a café, order a sandwich and use the loo.

Back in the car, I check my phone for messages – none – eat my lunch and set my sights on Conwy.

It's a clear run. The weather briefly improves. The rain is less beat and more trickle. A coastal road takes me near to seaside resorts like Rhyl and Prestatyn, which conjure up pictures of funfairs, fish and chips, candy-floss, dripping ice cream, sticky hands, sand in sandwiches and piers. Glimpses of foamy, choppy water peep out between trees and buildings. Drawing close, crossing into what is surely enemy territory, my heart tumbles in my chest. What am I doing here? It's no longer my fight, my relationship or my battle and yet I feel inexorably drawn. My lover's story both taunts and eludes me. Contained within his narrative, surely, the truth must lie? Not the reason he fled, but the reason a boy died and another got caught up in something he shouldn't.

Mid-afternoon light bleeds out as I drive over a designated bridge for motorists, the more ancient model, suitable only for pedestrians, lying parallel. Beneath, the river boils and roils after so much rain, Conwy castle ahead emerging spectral through the gloom.

Following the signs for a car park, I easily find a space, feed a meter and slap on a ticket for a couple of hours, which costs me next to nothing.

Conwy might be gorgeous in high summer. The castle, solid, ancient and imposing, looks terrific. My first impression in the wet, though, is of a land that time forgot around 1950. It's the kind of place where banks don't yet have outside or inside cashpoints and where, I suspect, affairs of the heart are less easily tolerated; consequences of the latter, if small-town living is anything to go by, potentially destructive. Nothing like the laissez-faire environment in which I grew up, in which people got together, hooked up, as the Americans would say, and then went separate ways with regularity, often with kids in tow.

Next, I find a café with wi-fi. Ordering a cup of tea, I use my Iphone to tap in Furlongs' Cab Service for an address. It turns out to be central, literally a street away from where I sit. Taking it as a good omen, I drink up and make my way through a sudden shower of rain that stings like needles of ice. Few people are about and those that are scurry, heads down, umbrellas up. Mothers herding children. Businessmen with briefcases, clicking and snapping to their next appointment. Everyone intent, purposeful and not the least bit interested in me. Despite this, I glance over my shoulder, see nothing out of the ordinary and, feeling ridiculous, stride on in imitation of the rest. What was that I mentioned about herd instinct?

The office for the cab company is the size of an old-fashioned railway carriage. Cluttered with newspapers, box files, old calendars, grimy paperwork and smelling of oil lubricant, especially pungent given the extreme level of heating belting out of an electric fan heater, it isn't what you'd describe as welcoming. I squeeze inside and am greeted by a bony stare from a thin little man in a short-sleeved shirt and, unaccountably, wearing a set of braces to hold up trousers that are too short in the leg and too high in the waist. If it weren't for the psoriasis on his elbows and winkle-picker shoes, he'd resemble an overgrown toddler in dungarees. I transfer my gaze from his clothes to his greasy comb-over and back to eyes that are the colour of sultanas. A radio crackles and he momentarily stops gawping at me and babbles something in Welsh into a microphone. I wait patiently, fish out the magazine from my bag. Eventually, he finishes and twists his suspicious gaze toward me.

"I wonder if you've seen this man? He called for a taxi last month." I supply the date and push the magazine in front of him. The little Welshman doesn't give it so much as a glance.

"No."

"Is it possible to speak to your drivers?"

"No."

"Oh," I say, because I can't think of anything else. I wonder why he is so unhelpful. Is it in his genes? Does he think I'm a crook, a snooper, both? I forge my best 'no problem' smile. "I wonder if I could—"

"Are you Heddlu?"

"Pardon?"

"Police," he says.

"No. I—"

"Journalist?" He draws out the syllables, giving the impression that he doesn't think much of them. I smile, lie and assure him that I am not.

"Well, then, best be on your way."

Crumbling under his stubborn gaze, I turn to leave. Almost out of the door, I turn back. "Have the police already paid a visit?"

He slow-blinks, tilts his chin, the briefest of nods.

Jane, I realise, thinking I need to be careful. 'Thank you for your help," I say, without a trace of rancour, about to go once more.

"They won't find him."

"Who?" I hardly dare to breathe.

"The driver. An immigrant, see. Moonlighting on the side. Had to get rid of him. Done a flit with the takings. Gone back to where he came from if he's got any sense."

"Right," I say, crumpled. "Don't suppose you know whether or not he gave this man a ride?" I tap the picture.

He tuts. "Police asked me that too."

"And?" I say, expectant.

"Like I told them, can't 'elp you."

# Chapter 31

Defeated, I step out into a gust of howling wind and walk quickly, half expecting the click of fast footsteps behind me, but there's nothing and nobody.

Eager to escape the weather and find somewhere for the night, I stroll into the first hotel that happens to be in the High Street. A former coaching inn, it has a wide entrance, lots of polished wood and lamplight that penetrates the overarching gloom. A reception area lies straight ahead. To my right: a bar in which a log fire burns. To my left: a restaurant. I check in for the night, fill out a form, giving my details and car registration.

"Do you have a car park and wi-fi?" I ask.

"We do."

"Thanks, I'll move my vehicle."

"Will you be wanting dinner with us this evening?"

"Please." I agree a time, take my key, return to where I parked a few streets away and drive back to the hotel.

My room is a little dated, although functional enough and has a great view of Edward I's architectural masterpiece, Conwy Castle, illuminated and ghostly in the gloom. I unpack my things, such as they are, and sit on the bed, wondering what to do next. I stand as much chance of finding Tom as organising a meeting with an MP in the Cabinet. As if to prompt me, my phone rings.

It's Jane. "I've been to your house. Where are you?"

"Out," I say, "obviously," I add with a shaky laugh. "Have you found Tom?'

"Not yet."

"You sound confident. Has something happened?"

"It's Garry Swain. He's dead."

One should not feel joy at someone's passing, but I want to scream and shout hallelujah because surely this means Tom's problems are over. But not all, I realise, a feather of fear grazing my cheek.

"Hello, are you still there?"

"Yes," I say, my elation brief. I need to push her, to ask what happens next. I'd like to know whether an associate bumped off Swain, or whether karma took its own course. I ask.

"That's all I have."

Glancing up, I see a large spider ambling down the wall.

"Are you all right?" she says.

"Yes."

Jane says that we need to meet, to which I say I have to go, and cut the call.

Lost in every sense, I stretch out on the bed, to think and not feel. One thing is clear: Tom must be found and told about Swain's demise.

Grabbing my phone, I hit speed-dial. Vick picks up after three rings.

"Where the hell are you?"

It's not quite the response I expect.

"Had some woman round here, a police officer looking for you. Seemed urgent. Asked me to pass on a message for you to get in touch."

Jane. "It's okay," I say. "We've already spoken. I'm assisting with an enquiry."

"What enquiry? Is this connected to Tom's disappearance?"

"Of course not." I gaze out at the illuminated castle, tons of black and silver reflecting off the water.

"Well, what is it connected to? I'm all ears."

"Vick, I'd rather not say." I make out I'm embarrassed.

"Roz, you sound strange."

"I'm fine," I lie.

She huffs, immediately grasping that I'm not being straight with her. I blunder on, "Can you think of anything about Tom, some clue into his background?" I want to say 'real' background, but daren't confess to what I know. "Something you think unimportant, but might be really important."

She goes very quiet. I can practically hear her processing. "I knew it," she bursts with jubilation. "You haven't given up on him at all. What the hell has that man done now?"

I screw my eyes up tight until they water. "Vick, please, I can't tell you. I wish I could but I can't."

Hoping I do enough to mollify her, I don't speak; let the silence do the talking. Vick doesn't say anything either and I think she's coming up empty. The spider progresses from the wall to the floor and is heading along, near the skirting board, at terrific speed, a genuinely athletic arachnid.

"You know those scars on his arms?"

I visualise the peppering of marks on his skin from numerous small burns. "From when he got splashed with hot oil in one of the kitchens he worked in?"

"I never believed it."

I swallow hard.

"Always looked more like cigarette burns to me. Occurred to me after Reg dropped a lighted fag on my sofa."

"Bet you were miffed."

"Stop changing the subject, Roz."

I'm not. I'm attempting to protect myself. "Bit of a difference between material and skin."

"Whatever."

"Are you suggesting he self-harmed?"

"I wondered if someone did it to him."

Shocked, I'm lost for words.

"You still there?" Vick says.

"Do you really think so?" I drag the words out, consonant by consonant, vowel by vowel. Every one of them sticks and, when each peels away, it stings.

"It would account for a lot, don't you think?"

Oh goodness, where is this all leading?

"Roz, I don't have a clue what you're up to, but if it's what I think, stop. Come back. Stay here for a while. I'm not leaving for another week."

I'm tempted. Swain is out of the picture, any threat to me receding to the same level of risk employed in crossing the road. Let the police do what they have to and get on with my own life. Except Vick's latest observation about Tom crushes me. What happened to him all those years ago?

"I'm all right," I say. "I'll call you the moment I get back. Promise."

# Chapter 32

I go downstairs to the bar and order a badly needed drink from a fresh-faced youngster, who doesn't look old enough to be serving alcohol.

"Be with you in a minute," he fires back, scampering off with a tray of drinks.

Somehow it makes my solo state more conspicuous. I guess it's a female thing. Blokes don't suffer the same indignities.

While he's gone I glance around the lounge, a combination of tartan and old dog, although there is not so much as a terrier in sight. The smell of wood smoke from the log fire drifts on the clotted, clubby air. Four tables are already taken. At one, a cluster of middle-aged women laugh and chat. There's a young couple sitting very close to each other, holding hands, knee to knee. An old boy, with a red face and a tumbler of what looks like Scotch, eyes me with curiosity and suspicion as the stranger that I am. Hailing from Devon, I recognise the 'League of Gentlemen' attitude. Nothing personal about it; anyone the local doesn't recognise as 'one of them' comes in for this type of appraisal.

Larded in sweat, the childlike barman dashes back and

doesn't seem to remember me, or what I ordered. We go through the motions again and I put my drink on a tab and take it out of the bar and through to a small lounge created from a wide corridor. A family spreads out on sofas near the entrance. Tables, all different heights, dot along the right-hand side. Tall bar stools squat in the middle, higgledy-piggledy.

I head for the only available spot near a window with dusty drapes, where I sip and think about those scars Vicky mentioned. 'Old' scars tell stories. I feed it into the sparse information Jane supplied that includes the death of a child and Tom's involvement in it. Guilt in a court of law doesn't always mean the person accused did it. Miscarriages of justice exist. The police don't always get it right. Did they get it right with Tom? Truth is, based on what Jane told me; I can't tell the difference between hard fact, circumstantial and lie.

I take another long swallow of vodka and let the alcohol fire the synapses in my brain.

If I hoped to crack Tom's whereabouts by coming here, I'm off-beam, and not thinking loosely enough. Going back to his recent visit, I'm as sure as I can be that he would not come all this way alone on a whim, for a few days of R&R, or as a means to escape me.

Without warning, I am hot with tears. He put up a fight, Jane said. He didn't want to leave Stephanie, yet he tore himself away to save the woman he loved and the daughter he treated as his own. Great love demands sacrifice and I meant what I said to Stephanie that grief is the very high price we pay. I sob for my own loss, stupidity and delusion. I cry fat tears of anger, catching them on the back of one hand as I drive them away.

*Stay angry.*

*Stay focused.*

*Be detached.*

Fiercely sweeping up my drink, I go through to the restaurant for a meal I know I won't enjoy. Heavily beamed, with thick curtains at the windows, wood panelling and china, the restaurant is exactly as I expect, mirroring the cavern vibe in the rest of the hotel.

Without appetite, I decide I'm in need of comfort food to tempt me and order a dish of belly pork with chorizo and apple chutney from the main menu. Offered wine, I decline. The moment the waitress leaves I recognise my mistake.

Dinner arrives. Halfway through, I am uncomfortably full and my brain feels sluggish. By carefully arranging my napkin, I conceal the leftovers and slip back to the bar. There, I order another single vodka and tonic and take it over to the fire. The old boy has two drinks on the go, a pint of beer with a whisky chaser. His glassy red-edged eyes fix on me. Below, his cheeks and nose flare with thread veins, only this time he smiles warmly, as if the alcohol numbed the demon he is fleeing. I smile back. He tilts his head in a gesture of 'hello'. I do the same.

"You're not from round here," he says in a richly accented, deep and cultured voice that sounds stronger than he looks; age and, I suspect, booze exacting their toll.

"No," I say.

"Come far?"

"Cheltenham."

"Long way from home."

I agree.

"Business, I dare say."

Unfinished, I think. "Business, yes."

Silence opens up between us. A chasm. The old man looks as though he's born and bred here. It's a closed community. Might he throw light on 'Runaway Tom?' I wish I hadn't left the magazine in the room, but don't want to nip out to retrieve it for fear of losing the connection. I roll the conversation again.

"You live here?"

"Yes."

"All your life?"

"Oh yes, I should say so. I was a doctor for forty years. This was my patch."

A thrill of anticipation sparks inside me. "Then you might be able to help."

"I'll do my best." The accompanying smile perfectly captures the predicament of the professional retired. He's only too glad to be of assistance, to be needed and useful again.

"I'm looking for someone. He goes by the name of Tom Loxley, but doesn't live here any more." Without proof of him ever doing so, I break off. Tom feels insubstantial and opaque, more shadow than person.

"Never heard the name," he says.

"But you might have heard of the case he was involved in," I finish. Awkward. Clumsy.

"A case? Sounds interesting. If it occurred between here and

Llandudno, I'm your man." He slaps his knee, taking a drink, the whisky buoying him.

"It happened a long time ago. A boy killed another."

His smile expires and his eyes slide to the door. "No." He firmly shakes his head. "I don't recall anything like that."

"In forty years, did you never come across a crime like it?"

He looks at me straight. "Absolutely not." His voice doesn't tremble. It is clear and unequivocal. He takes a gulp of whisky and replaces the tumbler back on the table with more force than necessary to emphasise the point. I catch an edge of anger in his expression, as if I've made an improper or inappropriate suggestion and cast a slur on the inhabitants. But he knows something. I'm sure of it.

"I must be mistaken," I say, making light of it.

"Indeed," he says. Do I detect a note of relief in his eyes despite the abrupt tenor of his voice?

"Wrong end of the stick," I add, gilding the lie.

"Easily done."

Strained, I look around the bar. A number of old photographs of yachts and sailors adorn the walls. I remember once having a conversation with a doctor who practised in the southwest. He claimed to be expert in removing fishing hooks from fingers. "I'm guessing a lot of your work centred on sailing injuries."

On safer ground, he lets out a fruity laugh. "You're right there. Boats are pretty dangerous environments. Far too many happy amateurs who don't have a clue what they're doing. I've delivered babies on board, treated crush and head injuries, serious lacerations, resulting in amputation in two cases," he says, eyes alight with recollection, "eye injuries – oh my God, lost count of those – and, of course, the more obvious burns, hypothermia and drowning, the latter exceeding my area of expertise, naturally," he says, reaching for his pint, which he drains.

"The man I'm looking for lost both his parents at sea."

The flesh around his veiny nose tightens and his eyes sharpen. "You ask a lot of questions, young lady. If I was a betting man, and I'm not, I'm guessing your interest concerns an affair of the heart. Am I right?"

There are times when lies work better than honesty. This wasn't one of those occasions because in one way the old man spoke the truth. I had to see Tom again. I needed to.

I offer a shy smile. He studies me carefully for a moment, takes a tentative sip of whisky, unable to make up his mind. I wonder if I can draw him out.

"He's in trouble." Urgency makes me slightly breathless. Like a hammer blow I also realise that Tom is in deep. Not for one second do I believe that Tom *intended* to kill. No way. Not ever.

Under the pretext of giving it serious consideration, he glances at the exit. I'm losing him. He drinks the rest of his whisky in one swallow. "I know of nobody here."

"But the couple," I say, tugging on an earring, my face assuming a picture of quiet desperation.

He rises slowly to his feet, limbs and joints cracking. "I recall a husband and wife, experienced sailors, who drowned, maybe..." he pauses, screws his eyes up tight in recollection, "gotta be twenty years ago, or thereabouts," he says, his voice a rich drunken burr. "I don't know the details, but they were from Llandudno. Now," he says, "I need to get home. My bed awaits."

"Thank you," I say. It's not much, but it's a start.

# Chapter 33

Sullen, threatening and moody, the sky pumped rain. Soaked through, jeans stuck to his thighs, hair plastered to his head, he cut a miserable figure. Made no difference. Nobody wanted to give him a lift. A boy-racer in a Mondeo sped past, engine thrashing, shooting a wave of filthy water up into the air. Too late, he stepped back, cursing. Nothing for it but to keep trudging, focus his energy on tracking down Linus, a man who would never leave home, never abandon his mother or his twisted desire to fuck up the life of the man known as Tom. Linus vowed it from the first time he started on him all those years ago to the last time Tom clapped eyes on him, before he left on his bike that grim, if memorable, day.

For almost thirteen years he had felt the after-shocks of Linus's malign influence. He had wanted to believe that time, which encompassed two generations, would loosen his hold. But he'd been wrong. What had happened to Linus, he wondered, to bring him slithering out of the shadows? Had Ursula died, or, more likely, was the scent of revenge hard in Linus's thin aristocratic nostrils? Cunning and shrewd, how Linus had traced him no longer remained a mystery. He pictured his old enemy catching a lead, making contact with Swain and visiting him in prison. Armed with fresh knowledge, Linus had worked it all out. For all Tom knew, Swain and Linus were working together.

Hugging the side of the road, something in the faded light reminded him of the grey dawn when he'd found Joshua. At first, he'd thought Joshua was sleeping. He looked so peaceful. Only when he crept closer, saw that Josh's eyes were not quite shut; the life behind the blue-tinged eyelids expired, did he understand that there was something badly wrong. Stretching out his fingers, touching Joshua's cold waxy cheek confirmed the worst, that his friend was dead.

And Joshua really was his friend.

Engulfed with remorse for hurting him, he tried to fathom which of his actions led to Joshua's ultimate demise. Was it the threat of physical force, or his taunting that drove Joshua, who was never very strong, into the night to exposure and death?

Afterwards was a blur. He didn't remember whether he'd run straight back home, or whether he'd hung back, fearing retribution. All he recalled were the swell of tears streaming down his face as fiercely as the raindrops dripping down him now.

Nothing had changed, he thought, miserably thumbing a lift.

# Chapter 34

I return to my room and trawl online for a husband-and-wife sailing team hailing from Llandudno who drowned off the Welsh coast a couple of decades previously. Zilch. There's a handy thing on Wikipedia that charts the demise by drowning of various celebrities that include death from drugs and alcohol in the bathtub, but nothing that chimes with Tom's past life. Frustrated, I turn in for the night and fall prey to patchy and restless sleep. By seven, I shower and chew over my next move during breakfast. I still consider myself a hack and who better to talk to than another journalist from the area?

I think it will take me five minutes to drive from Conwy to Llandudno Junction and the office of *The Daily Post*. I think wrong. The road ahead is closed. Two police officers redirect traffic.

Sliding down my window to ask what the problem is, my eyes water and I pick up the acrid tang of smoke and fire. This is swiftly followed by the smell of scorched building, smouldering remains of plastic and chemical.

"Fire at a laundry last night," a stocky six-footer explains.

"Had to evacuate the area. Nobody allowed through at present."

"Anyone hurt?"

"You press?" He asks it in the same tone he might adopt if enquiring whether I'm a member of a terrorist organisation.

"A concerned citizen."

"One chap treated for smoke inhalation. Now would you mind turning around and driving away, Miss?"

I head into town and park. A phone call to the newspaper office from my car generates a permanently engaged tone. Probably a small team and, no doubt, every journalist focused on the fire, a great news story, as far as the local media is concerned. If only they knew the kind of story I'm following. Truth is, nobody will have time to speak to me any time soon, supposing they even remember an incident that took place over twenty years ago. With a name, I could, no doubt, pull records and dig out the story via microfiche; something that Elliott told me was dying out because it was too expensive. Digital imaging is the way in which most records are now kept, but it's not raw data I'm after. I want story and insight and an answer for why Tom did what he allegedly did and why he duped and ditched me.

Dispirited, I cut down a narrow street and into the town centre. With its high-street shops, restaurants, cafes, bars, and its Regency-style architecture, Llandudno is to Wales what Cheltenham is to Gloucestershire, except the former has the benefit of the sea and a fabulous pier.

I wander along the wide seafront, the wind in my hair, flick of rain on my face and think about the old doctor's words, the shifty expression in his eyes, the fact that he started off proclaiming he knew everything and ended up knowing nothing. What was that all about?

Under grey, forbidding skies, the water looks satanic, but in summer, I imagine sparkling light cresting the tips of the waves, like millions of fallen stars.

Out of season, most hotels and guesthouses sport signs declaring 'No Vacancies'. Some are shut, others undergoing refurbishment. Only the hardiest remain open, playing host, no doubt, to businessmen from Liverpool and pensioners taking advantage of cheap deals.

I meander down side streets and pop into a ropey-looking establishment that looks as if it's been in town since its inception. The aroma of coffee stewing too long greets me. Inside the foyer, a young slow-eyed receptionist taps away on a computer keyboard. Glad of the interruption, she looks up with a broad smile.

"Can I help you?"

Her accent is heavy Eastern European. My immediate response is *No, you can't because you're new to the area* but I press on.

"I hope so," I say brightly. "It's an odd question but I was wondering whether there's anyone working at the hotel who's lived around here for the past twenty years."

"Twenty?" Her mouth tugs into a frown.

"Yes."

"Sorry," she says, drawing out the word. "I think not."

"It was a long shot," I say apologetically. "Thanks, anyway."

"You're welcome."

I make to leave.

"But wait," she says, eager to please. "Mr Evans, the proprietor, he is what you call local."

"Would he spare me a moment, do you think?"

"I do not know. He is very busy man." She flutters her fingers, as if Mr Evans is a butterfly flitting from one flower to the next. "Ah," she says knowingly, glancing over my shoulder.

I turn around and step aside as a short, overweight man with a yellow sweaty complexion hurries past. His expression below a large pair of spectacles is two parts harassed and one part startled. Not much of a butterfly, more of a busy bee.

"I wonder, Mr Evans, if..."

"You want coffee," he says in agitation. "Take a seat down the corridor and I'll be with you in a minute." And then he disappears.

I look back at the receptionist who shrugs. "He is busy man," she repeats.

"Tell you what, I'll pop back later." She meets my gaze. We both know I'll never return.

I double back to the promenade and walk towards the pier. Beyond is a monster-sized hotel that overlooks the bay. Well past its Victorian heyday, a little tatty and in need of a coat of paint, it's a fine example of shabby chic. Near the double-door entrance, a man in a top hat, wearing a three-quarter-length red jacket over black tailored trousers and highly polished shoes. Standing outside, like an old retainer, he is one of those rare creatures: a doorman – and not to be confused with a bouncer. Judging by his lived-in appearance, I estimate he is about seventy. He has kind grey eyes unaffected by drink and, as I draw close, he beams a warm smile and greets me with a deferential "Good Morning," followed by, "Not so nice today. Rain's made a proper job of it."

I can spot a Devonian accent within seconds and this man is the real deal. Briefly comforted by someone who reminds me of my roots, I engage him in conversation.

"You're not from this part of the world."

"Neither are you," he laughs.

"Totnes," I say.

"My word. Been a long time since I heard that name."

"And you?"

"Thurlestone," he replies. "Although I haven't lived there for nigh-on fifty years."

"Really?" My pulse skips a beat and my heart gives a little bounce. "How come?"

"The love of a good Welsh woman." His eyes mist over and I intuit that his wife is no more. Poor old boy. "The name's Roy, by the way," he says, offering me his hand, which I take and shake. "Roy Marchand."

"Roz Outlaw," I say.

He laughs and his eyes crinkle with pleasure. "Proper name to conjure with."

"My mum reckons we're descended from Robin Hood, but I think it's one of her more fanciful ideas," I confide with a grin. He laughs again, sharing the joke. "So you've lived here all your adult life?" I say.

"That's right."

"In that case, Roy, you might be precisely the man I'm looking for."

# Chapter 35

Almost sixteen miles on foot in horrendous weather, exhausted and crazed with hunger, he dared not stop. The closer he got to his destination, the more likely Mads would catch up with him. She'd no idea of the significance surrounding his solitary trip to a young boy's grave months before, but she wasn't stupid. If she had to look for him anywhere, she'd return to the place where it all started. In his head, he was on a timeline, his only focus to get to Linus before Mads got to *him*.

In the middle of a rural wilderness and with nobody willing to give him a lift, his best chance was to find shelter, rest up for the day and travel again by night.

On the lookout for a disused building, a barn, old garage or shed, he padded along the open road. The rain ensured that most people stayed in the warm and dry, but to a dog-walker, farmer, or someone who had to be out in the elements, he'd immediately be logged as a stranger. One call to Neighbourhood Watch and the next to the cops, he'd be sunk. He needed to get off the land. Swiftly.

Rounding a bend, he spotted a chapel two or three fields

away, tucked into a hollow on the hillside, offering genuine sanctuary – a miracle. Except the last time he'd experienced one of those it had inexorably led to dire consequences.

He remembered sounding the alarm. Nothing came out the way it was supposed to. It was as if he were speaking to other life forms from a faraway planet. He made little sense even to his own ears. Someone shook him. Strained faces. Wide then narrowed eyes. Screams, shouts and accusations next, including a threat to kill from his aunt.

*"For God's sake, you knew Joshy wasn't robust," Uncle Geoff blasted in his face. "You should have looked after him, not turned against him."*

*"It's his fault," Linus whined, cut and bruised, his spitfire eyes drilling right through him, tears squeezing out onto the planes of his cheeks, "his fault he's dead."*

His fault. That's what everyone said. And it was true. He'd been rough and mean and Joshua had died because of it.

A lot of cars came to the house, including an ambulance and police car with two officers. Aunt Ursula was given a sedative to make her sleep. A creepy silence, like a coffin lid, fastened over the house. Strangely, he could not remember much about Caro. But he remembered Uncle Geoff all right. Molten with distress and rage. Uncharacteristically so.

Time knee-jerked backwards and then forwards, missing a beat, losing its step, dragging him with it. Set aside, separated, banished, however it was described, he'd never felt so alone in his entire life.

*Finally, he found himself sitting in a room with Uncle Geoff and a severe-faced police officer. His uncle rested both his hands*

*firmly on his shoulders, looked solemnly and sternly into his
eyes and said in a voice he barely recognised, "What counts now
is that you tell the truth, lad, and only the truth. Leave nothing
out, do you understand?"*

He tried, but with every tongue-tied word, he felt condemned
already. He looked from the officer to Uncle Geoff, who sat with
him. The officer, brisk and threatening, said, "So you don't deny
hitting Linus?"

"Yes, I did but—"

"And you hurt little Joshua too?"

"Accidentally, and it wasn't only me. Linus started it. He
always did."

"Let's leave Linus out of it. I'll be speaking to him in due
course once he's feeling better. Let's stick with your part in what
happened. Did you push Joshua outside?"

"I never. I fell asleep. We all did."

"Was this after you weed on Linus's sleeping bag, or before?"

"That's not true. Linus did it to me."

"If that's the case, lad, why would he sleep in it?"

"Because I made him. As a punishment." As soon as the words
slipped past his lips he knew he was sunk.

"Like you made Joshua leave the bivouac, I daresay."

"Uncle Geoff," he burst in desperation. "I would never ever
hurt Joshua, you know that."

But he had. How else to explain it? It was true what they
said that he was guilty, that it was his fault, wasn't it? Had to
be. And he really was mean to Joshua. He really had disappointed
everyone.

The interview lasted for what seemed like hours. There was

talk of pressing charges, which he didn't really understand, places he might be sent where he could pay for his crime. The way the policeman had talked confirmed his guilt and, worse, that he was, in fact, a murderer.

People came and went. The boy, now known as Tom, was segregated. The police came back and spoke to him again, this time on his own. They talked to Linus too, he found out later, as they said they would. Timelines remained jumbled. At some stage he was told that he would not be sent to an institution, despite his aunt's insistence that he should.

Joshua's funeral took place, which he was not allowed to attend. From an upstairs window, he saw the front garden fill with flowers, a small white coffin carried in a procession of weeping grown-ups from the front door to a waiting car. It puzzled him at the time because it suggested that Joshua had been kept in the house instead of in the place where all souls wait for burial. Again, he found out later that Joshua had lain in state in the dining room, the thought freaking him out, not that he was ever allowed to eat in there again.

Every time he glanced at his uncle for reassurance, like he'd done when his uncle broke the dreadful news of his parents' drowning, Uncle Geoff dropped his gaze. If Uncle Geoff didn't believe him, he was lost forever. It killed him.

A car horn startled him back to the present. Ruefully crossing from one field to another, he realised that he'd been dead inside ever since.

# Chapter 36

I kill time and wait for Roy to finish his shift.

"Short hours this time of year," he sniffs, giving the impression that days outside work are long and lonely. From my point of view, this is good. Lonely people, particularly Devonians, like to talk to anyone prepared to lend a listening ear.

We are sitting over hot chocolates, my treat, in a popular café. This time I don't start my spiel in the usual way, but ask Roy about the couple who drowned. He doesn't ask why I want to know. His brow doesn't crease in recollection. He doesn't do that thing when people, who have absolutely no clue, cobble together random answers, take pot shots and burble educated, and mostly incorrect, guesses in a blind bid to be helpful. He comes straight out with it. "The Truebloods."

Dumbfounded to hear Tom's real surname, almost as whacky as mine, I can barely speak.

"Experienced sailors," Roy chats on, hitting his stride. "Used to run a small hotel not far from here. Lay empty for a while after the accident, then it was bought up and turned back into residential. Long time ago now," he adds dolefully.

Straight away, I wonder what happened to the proceeds of the sale. Did Tom inherit? Was he lying to me all this time about the state of his finances? Then I remember that Tom was only a teenager when he testified. Money from an inheritance would be more likely put in trust until he was twenty-one. In any event, a lawyer would make an attempt to track him down and come up empty. It didn't explain what happened to the loot.

"You said they were experienced," I say. "How did it happen?"

"Travelling back from northern Spain through the Bay of Biscay. Midsummer, it was. Weather good, not particularly strong wind."

"So?" I'm barely able to contain myself.

"The keel of their forty-footer dropped off."

"God, does that happen often?"

"Not if the boat is properly maintained, although a keel bolt failure isn't uncommon."

"And it would sink quickly?"

"Wind in the sails acts as a counter-balance to the solid-iron hull underneath, see? If the keel goes, a boat will go down in less than a minute."

"They never stood a chance," I murmur.

"Instant disaster," Roy concurs, stirring his drink contemplatively. "Similar happened with Cheeky Rafiki some years back. Thankfully, the Truebloods' little boy, Kit, was staying with friends of the parents at the time, otherwise he'd be a goner too."

*Kit. Kit Trueblood.* I try out the name for size, not sure it fits. But then, how would I know? Tom Loxley is nothing more than a ghost from my past. Pain creases the inside of my chest. Again, I remember Stephanie Charteris and how she spoke of the physical trauma of grief. For me, it's more about loss.

"What became of him?"

Roy glances away. Is this the moment Tom is deemed a murderer? If I go straight in with a direct question, will I spook my newfound friend?

"Bad business," he says at last.

I think I know this, but maybe I don't. Surely, by now, Roy must recognise that my nosiness and animation are not a direct result of his magical storytelling ability? I try to tone down my blatant interest.

"How so?"

"He disappeared."

"Disappeared?" I reiterate, hoping to draw out more information.

"When he was still a kid."

It takes all of me to stop my jaw from hitting the table. This doesn't compute with Tom the teenage witness. Maybe, Roy is mixed up. Maybe when you're seventy, eighteen seems more juvenile. Yes, that's it.

"Must have been a couple of years after his folks drowned," Roy explains.

I experience a sharp blast of fear. Too dumbfounded, I don't speak. I cannot.

"Like I said," he continues, warming to his theme, "Kit was staying with his dad's best pal, Geoffrey Verdi, and his wife.

They took him in after his parents died. Bodies never found, incidentally," he says, frowning, as if his omission displays a grave act of disrespect. "Brought him up as one of theirs." Not by an elderly aunt, then.

"Where?"

"Near Deganwy. Big house."

"Tom, I mean Kit," I hastily correct myself, "had no other family?"

"An only child, by all accounts. The Verdis had three children, so Kit acquired ready-made brothers and sisters."

I sip carefully through a layer of foamy milk to give me time to digest Roy's information. Perhaps the disappearance relates to time Tom spent in an institution. It fits with the picture Jane described. Seems she was speaking the truth. With a jolt, I recognise that I misjudged her and, worse, Tom is culpable. "You mentioned bad business earlier. Did you mean Kit's disappearance?"

Roy gives a shifty look and drops his voice. "Nobody knew what became of him. Some said he was sent away. Others, well..." he stops, stirs his drink, places the spoon on the saucer. I wait, praying he'll find the courage to resume. "Plagued with death, that family," he says finally. "One of the Verdi kids died. Only nine years old. A sickly lad."

I virtually squeak.

"Delicate," he explains. His lips wrap around the word with precision.

A sour taste floods my mouth, wiping out the sticky sweetness of chocolate. At eleven years of age, Tom would be stronger and more muscular. Was he the archetypal bully who betrayed the very family who opened their doors to him?

"Was the child ill? Is that what killed him?"

"Oh, there were a lot of rumours and suchlike, all sorts of gossip and stories, some of them not very nice."

I wait for Roy to elaborate, but he doesn't. He might like to talk, but he's no tittle-tattler. "And this happened *after* Kit disappeared?" It's vital I get the timeline right.

"No, no, the Verdi lad died and Kit vanished later."

I urge him to tell me more about the little boy's death. He blows hard across the foamy surface of his drink. His cheeks suck and pop. "The kids went camping. Daft time of the year, if you ask me. There were tales of abduction, all sorts."

"Abduction?"

"The boy was found outside the tent, apparently."

"You mean he was lured?"

He shakes his head, doesn't know, retreats to safe facts. "The boy is buried at Conwy parish churchyard. Like his dad."

"His dad?" And then I remember that Roy mentioned a plague of extinction. I ask him what he meant.

"Geoffrey Verdi committed suicide not long after the boy died – can't for the life of me think of his name. The dad couldn't deal with the sorrow, see?"

I nod humbly. "And Kit vanished after that?"

"Indeed." He gazes out through the window at sludgy-coloured waves beating against the beach. Not once has he asked me why I'm interested. Perhaps he senses.

A trace of a smile lights up his face and briefly lifts the

sombre atmosphere. "With all that death knocking about, no wonder one of the Verdi kids took to writing obituaries for a living. Fancies himself as an author." His tone suggests that the profession is a less than honest form of work. "Runs in the family or some such."

"And the mother, Mrs Verdi?"

Roy turns his gunmetal eyes to mine and stares at me straight. "With that woman taking up the reins, it came as no surprise when young Kit disappeared."

# Chapter 37

They wanted to make him sorry. For Joshua, for Uncle
Geoff, for breathing. A day after Kit's last supper with
him, his uncle drove his favourite car, a Lancia, into a clearing
close to where Joshua died, fed a hose from the exhaust into
the interior and gassed himself.

And Kit got the blame for driving a distressed man to the
brink.

Distraught, utterly alone, he barely noticed a repeat of
doctors, police and funeral directors. The only discernible
difference this time, his aunt did not scream distress. Chillingly
calm, with eyes that were cold and empty, she made a point
of listing his failings on a daily basis, lest he should forget.
Every time she glided into a room, she brought winter with
her.

With these thoughts tumbling through his mind, he
blagged a lift from a driver called Jed, a Christian outreach
worker with the symbol of a fish in his rear window. Probably
the same age as Kit, he had a shiny face that complemented
his shiny personality. Everything about him, from his trendy
rectangular black-framed spectacles to his casual jeans and

t-shirt shrieked *I'm a regular guy and just like you* when nothing could be further from the truth. Within moments, Jed was asking too many questions. Kit's monosyllabic replies did little to deter Jed's earnestness and belief that he had a live potential convert cooped up in his car, gagging for redemption. While Kit and his clothes steamed in the stiflingly warm interior, the young man preached, droning on about the love of God, the need for forgiveness of ourselves and others, and the inherent goodness in us all.

"What about the evil in us all?" Kit said.

"Brilliant point," Jed replied, because, with Jed, everything was fucking 'brilliant,' Kit thought sourly. Next, his lift launched into a discourse on the devil and the darkness within. Kit wondered how Jed would react if he knew how much the many demons messed with his passenger's head, how often they held all-night raves inside his brain.

Tuning out from his driving companion, he didn't remember the exact day it all went so horribly wrong. To cope, he went into shut down, retreated inside himself, for days, weeks, months and finally years. He was their dark secret.

And they were his.

And now he believed there was another.

Dropping him off, the man wished him blessings and shoved a pamphlet into Kit's hands. He ditched it at the first opportunity.

Crossing over by a roundabout, he headed down a road that led to the quay and marina, the oily, pervasive scent of seaweed and noise of clanking halyards assuring him that he was on familiar territory. Beyond, lay sandbanks divided from the sea by boulders, a cycle path and view of Llandudno.

Grey wind and rain hurtling through him, the astringent smell of sea water and ozone drifted in the sodden air, briefly comforting and reminiscent of times he'd spent with his mum and dad on the water. His best memory of a summer day, the sky a brilliant blue; sun high, splashes of light silvering the sea, the castle a feathery ghost in the distance.

Kit wasn't looking for a bed for the night. He had that worked out. With more gales forecast to blow in from the west, the likelihood of any boat owner taking their vessel out for a spin was minimal. This time of year, most people stayed holed up at home. Knowing the area well, it would take him no time to break into one of the boats moored on the quay, as he had done once before so many years ago. Then he'd dry out, make a brew, if he were very lucky, and get his head down. Next, he'd unearth the secret that meant he was worth more to the Verdi family dead than alive. After that, he would take revenge for the destruction of his life and all that had been done to him.

This time, nobody was going to stop him.

# Chapter 38

Close to the medieval church of Saint Mary and All Saints, Conwy parish churchyard lies right in the middle of town and reminds me of Saints Mary and Matthew's in Cheltenham. The latter sits tucked in off the high street, a little oasis of calm amid frenzied shoppers hell-bent on retail therapy.

At All Saints, I hope to find solitude and clear lines of thought – graveyards hold no fear for me – yet my quest for truth eludes and I find no solace in the 'Dearly Departed' and 'Fondly Remembered.'

Clouds scull across a darkening sky and Roy's revelations rattle around inside my head like dice in a game of a chance. I wonder about the people behind the names, the couple who drowned, leaving their only son, my former lover, and the Verdi family, whose son now writes obituaries for a living. I cannot get out of my head the number of deaths dogging Tom/Kit's relatively short life. Surely, this can be no accident, no coincidence? I cannot forget Roy's chilling last words to me: *With that woman taking up the reins, it came as no surprise when Kit disappeared.*

Disappeared where, how, when and why?

I find myself drawn to an unusual grave with a cover of wrought iron, on which seven crosses stand in line. Underneath there is a simple sign that states 'We are Seven.' Seven what? Sins, people, family?

Breaking away, in search of Verdi gravestones, I'm struck with the thought that, unlike the many mothers recorded here, I will never be one of them. It hits me hard, and a grey moan of frustration and dismay tunnels from the back of my throat, through my mouth, swallowed in one gulp by the wet air.

I shake myself, for this is not about me. This is about a lost boy and a dead child. Their journey. Their story. Ironically, it's the biggest news item that I will ever handle and one that I will never write.

Ancient graves cluster in one part of the cemetery, while new graves, some studded with fresh flowers, another. Stumbling blindly from one memorial to the next, an arrangement of out-of-season creamy yellow roses catches my eye. Glossy and healthy, they look so fresh I'm inclined to think that they were flown in especially. Drawing near, my eyes widen and I almost sink to my knees. For here, right in front of me, is the grave of Joshua Marco Verdi, beloved son of Ursula and Geoffrey, and brother to Caro and Linus. The inscription reads: 'Those who we have held in our arms, we hold in our hearts for eternity.' I stare at the sad little gravestone for several moments before glancing to the grave next door. Surely, Joshua's father must be close by.

Yet he isn't.

Puzzled, I take up the search once more and, eventually,

wander to an area of the churchyard where the silence is more ragged and the ground less nurtured. It's here that I discover Geoffrey Verdi's last resting place. Aside from his date of birth and death, there is no inscription. I press a hand to my mouth because it seems to me cold and unforgiving. The man was a husband and father, a guardian to his friends' son, a good man, surely, and yet he appears to count for nothing. On Joshua's grave, there are flowers, a potent symbol of memory and token of love. Here there is grass, weeds, brambles and dirt.

Instinctively, I pat Geoffrey Verdi's gravestone, my personal gesture of affection for a man I never knew because his loved ones disavowed him. At least, that's how it seems to me. And with a small backward glance, I make my way to my car, more bewildered than when I came.

Back at the hotel, I freshen up and head to the bar. It's quiet and I'm served a drink in record time. I take a seat near the window in clear line of sight of my drinking companion the previous evening, the doctor. He glances up with a hangdog expression and raises his glass. I nod back. To be honest, I'm surprised to see him. I had him down for running scared.

"Good day?" he enquires.

"Very." I flash an easy smile.

"Find that fella of yours?"

"Sadly, not."

He lets out a dolorous, commiserating breath and takes another drink. Neat whisky. No chaser.

"Plenty more fish in the sea, but it's always the nice piece of hake you fancy." He says it with fervour. I wonder about the doctor's wife. Perhaps the doc is a widower like Roy. Perhaps he is referring to a lost love. Not given to fishy comparisons, nevertheless, I nod in agreement.

"So will you be going back home tomorrow? Cheltenham, wasn't it?"

I'm impressed he remembers. "Not yet. Unfinished business."

"Sounds serious."

"Depends how you view it. Actually, I'm incredibly grateful to you."

"Me?" His cheeks flush rosy red. Must be a while since someone paid him a compliment.

"Thanks to you and your suggestion, I found out about the parents who drowned."

He smiles without commitment. "That's handy." His fingers grip the glass so tight it's possible it might shatter.

"I also discovered what happened to their son, although not a lot to tell."

"Is that so?"

"Apparently, he vanished."

"Good grief. Probably why I never heard of him." He half-laughs but his throat cramps and it comes out strangled.

"You're right," I say, no big deal in my manner. The doctor looks as though he might pass out with relief. He thinks he's off the hook. He has no idea that I'm only getting started. "Can I get you another drink?" To be perfectly honest, he looks as though he could use one. I am the very essence of amiability.

"Well, that's very kind of you." He pushes his empty glass towards me with an ancient hand that trembles.

I pick it up with a reassuring smile and head to the bar. "Same again. Make it a double," I murmur under my breath. "And I'll have a straight tonic." I put the drinks on my tab and, grabbing both glasses, join the doctor at his table. After all, it would be rude of him to allow me to sit alone. Any consternation he feels, he hides. Booze, apparently, is more important to him than batting me off.

"Lechyd da," he says. Cheers.

We clink glasses. I smile sweetly. "My name's Roz, by the way."

"Phillip," he says.

"So what do you do to amuse yourself around here?"

The lines around his eyes and mouth relax. "This and that. I like my garden although the weather isn't that special right now."

I nod, playing the game, wonder when to pounce.

"And, of course, there's my daily amble along the beach, not that my knees are much good these days. Important to keep active, mind."

"Of course."

He leans in. "As a young man I swam a lot in the sea. Had quite a body," he says with the narcissism that sometimes accompanies fond recollection. "Bit too cold for me now."

I laugh. "Ever sail?"

He catches my hard look and chooses to ignore it. "Never had the time."

We fall into what he believes is companionable silence.

"I also found out about the boy, you know, the one who died? Apparently, there were a lot of rumours about what actually happened."

His face drains of colour. "Really? I don't recall." He blinks rapidly and his voice is glazed with disquiet.

"I'm surprised. Seeing that this was your patch. Forty years, wasn't it?" My sly intonation is entirely deliberate.

"My memory isn't so good these days," he adds with a dry laugh that sounds like wood splintering.

"You *must* remember the Verdi family," I say, pushing a smile to disguise the hidden barb buried in my words.

His lips thin and tighten in response. Opening his mouth in denial, self-preservation kicks in at the last second, preventing him from seeming clueless as well as deceitful. "Everyone knows the Verdis." He takes a swig of booze to emphasise the point. Sweat pops up on his brow.

"Where do they hang out?"

He frowns as if I am speaking Martian.

"Where do they live?" I say to clarify.

With nowhere to hide, he stutters, "Vixenhead."

"Is that a place?"

He knocks back his drink. "Name of the house."

"Which is where?" It's a simple enough question.

"Henryd." He spits it out as if it's taboo.

"Far away?"

"No."

"Did you know the family well?"

Making no secret of his displeasure, he stands up and reaches for his walking stick. For a tense moment I think he might crack me over the head with the ivory handle. "No good will come of you raking up the past," he hisses in my ear, his breath stewed with booze and bellicosity. "I'd be very careful if I were you, young lady."

Breath catches in my lungs. Hair on the back of my neck prickles, and fear leaks out of my pores.

Limping slowly away, the click of his stick against the floor resembles the noise of a gun that's jammed.

# Chapter 39

Spying lights from a smart hotel, executive-style, with, no doubt, a conference centre and leisure facilities, he waited for nightfall before he made his move. Earlier, he'd selected a temporary home, a solid, if not show-stopping twenty-six- foot Westerly Centaur, going by the apt name of 'Castaway'.

If a trick works, it's wise to repeat it. All yachts carried bolt-cutters, to be used in an emergency. These were often found in cockpit lockers. Out of all the boats moored, there was bound to be one whose owner was less than security-conscious. Sure enough, he quickly located a willing victim. Helping himself and suitably armed, he set to snapping the chain and padlock securing the wooden washboard and entry to the Centaur. Busting in was easy.

What the boat didn't have in the oceanic equivalent of kerb appeal, it more than made up for in space below. Roomy, with good headroom, Kit was able to stand with only a slight dip in his neck to accommodate his height. After stripping off his sodden clothes, a basic recce in a storage locker under a bunk revealed an Aladdin's treasure trove of dry food. Aside from basics, like tea, coffee, sugar and powdered milk, a biscuit tin yielded a half-eaten pack of chocolate biscuits that he instantly demolished. The galley was small with only a single sink. A further hunt through one of the other bunks revealed dried pasta and rice, two tins of fish and one of corned beef, cans of tomatoes and sweetcorn. It didn't take him long to find a can-opener and rustle up a makeshift dinner, the first real food he'd consumed in days. Sheltered from the elements, warmth provided care of a single-burner stove in the starboard, he felt overwhelming exhaustion.

Unearthing a sleeping bag from a locker, he dragged it through to a berth in the forward cabin, shut the door between the fore and main cabin, and clambered inside. Before he turned in, he took out the fluffy seal he'd given to his young stepdaughter and, clutching it to his chest, slept the sleep of the nearly dead.

Ten hours later, he woke, disorientated, his waking dream one of home, the small hotel in which he and his parents had once lived. A smile spread across his face at the memory of happier times. Built in the 1920's, partially rendered, with Virginia creeper sending a blaze of colour across its exterior, and with a magnolia growing in the garden, the old place was his destination when his path crossed with Swain's. He never did find out whether new owners had extended, repainted or knocked it down; such was his isolation from the outside world.

While Caro and Linus went back to school, he was kept at home. A private tutor, a dour woman from Tredegar with a heavy South Wales accent, was appointed to teach him. The atmosphere in the house crushed. The air exhaled pain and sadness. Time limped slowly, without definition or meaning. Everything stuttered in his head. No matter how much he tried to recollect with clarity and accuracy, he couldn't grasp hold of any thought and retain it. Nobody came near. He was abandoned, forsaken and isolated. There was a great deal of anger, both open and unseen, some of it his.

Stumbling out of bed, he pulled the boat apart and dug inside compartments, where he discovered wet-weather gear and safety harnesses, a canvas bag containing two sets of wrenches, pliers, screwdrivers and a ball-peen hammer with a long handle, a pair of binoculars in a smart black case, sailing gloves and a single pair of man's leather gloves and, best of all, an old Norwegian-style sweater that was too big, but dry. Pulling it on, he set about breakfast – tuna straight from the can.

A quick squint outside a porthole confirmed that the weather had not changed. If anything, it had got worse. Every single halyard clanked in the force eight, a brutal cacophony of percussion and noise, chiming with his discordant mood. He'd only one desire after he left Ludlow. Physically, he was still focused, yet he could not gauge how he would react at going back to the place and people who had caused him such misery. Would his mental muscles hold? Would the truth derail him?

Disconsolate, random memories of his past returned to maul.

*"You'll be their fag. Know what that means? They'll jump you, hold you down, part your bum cheeks and stick their dicks up your arse." He couldn't imagine anything more awful, but*

*this is what they promised if he didn't comply. They had the ultimate drop on him, the threat to put him away where he belonged, to a reform school, an institution, where he would be brutally taught right from wrong.*

And then there were Ursula's grim friends with their braying drunken laughter, their superficiality and the way they sucked up to her, the lady of the manor, after Uncle Geoff's death. Everyone was taken in by her lies, including intelligent people like the doctor. Quick, he was called, although Ursula always called him Phillip. Kit didn't understand at the time but, through adult eyes, he suspected that there was a deeper relationship between them than doctor and patient, despite the fact that Quick was married. At the memory of Vixenhead, seat of power, that horrible house of shadows that beat to its own sick rhythm, he shook. It was as if the very bricks were imbued with evil and black smoke from the chimneystacks chugged out fear.

Before venturing there on the two-mile walk through the woods, he'd need to sort his head out. If only he had something to take off the edge. A couple of Paracetamol unearthed from a drawer were hardly going to touch him or the blinder of a headache brewing behind his eyes. Nevertheless, he chewed them both and swallowed.

Stepping outside, he loped along the gangway and out onto a road and into a small residential area. Narrowing his eyes against driving rain, he crossed over and past a row of down-at-heel shops selling tat and seaside paraphernalia that looked out of place now the season was well and truly over and the new one not yet begun.

*Vixenhead*

A self-styled antique emporium that his mum visited when he was a boy, had a closing-down sign even though it seemed to have given up the ghost a long time ago. Plastic chairs piled up outside a tatty-looking restaurant with a chalkboard outside proclaiming that the dish of the day was roast pork with trimmings. The only place that looked relatively okay sold designer clothes circa turn of the century. He felt as if he'd stepped back into a time warp, as if everything had deep-frozen the exact moment he broke free.

Arriving at a seedy underpass near a set of steps, a train travelled overhead. A big part of him wished he was on it.

Ahead, three bridges into the town towards the once-mighty fortress and medieval garrison. The newest consisted of two iron tubes, each weighing over a thousand tons and supported by towers, providing a vital rail link.

Crossing over and looping round, he headed for Llanrwyst Road, from where a public footpath cut through a nature reserve situated above a limestone cliff overlooking Llandudno Junction. Next: to Henryd and Vixenhead, with its fourteen acres of pasture and woodland.

Stepping up onto a steep track, trainers sliding in a winter's worth of mud and foliage, he thought that, despite the passage of time, the fact that he had rehabilitated himself as best he could, that he knew he could love and be loved, deep in the heart of his being he believed that he was tainted. Spoilt. Unworthy. Rotten.

Perhaps this would inspire him to do what needed to be done.

# Chapter 40

I clean my teeth in front of the bathroom mirror and wonder whether no news from Jane should be read as a good thing, or not. Pushy as hell, maybe she lost patience with me. I do not contemplate the possibility that she caught up with Tom. He's free. Still. I know it.

Bottom set done, I go for the top, brushing and scrubbing, as if dedicated dental care will somehow restore order to my life. Following my drinking companion's open hostility the night before I'm as certain as I can be that a conspiracy is in play and possibly for many years. With so many half-truths, lies and rumours, how can it be otherwise?

And there is something else.

What if Tom isn't running from Swain? What if he is running from something else, something bigger? Instinctively, I know it's connected to the dead child.

My skin suddenly feels shrunken, too tightly wrapped around my flesh and bones. Pressing me in. Squeezing my lungs. Crushing my skull.

I grip hold of the sink. Steady myself.

Roy never mentioned the word *murder,* let alone that

another boy committed the act. Roy said a boy *died.* Until I have verifiable proof and not simply the words of a stranger to my home, I *must* cling to the small hope that Tom is innocent. Somewhere in Vixenhead, I'm certain the truth lies and at least one of the Verdis knows what it is.

I spit out into the basin. If I uncover their secrets, will it set Tom and me free? Slooshing water into my mouth and swilling it around, I don't think so.

Too early to pay a visit, I walk through town in the foothills of the castle ramparts. History oozes from every stone and street from the thirteenth-century merchant's house to the finest example of a Welsh Elizabethan town house, Plas Mawr.

Down by the quayside that overlooks a natural harbour, the sea breathes reassuringly in my ear and I consider how strange it must be to write obituaries for a living. Not an average sort of job, I suspect it's one that finds the obituarist by happenstance than by design. What kind of person would sign up for talking to people about what most would rather sprint from?

Back to running again. Me. Tom. Us.

Walking past what, at six feet across and ten foot to the upper storey, is reputed to be the smallest house in Britain, I fetch up among a tangle of fishing boats, pots and lines. From there, the sombre walls of the castle eye me again; malevolent in the still morning light that promises another day of driving rain. Caving in under the weight of their gaze, I roll up the collar of my jacket and don't stay long.

Crossing a road back to the hotel and car park, I bowl into

the funny little man who runs the cab company. He flashes with recognition and mumbles a greeting mid-stride.

Almost past me, I fire a question. "Hello," I say. "Have you heard of a place called Vixenhead?"

He stops, as if someone put a bullet through his heart. When he turns around I notice the set of his jaw, the vein throbbing under his left eye. More than ever, he regrets his decision to speak to me the day before, it seems.

"You've heard of it?" I say. Sure, he has.

"It's an old school." His delivery is leaden.

"Marvellous. Could you tell me how to get there?"

Beady-eyed through his pebble glasses, he doesn't utter a word. Is this a Welsh thing? Am I not making myself plain? I give it another go.

"I could, but I won't."

"Why ever not?"

"You don't want to go there." He speaks quite softly, but there is no mistaking the warning in the message. The doctor's words: *No good will come of you raking up the past* snake around my feet and threaten to grab my ankles and bring me crashing down.

"But I do," I say.

He shakes his head, blows out through his teeth, making a whistling sound.

"Please."

"Stubborn miss, aren't you?"

I push an apologetic smile of agreement.

"You won't be allowed in. Nobody is."

"Then it won't matter if you tell me how to find it."

"What's it to you?"

"Like I said, I'm trying to find someone."

His eyes roll. I can see what he is thinking: Not That Again. "There will be no answers there."

"Won't you help me?" It's a cheap last shot, but it's all I have.

He shifts his weight, glances at his watch, eager to get moving, or so I believe. "When were you going?"

"Right away."

He sniffs and nods, raises his chin and narrows his eyes. "Take you ten minutes, maybe twelve, depending on traffic," he calculates. "It's set in fourteen acres of woodland, down a long drive. Could take you another five to drive along. Pot-holed, see?" I think about my poor car. I have no idea why the little man is consumed with the ergonomics of my intended trip. "Now," he says, the lenses of his glasses misting with damp or effort, or both. "As soon as you done whatever, you give me a ring."

"Pardon?"

"You got my card?"

"Well, yes, but I really don't...'

He puffs out his cheeks and chest. I catch a glimpse of his braces. "I'm tryin' to look after you. Make sure you're all right, see?"

"Oh," I say in astonishment.

"If you're not back in a couple of hours, I'll send one of my drivers to check up. Now I have to get going, else I'll be late."

Touched by his solicitousness, alarmed by his personal-safety measures, I stare after him with a mixture of emotions. "Your name?" I call.

He doesn't break stride, "Edwyn."

If Edwyn thinks a grown woman needs protection, what hope for a young boy called Kit?

# Chapter 41

He was fourteen when he wouldn't do as he was told. Again.

"*Drink it.*"

*Blinded by tears, snot running, Kit clamped his mouth tight shut. He couldn't move because Linus, standing behind him, had his arms manacled to his side.*

"*I said, drink it, damn you,*" *his aunt cursed, forcing the neck of the bottle between his cracked lips. Glass clashed painfully against his teeth and grated his gums.*

"*I'll make him, Ma, don't you worry.*"

*Kit stared into his aunt's soulless eyes. Either cosmetic procedures or genetics rendered her face emotionless, her expression as smooth as a mannequin's. Dark anger now gave her the cold appearance of a shark.*

*He twisted his head away, tried his best to thrash about, but with his upper body pinned and arms dead, he could do little to resist. So Kit did the only thing he could. Jerking his knee up, he scraped the heel of his shoe down Linus's shin.*

"*Ow,*" *Linus howled, releasing Kit as though he were molten metal.*

*Freed, Kit darted across the floor, his destination the door and liberation. Snatching at the handle, nothing happened. Frustrated, he jerked and pulled but it wouldn't budge. Didn't even rattle. Fear snatched at him. Panic grabbed hold and would not let go. Still he heaved. If will could bust down the door, it surely would spring open.*

*But his will wasn't strong enough against three inches deep of solid metal.*

*Doomed, Kit almost collapsed in despair. Behind him, Aunt Ursula let out a long drawn-out, tiresome sigh. "It's locked, you stupid little boy."*

*Neither stupid nor little, he rallied. Escape blocked, he turned and faced his tormentors, both of whom advanced slowly, like jackals around wounded prey. No way would he drink from the bottle. They'd done it to him once before and he'd been sick and ill for days, with no energy to crawl out of bed. The memory made his eyes sting and his gullet shrink.*

*"There's more than one way to skin this little runt," Linus goaded.*

*Nausea shooting through him in waves, Kit stood tall, raised his fists. If he could land a blow, it would hold Linus off, buy him time. Maybe then he could take on and disable his aunt. Kit had no reservations about decking the woman if it ensured his survival. The key was in her pocket. If he could get his hands on it, he would open the door, take to his heels and run and run and never look back. These thoughts shot through his head in seconds. His hesitation cost him. Pain blasted through the right side of his head, fleeing down his spine, cutting his legs from underneath him. Collapsing to the ground, he saw a supple smile glance across his aunt's thin lips for she, and not Linus, had delivered the fatal blow. The rest was a blur as Linus knelt on his chest, jacked open his mouth and half a pint of dilute cleaning fluid was tipped down his throat.*

That was the worst they did to him. Caro only ever watched when Linus stripped him naked, tied him up and whipped him with a dog lead. *"Friends are for other people, not you,"* she announced imperiously.

Kit allowed himself a dry smile. How prophetic Caro's words turned out to be. An attractive-looking girl, she was never short of friends or people who admired her. Perversely, a big part of him hoped that she had got away, sought redemption and found it. He didn't wish her harm in spite of what she'd done. This was something that he didn't understand and certainly did not want to admit. Not then. Not now. How can you feel something akin to gratitude for to someone who is a witness to your suffering, for to someone who exploits and takes advantage of you? What was wrong with him? The smile vanished at the memory of what always happened after Linus had reduced him to nothing. Her cool hands. Intense. Strong. Dirty laughter. Release.

He blanked out the memory for fear of what it would do to his resolve.

Progress was slow due to the level of rain. A landscape he once knew so well as a child now viewed incomprehensibly without comprehension through adult eyes. Over time, shapes and sizes had changed and evolved, paths blurred, new ones carved. With each step, he hoped to exorcise his ghosts and yet there were none to be seen. They all hid supine and still inside his mind.

He took the summit route, not a hard climb in the right boots, but muddy and hopeless in trainers. In the lower section, beech, sycamore and pine towered scarily over earth slashed with snowdrops and early-flowering primrose and crocus, the upper slopes dominated by old-timers: oak, ash and elm. With the weather this bad, the woodland setting offered the greatest protection. Nobody shared his journey other than the odd rabbit.

Emerging onto a designated footpath with a broken fence on one side, he passed a caravan site, dishevelled and sad in the rain, and next an abandoned horticultural centre with broken-down greenhouses. A rough track skirted a farmhouse overshadowed by a tall, ugly mast and dominated by a dung heap at its base. Passing through a gate into a field, he kept right to the edge to avoid loose cattle standing bedraggled and mournful.

Over a stile and through a gateway, he continued until the land dipped and he reached a familiar landmark. Standing at 118 metres, Bryn Locyn Trig Pillar punched a hole in the sky. From there, on a clear day, there would be views of both sides of the Gower. All he saw was murk and uncertain future.

Pressing on, his trainers squelching with moisture and rubbing holes in the soles of his feet, the surroundings became briefly more hospitable. Another farm, with traditional buildings converted into holiday homes and cottages, offered a rare glimpse of orderliness among the rural chaos, or maybe it was essentially his brain flipping out.

*You like it, don't you?*
*You like me touching you.*
*I know you do.*

*Don't look at Linus. Look at me. I said look at me.*
*Now don't snivel. Don't make a fuss.*
*See, there you go, my lovely.*
*There you go...*

Snatching back to the present, he entered Iolyn Park. From here, he knew the way blindfold. The fence. Dense vegetation. Gate. The mounds and incline leading to Gorse Hill. In the distance, Henrhyd Falls and Nant Llech Valley. With so much rain it would be spectacular. Another caravan park briefly represented civilisation. Except he wasn't going to civilisation. He was going to hell.

Crossing open country, wind howling, he picked up another footpath from where he could access the grounds to Vixenhead. It was going well. Then his luck ran out.

Barbed wire in the form of a perimeter fence blocked his path. Even if he blanketed it with his leather jacket, he was afraid of ripping his flesh on lethal spikes. Dispirited, he followed the line of the fence and met with an additional obstacle in the form of a single strand of wire pulsing with electricity. He swallowed. An image of cigarette burns and remembered pain attacked his nerve endings, sending a shiver of fear along his spine.

Reckoning barbs were a lesser evil, he retraced his steps and searched for a dip, where the barrier was less taut. Minutes later, he located a spot next to a post listing to one side, rotted from the ground up. Giving it a swift kick, it leant considerably more until he simply trampled it down and entered forbidden territory. If he thought his problems were over, he'd seriously miscalculated. The land was now his enemy.

Dense and uncultivated woodland sprawled like jungle before him. Mortified, he considered turning back and seeking a more direct route, jettisoning the idea almost immediately for it would risk exposure and give away any advantage of surprise. His only option was to use his fist and body as a battering ram and hack a path through.

Thickly overgrown and untended landscape made him lose his bearings. Fervently, he hoped he would not stumble into the clearing where he'd found Joshua, something he desperately wanted to avoid.

Oh God.

In truth, Kit had no clear memory of what was true or false when he'd discovered him. Sometimes, it was dark. Sometimes, it was bright. Wind swayed the trees and then there was no breeze at all. When his shattered mind tormented him, he thought Joshua had been alive, still with a flicker of breath in his lungs, pulse rate stuttering, his heart tripping and missing beats, winding down.

Could he have saved him?

The wind that howled now dropped to a thin plangent whine. Each step a major operation, bramble and weed caught at his clothes, begging and pleading with him to turn back.

He didn't listen.

# Chapter 42

Rattled by Edwyn's concern and following his directions, I drive the two-and-a-half-mile journey via Llanrwst and Henryd. The entrance to Vixenhead takes me by surprise and I almost miss it. In my mind, I see a grand pair of ornate gates set between stone pillars, with statues of Welsh dragons atop, and these presiding over a fabulous, if potholed drive, with manicured lawns on each side flanked by rolling, properly managed woodland. There are no gates. Columns, like two war-wounded soldiers perched on crutches, stand dilapidated and covered in moss and lichen. The way ahead is, indeed, crevassed, its edges practically overrun with waist-high grass and overgrown weeds. I wonder how long since someone drove down, except there are visible tracks, possibly belonging to a four-by-four, slashing a route through.

With a deep breath, I nudge the Fiesta gingerly into the mouth of the drive, which proves to be narrow, sinuous and winding. I have no idea what I will do should I meet a vehicle coming from the opposite direction, especially as my reversing skills are abysmal.

Little by little, I move the car along, apologising aloud with every bump and scrape for dragging it to this Godforsaken place. Entombed in a deep-green tunnel of foliage, it's impossible to view imagine how the landscape was once upon a time, when the grounds were in their heyday. To fall into such a state of neglect, after all the years it took to perfect, doesn't bode well for what I will find at journey's end. If I hoped to meet a rainbow, I could forget it. More likely, a derelict building braced for demolition.

I picture emptiness, voids and shrouds.

At last, I round another bend and blink. The contrast between the immediate entrance to the house and the potholed drive is staggering. It's as if I travelled through a minefield, no man's land, down Sniper's Alley, to reach safety.

To my left, redwoods and chestnut shout loud against a baleful sky. There is an upper lake, an old rock garden and stone bridge with steps leading down to grottos and waterfalls that cascade into a Victorian water garden with reeds and lilies. Cruising slowly past, I start at the sight of four dripping faces staring back at me, gargoyles with wizened features and pointed chins, green slime erupting from their ugly open mouths. It's not too late to turn back, I remind myself. The burning desire for truth convinces me otherwise. This is no reckless, shallow fascination. This has to be done.

Edging onto a gravelled area of chippings the colour of Cotswold stone, I park the car and stare through curved double wrought-iron gates beneath an ornately carved stone arch. Raised beds, a fountain that runs dry, and a wide path that cuts through a garden that is tidy, nurtured and certainly less overgrown than its surroundings. Expecting a building to rise up from the ground, grim and crumbling, like an aged face that is all eyes, wrinkles, shrunken gums and thin lips, I gaze upon three storeys, two of stone, topped by a third clad in decorative black timber. Infill panels, once painted white, are faded to grey. Gormenghast meets Dracula's Transylvanian pad, there are turrets and towers, chimneys and parapets. God alone knows how many bedrooms. Vast windows with leaded panes, like squares of Cadbury's Dairy Milk, jut out from its exterior and number eight. As I tilt my head, the house peers down, its gaze inscrutable. Gargoyles on the buttresses, different to the ones on the bridge, are half-female, half-vixen, sharp-eyed and terrifying, as if hurtling back to Hell, where they were conceived.

More mundane, a cement mixer and two skips are parked on the other side of the gravel next to a modern single-storey broken-down double garage. I have the impression that the house is a work in progress, a full programme of renovation already underway.

Trying to muffle the sound of my shoes, I move slowly towards the west of the building and, from this angle, see that it is deep and stretches back. Less tangibly, I sense something odd, off, that isn't right. There's an incongruous modern addition in the form of a tall metal gate, held up between two pillars, with spikes running threateningly along the top edge. Fortress Vixenhead. Under the house's watchful gaze, chill tiptoes along my spine. This is a place of dormant anger. Awake, it will growl, bare its teeth, snap at my throat.

As I edge back to the main entrance, my footsteps crunching, the house appears to stir. Risking a look to my left, on the ground, at its feet, a black cast-iron mailbox is propped against the border fence, drunkenly askew.

Metal grinds as the gate creaks open, raucous and loud, buffeted by a sudden gust of wind. Fear zaps me. Catching hold of my breath, I centre and anchor it inside, like Reg does when he smokes weed. Breathe, I think, just breathe. Briefly, I morph into my fearless mother. But I cannot hold on to it. I was never much good at courage.

A glance over my shoulder confirms that my car is ready and waiting. It would only take a few fast steps to reach it and safety. If I go now, I can scoot and hoof, drive away and go home, never to return. Then I think of Tom, his guilt or his innocence, everything that was ripped away from me, love and sex, family and chances, and what I came for.

Stephanie was oh-so right. There is no going back.

Steadying myself, I force my feet along the path to the stern, dark wooden door in which metal studs are inserted like cloves in a joint of gammon. On closer inspection, the paint, in common with the panelling on the top storey, reminds me of a manicure past its prime, peeling, bitten and chipped. The glaring anomaly in the faded appearance is the bell-pull. It's black, fashionably antique in style, made of iron and patently new. I tug it, step back and dance from one foot to the other. I wished I'd had a wee before I came. I don't think an immediate request to use the lavatory will improve my pitch.

Sharp footsteps and the click of heel on wood flooring. Next a minor curse as a chain is unleashed, then the door swings open revealing an exceptionally tall woman, mostly because she wears towering green stilettoes that accentuate her bony build. Her dress is tailored, navy blue, cinched in at the waist. She has very short grey hair, giving her a gamine appearance, and the smoothest skin imaginable so that it is difficult to tell her age. Only her hands, mottled like my mum's, suggest a woman in her late sixties, possibly older.

Her eyes are gaslight blue yet, behind them, the light is absent, not so her smile, which is wide, delighted and friendly. "Hello." Her voice claps in pleasure as if she is meeting an old friend and absolutely thrilled.

"Hi, I wonder if you can help…"

"No need to stand on the doorstep." She gestures for me to come inside. "It's far too cold and wet. I was about to put the kettle on. Won't you join me for a coffee?"

"Well…"

"I insist."

She throws open the door wide and with a flourish. Overwhelmed, I enter, as if on castors. The unexpected welcome is one thing, the interior another. I expect Miss Haversham-style cobwebs, litter and mouse droppings, cockroaches and damp, peeling ancient walls, dingy lighting and cramped conditions. Instead, in a twist of old meets new, I am greeted with chandeliers, sumptuous designer wallpaper, space and paint effects, and not a speck of dust in sight.

I gaze around the vast half-wood-panelled hall and massive stone fireplace; so huge you can virtually draw up a seat and sit in it. A log fire ticks and crackles in an enormous grate that looks as if it's been reclaimed from Conwy Castle's great hall itself. I imagine suits of armour, portraits of kings and secret passages. To the right, a wide, highly polished wooden staircase, the kind that movie stars in top hat and tails dance down in old black-and-white movies. Picking up on my obvious enchantment, the woman smiles widely in approval. I think her face will crack.

"Ursula Verdi," she says, extending a hand.

I take it, palm to palm, her skin slightly damp. "Roz Outlaw," I say.

"Come through." She walks with a sprightly step and takes me down a wide corridor with faded red carpets, carved timber panelling, and a lath-and-plaster ceiling, most of it ropey, past door after door, towards the back of the house, to a kitchen so gigantic you could fit my house into it several times. I gaze with envy at the modern industrial-sized range cooker, the cupboards and drawers and lack of clutter, not a washing machine or fridge in sight. Tom would love this, I think, before realising that this was his home long before I stepped into it. And what a home.

"Now where have I put the coffee?" She trills with laughter and I get the impression that she's as scatty as my mum.

"In the cupboard above the kettle?" I am in full-on people-pleasing mode. It's not difficult.

"Of course," she says, opening and finding exactly what she wants. "Cups and sugar here too," she proclaims, as if this comes as a surprise. "Do you take sugar?" she asks, twizzling around on perilously high heels. Her legs are so thin I think they might snap.

"One in coffee."

"I thought so. My Joshy loved sugar too. Always two

teaspoons in his tea. He had it in a baby's bottle until he was five, would you believe it?" For a moment her smile fades and she stares at the cups in her hands as if she hasn't a clue what to do with them. Desolation sweeps over her and puddles at my feet.

"Here," I say, feeling awkward, "Let me."

"Would you?"

She shoots me an expression of such gratitude I feel worse. Forcing a fake smile, I say, "Of course."

She collapses onto a chaise longue that has seen better days, as if she overexerted herself and run out of steam.

I take the cups and put the kettle on. A quick hunt for the fridge finally yields a four-litre carton of milk, too much for one elderly woman.

A few minutes later, we are sitting at a dark refectory table that pays homage to the building's roots while, overhead, a row of trendy hanging pendant lights in brass, the ultimate in modernity. She smiles sweetly and sips her drink. Despite her happy expression, she looks vacant. If any conversation is to take place, I must start it.

"You mentioned Joshy."

"My son," she says with a beam. "Such a lovely boy. Takes after his father, naturally. Gorgeous man. Dead now." Her smile loses its lustre.

"And Joshy?" I hate myself for this, but it's the only way I can extract information from her.

A shadow passes behind her eyes. She darts a look at the door and then to me. Her nervous gaze finally settles on mine. "Murdered," she whispers.

My throat shrinks. This is the boy's mother. She *must* know and speak the truth. My mug goes down hard onto the table.

"I'm so sorry."

Her bony hand shoots out and closes over mine. "He found him and then he killed him."

"Who?" I brace myself, fearful that whatever she says next, I will come unglued, undone.

"That wretched boy. Geoffrey took him in. Stupid, stupid, stupid. I never wanted him in the first place. I said no good would come of it. Why would I need that runt in my house?" Her voice rises in pitch, the eyes shoot wide, as if addressing her late husband and reliving the argument with him. "Why," she says, her chin trembling, "would I desire a reminder of all that I lost? The love of my life," she wails, tears springing to her ears.

"What the hell?"

We both twist around. In the doorway stands a man in running shorts and shoes. His white vest is dark with sweat. My eyes move straight to his haircut. Hair flat and black on top, the rest of his scalp shaved, Peaky Blinders' style. His muscles roll and glisten, pumped up, flushed with exercise and anger at my intrusion. He has nut-brown eyes, swarthy skin, grainy and in need of a shave. His lips are full and currently screwed in anger. Black eyebrows also express his fury. "Ursula, get back to your room. Now." He speaks slowly, convincingly and I detect a foreign accent, maybe French.

She recoils, fear shadowing her features. "I did nothing wrong, Raoul. It wasn't my fault. Please don't tell Linus. He will be so very disappointed." She speaks in a wheedling and whiny tone, eyes misting with fresh tears. There is something horribly coquettish in the way she reacts to him. Man-pleaser.

Raoul doesn't walk across the room. He struts. Commanding. His arm around Ursula's narrow shoulders, he changes tone and says soothingly, "Don't be upset, little one. Shall I call Philip? He can give you something."

"Yes," she says, looking up adoringly at Raoul. "I'd like that. Something to take the pain away. Philip is so very good to me."

Is this the same Philip I met at the hotel, the doctor who threatened me only last night? I shift uneasily, unhappy at the portrait of concern that feels false and anything but cosy. Comfort dispensed and received, they both turn on me. It's Ursula who delivers the blow that catches me straight between my eyes. "Look what she made me do, Raoul. Tricked her way in."

My jaw drops. Underneath her malicious expression, there is cunning and conviction. It doesn't sit snugly with her fluttery, smiley welcome or her confusion about making coffee. In a trice, I work out that Ursula has dementia. Can I trust a word she said? And who is Linus?

I get to my feet, not quick enough, judging by the glare in Raoul's eyes.

"You," he says, jerking his head towards the door a mile away, "Out."

"I can explain." I flinch, as eager to go as Raoul is for me to exit.

To make his point, he shoots forward, grabs my shoulder with his weighty hand, and propels me out of the kitchen.

He doesn't let me go. I squirm, but his grip tightens like a screw. Up against this muscular pile of flesh, I am powerless. I try to relax, but my shoulder kills me.

The inquisition begins as he marches me down another corridor in which ancient portraits grace the walls and another staircase winds its way to another wing.

Narrowing his eyes, he demands to know who I am.

"I, I'm a reporter," I stammer.

"Scum," he spits out. "Who do you work for?"

"Nobody. I'm freelance. Look, can you let go of me? You're hurting."

He digs his fingers deeper. "What are you doing here?"

I swallow hard, as much to kill the pain as buy me thinking time. "Chasing a story."

He repeats what I say with a black smile that quickly disappears. "You'll find no stories here."

"That's not..."

"You like harassing a sick old woman?"

"No, I..."

He stops, bears down on me, his face in mine. I try to look away, but he grabs my chin. I flick a glance to the side, disorientated, searching for an escape route. Walls close in around me, hiding their secrets, making cloudy what should be clear.

"I'm sorry," I gasp. "Please let me go."

"You have no idea how sorry you will be."

"I understand. Really I do." I sound as vulnerable as I feel.

He grunts and pushes open another door. Magically, we are back to where I first came in. The smell of wood smoke is no longer aromatic in my nostrils. It resembles a dirty old bonfire on which chemical waste is illegally burnt.

Grabbing me by an elbow, he pushes me to the door. "Now get out and don't come back." For emphasis, a slew of slime from the back of his throat hits my cheek and traces a glistening trail down to the corner of my mouth.

He releases me. He doesn't repeat the order. He has no need. Wiping away spittle and tears, I'm gone.

# Chapter 43

Oblivious to nettle, thistle and thorn, Kit slashed a narrow channel with his fists, knuckles tearing, fingers stinging. Each tendril and branch thrashed and bucked, putting up a terrific fight, in final death throes. With each step, he struggled with visions and words he'd rather forget. *Fat Kit/Kit Fat*, a play on the popular confectionery, except he was underweight all of the time and malnourished some of the time. Kicked out of bed at dawn, he was worked from early morning until late at night, cleaning and washing, cooking and serving. "For him who serves is greatest," his aunt regularly reminded him. If he yawned or expressed fatigue, he was struck and reminded that he should be grateful to have a roof over his sorry head. A modern version of Cinderella with an added twist of gender equality.

And so many had known. They must have.

From the teacher who came to give him a perfunctory education; Philip Swift, the doctor who regularly visited the house to tend Ursula, day and night; gardeners; delivery drivers; the local population. Nobody was deaf, dumb or blind. If Aunt Ursula's friends suspected, they either didn't care or feared a scandal. In his more charitable moments, he recognised that no whistle blower ever got prizes.

But he wasn't feeling benevolent.

With each recollection, unconsummated rage flared and pushed him on until, finally, with the house in his sights, he was raving. Blinded, he failed to notice the land levelling off, the emergence of a clear track, mown grass and grounds parading a more cultivated veneer. For him, they would remain forever afflicted, diseased and rotten.

Doubled over with stitch, sweat and rain dripping into his eyes. Furiously pushing it away with the back of a bleeding hand, he straightened up, stood breathless and wild, as if in rhapsody before a shrine. Except this place beneath a stone bridge and guarded by a defiant group of trees was neither hallowed nor spiritual. Amid weeping beech and willow, snow-drops and ferns and hellebores, stood a monument to the destruction of his childhood.

The sound of running water is supposed to soothe. He found no solace there. Weeds that could drag him under crawled out of the dank depths and clawed at his feet. Above: four malignant faces dared and goaded him to jump. How many times when things were really bad had he considered leaping onto the low wall and tumbling in, submitting his body to a similar fate that befell his parents? Pumped with adrenalin, he briefly considered it now.

Disappear.

No longer exist.

Stop hurting.

Disturbance from behind, Kit twisted round and watched

as a magnificent heron swooped down and, with the precision of a guided missile, flicked a fish out of the pool and made off with it wriggling in its beak. Enough to break the evil hold the place had on him, he shook himself free and took the stone steps two at a time, darting across the bridge and back into the safety of abandoned vegetation and trees.

Working his next move, he had no intention of making a direct approach. That risked danger. For now, he would stake out Vixenhead and find the best way to penetrate unnoticed for the final assault. He wondered whether they still used the customised priest hole, his private house of horror. Fetid and squalid, with mushrooms multiplying on the walls, there it had been easier to lock him in. Light had seeped through courtesy of a single barred window. During the winter months, he'd emerge, blinking like a newly born mole. Spring was better. Spring meant the suggestion of warmth and sunshine and hope that never lasted. Summer was a bastard. Suffocating. Stifling. Smothering.

He wondered whether from the inside there remained any suggestion of restraint, captivity and despair, or whether it had been cleared, whitewashed, all deeds contained inside airbrushed out of existence.

Tracing a path between the lower lake and upper, he passed a cedar, its lower branches no longer bearing the signs of where he and Joshy had once swung from a rope swing. Looking up, he swore faraway children's laughter briefly echoed on the breeze before finally bidding farewell.

Gut twisting, he moved around the remnants of the old

chapel and, using the yew trees for cover, inched his way towards the front of the house.

About to draw near, he heard an irate voice, one he didn't recognise. Manoeuvring around to get a better view, his jaw slackened at the sight of a flash of bright colour and an unmistakeable figure speeding down the path from the house and shooting across the gravelled patch, to where a bright-yellow car waited on standby. Flinging open the door and hurling herself inside, Roz, for it was definitely she, stalled the engine twice before pressing her foot on the gas. Tearing down the drive, pale and strained, she looked as if Lucifer himself chased after her.

# Chapter 44

Nerves shattered, I don't stop. The car whacks every lump and hollow, straining the suspension, knackering the exhaust. Who cares? In my head, nasty little men with wizened expressions and snarling women who are half fox pursue me all the way. A wave of anger only hits once I'm on proper tarmac and haring back to Conwy. Furious about what I didn't say, I fail to process what happened with any clarity until I'm at the hotel, parked in the bar with a soft, sweet, fizzy drink.

Raoul doubles as Ursula's carer and gaoler – that much is obvious. Maintaining the Verdi party line, he is also the keeper of stories and secrets. The aggressive way in which he manhandled me is living proof. But it's Linus to whom he reports. Linus who will be upset. Linus Ursula doesn't wish to disappoint. Is he the son, the obituary-writer?

And then I recall my conversation with Ursula before her minder stuck his beak in. Ursula's desolation at the loss of her beloved Joshy, 'the love of her life' and her damning words about the boy, meaning Kit, whom she never wanted in the first place. She's nuts, isn't she?

*What if she isn't?*

Oh God. I am tearing up inside.

Tears spatter my cheeks like hot fat from a pan. A little piece of me so wanted to believe that Tom was innocent of any charge, but I can no longer sign up for that version of events. How can I dispute a mother's account about the killer of her child? She would know, more than anyone, wouldn't she? Mad, or not?

Yet there are anomalies. If Josh resembled his 'gorgeous' father why would Ursula bury her husband Geoffrey so far away from his son? Is Ursula under orders because she is a danger to herself, or to others? Why would I be warned off with such venom?

From my car, I call Edwyn. "Furlongs," he pipes.

"I'm back."

"Right."

"And in one piece." Except bits of me are shredded and litter half of Wales. "Edwyn, who is Raoul?"

He makes a sound: part sigh and part click of disapproval. "Linus Verdi's friend. Thinks a lot of himself, that one. Manipulative. Devious too."

Devious is interesting. "In what way exactly?"

"After...' Edwyn pronounces it with a short 'a' and heavy emphasis on the consonants, "...the main chance." I want to quiz him but Edwyn continues, "You going home, then?"

"Why does everyone keep asking me that question?"

"Because you should go back to where you came from."

I splutter. It has no effect on Edwyn.

"You're an outsider," he insists. "You wouldn't understand. Bad blood there, see? Goes back decades. Any fool can spot it."

All right, I'm an idiot. Perversely, Edwyn's insult hardens my resolve.

A crackly noise from a cab driver to the office resonates down the phone line. Before I can say another word, Edwyn says he has to go and does.

Distracted, I take my drink and, finding the lounge area opposite the bar empty, plump down into a sofa near the fire. It burns and ticks and, this time, there really is a lovely scent of wood smoke. I tilt forward and warm my hands.

*Bad blood. Goes back decades.*

There is no sign of the doctor, no sign of anyone, even though it's lunchtime. My gaze swivels to the local newspaper seductively splaying its pages across a side table on the opposite side of the room. I get up, swipe it and sit back down.

A rough glance reveals that it's pretty standard fare. Local crime story on the front page and spilling over onto the inside cover, the rest a medley of good-news and bad-news business stories, mashed up with grinning faces of local dignitaries glad-handing, court items, what's on, motors toward the end, with dating and notices spliced between property and sport. Oh yeah, and in this week's jolly, there is an obituary of a former councillor written by none other than Linus Verdi. I drift through well-written, well-meaning prose. It's a rare person who writes ill of the dead. They might say it and think it, but there's no place for trashing reputations in a local lash-up – too many people to offend. Bleakly, I wonder what was written when Adam Charteris, another of Kit Trueblood's aliases, died.

Heavy-hearted, I pick up my Ipad, and Google Linus Verdi.

A photograph pops up of a man with a top lip that is so thin it looks non-existent. He has hooded, deep-set eyes that perch above cheekbones that are as sharp as a cliff-face. I have no idea how old he is but his patrician features, courtesy of his mother, don't connect with his hair, which is grey, prematurely so, I guess, and way too long to look cool. The man with the sneering smile looks as if he begs to differ. There is something rather hollowed-out and gaunt about him. Perhaps it's not a good snap. Maybe he is recovering from a debilitating illness. Morbidly, I wonder whether the nature of his work has a negative effect on his appearance. In essence, the self-satisfied exterior doesn't conceal the fact that he doesn't look like a well man. I wonder if Raoul looks after him as well as Ursula, although Edwyn's sly intonation, implying prejudice, suggests a closer relationship between the two.

*After the main chance,* Edwyn said.

When people make such claims they normally mean money. Instantly, I remember the hotel that belonged to the Truebloods. Surely, the proceeds from the sale after death duties would belong to Tom? What happened to it? Did the Verdis somehow intercept and thieve it for themselves? I wonder if this is what lies behind Raoul's anger and obvious desire to get rid of me. I do not simply smell the coffee; I sniff a bitter acrid brew that has been stewing for over a decade, if not longer. If Ursula is mentally compromised, what are the consequences? Who would have power of attorney? Linus, or another sibling? What will happen to Vixenhead when Ursula dies? Oh my God, I snag inside, thoughts spiralling with question after question, Tom is worth more to everyone dead than alive. I recall Roy's words: *He disappeared... When he was just a kid.*

No, he didn't. Tom *was* disappeared. And there's a huge difference.

# Chapter 45

In shame, Kit stood mute, a million images of Roz rushing through his head: Roz rescuing fruit flies from glasses of wine like her life, not theirs, depended upon it; Roz fucking up his best shirt by putting it on a wash that cooked it and rushing straight down town and buying him a new one that cost twice the price of his old one; Roz happy and quirky and never sad; Roz kind, never mean; Roz fun and adventurous and sexy; Roz true and loyal and worth more than him.

And she'd tracked him here? What was she thinking?

Except he knew. Of course, he did. Roz had come because she cared; about him; about the truth. Without strings or judgement. Shame on him for ever hooking up with her and not giving her all she deserved, someone way better.

The sound of tyres spitting gravel brought him back to his senses. He shrank behind a rhododendron bush and peered between its glossy wet leaves. He had no doubt that, if he waited long enough, Ursula's acolyte would show. Less sure, how he'd respond to seeing Linus after all these years.

Linus Verdi's six-feet-three-inch body unfolded and stepped out of a Volvo four-by-four. To Kit's surprise, the years had not been kind. The muscular physique had shrunk. Dark hair was straggly, long and grey, and his skin the colour of cooked pearl barley. But it was the eyes that spoke most eloquently. Not simply sullen and cold, but hard and void, like two black holes. At the sight of him, a pulse in Kit's temple thundered, pressing hard on an age-old wound, still raw and weeping. Tightness in his stomach and groin. Bile in the back of his throat. Dizzy, he retreated and leant against the trunk of an elm, smooth bark against his spine. Utterly diminished, he felt compelled to pray to a God in which he didn't believe. Prayed not to be seen. Prayed for deliverance. When Linus disappeared into the house Kit realised that for several seconds he'd been holding his breath, lungs bursting. It took pure will for him to let it out and pull himself together. Paralysed with fear, he'd virtually forgotten what he'd come for – to stake out the house.

Abandoning the front elevation, he dropped onto his belly and, crawling to avoid his silhouette being spotted, followed a line through the trees. From somewhere, the distant noise of a woodpecker battering a hole in a tree trunk to prise out unsuspecting grubs for its lunch.

Travelling slowly through 180 degrees, each movement minimum and controlled to eliminate the possibility of drawing attention, Kit finally faced the rear elevations. Brow popping with perspiration, he glanced up to check that nobody could detect him from an upstairs window. He was safe from the turrets. No one ventured there; too unstable.

Lowering his gaze, he skimmed the oval-shaped ornamental water feature in front, now drained. Shooting across on his elbows, he drew as close as he dared, using the shallow walls of the pond as cover. From here, he had a clear line of sight of the colonnade suspended between two wings of the house. The west side masked the exit from the priest hole and what had once been his home and prison for the best part of seven years. Vixenhead was much as he remembered and he took perverse pleasure in seeing that, in common with Linus, it had not stood the test of time. With flaking paint, rotting window frames, damaged guttering and stone that needed repointing, the fabric of the building looked exhausted. It made no difference that the immediate grounds surrounding the Jacobean-style edifice had been prettied up. To him, it would always remain ugly.

Belly flat, wet and cold, jacked up on his elbows, with an icy breeze dying to a whisper, Kit remembered only too well the dark, the murk in front of his face, the dusty, tarry air that filled his eyes, ears and nose. In recollection, his heart rate shot up and he pressed a hand to his chest to still a weird thrumming sensation underneath his ribs. Nothing could prevent tears that had stayed in check for more years than he cared to remember from spilling down his stubbly cheeks.

Without warning, double doors sprang open. Next, raised voices, the sound of slapped flesh, a noise he recognised so well, and a man's gruff protest. Dragged back to the here and now, straining his ears, Kit heard two male voices, one familiar, one foreign, like birds of prey in the wind, squabbling over a defenceless baby rabbit.

Tilting his chin to get a clear eye line, he saw Linus emerge first, followed by another man dressed in shorts, t-shirt and running shoes. One side of his face bore the livid marks of Linus's handprint.

Agitated, Linus flailed his arms, fists clenched. In response, the stranger, muscular and conciliatory, patted the air with his palms flat, fingers splayed in a gesture of calm.

"I told you never to leave her alone," Linus bawled in the man's face. "My mother is old, frail and ill."

"I went for a run. I was only gone ten minutes."

"And look what happened. Don't you understand, you moron?"

"Sure, I do. We are this near." To demonstrate how close, the man raised a hand, thumb and forefinger pressed within a millimetre of each other.

Linus's face fell in derision. "There is no 'we' about it, Raoul," he said, jabbing a finger in the other man's chest. "You'd best remember that."

Raoul backed away. "Of course, I'm sorry. I did not mean anything by it."

"I don't need cock-ups and some bloody hack snooping."

"Linus, she won't be back. I made sure of it."

"And that's your mistake, Raoul." There was no misunderstanding the deadly intent in Linus's voice.

"What? I don't..."

"You should have *made sure*," Linus said with heavy intonation, "that Kit's woman never left."

"But—"

"We could have staked out the bitch as bait."

Kit felt as if someone had dropped a bag of cement on his chest from a great height. Linus was on to Roz. Thank God she got away. As worrying, was it his fault for running? Had he drawn attention and provided Linus with a lead?

"But how do you know he would come?" Raoul said.

Linus turned and looked straight towards the pond, sniffing the inert air. With a gasp, Kit dodged down.

"He'll come," he heard Linus say. "I sense it. Especially now that Swain is dead."

Swain dead? Kit hugged the sides of the pond. An answer to a prayer, he should feel elation. Instead, his thoughts slipped and slid. One foe vanquished, another more deadly to take its place.

"Then this is good," Raoul said, a smile in his voice, eager to deflect Linus from his own shortcomings. "I'll make you lunch. Frittata, your favourite."

Kit poked his head up enough to watch as Raoul placed his hands on Linus's narrow hips and kissed him slowly on the mouth.

Long after both men went inside, he stayed down. Thinking. Processing. Headline news: Swain was dead and Linus, who would always love his mother, was out to get him. Just like he knew he would.

Crawling back the way he'd come, slipping from one shrub to another, he slunk around toward the front of the building and viewed it with more clarity. The gates that seemed imposing when he was eleven had diminished in size. Scoping left and right, he spotted something different about one of the pillars. There were indentations in the stone from where the mailbox had sheared off. Switching his gaze to the ground, he spied it propped against the fence and obviously damaged by the fall. About to move off, the approach of a vehicle froze him to the spot, a red post van rattling across the gravel.

Hurrying against a blast of wind and rain, the 'postie' squatted down in front of the mailbox, crammed a bundle of correspondence into its mouth and scooted back to the car. A fast U-turn and he was out of there.

Kit let out a long breath. In front of him was a prize that must be taken at all costs. He did not think. He did not plan. He stood up and broke cover. Dashing across the gravel, he swooped. He was clumsy and it was heavy. He hardly noticed, so great was his triumph. Retrieving and carrying it in both hands, he tracked back the way he had come.

Through the wilderness.

# Chapter 46

I'm like a train that veers wildly off course when it's supposed to be slowly approaching the signal box. If Tom committed murder, he would not *disappear*. He would do time in an institution. He would hopefully rehabilitate and come out. Afterwards, if he did what Ursula claimed, he would go and live somewhere else, far away. He would not hang around in a place in which he committed the crime. In common with Roy, my lovely Devonian doorkeeper, at no time did the crusty old doctor mention the word 'murder' or 'manslaughter'– and he should know. With a thud, I register that the doctor could be an informer for the Verdis. Did he play me?

Setting aside the thorny complication of senility, Ursula's belief about Kit's guilt could all be in her twisted head. Often grief needs someone to blame. I have no experience of bereavement, so it's difficult to gauge.

Alternatively, Geoffrey Verdi was so immensely powerful that he glossed over what Tom did and shielded him from a full-on police investigation. It would take considerable skill, determination and influence. But why on earth would he exert such power when Tom allegedly killed his youngest son?

Confused, I consider phoning Vick, but dismiss it because she'll order me to pack my bags and come home. I think about phoning Jane and do what, confess to my meddling? Could the police charge me with interfering in a police investigation? Probably. Bang on cue, Falconer's blind eyes rear up in front of my nose. I mentally back away. Quick. Skedaddle.

And then I recall Mike Shenton, his pained expression and plea to leave well alone, the way he reached out, touched my sleeve, his fingers on my hand, his assurance that he believed me. How much did it cost him to reveal this? He was taking a hell of a risk, and for what? Because he cared? Because of professional pride? Was this what I, too, was doing? Messing in things and people that had no bearing on my life?

Shenton, of all people, would understand.

Toying with the thought for ages, I go back and forth, weighing up the arguments on both sides, my Libran personality given a thorough workout. Hunched over the fire, I stew like this for the entire afternoon. When evening comes there is no sign of the doctor with his thread-veined features and hate-filled mouth.

Without appetite and without anyone to berate me, I order hot chocolate topped with cream and marshmallows, and a slab of carrot cake for dinner. The place is as empty as one can expect for a cold, wet day in early February, so I eat alone, in silence. Zapped with a sugar hit that is as pleasurable as it is instant. Pinching crumbs from my mouth and dusting them off my lap, my phone rings from a number I don't recognise.

"Roz?"

"Mike?" I choke and then cough. "Sorry, I'm eating."

"I'll call you back."

"No, it's all right."

He pauses. If he rehearsed a speech, he forgot it. "You didn't seem well the last time we met."

"I was in a hurry."

"You virtually ran over my feet."

Did I? Honestly, I don't remember. "Are you threatening to do me for dangerous driving or is this a social call?" My laugh is shaky, exposing my nervousness.

"I'm not threatening anyone."

"Good, because I'm really fed up of people intimidating me." Oh no, I think. Should keep my mouth shut.

"What people?"

"Oh, nobody important," I say, backtracking quicker than Reg when caught in a big fat lie.

"Roz, are you in some sort of trouble?"

I make a sound that isn't *yes*, but isn't *no*, either.

"Come on, what's going on? Trust me."

A dirty great fight erupts inside my head. He's a policeman. He's warm and friendly. He exudes trust. He played straight with me. He probably knows things. I could tell him, couldn't I? I could put my faith in him. It would be such a relief to talk, to confide. Perhaps I could give him a thin slice of information, see how it plays and gauge his reaction. And, damn it, I *like* him.

"Nothing's going on." I spit each word out as if I'm ejecting loose teeth.

"All right," he says composed and calm. "You aren't the only one being stonewalled."

Something tells me he is about to deliver a punchline. "I don't know what you're talking about..."

"Weeks before Tom's alleged death, a copper with close connections to Garry Swain, a criminal..."

"I know who Swain is," I bark, unnerved that Shenton reveals so much.

"You do?"

I ignore the surprise in his voice. "Does the copper have a name?"

"A guy called Chace was arrested on a corruption charge and, around the same time, Swain was gunning for a young man who put him inside. I think that man..."

"What?" I yelp. "Why are you telling me?" What I really mean is how do you know, how did you find out? When it comes to witness protection, the police have separate computers, separate files.

"Because you're in way over your head."

"I have to go," I squeak.

"Roz, don't hang up. Don't...'

Cutting the call, I think *Shit* and clasp the phone to my chest as though it's a defibrillator. Aren't one dead boy, one missing and one suicide, enough? Is Shenton looking out for me, or feeding misinformation? I bubble with alarm. My thoughts gabble. Oh God, have I made things worse? Surely, my cagey, elusive response gave the game away. What if there is something really weird going on? Something immense? Or is it all one big irrelevant diversion?

With a big breath, I speculate that Tom remained at Vixenhead after Joshua Verdi's death, unseen, hidden away for the freak they thought he was. I 'think' the road-rage incident was Tom's ticket to freedom. So why are the Verdis so damn jumpy now? As far as they are concerned, Tom, or Kit as they knew him, is no longer on the scene. Good riddance.

I should contact Jane and reveal what I know. On balance, I think it best to stay silent. Best do nothing. That way I cannot be involved, blamed, interrogated, arrested. *Hurt.*

Sod hot chocolate. I stride to the bar, where I order vodka, a double, with tonic. Spiriting it up to my room, I run a bath that almost meets the overflow, throw in hotel toiletries, strip off, sip my drink and soak.

Ursula's remark about Joshua and her husband, *the love of her life,* flashes through my mind. I think about Geoffrey's vow to take Tom in after his parents drowned, honouring a promise to a friend. It's a big, bold step to take care of someone else's kid. According to Ursula, the child bit the hand of those trying to feed him in spectacular fashion...

I take another gulp of vodka. Did grief drive Ursula demented? Or is her senility a sad consequence of a diseased brain?

*Bad blood.*

One thing I know. If there is the slightest chance that Ursula is lying, or wrong in the head, then Tom was, and is, a victim. Tom is in danger. Not from Swain but from the Verdis.

I don't understand why he is worth more to them dead than alive, but I have a feeling.

To hell with my fear and the terror that bloody man, Raoul, rained down on me. If I'm ever to discover the truth and see Tom alive again, I need to shake things up.

# Chapter 47

I spend a lousy night tossing and turning. When I partially surface I'm freezing cold, bleary-eyed and dry-mouthed. Fear set in, I don't feel as ballsy as I did the night before.

Too early to get up or summon room service, I stumble from the bed, make myself a cup of coffee with 'pretend' milk, and snaffle the tiny hotel-sized pack of biscuits from the welcome tray. My stomach growls and that's my own fault for eating cake for dinner. God, what would my mum say? My blood sugar must be hitting stratospheric heights.

Suddenly, my chest hurts and a sob catches me unawares. Why does this have to pain me so much? Did Tom ever love me, or did he only use me? Four in the morning, tears fall properly this time, trickling from the corners of my eyes, streaming onto the pillow and soaking through the pillowcase. A wet and pathetic snivelling mess, I hate to think what Reg would say if he could see me now.

*Get a grip.*

I exchange the top pillow for the one underneath, punch it hard and, like a meteor dropping from the sky, make a number of disparate sobering observations. Borne out of my 'hey man' hippie upbringing, sodding about for decades, and lethargic slide into the world of work, people-pleasing is part of my DNA. Inextricably linked, my need to fix people who cannot be fixed. People like Tom. With a faulty gene, his mutation, I realise, cannot be manipulated. Idiot me for trying.

And there is more: I might not be a mother but I have a mothering instinct. If any proof were needed, look no further than my relationship with my little brother, Reg. I might not be ambitious, but I'm a pretty good cheerleader for those who aim to achieve something magical. Vick would tell you that. With Tom, too, I did my best to bolster him because, deep inside, I sensed he was broken. If I smiled and laughed and loved him enough, I would reach and reclaim him, or at least that was what I sold myself. Sadly, my desire was not borne of simple altruism. Like everyone else, I have an agenda, even if it's the satisfaction accumulated from helping others. With time fast running out on me, I yearn for stability and children. Another stint of snivelling erupts and I curse the fact that I've gone all emotional, as if I spent the night tanked up on Tequila. Odds on, I'm slipping into the sticky swamp called depression. Mum was right about that. Sombre and downcast, I eventually fall asleep.

Dozing fitfully until daybreak, I get my head together and finally do something I should have done sooner. Prowling through Google, I check out Geoffrey Verdi. Suicides make good copy and it doesn't take me long to find a short piece that reveals he made his money in the City, before decamping to Wales and dabbling in the hospitality industry, explaining how his path crossed with the Truebloods. The article paints him as a philanthropist, so he clearly wasn't short of loot. I let out a sigh. How glorious that must be. I don't dwell on it for very long because my mind hooks on the method of dispatch – good old carbon-monoxide poisoning – and a very blokey way to go, with no if's and but's. Poor sad man.

Galvanised, I send a text to Jane, who will be my backup plan should things disintegrate. As for personal consequences and sledgehammer of the law coming down on me, what do I care?

I get up, shower and dress. No longer hungry, I don't hang around for breakfast and go straight out, pick up my car and drive to the big house, with its watchful stare and open jaw. Light filters through the trees as I head up the long and winding drive. My emotions are all over the place and take a circular route: *up for it, scared, numb* followed by *up for it, scared, numb*.

It's 8.30 a.m. when I arrive, the sun is barely up and just pottering about. This time, I park facing the drive, primed for a quick getaway.

About to climb out, I hear the scatter of feet on gravel, a rear door flies open and, with a cry of help, a figure shoots inside, slamming the door shut after it. Bewildered, I twist round and meet Ursula's wild, manic gaze and pleading expression. The residue of yesterday's makeup smudges eyes that are dark against the deathly paleness of her complexion. Her lipstick crosses the natural boundaries of her mouth and seeps into surrounding cracks and wrinkles. She wears a pastel-peach negligee and not much else. Her feet are bare, the nails thick and yellow, and she has bunions. Her skin, slack and purple and mottled with cold, looks too big for her arms and legs, like a dress size sixteen for a body that is an eight.

"Please, take me away from here," she cries, her sour early-morning breath contaminating the inside of my car. In agitation, her fingers clasp the edge of the driver's seat like talons on a bird of prey.

"Ursula, I can't."

"You can. You must," she shrieks. "I will be beaten again. Look." She slips across to the opposite side and hitches up her negligee, obliviously exposing her genitals. The bruise on her thigh is livid and a couple of inches in diameter. God alone knows what was used to inflict such damage. Instinctively, I reach across and pull her nightie down.

"I can't drive off with you."

"You have to."

"It's out of the question."

She puts her hands to her head and tears at her hair in distress.

"Hush," I say, reaching around and touching her knee. "We do this the right way. We'll go in together. I'll make sure nobody hurts you."

"No, no, no." She howls in despair and presses her hands to her temples. "You have to get me out of here. They want to kill me, don't you see?"

"They? Linus is your son, isn't he?"

"My lovely boy," she says, almost dreamy, with a wistful smile, before it vanishes into the morning mist. "Raoul wants me dead." Her wet eyes pop with terror.

Breath hitches inside me. "Why?"

Ursula's lips thin. Her eyes narrow to two slits. "You stupid girl," she barks, "He wants my money. Not that I have any. My bloody husband took it from me."

I scratch my head. "I thought he was the love of your life."

Darkness enters her expression. Ursula wags a wizened finger in front of my face. "I said no such thing. How dare you compare Gareth to Geoffrey."

"Gareth? You mean…"

Cold air blasts in. My elbow grabbed, Raoul drags me from my car. Simultaneously, another man I assume to be Linus, scoops Ursula from the rear.

"Come on, mother. Come, my sweet." Raoul doesn't say a word, possibly because, while I protest, Ursula screams at the top of her lungs. I'm surprised they can't hear her in Llandudno.

"Get your damn hands off me," I cry, the heels of my boots skittering across the gravel. Once I'm inside that house, I fear it will swallow me whole and I might never climb out. As I twist around, Linus's cytoplasmic gaze meets mine.

It spurs me on, yet the more I struggle, the stronger Raoul's grip. He has his beefy arms wrapped around mine, pinning me to him. Still, I shout. Thank God I had the wit to contact Jane. "You can't do this," I rage. "The police know I'm here."

"Shut the fuck up." Raoul marches me down the path and physically shoves me into the cavernous hall with the large chandelier that now looks tawdry.

Ursula is still going for it and although Linus does his best to calm her down, she does the opposite so that when he speaks, I can barely hear him.

"Take her in there," he yells to Raoul, jerking his chin in

the direction of a door on the opposite side of the house. "I'll take mother upstairs and settle her. Now, it's all right," he coos to her. "Linus is here to take care of you, darling." The way he says it produces a creepy image of forced sedation. I wonder what Philip left for Linus to administer.

Raoul pushes me into a room that has escaped cosmetic attention. Old chintz drapes adorn the windows, dark mahogany furniture and a rug that is worn and thin and stained with age-old spills. Not here to view the décor, I stare at Raoul with contempt. Muscly, with little in the brain department, he oozes streetwise cunning. It's Linus I need to talk to, to spell out how much shit he's in. Abduction is a serious business and I can't wait for Jane to arrive and take charge. The thought lifts my spirits because justice will be done, we'll all be protected from these bastards, and I will be free.

The screaming stops with the abruptness of a circuit shorting. Footsteps above my head indicate that Linus is on his way back. Something about his slow, deliberate tread, the way he enters the room and closes the door behind him dashes my optimism. A shard of fear stabs me deep in the stomach. Alone with two powerful men, what the hell will they do to me?

# Chapter 48

I cannot believe it. My ankles and wrists are bound and I am tied to a chair. Barring verbal protests, I put up no struggle because I don't want to get hurt. Hyperventilating, I cobble together a mantra my mum once taught me, and try to steady my breathing because, if I don't, I might pass out in terror.

Silently, Linus trawls through my phone contacts and reads my texts, including my most recent to Jane. If fazed, he doesn't show it. At any moment I expect her to blast in with the equivalent of a posse. *Please.*

He slips my phone into his pocket without a word. Raoul eyes me with gloating satisfaction. I glower at the pair of them. "You will never get away with this."

"I think you may be wrong," Raoul says. Cocky. Arrogant.

"Any minute now, the cops will be all over this place." I sound better than I feel. Raoul doesn't so much as blink.

"Where is he?"

"Who?" It's Raoul who demands an answer, Raoul to whom I speak, but it's Linus who I watch. The silent man is the scary man. With his pale vampiric features, I reckon when Linus looks in a mirror he sees absolutely nothing.

The slap comes hard and fast. Shocked as much by the speed as the pain accelerating across my face, I shout, "The police are going to have a field day with you." When I fling 'you' I look at Linus. Definitely the guy running the show, his face remains impassive.

"They would have to find you first," Raoul sneers. "We simply tell them that you came and then you left." He flicks his fingers in a dismissive gesture that confirms I'm toast.

In a maze of corridors and hidden spaces, I'm acutely aware that I can be as easily disappeared as Tom. I flash with panic. Maybe they already sent Jane away. No, she's smart. She wouldn't take their word against mine. *Would she?* "My friends will come looking for me," I insist. Except they won't because nobody, other than Jane, knows I'm here. "And my mum and dad." This, too, is rubbish. Fleetingly, I wonder whether Reg would abandon his legendary complacency and come to my rescue if he knew the state I was in. How I wish I told Edwyn about my return to the mausoleum in the middle of the woods. And why the hell didn't I come clean with Mike Shenton? My heart catches at 'if only's'.

Raoul reads the anxiety and recrimination in my eyes and calls my bluff. "Nobody is going to rescue you."

My breath breaks free, sprinting hard and fast, in spite of my every effort to drag it back and contain it. Without a deterrent, what will they do?

"We know that Tom Loxley is your boyfriend. No point in denial." Linus's words emerge from deep inside a core that is rotten; wriggling and squabbling like fat maggots.

I picture him slip-sliding from one street corner to another.

My imagination did not play tricks on me in Ludlow. He was there. Always there.

He nods, no smile, as if he can read my mind. "And you, Miss Outlaw, have been following the man you know as Tom."

"He left no trail."

"So you keep saying." He rests his rear against a tall Gothic cabinet with fancy inlay in the doors. It manages to be stark and forbidding, yet over the top and tawdry at the same time. If Linus were a piece of furniture, this would be it.

Raoul rolls his dark eyes. "You really expect us to believe this crap?"

"Shut up, Raoul."

At his master's command, Raoul drops his head, practically genuflects, Linus's domination over him supreme.

"Miss Outlaw," Linus says, demanding my full attention. "You must have some idea where he is, where he might go, otherwise you would not be sitting here with us."

"You make it sound like a leisure activity," I say. Sulky. "Let me go. Now. I insist." Neither man flickers. Silence inhabits the room. No friendly clock. No white noise. No sound of human activity at all. Only them and me, a mad old woman conked out upstairs, and DANGER. "Look, if I knew I..." My words trail because I can't admit that I would never tell them where Tom is. In a million years, they would not understand that my 'innocent until proven guilty' sense of justice is greater than the fear they inspire.

Linus slinks across the room and draws up a chair very close. Sitting down, he rakishly crosses one long leg over another, the very picture of reason and fair-mindedness – a filthy lie. Chill breath, tainted with strong coffee, circles me. I'm tempted to spit in his face but, thoroughly intimidated, fear the consequences. He tilts his head, studies me, mapping my every facial move. Creeps me out. When he speaks I instinctively draw my head away. "Will he come for you, do you think?"

"I wouldn't bank on it." I want to give the impression of strength and composure. Up against Linus Verdi, I am a pathetic and feeble wreck. The man has a force field that Mum would consider negative energy, blocked chakras and nothing short of evil.

Trading looks with Raoul, Linus nods again, his poker face giving nothing away. Raoul slips a flick knife from his pocket and leisurely exposes the blade, examining it. Rapt with fear, in a frenzy of anxiety, I glance around the dusty room. Supposing I could wriggle free, I have no clear idea of the best escape route.

"You won't get away," Raoul says chillingly, retracting the blade and sliding the knife into a jeans pocket.

Storming inside, I look from Raoul to Linus. "What do you plan to do with me?"

Linus answers. "Whatever is necessary." He fishes out a packet of cigarettes, taps one out, slides it between bony fingers and lights up. Immediately, I think of the numerous scars on Tom's arms, cigarette burns, according to Vick.

If I thought begging would do the trick, I'd try, yet I know any appeal to Linus's better nature won't work because he doesn't have one. His only weak chink is his mother. Unlike Raoul, he was firm yet kind with her. He didn't pinch or threaten. He wasn't rough. There was tenderness there.

I jerk my chin in the direction of the door. "If your mum was in her right mind, what would she make of this? Think she'd be proud of you?"

His eyebrows draw together and his mouth tugs and carves ugly lines into his face. "Don't ever speak of her. She did everything for us. *Everything.*"

"And not your father?"

"My father was a deluded, sentimental bastard and he forgave your precious boyfriend."

Fresh fear flares inside. Explains why Geoffrey did not receive star billing in the graveyard.

"Afterwards my fucker of a father disinherited his own flesh and blood." Linus's face is shadowed with decades of resentment and hatred.

"So that's why you stole Tom's inheritance from his parents. You can't bear the thought of him alive and ready to demand its return."

Linus smiles in a way faintly reminiscent of D.I. Falconer – no warmth reflected in his eyes. "Not bad, Miss Outlaw, but you're wrong. Tom, or as you very well know by now, Kit, doesn't have a pot to piss in. Never did."

I blink in confusion. It's freezing in the room yet I pool with perspiration in the small of my back, underneath my arms and down behind my knees. "Then I don't understand."

"Of no consequence." His smile is cold.

While Raoul is physically violent, Linus's brand of brutality is more refined and twisted. What the hell is keeping Jane?

"I have waited almost a lifetime to have what is rightfully mine, my birthright." At the mention of entitlement, Linus's voice assumes an edge sharp with malice. "Waiting a few more days will make no difference to me. Can you wait too?"

I nod blindly.

"It won't be for long. When Kit is dead all will be revealed."

"No," I bellow, "You're crazy. He won't come. You won't ever find him."

"I hope you're wrong, Miss Outlaw. For your sake."

# Chapter 49

The sky was a deadly flat grey by the time Kit returned to the boat. Before he took one step down the pontoon, he hung around and checked to see that his bolthole was safe. Only then did he move.

His arms ached with strain at hauling his booty along a path carved out of a jungle of bracken and nettles. Back in the safety of his nautical lair, he dumped the mailbox on the floor, plumped down and eyed it. Would this unearth treasures, reveal clues, open Pandora's box, a can of worms and all those other idioms? Or would it simply disclose banal day-to-day stuff, meaningless to everyone bar the recipient?

Reaching for the canvas bag he'd found on his arrival, Kit selected a hammer. A ball-peen with an exceptionally long handle, he swung it high and, aiming along the line of the existing aperture, brought it down hard twice, puncturing metal. Next, he dug in with a screwdriver. Finally, using a wrench, he jemmied the facing open enough to extract the mail clinging for dear life inside. Out of seven items, he ejected two straight away on the grounds that they were addressed to 'The Householder'. To be certain, he opened each; one an offer for insurance cover for a boiler, the other a request for support of a charity. The rest, he spread out like a Chinese meal, not quite sure which to sample first. Studying each envelope, four had the plain direct appearance of bills. Of these, three were addressed to Linus, one for Raoul Hernandez, the final communication a letter addressed to Linus from a solicitor based in Llandudno. Kit didn't need a crystal ball or second sight. The stamp on the back told him so. This he would save for last.

Ripping open the first to Linus, he discovered a request for payment from an electrical contractor. Kit's eyes roved through what appeared to be an entire rewiring project. It included RCD protectors, cooker and shower circuits, outside light and power, inside down-lighters and replacement of faulty wiring, certificates of every denomination, and four chandeliers and connection for the same. The total bill was an eye-watering twenty-nine thousand pounds, excluding VAT. Next, a bill for plumbing, covering dozens of items that indicated the entire house had been ripped apart and every flue, feed pipe, cylinder and membrane replaced. In addition, there was an itemised price for a brand-new oil tank and fitting. Sanitary ware took up a second sheet. On a third sheet, a more modest sub-total for guttering and downpipes. The lot rolled in at a shade under fifty thousand pounds, in other words a small fortune.

The third was an estimate for carpets and flooring that ran into a similar amount. Spreading them out before him, Kit simply stared. He'd considered it before but now he had proof: Ursula was dying and Linus was already spending his inheritance.

The envelope marked for Hernandez revealed that he owed several hundred pounds for a selection of Victorian-style mirrors and for paint from a high-end manufacturer. Linus never had a creative bone in his body, so Kit could only surmise that Hernandez was the driving force behind the extensive programme of renovation. Would building works hide the rotten fabric beneath? He didn't think so.

Busting for a pee, he used the head, after which he returned to the legal missive. Exercising care, he poked an index finger underneath the flap and pried it away from the seal, his fingers sliding inside the throat of the envelope to extract the contents. Dated the week before, the letter-writer, a Mr Wyndham Jones, a probate lawyer, firstly thanked Linus for calling in to discuss the position regarding Mrs Verdi and any claim that could be legitimately made on the estate in the event of her demise. Sympathy was offered to the family. *'I was so sorry to hear about Mrs Verdi's failing health...'* Jones then referenced a meeting that had taken place and, *'for clarification's sake, the following is a précis of what was discussed...'*

*'As you will recall, your father's unfortunate suicide does not render his will null and void. It was his express wish for his estate to be put in trust for Ursula Verdi's lifetime, to allow her to live at Vixenhead until she so chose to vacate or downsize. She will live there rent-free as long as she desires, paying council tax, utility bills and outgoings and keeping the house in good repair and insured against fire and other usual risks...'*

Kit tuned out. Why would Geoffrey leave Vixenhead in trust? Why not leave Vixenhead to his wife for her to pass on to Linus and Caro? After all, she was the mother of his children. Kit scrabbled inside his head for a memory that would shed light on his uncle's motivation. It would not come.

He returned to the letter. '*On Mrs Verdi's demise, all property and assets, at the request of Mr Geoffrey Verdi, will be transferred to Kit Trueblood, either to retain or sell…*'

With a stab of realisation, Kit's eyes widened. He gripped the letter so hard his thumb left a dirty mark on the paper. Fuck, Linus and Caro's reaction to such a momentous decision would be explosive and, perhaps, rightly so. No child expects to be cut out of a parent's will. In other circumstances, he would feel sorry.

In these, he didn't.

Feverishly reading on, the killer paragraph occurred on the last page. '*As discussed, Mr Trueblood's whereabouts have not been known for some time. In the event of Mrs Verdi's death, this firm will undertake to make strenuous efforts to contact him. Should we, during the course of our enquiry, discover that Mr Trueblood is deceased, then the estate, in accordance with the terms of your father's will, will be split between yourself and your sister, Miss Caro Verdi.*'

Kit rocked back. All along, he'd been wrong about Linus. He'd believed Linus's sole reason to team up with Swain sprung from obsession and pure malice. Now Kit understood that Linus had more solid and rational reasons for wanting him gone. As long as he was alive, he posed a risk to Linus and Caro's inheritance and future.

Suddenly, the last conversation he'd had with Uncle Geoff before his death emerged from the recess of his mind and formed ice chips in his blood.

He was in his room, alone, as usual, staring at the wall, when he heard a mild tap at the door before it opened.

*"Mind if I come in?"*

*He looked up to see Uncle Geoff 's hesitant, embarrassed expression, and nodded.*

*Straight away he could tell that his uncle was in a funny mood and, given the prevailing climate of desolation, this was quite exceptional. His uncle viewed him with hangdog eyes, crossed the room, patted the bed, gesturing for him to sit close, like they always used to. His boy heart leapt. He did as asked.*

*Immediately, Uncle Geoff put a firm arm around his shoulder and asked him to talk about Linus and how he behaved the night Joshy died. At this, he flinched, rounded his shoulders and stared at his shoes. He'd been through it so many times, both inside his head and to those in authority. Fearing a trap, the last thing he wanted or needed was to go through it all again.*

*"It's all right, Kit," Uncle Geoff said softly, giving his shoulder a gentle squeeze. As soon as his name was mentioned, rather than an anonymous reference to 'the boy,' his pulse raced. He knew things would be all right. "I'm afraid I overheard Linus talking to Caro," Uncle Geoff continued solemnly. "I have a terrible feeling that I've misjudged you. We all have. Am I right?"*

*The dead weight that had hung around his heart slipped its anchor and drifted away, the relief so great that Kit burst into tears. Uncle Geoff pulled out a big white handkerchief and handed it to him. When he stopped crying, little by little, it all came out, the real truth, this time, including the bullying that led up to the fight.*

*"Thank you," uncle Geoff said. "And I promise I'm going to*

*make it right for you." Kit had no idea how his uncle could square it with everyone, but he trusted his uncle with his life. "Now why don't you run outside, take your bike out for a spin around the grounds?"*

*Banned from cycling as part of his punishment, Kit beamed in jubilation. Allowed to ride again meant that he was truly forgiven.*

*He thundered downstairs, slipped outside through the back entrance and galloped across the gravelled drive to one of the barns, where his beloved bike was kept. One look told him he wouldn't be riding any time soon. Both tyres were slashed. Odds-on this was Linus's work, a final 'screw you' before he returned to school. Even this could not put a dent in his mood.*

*Strolling back the long way round, through the extensive grounds, he climbed a tree, hung out there for a bit and then, intent on seeking out his uncle about getting his bike fixed, Kit returned to the house, from where he could hear the mother of all arguments going down. It started on the landing and finished up behind closed doors. Joshua's name was mentioned and so was his. His uncle yelled something about a secret, after which he heard his uncle swear, and that was really rare.*

*A day later, his uncle went into town to attend to what he described as important business. That evening, Uncle Geoff brought a tray of food for both of them to his bedroom, to which he'd been reinstated. Fish and chips washed down with Vimto. Afterwards, they played board games until long after Kit's official bedtime.*

*"Goodness, high time you were in bed, young man," Uncle Geoff said.*

"One last game? Please?"

"Oh, I've already played my last game, Kit," Uncle Geoff said, a sad smile on his face.

"I'll let you win this time," Kit said, drunk on happiness.

"I've already won. You'll see."

Kit never understood what his uncle meant. Not then. Only now.

As Adam Charteris, he was officially deceased, but should he return from the grave and prove it, he stood to benefit on a scale that left him speechless.

Judging by the spending spree, Linus and his boyfriend needed money more than ever. Which was why Linus would stop at nothing to ensure that he stayed dead. Boy, was the bastard in for a shock.

# Chapter 50

Like a high-court judge passing sentence, Linus pronounces, "Take her down."

Raoul unties my ankles and releases me from the chair. If fitter and stronger, I'd make a dash for it. Or would I? There is still the blade to consider and, with my wrists bound, Raoul's powerful body practically manacled to mine, I have little choice other than to comply and let him propel me out of the room, down a wide corridor I don't recognise. Through a door, from which stone steps connect to a musty bottom storey, another door opens out to a narrow passage. Every inch of the way, I memorise.

The air feels static, as if this part of the house is never open to the elements. There is a strong smell of plant mould and decay, like catacombs.

We finish up at a dead end. Nothing but panelling with a fancy design of fox heads carved into the wood. Puzzled, I wonder what happens next. Maybe standing here is a joke designed to wrong-foot me. Or Raoul, with his black eyes and blacker soul, is playing mind games right out of Linus's play list. Sensing this is no time for complacency or acquiescence,

I flick my head hard, smacking Raoul on the chin. Startled, he lets go and I seize the moment and turn. Head throbbing, heart beating, it's as far as I get. Raoul catches hold.

Fear assaults my body. I think about the knife, what he might do to me...

Bright pain explodes across my stomach and I double over, retching.

"Next time, it will be a punch to your kidneys and, believe me, it will hurt more."

Gripping my elbow, dragging me upright, Raoul shackles me to him with the cruel determination of a slave trader. Tears streaming down my face, barely able to breathe, I hobble forward.

Raoul leans toward the fox carving and pushes the flat of an index finger against the vixen's nose. Immediately, as if I'm in a Harry Potter story, the panel slides sideways, creaking and complaining, to reveal an aperture wide enough for two people to walk through side by side. There are stone steps. Dark and rotting. A dungeon.

"No," I shout, my legs rigid, shoulders twisting, shoes sliding; my whole body one big protest. Pointless. Raoul is a citadel whose fortifications can never be breached. Desperate, I sink my teeth into the soft flesh above his arm.

"Bitch," he howls, delivering the promised blow.

Sharp and deep, a combination of stitch and period cramp, the pain is like no other. Had he attached my lumbar region to mains electricity and jump-started me, it could not feel worse. I collapse in agony. Hauled to my feet, Raoul throws me over his shoulder and steps through the entrance to what

I'm sure will be my prison and last resting place. I'm too out of it to think, or see or observe. I am one throbbing mass of writhing agony. Dumped down, white spots dancing before my eyes, the ground rushes up to meet me.

When I come round I'm mercifully alone, the bindings around my wrists are gone, red, angry stripes all that remain.

I lie curled. Muscles in my body spasm and object. Nausea is intense and I fear spitting and peeing blood. I hate Vixenhead. I hate Linus's henchman. I hate Linus Verdi. I hate Tom for ripping up my life. Hate, hate, hate.

My face is cheek-down against a veneer of carpet. There is grit and dirt, and all manner of detritus beneath. Rolling carefully onto my back, I stare up at a single naked illuminated light bulb. I don't think Raoul lit the room as an act of kindness. He did it to enable me to see the mess I'm in. Tears squeeze out of the corners of my eyes and drip, glancing off my chin and onto the floor. I am so very very tired.

Minutes pass or maybe hours, I cannot tell. Eventually, I stir. Pain is chronic rather than acute. Still hurts like nothing I experienced before. Perhaps I'm not cut out for childbirth. Perhaps this is a higher power's way of telling me I'm not fit for purpose.

In misery, I angle my head. Thin light seeps in through one window, which is barred. Beneath it, a camp bed with a dirty sleeping bag folded neatly. There is no pillow. Against one wall, stacked, three deep, cardboard boxes, the type used by removal firms. An old bicycle with slashed tyres rests against another. There's also a metal bucket and, heartbreakingly, an antiquated child's school desk and chair, on which sit a pile of old hardback cookery books, and, fleeting joy, a torch.

Slowly and horribly, I realise that there is no exit. A metal door divides me from the Verdis and the rest of the world. If I scream my lungs out through the bars of the window, nobody will hear. When Jane comes, she will be turned away. When she stands her ground and insists on searching the place, Linus will tell her to be his guest. I am buried alive. And this is what those monsters did to Tom. A kid. A boy. I'm sure of it.

Sharing a snapshot of Tom's real past, his incarceration and isolation, I'm mortified and terrified in equal measure. How fucking dare they.

Sparking with fury borne of despair, I cautiously stagger to my feet. My back and stomach are tender and I find it difficult to move without wincing and triggering a river of pain.

Checking the pockets of my coat, I find a tissue and loose change. My jeans contain an emergency tenner and the cigarette I retrieved from the porch of Stephanie Charteris's house. Crushed and broken in two, it could be construed as symbolic of my situation. I don't carry a penknife, pepper spray or anything I can conceivably use as a weapon.

With a heavy sigh, I think of Tom and wonder if he might come for me. Right now, I want him to get me the hell out of here, for my sake, alone. Real life is tougher than fiction. If I ever escape and see the sun again, I will, like the saying goes, wield my pen, a mightier adversary than the sword.

And whether or not Tom killed Linus's little brother, Joshua, like Ursula said, Linus believes it with all his dark heart. No wonder Geoffrey Verdi was banished to an unloved spot in the graveyard.

Feeling a little more purposeful, I determine to find a way to breathe new life into hope and keep it living. Somehow. Anyhow.

Galvanised, I try the torch. It doesn't work. Inside, there are no batteries. I flip open both desk lids and stare at exercise books for Maths, Geography, History and English. I can tell from the way the writer forms his capital 'D' and lower case 'r' that it's written in Tom's hand. Years span to GCSE level. Textbooks too, including a Welsh primer. If there are any secrets to discover, I won't find them here. Next destination: those cardboard boxes. They could contain junk, bank statements spanning decades, old irrelevant details of ancient lives. They could also conceal evidence that will damn them all to hell.

# Chapter 51

Kit had it worked out: contact Mads and reveal Linus's true agenda. It wouldn't be difficult to spell out exactly why Linus needed him dead. He had no doubt in his mind that, if he broke cover, Linus would attempt to kill him. Only when everything was sorted legally could Kit afford to breathe easy. Even then...

A rush of nausea overwhelmed him. Post-adrenalin dump or fear, he couldn't tell. He did his best to steady himself.

With Mads in tow, he would visit Wyndham Jones in Llandudno and prove through DNA that he was Kit Trueblood, the genuine article, and inheritor of Vixenhead.

He said it out loud. Him. Who would have thought it? What would his mum and dad say if they were alive?

His eyes shut tight to stem a sudden rush of anguish. Screwed his hands into fists, nails biting into soft flesh to ward off memories that howled around inside his brain. Sailing at top level was an expensive business and his father might have been a terrific hotelier, but he wasn't great with money. Too much of a bon viveur, it was rumoured. By the time the debts were covered, there was nothing left. For years he'd been taunted for his parents' lack of financial competence. One of Ursula's many moans, she blamed his mother for her, as she put it, 'gaudy, expensive tastes,' although Kit never understood how she'd arrived at the conclusion – unless there was something he didn't know. And this brought him to another thought that dug in and niggled and would not break loose. Grief was the reason stated for his uncle's suicide. According to a coroner, his uncle had been of unsound mind following Joshua's death. Everybody bought it, including Kit. In the light of his recent discovery, was Uncle Geoff mad when he ensured that Vixenhead and all its assets eventually found their way to his ward? Kit didn't think so and it begged another question: why did his uncle take his own life so soon?

The need to know was as strong as his desire to watch the old house go up in smoke and burn, twisted, charred and blackened, to the ground.

Instinctively, he recognised that such destruction would not help him. This would not be like annihilating the potting shed, as he'd done all those years before, in a cry for help symbolic of his pain. If it were possible for good to emerge from something that was essentially evil, there was no better time. The people not the place were at fault. And they, he thought darkly, would surely pay. Reputation was everything to the Verdis and this he would publicly destroy.

With the money from the sale, he would go to Roz, come clean and beg forgiveness. She would forever retain a special place in his heart and he needed to tell her and she needed to hear. Kit blinked. Roz had been, and still was, an angel on his shoulder. Shame stalked him again for her loyalty in the face of his treachery and for her love when he couldn't love her enough and in the way that she most desired.

Resigned and, with everything mapped out, he allowed the waves rocking the boat to lull him to sleep. His last waking thoughts, before finally dropping off: there were secrets stowed in Vixenhead's ruined heart yet to be revealed.

He had no idea for how long he was asleep. Judging by the light bleeding through the hatch window, dawn had long broken and worked a full shift. There were things to do, chapters to close, but he lay awhile, marvelling at the spectacular turn of events, daring to dream of futures and not the past.

In a moment of reverie, he imagined starting over, knowing those he loved would all be safe, heart swelling with rapture at the thought.

Scratching his head lazily, the hair on his shaved scalp was already growing back and itched. His chin had several days' worth of beard. With his smelly clothes, now too big for him, he looked a right heap. He planned to ask Mads to bring him a clean sweater, jeans and underwear. Pushing himself up, he crawled out of the bunk, pushed open the double doors and...

"Hello, Kit."

# Chapter 52

I am weary. Cold. Hungry. Despondent.

I hoped for handwritten notes, photographs and letters. I found old Christmas decorations, camping gear, a brown-leather school satchel circa 1960, cut-glass decanters and porcelain, light bulbs, paintings that look as if a five year-old had knocked them up, six boxes of cheap paperbacks with covers depicting women in jeopardy and with brown and curling inside pages, general tat and crap that should be stored in a skip. I was deluded to ever imagine a smoking gun.

I need a pee. I view the bucket with disgust. Then I have a better idea. Picking it up, I bash it long and loud against the fortified door. Metal against metal. Surely, someone will hear? I keep the din up until my arm is aching and I am bursting. Dismayed, I give in, squat and use my only tissue. Urinating hurts like hell, as if I'm pissing glass. I want to cry and do.

Tears reduced to dry sobs, I glance at my watch. Coming up for noon, and with nothing to eat since yesterday, no wonder I'm starving, although time has no relevance down here. No day, no night. Simply one hour drifting interminably into another. I'll probably go mad first, like Ursula upstairs, before my heart gives out or I starve or die of thirst.

Noise.

I glance towards the source, the entry to my tomb. Two bolts shoot back. The door chimes opens and Linus stands before me. No match for Raoul's physicality, a tall and skinny man, he should be less frightening than he is. Saliva dries on my tongue. I find it hard to swallow and, involuntarily, take three steps back.

"Come with me," he orders.

Part of me wants to stay right where I am. In here, I'm safe from harm. In here, there are no tricks. If I go with him, it must be into a trap. I remain rooted.

"What are you waiting for? I won't hurt you."

His smile is vile and I don't believe him. He has something planned. I know it. With Raoul, I understand where I am. Violence is his beat. Linus is different. A destroyer of minds, not bodies.

The smile falls off his face. "Don't vex me. There is no escape. Every exit is locked, including windows. Your only hope would be to depart from one of the towers, a drop of at least thirty feet. Now move." He steps aside and gestures for me to go first, curiously and worryingly polite.

I do as I'm told. When I pass Linus to climb the steps, I feel his rank breath on my face. My knees clash together and tremble.

Light from the corridor spills down the staircase, guiding my way. When I reach the top, I hesitate, unsure.

"Keep going." Linus digs into me hard with blunt fingers.

Pain discovers a circuit along my back, flashing through nerve endings and fusing my injured kidneys.

I walk mechanically, taut and tense, primed for a blow from behind, another blitz of pain.

Following the route I took with Raoul earlier, I reach the ground floor and corridor with ancestral portraits. At one end is a staircase. Linus indicates that I take it. From somewhere above, I catch the sound of music. With each step, the volume grows louder. It's Old Blue Eyes, I realise, singing 'My Way' and rambling about having 'few regrets', Tom's strange hang-up to the point of phobia suddenly explained. With dread, I stumble on.

The house slowly wakes. It has a rhythm of its own, offbeat and out of time. Walls writhe. Carpets the colour of blood murmur. Starved of heat and hungry, fireplaces open their jaws wide. Everywhere I hear the taunts of children, the bully's whine and victim's cry.

Opening out onto another corridor, Vixenhead is a Rubik's cube and as impossible to fathom.

Linus creeps past me and opens a door to a small room, by which I mean it isn't as big as the rest. After the prison experience, it's like a palace. Inside is a Minster fireplace, the grate and log basket empty. A stepladder perches against a wall and half the ancient wallpaper is stripped and in tatters on the floor. Black mould dapples the area beneath the coving. The air stinks of it and it outclasses the aroma of sugar soap.

In hope of spotting a sharp-edged scraper, I scope the room – nothing other than a sponge and cloth. Better news: a refectory table and a small tray of food for one.

My stomach growls in anticipation. To stay in the game, I must eat and drink. Silently requesting permission, I glance at Linus. He nods with a grave expression. Controlling. Not only lord of Vixenhead but master of all who enter its portals, dominator of my digestive tract too.

I fall on the food. There is bread and butter, two Rich Tea biscuits and a glass of water. I consume the lot in record time, concerned that, at any second, Linus will whip it away. Next, I attempt to engage him.

"How did Kit ever escape this stronghold?"

Linus flicks a smile. He appreciates my description of his fortified home. "He tried many times. Many times I brought him back." Pride swells his sharpened features.

"Apart from the last occasion."

"He got lucky," he glowers. "Fortune smiled on him in the shape of a violent criminal. Ironic, really. In a small community like this, it's impossible to hide an event like that."

"You mean too much of a coincidence that Kit should disappear on the same day as a road-rage incident?"

"It claimed a local man's life. The place was alive with chatter. When police appealed for *other* witnesses, my mother realised that there was at least one. Didn't take much to work out who."

"So the law spirits Kit away."

"Only for a while," Linus said, cunning in his eyes. "Swain used every contact he had." Including a man called Chace, I remember. Mike Shenton was right about that. So right about many things. Mike doesn't have a corrupt cell in his body; he was simply trying to hammer home the impossible odds stacked against me. "Swain never bought that Kit was dead."

"You struck up a friendship with Swain?" Keep Linus talking, keep him engaged.

"Only until his ticker gave out. Kit made the mistake of coming back. Had Kit stayed dead, like he should have done, we might have spared him."

Surprised Linus discloses so much, I realise bleakly that he has no intention of me leaving.

The music abruptly stops and the ceiling shakes, plaster cascading down like face powder. Someone is dropping heavy items and smashing glass. It sounds as if upstairs is being torn apart by ram-raiders. I glance up at the fearful commotion erupting above my head. The loudest noise, by far, is Ursula screaming. And it's getting louder.

"Stay here," Linus commands, stalking out, slamming the door shut after him.

I fully expect him to lock it. Distracted and furious, he doesn't bother. I count to ten and then move.

# Chapter 53

"Mads," Kit gasped. "I've never been so pleased to see anyone." From the expression on her smooth features, he couldn't claim, hand on heart, that Mads felt the same way. To be fair, most times it was hard to tell what she thought. He never knew her real name and wouldn't be surprised if she had as many identities as the people she was paid to protect. It added to her generally elusive persona. "How did you find me?"

"It's my job to find you."

"Were you followed?"

"Not that I'm aware of."

"Did you see anyone, anyone at all?"

She thought for a moment. "A kid on a bike, an old man walking a dog and a woman my age on a mobile phone walking away from the hotel. Nothing spooky. More to the point," she said, glancing around the interior of the boat, "is this yours?"

He hung his head.

"Thought so. Christ, do I have to add breaking and entering to your—"

"Sod that. Are Stephanie and Zoe okay?"

"Like I told you on the phone, relax. They're fine."

Kit briefly felt the strain release from his body. Then another thought occurred. "Does Steph still believe I'm dead?"

"She does."

"Then how did you explain the need to protect her?"

"With a little verisimilitude. My stock-in-trade," she said with a short smile. "Told her that we'd received information about an anonymous threat. Nothing that would get Stephanie too rattled."

His face fell. "She'll be petrified."

"She's more grounded than you appear to think. Like I said, everything is cool."

"Is she seeing someone else?" It was stupid to enquire. Couldn't help himself. Selfish of him, too. He genuinely wanted Steph and Zoe to be happy, but...

"Funnily enough, she never said," Mads said tartly, leaning back, her leather jacket creaking. "The good news is that Swain's dead. Heart attack."

"I know. Read it in a newspaper." Kit met her eye. It was the only way to deal with Mads. Brazen it out. Lie for Lie. He didn't want her finding out that he'd been drawn to Vixenhead to eavesdrop, to spy, to plot vengeance.

She looked him up and down and arched a perfect eyebrow. "You have a nice body, but are you going to put on some clothes?"

Kit flicked a smile. Same old Mads. Straight to the point. "I was going to contact you so that you could bring me some new gear."

"I assume you mean jeans and t-shirt and not drugs?"

"I'm not using."

"You've certainly lost weight." She said it in a way that implied she didn't wholly believe he was clean. That was the other thing about Mads, Kit thought, meeting her level gaze. Cynicism was built into her DNA. Queen of Cool.

"Go on, shove a sweater on, at least. Is there anything to drink around here?" She dubiously eyed the surroundings.

"Used the last of the water for a brew, but there's a couple of bottles of soft drink." Kit reached across and into a locker. Taking a bottle-opener from a drawer, he popped the lids.

"I see you've made yourself at home," she said dryly.

He shot her a wonky smile. "Here," he said, pushing a Sprite into her hand.

She chinked her bottle against his, took a swig and fixed him with a penetrating gaze. "Like to tell me what the hell is going on?"

"Let me get some clothes on first," he said, snapping another smile.

"Be quick. I don't want some irate boat-owner catching me."

He was.

Sitting down opposite her to better study the generous mouth that so rarely smiled, he said nothing for the simple reason that he felt empowered for a change.

"Well," she said. "I'm waiting."

"You, first."

"Dear God, you know that isn't how it works, Kit."

He did. Mads would only tell him what she wanted him

to know in any case, but he felt drunk on opportunity and the possibility of getting his life back. "Roz followed me here."

Mads shook her head. "Too bad."

"Won't do," he said sharply. "How come she didn't get the same treatment as Steph?"

"My first priority was, and is, you."

It didn't answer his question. It barely even made a damn stab at it. "You left her twisting in the wind." There was more than an accusatory note in his voice.

"We did everything that was necessary," she said, throwing him a direct *don't fucking challenge my judgement* look. "Sorted a backstop for when she asked police too many questions in Gloucestershire."

Kit jolted in astonishment. "She went to the police?"

"Not that this deterred her."

"What do you mean?"

"She traced Stephanie."

"Jesus Christ." Kit flashed back to the moment Roz caught him in the kitchen with Reg's laptop. Him: unable to resist a look at Steph on Facebook; Roz: unable to resist seeing what he was up to.

"Amazingly, she didn't play the sisterhood card or claim to be a wronged woman," Mads continued. "Stephanie has no idea who Roz is."

Yet still she tracked him down, Kit thought, overwhelmed once more by the strength of Roz's passion for truth, and yes, for him. Isn't that why he was drawn to her in the first place?

"My only interest in Roz," she said, "was to get a lead on where you might go and how to find you."

"And did she deliver?"

"No."

Mads's plain denial was deliberate. It begged a question to which Kit already knew the answer. Linus provided the clue, not Roz. Mads had simply followed his trail. He *thought*.

"Something I need to know," Kit said, "What happened before, when you moved me on the first time?"

"You know what happened."

Kit shook his head. "There was no administrative error, was there?"

When Mads replied, her mouth was so set, the words struggled to pass through her teeth. "Okay," she said shortly, "Someone on the original team had a connection to Swain."

"A copper? Jesus."

"Dealt with."

"Are you sure?"

"Certain. Corruption is not responsible for this," she said, eyeing his surroundings.

Still didn't explain how she'd rumbled his new nautical sleeping quarters. He asked her.

"I have Edwyn Thomas to thank for that."

Every blood capillary in his face drained of colour. Mads placed the bottle carefully on the galley table, folded her arms. "Don't pretend you don't know who I'm talking about."

"What have you done to him?"

"Nothing yet. I'm still thinking."

"You can't charge him."

"I think you'll find I can. Perverting the course of justice is my current favourite."

314

"He's an old man, a good man. He pretended to be my guardian to protect me. If you'd found out I'd been living with the Verdis, you might have talked to them. I couldn't afford for you to gamble with my life, to take that risk." His composure gone, he was blabbering.

"Why didn't you tell me the truth in the beginning?"

"You would never have believed it."

"Because," Mads said, her voice a blunt instrument, "you had something to hide."

Kit raised his hands, palms up. "I can explain."

"You damn well better. And you can tell me about Linus Verdi too. I want to know precisely why he visited Garry Swain in prison."

# Chapter 54

All hell breaks loose, Linus drowned out by Ursula's sibilant high-pitched screams. Tip-toeing, I creep along the passage and then run, scooting down the staircase, mentally ticking off landmarks: the grandfather clock, the chandelier that hangs in the great hall, the huge Inglenook, each of them staging posts for the journey in and, now, the journey out.

The front door is all that stands between liberation and me. I'm like a tuning fork, quivering head to toe with feverish anticipation. Consumed by the thought of flight. My hand reaches. I flick back the Yale lock, depress the handle, fling open the door, inhale the scent of familiar perfume, and gasp.

"Thank God," I say, spirits lifting and flying high. I pay no attention to the military-style coat with the epaulettes on the shoulders, the super-high stilettoes. I'm saved. That's all I think. "Quick, we have to get out of here. I'll explain, but we must go right away."

Behind me I hear Linus call, "For God's sake, what does Miss Houdini think she's doing? Stop her, will you, Caro?"

Jumbled thoughts crash into each other. I mentally screech to a halt. The woman I know as Jane closes in, dagger heels clicking. She gives me an almighty shove in the middle of my chest with a fist inside a leather glove, brick-red and similar in hue to her lipstick. With Linus behind me, I have nowhere else to run.

# Chapter 55

"They locked you up for six years?"

"Almost seven."

After he told his story he thought Mads would recoil with shock and disbelief, perhaps a long, slow sigh. Her cool-blue eyes simply drilled into his. "Nobody knew?"

Kit shrugged. "People suspected."

"Like Edwyn?"

He swallowed. Without Edwyn backing him up, he was sure the Verdis would have found some way to prevent him from testifying so that they could keep him as their slave at Vixenhead for the rest of his life. "It's why I confided in him."

"Before or after you first came to us?"

"After." It was Edwyn who found a boat for him to hide in for a week, Edwyn who brought him food every day.

"Hmm." Mads tapped the table with her fingers. Maybe she bought it. Maybe, she didn't. "And the kid?"

"Joshua," he reminded her sharply.

"You played no part in his death?"

"How many more times?" Kit burst out. "See, I knew you wouldn't believe me. That's why I never mentioned a word.

318

Nobody ever *listened*. Jesus Christ, Mads, don't you think I haven't gone over it a thousand times? When everyone believes you're guilty, and you're only a child, it's hard to maintain your innocence. That's why I felt responsible. I still do."

She leant forward, raking his face for lies. "But you said you didn't kill him."

"I did not kill him."

"You harmed him."

"Yes, yes, yes."

"Calm it, Kit, and for God's sake, sit down."

Belligerently, he obeyed.

Mads looked at him for a long long time. "You must understand, I have to nail the facts."

"Yeah, yeah, your job on the line and all that."

She shot him a caustic look. "That's beneath you."

Jaw grinding, teeth hurting, blood rising, he stared her down, *fuck you* scrawled all over his face.

Seemingly impervious, determined to break the deadlock and get what she wanted, or so it seemed, she reminded him with two words. "Linus Verdi."

"What of him? I've told you everything you need to know."

"Do you have the letters?"

"Yes."

"Show me."

He disappeared into the fore cabin, retrieved and handed her the mail. Watching her; left knee jabbering, fists air-drumming 'Stockholm Syndrome', a track from his favourite Muse CD. Mads read each in turn carefully and without expression.

"Okay," she said, spreading them out on the table. "Much of it's circumstantial, but I see what you mean."

"Can you at least vouch for me with the solicitor?"

"I can, but we need to think this through."

"Fuck it, Mads, what's there to think about? I've wasted enough of my life already."

"For a start," she said, tapping the solicitor's letter, "Ursula Verdi isn't dead. Only when she pops parks her clogs do you inherit Vixenhead."

"But I need to let Jones know that I'm alive and kicking now." If only, to scupper Linus's plans and wipe the smirk from his sad fucking face.

"But there's no mad rush," she said smoothly. "Never let irritation cloud judgement."

Kit silently cursed. It was all right for Mads. She didn't have his life.

"Seriously, Kit, you have so much anger in you."

Her supple smile and poise in the face of his rage nearly did him in. "I don't have anything else."

"If you're to survive in the real world, it needs taming."

"It's anger that's kept my heart beating."

"And will give you a heart attack."

"I'm not Garry Swain," he shouted in her face, catching taking both of them off guard.

He caught a flash of fear in her eyes, which surprised him. Is this how others saw him? To be walked around and feared? Would he ever fit in? Damaged, could he ever go back to Stephanie? Would she want him? What about Roz? Could they still be friends? He couldn't blame her if she never wanted to see him again. He scrubbed at his face with his hands.

"I'm sorry," he said. "Truly. I just need a moment."

When Mads spoke next she softened her voice, dialled back the tone. "I'm speaking to you as a friend, Kit, for your own good."

"You're not my friend, Mads," he said, sober and without emotion. "We have a working relationship. That's all."

She shook her head, as if she didn't have a clue what to do with him. "Come on," she said, standing up. "Get your stuff and then you need to get your shit together. We'll figure a way out of this, I promise."

Reluctant, he glanced up, briefly closed his eyes, let out a breath. In the end, he had to admit that Mads was all he had.

"How does a long soak and a hot meal sound?"

"Where?" he smiled doubtfully.

"Llandudno?" Her eyes sparked with humour, a rare sight.

Eager to get going before she changed her mind, he stood up. "Give me a tick."

"I'll take these," she said, sweeping up the letters, sliding them into her bag, "See you outside. It stinks in here."

Kit flicked her a grin, grabbed his rucksack and, gathering up his things, stuffed them inside. As an afterthought, following Mads' lecture, he rolled up the sleeping bag. Picking up the remains of last night's makeshift dinner to put it in the trash, he heard a dull thud and turned.

Mads gaped back, wide-eyed, as if she was as startled as he to find herself back inside the boat. Staggering, she tried to speak, but blood filled her mouth and coated her teeth. More blood pumped from a gash to her neck. Her right hand clutched at it, but nothing could stop the dizzying flow of bright, oxygenated gore. He started toward her. Didn't think how it had happened, only that it had. He caught hold, taking her full weight as her legs buckled.

Laying her down in the galley, he grabbed a tea towel, pressed it hard to the wound. It soaked through within seconds. Immediately, he flashed back to the road, Jack Prior fighting to stay alive. Blood. Blood everywhere.

Mads' breathing was ragged and shallow, her face ashen, life and vitality draining out of her. "Stay with me, Mads," he shouted, desperate to keep her conscious. He looked for her bag but it wasn't on her. Burrowing into her pocket for a phone, he discovered it wasn't there. "Shit," he cried, "Shit, shit." Even if he could make an emergency call, he recognised it would be too late.

Her eyelids flickered and she tried to say something again. It came out as a gargle.

"Hush," he said, gathering her to him, cradling her head. "It will be all right. It will be all right." With so much sudden loss of fluid, her temperature plummeted. He hugged her to him, trying to share warmth from his body with hers. Pressure on his chest, he sensed she was trying to move and drew away. Her bloodied hand briefly gripped his sleeve. He watched her eyes roll, glassy and unable to focus, drifting off into another time zone, another universe, infinity, heaven.

With a tiny shudder, her hand dropped and her head lolled to one side. When her half-closed eyes assumed a similar dull, opaque hue to Joshua's, he thought his mind would break in two.

Clutching the dead woman to him, Kit howled with impotent rage. Crazed, he was more than ready when a shadow walked along the pontoon and prepared to enter his world.

# Chapter 56

Kit lunged, grabbed a pair of man's legs and dragged the rest of him down into the boat with a crash. A blade missed Kit's eye by a feather's depth. First principle up against a weapon: run. Kit would have run like hell, but was effectively penned in, with nowhere to flee. Those who wield a knife rarely stab, the idea to frighten and intimidate a victim. Bollocks to that. The man squaring up to him was a determined killer, the evidence lying bleakly on the bunk beside them. Raoul was not going to stop now.

Kit backed away from the stern towards the bow. With so much blood, his trainers slipped and slid along the galley floor. In an effort to maintain his balance, he didn't glance left and right, his eyes fixed only on the man in front, a muscular towering presence, heavier set and more fit than Kit ever could or wished to be.

Adrenaline pooling around his kidneys, snarling and snapping through his bloodstream, jacking up his heart rate, Kit danced from one foot to the other, doing his best to look tough, playing to the man's ego, hoping Raoul's arrogance would be his undoing.

Dark-eyed, Raoul jabbed the air and came at him. Speed his ally, it became his enemy as Raoul slithered, caught the galley stove with his boot, bounced off and fell down onto one knee. Frenzied, Kit thrust out his leg, the top of his trainer connecting under Raoul's chin. Powerful enough to stun, it was nowhere near enough to disable his adversary, but it dislodged the knife, which skittered along the floor. Tempted to stoop and grab it, yet fearing it would give Raoul an opportunity to sweep him off his feet and onto his back, Kit trapped it with his foot, kicking it away. Buoyed by his insane good fortune, Kit returned for an encore. He twisted to the side, rotated his hips and swung his leg again, attacking with the side of his foot, smacking the centre of Raoul's forehead.

Punch-drunk, Raoul dropped to his other knee, body swaying. Fired up, Kit grabbed the other man's ears, pulled his head down sharply as he brought his own knee up to greet Raoul's chin for a second time. The effect was immediate and overwhelming. Raoul toppled over backwards, eyes tight shut.

Breathing hard, Kit bent over, kneecaps throbbing, stress hormones dumping their payload all over his body, but chiefly his gut. Should be the end of it. Should do what all sensible men do and leave. He had seconds rather than minutes and in seconds he could make good his escape. He knew this. He also knew that, with Mads dead, his position was significantly weakened. He looked at her, lying there. What was she, thirty-eight, forty? He'd known her for a decade and knew not the faintest fact about her. He didn't know whether she had a man or husband, a child who would miss her, whether she was straight or gay. How crap was that? The horror and waste of it struck him with the force of a volcano erupting after a century's long sleep.

Pumped up, seeking vengeance for Mads, for him and his shitty life, Kit dropped down on top of his enemy, energy powering through, with the intention of using his weight to smash the prone man's ribs.

Pain shot through his testicles. He screamed out as Raoul raised himself off the floor, features blurring into a stagnant pool of snarling hate. Next, a blow to Kit's temple sent him sprawling. Face down, breathing and inhaling fresh blood that did not belong to him. He raised his head, shook it, tried to concentrate and blot out the fire raging through his genitals. If his adversary got to his feet while he lay prone, he was finished. Raoul would not hesitate to snatch the knife and go in for the kill.

Raoul stood up. Mighty. Vengeful. Triumphant.

Using the confined space, fighting against the burning in his balls, Kit rolled to the side and pressed his back hard against the bunk, thrust his leg out and caught Raoul sharply on the shin. Raoul dropped his head, hesitated for a fraction of a second. All it took for Kit to jack himself up enough to launch his fists at his enemy's groin. As the Frenchman screamed, Kit shambled struggled to his feet.

Darkness in his eyes, death in the snarl, Raoul miraculously found and changed up to sixth gear. Went for him. Kit felt the air close in, as Raoul inhabited it with every fibre of his being. Kit could smell and virtually taste the man. Blow traded with blow, knuckles cracking, bleeding, bruising. The restricted space filled with the noise of men grunting, slugging it out. For Kit, it was like hitting an ox with a peashooter. Raoul was stronger, more skilled and knew where to land a punch.

"Come on," Raoul taunted, palms up, fingers curled. "Let's see what you've got."

Fired up, desperate, and losing all sense of reason, he took a swing. Mistake. Raoul dodged, grabbed hold and linked one arm around Kit's neck, the man's bony wrist pressed hard against his throat. Kit twisted and turned, sank his nails into Raoul's arm, but nothing could break the man's grasp.

It got worse. Clasping his hands together for maximum effect, Raoul pulled back, severely limiting Kit's chance to retaliate.

Pressure. Vanishing air. Spots. Floaters. Eyes popping. Throat closing. Feet sliding. Dying, Kit thought, I'm dying. In seconds I'll be with Joshua, Uncle Geoff and Mads in whatever passes for an afterlife. Instantly, her words haunted him. *Never let irritation cloud judgement.* Flicking a glance to the right towards the cooker and, fighting every survival instinct, he let his body relax, his limbs weaken, feigning supplication and death. When Raoul's hold slackened, releasing his grip, Kit lurched backwards and whiplashed his skull into Raoul's nose, with the accuracy of a bull's eye. There was a loud crack followed by a scream of rage or pain, or both.

Blood pouring.

Raoul yelling.

Everything accelerating.

Kit made a grab for the fire extinguisher to his right, unhooked it and swung at Raoul's head.

Collapse was instant, the noise of a strong man falling unconscious like the sound of demolition. Kit shot a hand to his throat and gulped in air.

Shaking himself together, he picked through Raoul's pockets and found a wallet stuffed with twenties, a credit card, driving licence and mobile phone. He scrolled through contacts, found Linus on speed dial.

Slipping wallet and phone into his rucksack, he stripped off Raoul's jacket and hoodie, slid his arms underneath Raoul's armpits and dragged him into the fore cabin. Hefting him up on the bunk, he put him in a recovery position; he didn't want him dead for the sole reason that he wanted Raoul to take the full weight of the law for the murder of Kit's protection officer. The hatch was too small for Raoul to escape through when he regained consciousness and, not for one second did Kit imagine him shouting for help with the body of his victim lying close by.

Closing the door, Kit secured it with rope, running one end to the single tap over the sink, tying it off, and the other looped over a rack for books and magazines fixed to the cabin wall.

A furtive glance outside and, waiting for two women to pass along the quay, he darted on deck, grinding his jaw at the spatter of fresh bloodstains, the trail of a dying, wounded woman plain to see.

Stepping around them, onto the pontoon, he jumped onto the gangway and, lying belly down, trailed his hands and arms in the water. Mads' blood mingled with his, briefly turning the blue-green water red, and, eventually, dispersing.

Dipping back into the boat, he changed into Raoul's jacket and hoodie. Tempted to take the knife, he left it where it fell, leaving the police to join the dots. Then he climbed the steps without looking back.

He struck out for the quayside and open road. A single yellow line to prevent parked cars did not dissuade the driver of a yellow Ford Fiesta. Roz, he realised, recognising the registration. Amazed at her sleuth-like powers of deduction, he angled his head, scanned the surroundings, expecting, wanting and needing to see a bundle of darting energy underneath a bright-red mane of hair. He saw seagulls wheeling in the wind, a guy in black with a hotel logo on his fleece, a delivery van and a car with a Belgian number plate. No sign of the woman he'd so recently abandoned. No sign of his lover.

Using Raoul's phone, he made two calls: the first to the police to anonymously report a crime at the marina: the second to Roz.

# Chapter 57

'Jane' is Caro Verdi.

If someone told me how I would react in a situation like this, I'd put money on me losing the power of speech and movement. Correct in every detail, bar the terrible sense of revulsion I feel.

Instantly connecting events, timelines, truth and numerous lies, a more sobering realisation is that there is nobody to rescue me against two devious and deadly individuals. I take a smart step sideways, Linus and Caro flanking me, the door impossibly out of reach.

"I see you've already had the pleasure of my brother's company," she says, with a condescending smile.

"Bitch."

"Watch your mouth," Linus threatens.

"Screw you, you freak."

He takes a swing. Caro grabs his arm. "Stop." Practical. Imperious. Cool. "Where's mother?"

"Upstairs," he says, panting at me with hatred. "Had to heavily sedate her after she smashed up her room again. Poor darling is quite distressed."

"Looking for those bloody letters, I daresay. She'll have a job. I hid them well."

Linus shoots her a look. If one expression could say *Shut the fuck up*, Linus wears it. Caro casts him a haughty stare in response.

"Where's Raoul?"

"Following your orders, as agreed."

I blanche and glance from one to the other. What orders? Caro nods with a slow, satisfied expression. There is strange chemistry between these two. Caro is dominant but, like spree killers, each feeds off energy from the other. God only knows what they plan for me. Whatever it is, it cannot be good. A tremor of panic seizes hold, narrows my airways, caving in my chest.

"Let me go," I plead. "If you release me, I swear I won't go to the police. I won't say a word." It's like talking to chairs. "Nobody got hurt," I stress, flashing a frozen smile, attempting to prevent my voice from wobbling and climbing higher.

Caro tugs at the fingers of her brick-red gloves, slips them off and smiles. Really smiles. Teeth on display. A younger version of Ursula in appearance. I wonder if she too will lose her mind when she's older. I bloody hope so. "Shall we tell her, Linus?" she says. There's a grim flirty twist about the way she talks to her brother. Again, I'm reminded of Ursula and the way in which she made eyes at Raoul. 'Dysfunctional' does not describe this family. Sickened, I imagine all sorts.

"Tell me what?" I stammer.

"You are the remaining loose end," he says.

"And loose ends must be tied off," Caro chips in, as though

I am a boat to be tethered to a mooring, except I believe they plan to sink me.

"Why?" I burst out. "I haven't hurt you. I've done nothing wrong. I never breathed a word to the police. I did as you said."

"Not the point, I'm afraid," Caro says, not sounding sorry at all. "It's like this…" A phone rings, the tone familiar because, I realise, with a start, it belongs to my mobile. I pray it's Vick, or Reg, or God help me, Mum – anyone who can fathom that things aren't right and sound the alarm. I fill my lungs with air, ready to scream.

Linus and Caro trade puzzled looks. He slips my phone from his pocket, glances at the number on the screen, and relaxes. "Raoul," he explains to Caro. "Presumably to announce mission accomplished."

Caro arches an eyebrow. "Why doesn't he phone your mobile?"

Breath popping, I wonder the same. Linus shrugs and, raising the phone to his ear, listens for a few seconds and frowns big time.

"What's the matter?" Caro says.

Linus mutters darkly, puts the mobile on speakerphone and places it on a circular table the size of a child's paddling pool. At its centre, an antique Chinese vase containing a lavish flower arrangement. In a savage moment, I have an urge to sweep it off and smash it into dozens of expensive pieces. I want the carpet soaked. I want broken, exotic flowers strewn. I want chaos wrought on these nutters.

"Who is this?" a voice demands. "I want to speak to Roz."

When I hear Tom my heart somersaults and backflips. "Tom, it's me," I yell, intoxicated and irrepressible. "I'm here, at Vixenhead. The Verdis have kid…"

"Shut up," Linus snaps, silencing me with a look that could freezes plasma in major arteries.

"Linus, you bastard," Tom's voice bellows. "If you hurt one…"

"Where's Raoul?" He eyeballs Caro, who doesn't speak.

"Talking to the police, Linus." Thank God. First, I thrill that Tom has the drop on them. Second, imminent liberation waits around the corner.

Linus's features narrow to a collection of slits and edges. "Telling them what exactly?"

"You really need me to spell it out? How you gave the order to kill me."

My brain thunders. Were these the orders that Linus mentioned, *Caro's orders*? I stare at her cold, bloodless lips. Devoid of lipstick, they recede into her face. She stares straight back with such power; I shrink inside.

"Impossible to kill a dead man, Kit."

"Is that why Raoul murdered my protection officer instead?"

Oh God. My eyes snap wide. Linus's translucent cheeks change to the colour of mushroom skin. Caro doesn't look too well either. Not part of their plan. Anxiety drips off the pair of them and stains the furniture, the carpet, the works. Hurrah.

"I'm not responsible for his actions," Linus blusters, standing his ground. "What Raoul does has no connection to me."

Not *us*. Not *my sister and me*. Linus is the worst sort of creep. Always getting others to do his dirty work. Always shifting the blame. A thought ignites. Did Linus play a part in Joshua's death and point the finger at Kit? Little Joshua was found outside the tent, according to Roy, the doorman. Did Linus trick the lad? I wouldn't put it past him. But then I remember him talking about Kit killing 'my little brother.' A genuine endearment, or smokescreen?

"It has everything to do with you. Don't make things worse. Let Roz go."

Linus stalls, looks to Caro, who leans across towards the phone. "Kit, it's me," she says.

I want to cheer him on, tell him not to lose his bottle, that these weirds can be defeated, including Caro uber-frigging-cool Verdi. Yet, from the ensuing dramatic pause, Caro's intervention shakes things up in Kit's world.

"Linus is right," she continues silkily, ignoring the grimace deforming her brother's thin lips. "Neither of us wishes to hurt you, or," she says with a dead-eyed stare, "Roz, for that matter."

"Liar. She's a liar, Kit." Addressing him by his real name for the very first time feels awfully strange. I hope it doesn't go unnoticed and creates the greatest impact. Fully expecting him to respond, to reassure, he says not one single word.

"However," Caro says, filling the gap and darting me a look that would snap steel. "There are things that need to be discussed. Family matters," she adds delicately.

"Like ignoring your father's wishes and removing me from the line of direct inheritance?"

Caro locks eyes with Linus. Reeling, I see it all. Geoffrey Verdi left Vixenhead to Kit. The revelation unlocks other possibilities. What other secrets are contained inside Vixenhead's dark, malfunctioning heart?

"We have no desire to be draconian," Caro says, oh-so reasonable and matter of fact. "We simply wish for Vixenhead to remain in the Verdi family. I'm sure we can come to an arrangement that works for all of us."

"Like buying me out?"

Linus shakes his head so hard, I think it might spin off his thin shoulders.

"Why not?" She flicks a cool smile. "We're open to suggestions," she says, persisting under the flow of negatives discharging from her brother. Crossed arms. Rounded shoulders. Veins popping in his neck. His face one big fuck-off NO.

"You're lying, Caro."

Exactly. Why doesn't Kit acknowledge me? Why doesn't he say my name? *Because he doesn't love you. Because he never loved you. Because you were simply there.*

*Fuck him.*

*But he's my only one-way ticket out.*

"I'm telling the truth, Kit. We all have so much to gain," Caro says.

"Aren't you forgetting something?" I hear Kit say. "Ursula isn't dead."

"Her health isn't great. She's a sick woman."

I open my mouth to blurt out that Ursula is being drugged and catch Linus's haunted, pained expression. Caro might

335

plan to hasten their mother's death, but Linus would stand in her way. I look straight at him and speak.

"Caro will k...'

The air disturbs and a sharp-nailed slap to the side of my face powers through my jaw, splitting my lip, rattling my teeth and briefly blurs my vision.

Caro stares through me and continues, as though nothing happened. "Look at it this way, we all get to benefit." For a moment I forget that she is talking about the death of her mother. She sounds as if she is discussing a trade deal.

"I have no love for Ursula," Kit says gravely, "but..."

"Remember how you loved me? Remember the fun we had? I miss you, darling? Don't you miss me too?"

I freeze. Tension wraps a chain around my head that bites into my skin. When Kit doesn't respond, she laughs, a strange hissing noise, as though her brain is unaccustomed to sending messages to contract her diaphragm and express joy.

"What's there to miss? You and Linus can go to hell. I'm never setting foot in Vixenhead."

Caro's laugh vanishes. Me? I'm horrified. Kit doesn't love me – I get that – but how can he abandon me to a couple of depraved ghouls? The chain around my head tightens. *Because that's what he does. That's how he operates. He's a runner not a keeper.*

"Not wise, Kit. You forget that we have Miss Outlaw."

"Kit, please," I burst out. "Don't leave me."

"Sorry Roz, but I can't help you."

"You must," I plead. Tears spring from my eyes. Snot oozes from my nose. I rave with panic.

Caro speaks, "Kit, you know very well what..."

"Damn you, Caro. Do as you please. I have an appointment to keep with Wyndham Jones."

The call ends.

Lightheaded, struggling for mental footholds, I tell myself that I'm delusional. Kit didn't really say those words. He didn't mean them. He probably already informed the police, explained the urgency. They'll arrive in double-quick time, right? Yes, that's it. He's staying away so that the police can swarm all over the Verdis and their blasted haunted house. Then I remember what Raoul said, that the Verdis would simply lock me up, fabricate a story and send any cops making enquiries on their jolly way. And where is Kit now? Why isn't he with Raoul and assisting the police? Please God, make Mike Shenton come to the rescue. Why oh why did I cut him off? Inwardly, I scream HELP. Outwardly, I stare ahead in stony silence. Shocked. Gaunt. Devastated.

Linus flashes a look in Caro's direction, as if to say *What now?* She doesn't miss a beat. "He'll come," she says. "He can't possibly resist."

She sounds certain. I disagree. Kit's words scorch, burn and blind me. He meant what he said.

"And her?" Linus says, without giving me a glance.

"Put her back where she belongs."

"But..."

"I told you, Linus, Kit will come."

"I'm not sure, Caro. You heard him. He's bold and he's

cocky. The second he sees Jones, the probate lawyer, we're sunk."

"Have faith, little brother."

Linus hunches his bony shoulders. He isn't persuaded. Sadly, neither am I.

# Chapter 58

Swollen and bruised, after Caro's sharp-nailed assault on my face, I'm ridiculously obedient. Physical blows, a new and strange phenomenon, are fast becoming a regular occurrence. Upsetting and frightening as these are, the mental pain and anguish is what does me in.

*Do as you please.*

Assault and torture; imprison and starve? Surely, Kit knows this is what they have in mind. Is this what Kit has in mind? What did I ever do to elicit such a cruel reaction? Did his years in captivity kink his mind? Is he as sick as them? Maybe he *did* kill Joshua Verdi.

I pass like a wraith down corridors blighted by human decay and absence of hope. I'm glad when we reach the secret door. At least in there nobody can hurt me.

The panel springs to the side and I enter, wordless, my dignity like a threadbare cloak. I will not beg. I will not plead. They cannot rob me of my sense of self. They will not remove my identity as daughter, sister and friend.

I will not let them.

Alone again, I trawl the contents of the remaining cardboard boxes. There are three. One contains old bed sheets, handy should I want to hang myself; another, old cushions that smell of cats, perfect for smothering; the last, a complete set of coarse earthenware pottery. No use to anyone. Except…

I drop a plate on the floor. Sturdy and truculent, it bounces, spins and glares up at me, flat and defiant. Enraged, I pick it up and hurl it against the wall. I do the same with five of its brothers and sisters. A soup tureen and teapot follow. Liberating and 'feel good', this is no form of anger management. My only desire is to arm myself with a sharp-edged weapon to ensure that I cause as much damage as possible to my captors. Stooping down, I select a fine specimen of pottery. It has a jagged edge and pointed tip. I slip it into the back pocket of my jeans.

Spent and light-headed from the sudden release of energy, I sit on the child's desk. Idly, flipping up a lid, I see a collection of exercise books. I take one out, flick through and do the same with others, throwing each on the floor, on top of the sea of broken china, a sanitised version of a dirty protest.

Kit's broad handwriting lifts off every page, misery scribed in the gaps and spaces. There is no mention of what happened to him, no code to break, no hidden message to interpret.

Burrowing to the bottom, my fingers touch something shiny. I fish out a folder bound with red ribbon. Expecting to find drawings or pieces of homemade art, I discover a sheaf of letters. I suspect they were stored, possibly hidden, after Kit threw himself on the mercy of the police after the road-rage incident.

Written to Ursula, they start with 'Cariad', Sweetheart, and they are signed, 'With all my love' from Gareth.

My mind plays back to the conversation in my car with Ursula about the 'love of her life'. *How dare you compare Gareth to Geoffrey.* My pulse jives.

I see that they are compiled in date order. The address at the top of the first reads 'Wisteria House Hotel.' Perhaps Gareth stayed as a guest. Perhaps they spent dirty weekends together there.

I begin with the earliest, when the affair was in full swing; love was blind and lust high on the agenda. There are many references to '*I can't stop thinking about you,*' and '*I can't wait to touch you/smell your exotic perfume, feel you next to me/ see you again*'. Strange reading a stranger's endearments, I read on. Gareth, it seems from his response, received letters from Ursula along similar lines, expressing mutual feelings. Like a voyeur, entranced and fascinated, I drift through the lot, scene by scene.

Gareth has a silken tongue and fine turn of phrase. He knows how to woo and, laced between passionate overtures, he promises Ursula all sorts, mainly weekends away, where he can 'spoil her', and do all sorts of things to her in stolen moments in stolen places. There is no mention of a ditched wife and, consequently, no doubt or guilt. Whether the same can be said of Ursula, I have no idea. Somehow, I don't think so. The only sign of discord and second thoughts appear around two years later. I continue, rapt.

'*Cariad,*

*You know how much I love you, but are you sure the child you carry is mine? I won't be angry if you tell me that it isn't so. I can't expect you to forego relations with Geoffrey, no more* than I can with Menna. I wish, with all my heart, the child was ours. As we've both discussed many a time, neither of us wants to smash up our marriages. Too many people would suffer as a result. It's enough that our great love remains secret.'

Feverishly, I turn to the next letter: 'I'm overjoyed and so sorry to doubt you. I so wish I could tell Kit that he is to have a little brother...'

The letter tumbles from my hands. Gareth was Kit's father, Menna, his mother and Joshua his half-brother. To be certain I'm not delirious, I check the address on the last letter: Wisteria House Hotel. Gareth wasn't a guest. Gareth Trueblood owned the place.

# Chapter 59

It takes me a while to recover and assemble my thoughts. Linus and Caro must know about their mother's extra-marital activities. *Looking for those bloody letters, I daresay.* Caro's cruel words course through my mind. That's why Caro wants to punish her. Linus is different. He has a closer relationship. Whatever his mother did and whoever she slept with, he forgave that a long time ago. He also viewed Joshua as her flesh and blood and, by default, his own.

Returning to the rest of the correspondence, an idyllic era begins when father and child share illicit time together. Sometimes it's clear that these are family occasions when Verdis and Truebloods meet legitimately for social occasions. My heart goes out to poor Geoffrey Verdi, cuckolded husband, and Menna, betrayed wife. Kit's dad also betrayed Geoffrey, the good friend who promised to provide a home for his son, should the very worst happen.

To be charitable, Gareth appears to be a good and caring father. In one letter he is anxious about Joshua's poor health following a serious viral infection, evidence that he loves Joshua as much as he loves Kit.

But things turn sour around four years after Joshua's birth, although Gareth Trueblood's feelings for his son, it seems, remain undiminished. From the tone, he is definitely a man trying to extricate himself from a close relationship that no longer works for him. Like father, like son, I rail to the walls. Full of shit, Gareth comes up with cheap, clunky lines straight out of the dumper's handbook: *'You will forever be precious…'* *'Our son will always maintain a strong bond between us…'* *'When I look on him, I remember you, but…' 'I will always care for you, but…'* Incredible to think that three little letters can inflict maximum damage. I bet Kit was *butting* his way out of my life long before I knew it.

Sliding off the desk, I flip open the other lid, and remove the textbooks to see if there are extra nuggets of information hidden within. A sheet of lined paper drops out of one, the ramblings of a small boy enthusing about a camping trip to the woods with Linus and Kit during half-term week. With a start, I realise that it's a letter written to Caro from Joshua. He signs it with kisses, obviously fond of his half-sister. I think about that. Was Caro once a nice person, someone for whom it was possible to feel affection? Was she ever a girl with conventional hopes and ambitions? My brain blots out the way she spoke to Kit in front of me. It's too unnatural.

I'm about to chuck everything back when I notice something odd. The interior space contained within each side of the desk is different. The one I sat on is around a couple of inches shorter in length along the back panel. Both would need to be empty to spot it, but there is definitely a discrepancy.

I put my hand inside and run my fingers along as if I'm blind and reading braille. On the left, there is a slight depression. I push and fiddle and a spring opens so that I can pull out the panel as an entire unit. Contained inside, a sheaf of papers bound together, like a report, and a separate single sheet, weighty and authoritative, brimming with seriousness and officialdom. I remove both.

Nervously, I view the document first and my breath hitches for, in my hands, I hold Joshua Verdi's death certificate. Divided into columns, there are obvious details like his name, age and sex. He is referred to as son of Geoffrey and Ursula Verdi, implying that Ursula never revealed that Gareth Trueblood fathered her child. Under the column headed 'Cause of Death', the finding of an inquest is noted, the verdict 'Misadventure'. I murmur it aloud. It feels out of kilter and inadequate, as if Joshua were off on an adventure and some mundane event cropped up to make him miss it.

I have no idea whether the certificate and its contents counts as ammunition, but sense its grave importance.

Picking up the report, I turn to the first page and letter from a coroner. It states that there is to be a post mortem. A second letter, a copy, is written from Ursula Verdi, in which she protests in the strongest terms that no post mortem should be carried out on her son. The third, from the coroner, a Mr Kenneth Davis, respectfully points out that, due to the circumstances surrounding Joshua's death, he has no option but to recommend a post mortem and that next of kin must comply.

Next, a letter to Dr Philip Swift and results of the post

mortem examination, a long medical treatise, peppered with medical terms that, initially, I fail to comprehend. Reading it through a second time, I pick up that Joshua's heart was three times the normal size, this due to the fact that it was forced to pump harder than average because of poor blood flow from a valve. Instead of the blood flowing in, it flowed back, or, at least, as I have so little knowledge, that's how I understand it. Scanning the text, the earlier viral infection Joshua suffered is mentioned but this is not as significant as the *congenital defect he carried from birth*. My mouth drops open at the implication. Joshua's lifespan was already limited. My pulse quickens at the memory of my conversation with Roy. The children went camping on the night Joshua died. Not a strong lad, exposure to the elements would affect him more swiftly and dangerously than most boys his age. Kit had nothing to do with his death.

Another more worrying thought erupts, as if from nowhere.

I stare blindly at the door. I have verbal, written and physical ammunition. If I fling it at them, catapult raw truth into their eyes, will it protect me?

Or will it simply make them mad and hasten my death?

# Chapter 60

Anger surged through Kit's veins like a river breaking free, overwhelming and smashing everything and everyone in its wake. *I'm coming for you, you bastards.* He prayed he'd fooled Linus and wrong-footed Caro enough to buy Roz time. Caro would bank on his return, but it was Linus, physically stronger, who Kit needed to harbour doubts about. It was the only element of surprise he'd have on someone he still feared.

Poor Roz. He'd so wanted to reassure her, to tell her he was on his way and that things were going to be all right. To maintain the bluff, he'd dug his lengthened nails into the soft palms of his hands until they'd bled.

He broke stride, his soul lurching at what he'd done to her. He, of all people, knew what it was to endure without hope. Isolated and with no promise of rescue, she'd be out of her mind with fear. He had no need to guess where she was held. He knew. His place. His prison.

Despite the beating and dull ache deep in his groin, he moved quickly. The voice in his head that accompanied his journey to Vixenhead did not belong to his aunt, Swain or Linus.

Remembered instances of cruelty, and there were many, did not take precedence in his mind. He had only one silken voice, only one act that was committed against him again and again.

He gasped in horror. Shame and humiliation, he had *enjoyed* it. *Had,* he reminded himself, confounded. What she'd done to him was no act of kindness and it wasn't sex. It was control, manipulation and gross exploitation. Yet, when Caro spoke, he found himself reduced to a young adolescent, tongue-tied, confused, yearning for a kiss goodnight, someone to put her hand in his, to be affectionate, to...

Furiously banishing the memory, he strode on, heels crushing weeds, brambles and earth, vanquishing them in the same way he expected to conquer those who had subjugated him.

Wind from the east picked up and the sky grew leaden with rain and more rain, darkening the sky, turning what should be day to night. Gave him an edge. His biggest asset was his intimate knowledge of the house. There were other places to hide – he'd used them all – other corridors and exits and entrances. If he could get to Roz, spring her from the priest hole before Caro and Linus noticed, then he stood a chance of making sure she was safe before the police got there.

By now, he reckoned they'd be swarming all over the boat. He wondered how long before Raoul confessed and pointed the cops in the direction of Vixenhead. Or would his loyalty to Linus and desire to protect his lover render Raoul ignorant and stupid?

If so, Kit thought with cunning, he'd have the opportunity of a lifetime to exact revenge. Question was: would he have the balls to take it?

# Chapter 61

Shaking with cold, I stuff the letters, report, with all its contents, and Joshua's death certificate into the old school satchel I unearthed from one of the cardboard boxes. I climb into the old sleeping bag. Thin and dirty, it stinks of feet and stale sweat and makes no difference to the chill seeping through the walls and oozing all around me like poison gas. There is no sound other than the wind getting up and shouting through the trees.

Obliterated, I sleep. When I wake dribble slides out of the corner of my mouth, my lips crusted and cracked. I am thirsty and my bones ache. My watch stopped at 1.23 p.m.

Standing, I flex my muscles, wave my arms around like windmills, jump up and down a couple of times, in a hopeless attempt to kick-start my circulation. I feel no hunger, no appetite. I feel sick and a little dizzy. In virtual darkness, I flick the light switch, but there is no light. Linus, I imagine, cut off the power, the sick, manipulative tosser.

Walking up and down, I try to think, but my thoughts are disjointed, flyaway and brittle. Vixenhead gave up her secrets to me. Should empower. Doesn't.

A clicking sound, like fingernails drumming against metal, taps a spooky tune.

Fearing a hoax, I pause, try to make it out, and turn in the direction of the noise, to where a huddled figure stands on the other side of the bars of the window. It beckons. My heart performs cartwheels and I open my mouth. "Don't speak," it hisses, "Move closer."

At the sound of the voice I know so well I want to scream aloud and dance. Survival dictates I obey. Wide-eyed and joyful, I look into Kit Trueblood's tired and weary eyes. A stupid smile pasted on my lips, I push my fingers through the bars and touch his stubbly cheek to make sure I'm not dreaming.

"Are you hurt?" His face is pinched with anxiety. I can't help it but I want to throw my arms around him and hug him so tight he cries out in protest. *See, I'm brave and dutiful and all the things you need me to be.* I shake the thought away.

"Good," he says. Urgent. Wise. "Now listen carefully..."

"Wait," I say. "Did you do it?"

"What?"

"Did you kill Joshua?"

Pain carves deep creases in the corners of his eyes. His mouth droops and his lips tremble. "I loved Joshua. He was my only friend."

I read truth in his eyes. Thank God.

"You believe me?" he gasps.

"I do."

"Oh Roz, I'm so sorry. Thank Christ you're in one piece. Will you ever forgive me for leaving?"

350

I want to tell him *yes,* but I can't because I know that whatever happens, he is never coming back. Not to me.

"I *will* get you out of here, Roz. I promise." He speaks more than words; more than intention; his is a solemn vow. Maybe he needs absolution. Maybe he seeks redemption. What do I know? I itch to get the hell out. The time for talk comes later.

Another thought flashes and, although Kit tells me to stay silent, I can't help but whisper, "The police are coming, aren't they?"

Light outside is shadowed with foreboding. There is no moon or sun. I cannot see what travels across Kit's face and yet I know instinctively that he doesn't want them here. If he ever summoned them, he's praying for a delay. At once I recognise why and it scares me.

"Kit, listen to me. You don't have to..."

"There's no time. Be ready."

And then he vanishes.

I stand open-mouthed. Seconds pass. Nervously, I pee in the bucket and get my act together.

*

Confused that he still cared, destroyed that she could not forgive, guilty that she saw right through him, Kit slunk away and made for what was known as the garden room. Tacked on, a late addition, it was where Ursula kept produce from the garden and where she arranged flowers, lavish blooms that exuded wealth and social standing, for parties held at

Vixenhead. The door would be locked but it was old and he had an idea that did not require busting it down and making a racket.

Looking up, Kit noticed lights on upstairs; the downstairs enshrouded in darkness. He pictured Caro waiting, Linus worrying, Ursula out of it.

Slipping Raoul's wallet out of the rucksack, he extracted the credit card and slid it between the doorframe and lock, wiggling it so that the card sat above the point where the lock entered the frame. Angling down, the card at right angles to the door, he slowly pulled towards him with one hand and turned the handle with the other, the effect to push the bolt away from the frame. The first time, it didn't catch. After another go, the door creaked slowly open.

Stepping inside, he sniffed the cold, musty dead-flower air and scooted across to the next door that would lead him into the main body of the house. Caro and Linus could not guard every entrance. He'd put money on them watching the main thoroughfare to the fake panelling and priest hole.

Tilting on the balls of his feet, he sneaked from room to room, edging down corridors, peering around corners, passing alcoves and cubbyholes, nooks and staircases until, ahead, the dead end and entrance to Roz's prison. Once the panel slid back, a short flight of steps to the reinforced door. This was the choke point, where Kit's journey grew most perilous. If Linus or Caro beat him to it before he got Roz out of there, he and Roz would be entombed together for the rest of their days. Tremors seized his body at the prospect. He couldn't go back. *Couldn't*.

On heavy legs, he moved forward. Slowly. Silently. Nimble. Doing okay. Doing all right. So quiet, he could hear his own heart pumping, his own breath seeping from between dry lips. The house was peaceful too. Calm. Obedient. Deceitful.

Without warning, noise snapped down through floorboards and ceilings, penetrated plaster and paint, and chomped at both his ears. Half paralysed with fear, he stood as if his feet were nailed to the floor, Frank Sinatra's jaunty voice singing, at top volume, 'Mack the Knife'.

Had to escape. Had to run. Sweat exploded across his brow, trickled down his torso, gathered between the cheeks of his buttocks. Horrified, in confusion, he shot out his arm, smacked the flat of his hand on the vixen's nose to release the catch. Ahead, smothering ebony. Ahead, pitch-black. He didn't care. It held no terrors. Anything to escape a sound that held more significance to him than anyone would ever know. Willingly, he stepped over the threshold, embracing the darkness, allowing claustrophobia to tramp all over him. Pressing another catch, he closed the panel. The sound shut off and Kit took a couple of deep breaths. Steady.

Feeling his way, he counted thirteen steps. The wall of metal with its heavy bolts lay straight in front. The lock could prove to be a problem. Would Ursula still have the key or, over the years, had it been lost or abandoned?

He released the bolts, felt the door give. No extra lock, thank fuck. Opened it. Blind light bled through the bars and weakly illuminated a room that had been his home for too many years. In a flash, he remembered crying himself to sleep, doing his homework at a desk too small and fearing that if he didn't get his sums right, he would be punished. He recalled long summer days when he yearned to be outside to escape the stifling heat, winter days when he froze. So many memories and none of them good.

Everything remained the same apart from the chaos that littered the floor. Books. Upturned empty cardboard boxes. Broken plates. Rubbish. And in the midst of it, dishevelled, big-eyed, with her mad, brightly coloured hair, Roz stood before him. She threw her arms wide and smiled.

And so did he.

# Chapter 62

Overwhelming joy lifts me off my feet. I am a castaway on a desert island when the pilot flying the helicopter in the hot sky above spots my fragile figure, descends, and lands in the sand dunes. I am a Lottery winner of squillions. I pass a degree in a proper subject with first-class honours. I produce not one but four children and they are all well adjusted and have no issues with drink or drugs. And Tom or Kit is here and what does it damn well matter what he is called? I want to run to him, hold him and squeeze the frigging life out of him.

But Kit's arms, once wide, drop to his sides. His smile flees. His focus is off as though teleported back to another time. A man no longer stands in front of me, but a boy, mute and zombified. I presume it's the shock of the place and not surprise, or dismay at seeing me, and do the only thing I best know how, the right and most instinctive thing; I open my arms wider still and he comes. He bloody comes towards me, takes me in his arms, presses my cheek to his chest, his hand in my hair, and hugs me tight until I think my bones will break. Sweet Jesus.

"Roz," he says, his voice cracking. "I'm so pleased to see you and I'm so sorry I lied to you. I'm sorry. I'm so sorry."

"It's okay," I gasp, burrowing my face into his broad chest, inhaling man and sweat and everything that turns me on. How many times have we stood like this? Body against body. Skin against skin. "None of it matters. I'm safe now."

He pulls away, looks into my eyes. Sober. "Not until I get you out of here."

'You' not 'Us' and with one singular word, I know how it will roll. It doesn't devastate because I sensed it already, but it crushes and makes me sad.

"What's that?" he says, eyeing the school satchel, its leather strap slung over my shoulder.

"A memento." I do not tell him what's inside. Wrong time. Wrong place. Maybe it belonged to Caro or Linus and stirs up unwelcome memories in Kit. At any rate, he doesn't question it, probably puts it down to my ditzy personality.

He shoots me an odd look and takes me by the hand. "Come on. Stay close behind."

We travel in tandem up the steps and huddle beside the panel and entrance to God knows what.

"Ready?" he says.

I gulp and mouth 'Yes'. I'm ready to get out of here, braced to breathe fresh air, set to be liberated. I'm not prepared for what might obstruct my path to freedom. Crazy to think that Caro and Linus will let us stroll out easy peasy.

The panel slides back, open sesame, and we dart into the corridor like a couple of thieves fleeing a heist. Kit puts a finger to his lips to ensure my silence. I agree with my eyes.

He presses the mechanism again. I hear a whirr and hum I didn't notice before. It sounds terribly loud in the charged silence. The panel closes so that, hopefully, nobody will detect anything amiss.

Fixing on his broad back, I follow him down the corridor. Instead of going upstairs, Kit opens a door to the left that I missed first, or is it second, time around? I cannot remember. Time travels in no chronological order in here. We move down another corridor past a door with a fire escape sign above. I fully expect to go through it. He shakes his head. "Steps removed. Sheer drop the other side." I nod dumbly. The place is a maze of falsehoods, traps and tricks. I could so easily take a fast route to eternity. Hitching a nervous glance over my shoulder, I see and hear nothing.

Surefooted and certain, Kit moves one way and then another. Too many doors to count. My bearings adrift, I doggedly follow. Terror, a naked white-hot flame, scorches the back of my legs.

At any second, I think our path will be crossed and we will be stopped. Mixed up, slightly unhinged, I have no idea where we will fetch up and don't care as long as we get the hell out.

"Here," Kit says, pushing open a door to a dilapidated room, an old larder, by the looks of it, like one of those pantries you see in grand country houses. Rectangular-shaped windows, high up in the walls, with fine mesh spun across the panes to provide a last resting place for bluebottles and wasps. Made of stone, work surfaces jut out on two sides. There's a shelf lined with jars of homemade preserves and lots of old vases and jugs. All are covered in cobwebs and spider poo. The smell inside the room is appalling, a combination of dead flowers and the pong you get off rotting potatoes. Fear also has its own unique aroma and it's strong. I smell it now. Kit halts and, buckling up, I bash straight into him.

Peeping out from behind, I spy Ursula made up like a marionette, standing with her back to a big, deep sink. Round blobs of rouge on her cheeks. Grim blue eye shadow and dirty great black lines above the natural contours of her sparse eyebrows. She wears a pink quilted housecoat that clashes magnificently with her bright-red painted lips. On her bare feet, fluffy mules. Her hands are encased in a pair of Marigolds, as if she is about to wade through a ton of washing up. Perhaps she has those jugs and vases in mind. I don't know what she thinks she is doing but, whatever it is, she scares the living crap out of Kit. Welded to the spot, he cannot take his eyes off her rubber gloves.

I step aside and walk forward purposefully. No way is this old woman preventing us from reaching safety.

"It's you," she says, bright-eyed and smiling. "I'm preparing the cleaning fluid. Be a darling and give me a hand."

Kit groans, half staggers, close to collapse. Sod this, I think, tugging his sleeve, barging ahead. A bony hand shoots out, grips my arm and spins me backwards.

Ursula's features contort, an angry clown. Screeching repeatedly in my face, she drags both of us towards the open jaws of the main house with more strength than I think is possible for a sagging bag of bones. She tries to push us through, and Kit, impossibly, fails to resist, as if she cast a spell on him.

Demented, spun out, I belt her as hard as I can with the flat of my palm. She lets go. Blood trickles from her mouth. Eyes shoot wide, but her focus is not on me, or Kit. It's over my shoulder, on the door behind, the exit. Her expression crumbles and whimpers. I turn to follow her gaze. Our only way out is barred.

Linus, and Caro in her lofty heels, stand side by side.

And Caro holds a gun in her red-gloved hand.

# Chapter 63

Ursula squeals. Linus shoots forward, catches hold of his mother's arm and, with soothing endearments, escorts her out.

"Move it," Caro says, indicating with the barrel of the gun that we step into the bowels of the house. Lost in whatever dark place he entered, Kit is suspended in another time. I read despair in his eyes. Petrified, I tug at his sleeve, gesturing that we return the way we came.

Close to losing it, he allows me to guide him, Linus, with his arm linked through Ursula's, leading the way, Caro bringing up the rear.

We do not return to the prison. Our destination is the great hall, where a log fire chugs out smoky heat from wet wood. All I can think of is my little rental in Cheltenham, my family and friends and the fact that I am here with Kit, against our will, and am unlikely to see those I love again.

Linus helps Ursula into a chair with horsehair sprouting from the seat like an old woman's chin. She looks up sweetly, their gaze a shared moment between mother and son.

"Linus," Caro barks. "For God's sake, wake up." Linus

springs apart. Ursula drops her gaze, sits quietly, head bowed, scrawny and submissive. I recall the vivid bruising on her thigh. By Caro's hand?

Linus advances on Kit and roughly frisks him. My pulse stutters. Kit does not protest at the personal invasion. Linus grins and with his long fingers pulls out a phone. Dropping it on the floor, he stamps on it and retreats back to his mother's side.

In a crisis I am known to laugh. This is not a crisis. It's a catastrophe. Detached, out of alignment, I'm struck by the absurdity of the situation. Our little gathering could be taken straight out of an Agatha Christie novel and the scene in which Hercule Poirot unmasks the murderer. With an ache in my heart, I think of Vick and a tear rolls down my cheek. Kit stirs, touches my hand. Back from the brink. I hope. Maybe.

A fag paper apart, I hear Kit's rapid breathing. I don't know of whom he is most afraid. It's difficult to tell. Caro, I think, and not because she has a weapon in her hand. Having never seen a firearm up close before, she certainly has the edge for me. Slim-line in design, it's sleek and black. There are markings on the side: Glock 36 Austria. I am transfixed and consumed by what it might do to a body. To me. How on earth Caro laid her hands on it, I have no idea because I think getting hold of firearms is difficult, unless you're a gangster like Swain. In a heartbeat the conundrum is solved: through Swain's underworld connections a weapon was sourced for Linus's sister.

She swings a high-back chair into the middle of the floor, close to the table with the Chinese vase I long to smash. Flexing my muscles, I feel the shard of pottery in my jeans pocket complain. "Sit" she says. My gut tightens. I don't want to move away from Kit. With him by my side, I feel a little better, which isn't saying much. "I said sit," Caro snarls. Kit touches my hand again, encouraging. I do as I'm told, cross the floor and park myself carefully so that I do not pierce my rear. I'm more likely to injure myself than Caro.

"You, Kit. Stay right there." Next, she addresses her brother by elevating a lofty eyebrow. Linus grimaces. I don't think he cares for being pushed around by his sister. Still, he complies and moves like a wraith to a fine big desk under the window. I realise that they have choreographed this scene to within an inch of its life. They know exactly how it will roll. It's preordained.

"I have papers for you to sign." Caro strips Kit naked with a single steel-plated look.

"I'm not signing anything."

I almost keel over at Kit's courage in standing up to his tormentor and now mine. It's engraved on his pale and terri-fied features. I have a sudden image of a small boy, weak and vulnerable. My throat closes at the thought of Kit then.

"If you want Ms Outlaw to live, you will."

She swivels the gun in my direction. The hole through which the bullet will pass seems impossibly large. Too stunned to gasp, my insides gag and sag. Will it hurt, I wonder madly? Because I have no doubt that Caro is capable of pulling the trigger and blowing holes in my body without hesitation or remorse. I turn my pleading eyes to Kit. I know what is being asked of him – to sign away his inheritance. I also know that when he does, the likelihood of us both getting out alive and sailing off into the sunset is remote. But I want him to at least give me a sporting chance.

"Look, can we stop the bullshit productions, please?" False swagger in his voice alarms me as much as the Glock pointing in my direction. *Don't do this. Don't give her any reason to hurt me. Don't.*

"I always said he was a rude boy," Ursula pipes up; currying favour, keen to be on what she presumes to be the winning side.

"Quiet, darling," Linus soothes.

"You're too good to the old bat," Caro snipes.

Ursula folds back in on herself with a whine. Bony hands claw at the quilted fabric of her housecoat. Linus glowers.

"I won't ask a second time, Kit." Caro speaks with deadly intonation.

I swallow and a knee judders. With my eyes, I beseech him. A man has never appeared more wracked with indecision, more torn between courage and cowardice. Will he call her bluff? Is he calculating the odds? Don't take too long, I want to scream, my nerves on fire.

I glance from one to the other. Caro's smug, indecent gaze is fixed on Kit. God alone knows what she is thinking. Suddenly, she snaps from her reverie, locks on me, and frowns. "Why are you wearing my satchel?"

I jolt with triumph. This is my moment. Hanging on my shoulder, I have in my possession the secrets of the past. It's in my power to dish up the dirt, stun and crush them into submission. But, staring down the barrel of the gun, I am aghast and speeechless.

And then she fires.

# Chapter 64

I hunch forward. My ears ring. Lumps of plaster and wood shower down from the ceiling, sending up clouds of noxious dust. Kit lunges. Linus blocks his path and pushes him away with an almighty shove that sends him spinning. We never had a better chance of turning the tables and now it's gone.

Flying to pieces, Ursula screams; hands clasped over her head, body rocking from side to side, drool spewing from her mouth.

"Sedate her," Caro growls, staring blackly at her mother, then her brother.

"But..."

"Do it."

Leaving the documents on the desk, Linus nods – curt and tight – and scurries out. Unappeased, Caro calls after him. "And make sure it's a big dose."

"I want Linus," Ursula wails. "I want Raoul."

"Raoul isn't here," Caro says, glittering with malice.

"Oh," Ursula says, plaintive. "I'll be good. I promise. Please. I'll be quiet," she sobs.

"You will."

Kit squares up to Caro a second time. "You twisted bitch."

She tosses her head with a lascivious smile and directs her gaze at me. "He loved me for it. Wanted it. Did he tell you?"

With a gun in her hand, Caro is invincible, yet her words and the barbed wire in which they are wrapped, do me in. Visibly, Kit shrinks, retreats, his vigour and daring all gone. I have a terrible image of Caro, the paedophile, and her long fingers all over him. Eliminating the monstrous picture in my head, I snap back to Caro, who is speaking to me.

"The satchel. Were you planning on keeping it as a keepsake to replace the kids you won't ever have?"

Something comes loose in my head. I don't see red. I see a vivid kaleidoscope of earthshattering colours, something akin to an LSD trip I never took. And I feel rage. Power. Spying on me, she used what she found to expose my private grief as well as my private life. "Inside are letters to Ursula," I announce. "They make for powerful reading." I think this will shame Caro. Not a chance. Her smile is one of cool and confidence. At the mention of her name, Ursula stirs.

"My letters? From Gareth? My love?" She clasps her hands together, shiny-eyed and dreamy. "I wondered where they'd got to."

"Gareth," Kit blurts out, astounded.

I feel so bad for him I want to hurt them all. And I will.

"Your father, stupid boy." Ursula glares. "Who do you think I meant?"

To me, she snarls, "You're a thief. They don't belong to you. Give them back."

In two bounds Kit hauls Ursula out of her seat by the

collar and shakes her in the same way a terrier dispatches a rat. I think she might snap a vertebra.

"Get off me." She struggles, drumming her small fists against his chest. "Help me. Help me," she squeals, eyes searching wildly, fixing on Caro, who stands by, stony. Enjoying the spectacle.

"Is that what the row was about?" Kit yells. He shakes Ursula so hard, loose skin on her neck wobbles. "Uncle Geoffrey found out, didn't he? You as good as killed him, you mental old woman."

"You killed my son," Ursula bit back, monstrous in her bearing.

"No, he didn't." I stand up, slip the satchel off my shoulder and hold it aloft. "Would you like the post mortem report, too? Joshua was sick. He had a pre-existing heart condition. Exposure finished him off. Kit had nothing to do with it. And you bloody knew it," I say, eyeing Ursula and then Caro.

"Ancient history."

I glance to the door, from where Linus enters with a syringe in his hand. One look at Kit and he crosses the room in two strides. For a vile moment I think he will plunge the tip straight into Kit's neck. Kit sees it too and loosens his grasp on Ursula and backs off.

"We've known it for years," Caro says.

"You knew?" Dumbfounded, Kit looks from Linus to Ursula to Caro, who remains serene, in charge, composed. "Is this true?"

"Every word." Caro says.

How the hell can these people be so cruel? How did they get to be this way?

"Not quite the whole story," Linus says malevolently to Kit. "If you hadn't started that fight, Joshua would still be here."

Kit's arms slap to his side and he backs away. Defeated. Beaten. Feeling similarly, I slump back down. *What fight? What didn't he tell me?*

"Oh, one other detail," Caro smiles nastily, "Joshua was your brother, Kit."

I practically short out at Caro's brutality. So does Linus, who looks to his mother. "Caro," he warns. "Not in front of mother."

"Why not? It's the truth."

Cowering and pale, Ursula tries to speak, to mount a defence, but nothing intelligible comes out of her mouth. In agitation, she trembles. I don't look at Kit. I can't bear to.

"For God's sake, Linus, give Ursula a shot."

He doesn't respond.

"Must I do it myself?" she asks, advancing.

"No," he snaps. He raises the syringe, fully loaded, squirts out a thin stream of liquid, expertly erasing air bubbles. Any moment now, and if he's not really careful, he will do his sister's bidding. Or will he?

"Kit, look at me," I say urgently. "That night, you were camping with Joshua and Linus."

"What of it?" Linus hovers. I don't look at him. My eyes are only for Kit.

"There was a fight, yes?"

"A scuffle," Kit pleads. "I never hurt him. I wouldn't."

"Okay, so why did Joshua go out into the cold?"

"What the hell are you saying?" Linus bursts out.

Kit frowns. My eyes flick to Linus and back to Kit. "Why would he walk into the darkness alone?"

His frown widens and then vanishes. Knowledge sparks in his eyes. He gets it, raises his hands to his head, clasping his skull in shock, as if he's just emerged from a car wreck.

"Don't listen," Caro snaps.

"Stop telling people what to do, Caro." Linus speaks quietly, through his teeth. There is no doubting the menace in his voice.

"She's playing us, Linus."

He looks at me straight, each word measured. "Then let her play."

I have Linus's full attention. Amped, I keep going. "A small lad, nine years of age, weak and vulnerable, Joshua was scared of the dark, like you, wasn't he, Kit?" Kit's features contract. A primal groan escapes him.

"He left because a person was there who was kind to him, made him feel good," I say, inferring something vile, "who took him by the hand, someone who *wanted* him..."

"Shut up," Caro spits, a nervy ring to her voice. The gun in her hand wavers. Malevolence oozes out of every pore in her body. Christ, I think she will shoot me this time.

"Caro?" Linus says sharply.

"She's making it up." Her eyes roll in injured indignation.

"Am I? Lies are more your speciality," I say.

The fire crackles in the grate, casting smoky shadows over the room. Joined in unholy union, both men say nothing, thinking back, calibrating and wondering. Perhaps this is not the first time Linus thinks about why Joshua, a frightened boy, willingly stumbled out into the cold night. Maybe he truly believed that Kit was responsible. Ursula, too, sits, a hand over her mouth, eyes still and focusing on the past, that familiar terrain where Ursula can retreat and be great again.

There is fear in Caro's eyes. Sensing danger, she attempts a laugh. It doesn't work, simply explodes in a flash and tumbles, smoking, to the floor. Everyone and everything stares at her. Even Vixenhead, the host of decades-long anger, deception and cruelty, bears down in judgement.

"What did you tell him, Caro?" I say. "Did you promise to take him back to his mummy, or did you do to him what you did to Kit?"

Called to account, this might alarm others, but Caro is a fighter. "Tell me," she fires back, raising her head and her game, fronting it out in the same manner she misdirected me in my own home in Cheltenham. "Why would I do such a terrible thing?"

"Because you were jealous. Because once you get your claws into someone, you can't let go. Because you're a walking perversion. And," I say breathlessly, "Because you want Vixenhead for yourself and screw anyone, including," I look in triumph to Linus, "your own brother. You have no intention of sharing it. You want it all for yourself. That's how you operate. Look at you now," I sneer, "bullying and controlling your own flesh and blood."

Bled of colour, Linus stares at Caro as if he doesn't know her. All the time they plotted and schemed, shared confidences and secrets, she never told him what really happened that night.

"Is this true, Caro?"

She breaks into an edgy smile. "Don't you see? I did it for us."

I do not know whether Linus Verdi cares for his sister, but I know he was fond of his little half-brother. It's there in his eyes when he talks to his mother, when he mentions Joshua.

"You led Joshua to his death?"

"He was never a true Verdi."

Ghostly pale, yellow in the fading light, Ursula slides from the chair and onto the floor. Out cold. Linus barely gives his mother a glance.

"And Vixenhead?"

"As much yours as mine. I swear it."

"Okay," he says. "All right." Shaky, he looks at the syringe as though he hasn't a clue how it got there. "Not needed," he says with a chuckle and smile that would sour a bright summer's day.

Caro lowers the gun. High drama over. Enforcement back on the agenda. "Get me those papers," she orders Linus. He hesitates, his expression briefly mutinous.

"Please," she says with a strip-light smile. Blinding. Manufactured.

Linus relaxes. "On it."

A little of me dies. I gave it everything and failed. I think I'm smart and I'm not. We are back to the beginning. Kit is so out of it, he looks stoned. He will sign those papers. Caro will kill him and then kill me. Maybe the other way around. Yes, I think this more likely because it would be a final torture for Kit.

The atmosphere in the room switches from dread to Gothic horror. The air shifts. Walls close in. Vixenhead snarling and baying, hungry for more blood.

All is in slow motion. Linus has his back to me. There is a dull 'oomph.' I think Caro shot him, but there is no snap and crack, like I expect. Caro tumbles. The gun spins away. Kit starts forward, snatches it up. Linus glances back over his shoulder, spots Kit, sees the weapon. His long body telescopes, folding in two, head down. Moving at speed, Linus rips open the door and tears outside, Kit after him.

I run to Caro. Kneel beside her. The cannula of a hypo-dermic sticks out of her neck. Driven into a vein, the plunger is all the way into the barrel, its contents, whatever they are, fully discharged.

Whether its shock or the effects from the drug, she is short of breath and when it comes, it's rapid, like a fish out of water. Maybe she has a weakness in her heart, after all. Suddenly, her limbs tremble, her body convulses. My jeans are flooded with warm liquid and I realise what it is. Caro wet herself. I pitch back on my heels, my hands outstretched, not knowing which part to grab and how to restrain a body that refuses to be contained.

My mind blurs. Never saw someone like this before. Outside my experience. Don't know what to look for. Don't know what to do.

Skin around her mouth tinges blue. Saliva foams and

gathers on her lips. Her eyes, once so blue, film, lids heavy and begging to close. She is dying, I realise, stunned.

Ursula stirs behind me. A draught blows right through from the open front door.

A gunshot rings out. Once. Twice.

*Kit shooting Linus.*

Pitching back on my heels, I leap to my feet. Leaving the dead and as-good-as-dead behind me, I take off after the living.

# Chapter 65

Kit clattered through the gates, shot across the gravel. Intent. Determined. Murderous.

*I will make him suffer.*

*I will kill him.*

*I will shatter his brain in the cool way he shattered my life.*

*Nothing else counted.*

Linus made for the four-by-four, parked at the farthest edge of the forecourt. Exactly what Kit would do in the same situation; grab the motor and run. Kit's one desire: to prevent that from happening.

A vehicle door wrenched open, sound of jangling keys, the heels of Linus's shoes skittering as he cursed, fumbled and dropped them. On a reflex, Kit fired, the recoil snapping, lifting his weapon hand, the gun emitting a loud metallic crack. He fired again. Cordite gilded the shadows, sucked away by a sudden current of chill air.

A wall of silence enveloped him. No moans of pain. No pleas for mercy. Gingerly, he edged forward, keen to see the damage done. In twilight, the air seemed less solid and yielding, the ground beneath his feet shifting. A figure moved and, in strides, Linus, coiled with fury, leapt out, crashing through the undergrowth, and headed east, in the direction that Kit least wanted to go.

Doggedly, he took to his heels, gave chase along a narrow trail, all bumps and bracken. He had no need of illumination. Could do it blindfold. Snapping and cracking, pummelling every twig and clump of earth, he ran for Roz, for Steph and Zoe, and most of all, for Joshua. He didn't know for whom or what Linus ran, but run he did. For a man who looked as if he toyed with death on a daily basis, Linus was impossibly fast, long-limbed and lithe. Kit pushed every muscle and sinew, yet he struggled to keep up.

Blood thundered through his veins as they headed through the meadow where ox-eye daisies once grew. Along a stone bridge and water, deep and dangerous, oozing below. Next, open ground and the hut Caro had commandeered, in which he'd been so often abused. Linus didn't simply choose this route by accident or as the best means to make good his escape. He deliberately led Kit there to taunt, crush and confuse; dark symmetry in his final 'Fuck you.'

Jaw grinding, rage propelling, Kit fired, the shot winging high and wide. Dispatching another, he found himself unable to shoot and run. Kicking off his back foot, he sprang forwards and accelerated past the tree where he'd hung out with Joshy, the rope long gone. In his mind, Kit saw bivouacs and make-shift dens, places he'd played hide and seek with his friend, hollows where he'd sheltered from the rain and, most of all, from *them*. Thundering through a clearing, he stopped. The atmosphere was different here. Contained. Eerie. The ground morphing into ghostly hues. Everywhere, ancient graves of deer and woodland creatures.

Linus was nowhere to be seen.

Flicking his eyes left and right, Kit realised exactly where he stood and sank to his knees, one hand clutching dirt, the other hanging on to the gun.

"You sad fuck," he hollered. "I'm coming for you. I'm going to kill you, Linus."

A silhouetted danced across his peripheral vision, followed by something hard and heavy powering through his head that blinded him with pain and sent him sprawling. Teeth biting down into his tongue, he tasted blood, earth and old rain. The only weapon he had was gone.

A shadow loomed over him. Something rotten and putrid filled his nostrils. He knew what it was: the smell of an empty, meaningless and lonely life, and it wasn't his.

Compression on his chest, hands on his throat, Kit gagged and choked and struggled. Sinewy and determined, Linus was stronger. His hate-filled eyes burrowed into him and Kit felt as if he were being eaten alive by army ants. This could not be his last image before he died, he thought, desperately casting his gaze above. A strange halo of light encircled the moon, red on the inside, blue on the outside, sparkling in the sky, bold and beautiful, and life-affirming.

Kit shot out an arm, fingers extended, reaching, scrabbling, nails digging for the Glock. Closing around the butt, lethal and deadly, and...

# Chapter 66

I run outside and spot the open door of Linus's four-by-four. There is nobody there. Beside the Volvo, the gravel is rucked up and scuffed, and I see where two pairs of feet kicked up the dust, spun away and scythed a passage through the woods. This is definitely the route they took.

Fear licks along my spine. I have no choice but to plunge after them.

Broken-down vegetation paves the way. I find myself in a meadow, unkempt and scrubby. Strange diaphanous shapes flutter and scatter. Sure they are spooks, I frantically increase pace. Careering down the track, the bleat of sheep echoes in my ears. Mocking.

I fly along a path that leads to a stone bridge. It's slimy to cross and I skid on moss and lichen, almost miss my footing. A malevolent gargoyle, cresting a pillar, leers at me. Terror spurts along my veins. Do I hear it laugh as I speed past, or is my imagination running loose and wild?

Wind picks up and fresh rain spits at the oily night. It's cold but I am hot.

Sure as hell, I wish I were fitter. Dizzy from exertion and

lack of proper food, extra flesh hangs from my limbs, reminding me that I carry too much timber. Dragged down, my feet are a couple of breezeblocks.

A building looms out of the faded light. It's small, wooden, with a pointy roof, a witch's hat. I feel like a passenger aboard the Vixenhead ghost train. Ghouls and 'wildings' and stuff that goes bump in the night everywhere. The ground, too, is alive with insects and creatures you never see in town: voles and moles, weasels and water rats. I don't think *Tales from the River Bank*. I think stories from *The Pan Book of Horror* I nicked and read from my Dad's eclectic collection.

Scrambling past, my foot catches. I hit a stump and yelp, land awkwardly, stumble. My ankle rolls and pain blooms, flares and shoots through my toenails.

Dropping down on my haunches, I clutch my leg. It throbs and hurts. Queasily, I check to see that nothing is broken. My boot is tight. If I take it off I will never get it back on. Tentatively, I stand up, put some weight on my poorly foot. The flesh feels swollen and dull.

Horribly alone, as naked and solitary as the moon shining down on me, I glance around. Rigid. On edge. Cracked. I swear there are bats and flying things that will flap into my face. Pulling the sleeve of my sweater down over my right hand, I slip the jagged shard from my pocket and hold it carefully. Just in case.

A couple of deep breaths and on I limp. Don't panic. Don't give in. Fear weaves a web around my mind. If Kit kills Linus, we are all condemned.

More trees. More bushes. Brambles lie in wait, ripping

at my clothes, tangling in my hair, their claws desperate to dig in and slow me down. The woods waken. Owls hoot. Badgers lumber. Vixens scream. Above it all, I think I hear Kit's voice. Can't be sure. The wind whines. Maybe it deceives me. Are there others here or only the ghosts of the Vixenhead dead?

The trail forks and widens. Wracked with indecision, I have no idea which one to take. Out of the dead light, yellow-green eyes emerge. I let out a startled cry. In fact, I might simply die of fright there and then on the spot. The eyes blink, glance away and a red, bushy tail slinks down a track, a fox loping through his kingdom. I follow.

More noise. Men. Fighting. Commotion.

The air around me narrows. The moon above is haloed with blue and red.

Dread grips my soul, as if I have entered a place of sanctuary, a church or monastery, where innocents were slaughtered.

Breaching a clearing, a shot rings out and, a few seconds later, another. I do the stupidest thing possible. I run towards the sound.

\*\*\*

... and Linus shifts his weight and pounces for the gun.

Freed, Kit rolls, tussling with Linus. Snatching. Grabbing. Unfettered. A shot rings out, Linus's hand upon the trigger. Snap and crack of a bullet hitting a tree.

In fear, he's struck out. In fear, he's cocked up. Dozens of memories of spectacular losses race through his mind. Can't let it happen again. *Can't.*

Rabid, Kit swings one leg over, levers himself on top of Linus and uses his body to press him into the dirt. Gripping Linus's wrist with his hands, fingers and nails gouging, he yanks, wrenches and twists.

Linus emits a yelp of pain. Another shot rings out, pointing away, ripping a hole in the night sky. Kit absorbs the recoil, digs deep with his fingers, excavating Linus's soul. He clings on, Linus hot and sweaty beneath him, body juddering, fingers slipping, until the man finally releases.

Like an eagle selecting lunch, Kit swoops, plucks the Glock and leaps back onto his feet.

"Get up." Kit wipes the back of his hand against his mouth. Just him and me and the sweet perfume of revenge, he thinks.

Nursing his wrist, Linus jacks himself up on one knee. He climbs to his feet, both arms up, palms flat in surrender.

"Turn around. Slowly."

Linus turns. Moonlight illuminates the planes of his cheeks. He looks more apparition than man.

"Phone. Take it out. Throw it towards me."

"For God's sake, who do you think I'll call?"

"Do it."

Linus obeys with a heavy sigh. Kit traps it with his foot. "You won. I lost. That's all there is to it."

"All?" Kit explodes. Blood flushes his features. He feels unsteady, irrational. Mental.

"Can we skip the histrionics?" Linus said.

"You arrogant fucker. You think you can talk to me as though you did nothing wrong."

"What are you going to do? Shoot me?" Linus says with a sneer. "You don't have the bottle."

"Don't I?" Kit feels the icy calmness of composure. He knows precisely what he will do. Linus sees it too. Kit reads it in his body language. A tall man, Linus curves his shoulders. Knees bent. Waiting. Knowing. Best of all, afraid. Really afraid. Kit savours every second, his finger tap dancing on the trigger for the sheer hell of it. Taking aim, he hears a crack behind him and Roz's voice crying out, "Don't shoot."

# Chapter 67

"Please, Kit, don't do it," I beg.

"He ruined me." Kit doesn't howl. He doesn't yell. He is serene and dispassionate and scary. He wants to kill Linus with all his being and I don't think I can stop him.

"If you shoot him dead, you're no better than him."

"Maybe, I'm not."

"That's not true."

"I fought him and Joshy got hurt."

"An accident," I say. I hope. I beg.

He makes a sound I don't recognise. It's filled with self-loathing and despair. "I deserted all the people I love."

"Because you had to. *To survive*. Please, Kit. You have a life. His is over." I jerk my chin in Linus's direction.

"Something we can agree on."

I have nothing but contempt for Linus. He is diminished and pathetic, a shadow in the gloom, but I know I must save him. From his strained, taut expression, he, too, understands that his fate lies in my hands. As much as I detest him, I creep closer. Kit won't shoot me. I know it.

"But this isn't the way," I say. "Caro is dead, Kit. Let the law take its course."

"The law that allowed Swain to stalk me and destroy my life? Give me one good reason not to finish him now?"

"Because you wanted my sister dead as much as me." Linus's venomous voice splits the night in two. I rattle with nerves. Does the man have a death wish?

"Shut up," I snap, edging forward. "Kit?" I murmur, desperate to reduce the tension. "You're a good man."

"Not a step closer," he barks.

"Okay," I say softly. "Okay." From far away, I hear the sound of sirens. Police. Thank God. Surely, Kit will come to his senses? I shift my weight from one foot to the other.

"Don't move a muscle," Kit growls. His gun arm shivers. Any second now...

"I'm hurt," I blurt out. "So I'm fine with standing still."

He doesn't alter his stance, doesn't drop his gaze. "Hurt?"

There is tenderness in his voice, concern. A breakthrough. "My ankle is a bitch. Rolled it."

Wind picks up, snatches at the trees. The woods recharges with negative energy. Suddenly, I want my mum.

Kit's laugh is dry. No fun. No shine. "I know your game. No point appealing to my better nature. I was separated from it a long time ago."

Affronted, I all but gasp. "I never play games." My voice is a knife. "Okay, shoot him. See if I care. You're absolutely right. Your life is ruined. Go ahead and destroy Stephanie's and Zoe's too. You think they'll come and visit you in prison because, sure as hell, I won't."

*

Her words stab him in the chest. Kit's whole life shoots before him like chapters in a novel. He flicks through the earmarked pages on Vixenhead and turns to the story of Steph and the little girl who'd called him 'Daddy'. And, yes, there are whole paragraphs on the strong, wild and sexy woman standing beside him now.

He's no believer, not a spiritual man, but something strange occurs. As he remembers the good, he finds himself bathed in love. The women in his life, not Caro with her perversions, has taught him fire and passion, blood and courage, decency and goodness, those qualities that Linus will never know in any number of lifetimes.

Awed, he stares through him. Revels in his weakness.

A final farewell, a last hurrah, Kit closes the book in his mind's eye, raises his arm high, points to the moon and fires.

*Click.*

And with a roar, Linus sprang.

***

Crashing in my ears, my body arcs. The broken shard is all that sits between Linus and Kit. In a second, I picture how Linus will strike down and trample me. It's written in his murderous eyes, yellow and sickly under the moonlight. So I aim right there. I punch off my bad foot, thrust forward and plunge deep. The tip penetrates. I'm astounded by how easy it goes in, like sticking a spoon in the yolk of a softly boiled egg. Stuff spurts, blood and indescribable matter. Some of it trickles warm down my wrist. Linus lets out an agonising scream, clutches at his face and staggers, howling and yelling, retreating and vanishing into the trees.

"Roz," Kit cries, catching hold of me. "Oh Roz, are you all right?"

I tremble all over. My teeth chatter. I think I might throw up. "Phone?" I say.

Kit nods, looks down, eyes searching the ground. "Here," he says, stooping down and handing me a mobile. It's mine. I don't question how it got there. I assume Linus dropped it. I scroll through contacts, press a number. After two rings it's answered.

"Roz?"

"For God's sake, Mike, can you get me? I'm in terrible trouble. Please. I've done... I've... " I break down and sob my heart out. Kit takes the phone and explains with more lucidity than I think him capable. Brisk. Brusque. He gives the address and ends the call.

I blubber. I cannot help myself. I have no idea where Linus is. He slunk away, a wounded beast, into the night. Will he return?

Kit slips his arm around me, not like he used to, and draws me close. Dissolving in relief, I should be happy with my head pressed against his shoulder, his hand stroking my hair. I should feel joy that he holds me so very tight. Undoubtedly, there is a physical connection, emotional too, but it isn't enough for either of us. He tells me I did good. He tells me that I'm the best. He declares I saved him. He doesn't tell me he loves me. He declares I'm special to him. Always will be and I believe him. Call it nerves, excess emotion, loss but I'm so unhappy I sob louder and longer, for I know it's finally over between us. Eventually, he walks me back through the grounds to where the light shines bright.

# Chapter 68

Vixenhead is febrile with human activity.

I count four police cars, two ambulances, a van and a fire engine. There is no fire, no smoke or burning. I look around for my car and notice that it's missing.

We cross the gravel like a couple of walking wounded, which I guess is true, and enter through the gates. Lights illuminate the path from hastily erected spotlights. Crime-scene tape flaps in the breeze. A white sheet covers something on the ground. An outline of a body. I left only one woman alive, Ursula. I look up, measure the massive drop from the nearest tower and shiver.

A uniformed female police officer bars our way. She takes one look, shouts to a colleague, "Get the Gov," and signals for backup. Magically, someone puts a blanket around my shoulders, Kit's too. Soft-limbed and warm, I flake with exhaustion.

"Are you Linus Verdi?" she asks Kit as two uniforms flank and stand behind us.

"Linus Verdi is heading towards Conwy. On foot," he adds. "I'm Kit Trueblood."

The female officer talks into her radio, issues instructions.
"Verdi is injured," I say.

"How so?"

I feel Kit's elbow in my ribs. "His eye. He hurt it," I blather.
She follows up with a fresh order for paramedics to be on
standby. The WPC's eyes sharpen. "And you are, Miss?"

I think twice before I reply. Will they do the equivalent of
clapping me in irons? Tempted to lie, I stutter an honest
answer. She notes it down. Duty done.

A plump male officer in uniform, with a shaved head and
thick neck, rolls towards us. He asks Kit to, "Step this way,
sir."

It's me you want, not him, I think. Kit squeezes my hand,
throws me a castaway smile and slowly leaves. Not long afterwards, I hear a car start up, Kit going for good. No way to
say goodbye, I cannot bear it.

Three police officers surround me. My natural default is
to jabber, crack a joke, break the ice. The ice is six feet deep
and impenetrable, the only jabber from the voice inside my
broken mind.

I stand lost and alone.

People in white suits and facemasks go in and come out.
One clasps a phone to an ear, his voice low and urgent. Others
carry bags and boxes. I think of Caro dead inside. I have no
need to ask what happened out here on hostile ground.
Ashamed to admit, I don't know if I think Ursula's violent
death a result, or not. In Vixenhead, there is no moral code.
Perhaps, I too, lack scruples.

When a tall man wearing a sober suit asks me to accompany him, I jump at the chance, for I never want to see or set foot in the place again.

I have a hell of a lot of explaining to do.

I am taken to a police station, where I'm offered sweetened tea. Allowed to use the lavatory on my arrival, I catch sight of myself in the mirror. With bruises and cuts and deep hollows under my eyes, I would frighten small children. My roots show through and my hair sticks up, whacky-badger style. I also stink of piss. Nice.

"Your ankle," someone reminds me, noticing my limp, and I am asked if I require a doctor. Automatically, I think of Philip Swift, Ursula's quack, and quickly decline.

The tall man in the sober suit is a Senior Investigating Officer called Finn. His surname, I mean. He rattles on about formal statements and courts and testifying and other things. I can't keep up. I'm tired and wired and quite possibly off my head.

"Do you understand, Rosamund?" He looks at me in the way he might view a rare, soon to be extinct, creature.

I nod furiously.

He switches on a recorder, explains who he is, who I am (in case I don't remember) and why I'm there.

"So, tell me what happened. From the beginning. Can you do that for me?"

I can and do. Once I get going, I cannot stop. It pours out of me. He doesn't shut me up even when I go off on one about being held captive, threatened, attacked. He asks me about Raoul and I answer. And, boy, do I shove it to the Verdis for all I'm worth. I don't care if two of them are dead. I tell Finn that Linus murdered his sister. I tell him what they did to Kit, how they tortured him, and why, except I don't really know the truth of it all. I mean, how do you begin to explain why grown-ups hurt a child, let alone one who already suffered, whose parents are dead? How do you start?

I reveal that Caro planned to kill Ursula and that Caro gave orders for Raoul to kill Kit. I speak of Joshua, of his death and the way it was portrayed – a far cry from the truth, except I still don't know whether a fight in which Joshua got caught up was a contributory factor. "There are papers to support it," I say, remembering the satchel I left in the great hall. Finn nods, as if he knows what I'm talking about, although I don't think it likely. I've only been there five minutes, or is it five hours? It feels like five days. Knackered, spent, I have no firm grasp on time. He indicates for me to continue. I talk and talk. Finn nods. He has the rare demeanour of someone in authority who is also highly intelligent.

"You mentioned a gun," he says.

"Caro's, yes."

"Where is it now?"

"In the woods. Somewhere."

"How did it get there? Who took it?"

I swallow. If I say Kit, it will get him into trouble. If I say Linus, I'm lying. "I close my eyes and cross my fingers. "It was so confused, it was tricky to see."

He frowns and I cave in. "Linus wanted it. Kit took it, to stop him killing us. By the time he got his hands on it there were no more bullets."

He goes over it again and, eventually, confirms that I will be spoken to at a future date as part of the ongoing investigation. He takes my contact details and tells me I'm free to leave. Strangely, it isn't a comforting thought. "My car," I say. "Where is it?"

"Oh, sorry, we're examining it for evidence."

I baulk inside. "I don't understand."

"Raoul Hernandez stole your vehicle. He is currently under arrest for the murder of a police officer."

I don't ask about the dead officer. Too overloaded with drama; too much horrific news to process. Ridiculously, the thought of having no wheels seems like a massive blow, which is stupid after all I went through. "Then how do I get home?" I'm close to tears.

Finn gives me a wonky look: part frown, part smile. "D.S. Shenton is here, waiting for you."

"For me?" I say, stupidly grateful.

"Yes."

He came. Goodness. A warm, fuzzy feeling smothers me like a cloak of fine down. Tears prick my eyes. *Again.* "Is Kit all right?" I ask.

"Being dealt with by other officers."

I don't want to be rude, but any five year-old could spot that this is not an answer to my question. "But he is all right?" I insist.

He smiles a nice smile. "Nothing for you to worry about."

"And Linus Verdi?" Fear sneaks along my spine.

"In hospital."

"Oh." I swallow.

He looks at me closely. Does he know? Did Linus say? "Lost the sight in one eye. Would you know anything about it?"

A hopeless liar, morally bankrupt, I meet his gaze.

"Self-defence?" he says.

I hang my head and whisper. "Yes."

"Jesus."

Nerves tripping, I give it to him straight. "He was going to kill Kit. What choice did I have?'

\*\*\*

The folder on the desk was as thick as Kit's arm. There were plenty of questions to answer about the woman Kit only knew as Mads. He gave his account truthfully to a police officer called Joseph, a giant of a man with jet-black hair, ebony skin and laughing eyes. Joseph had informed him that he was Mads' replacement.

"You believe Raoul was following Linus Verdi's orders?" Joseph spoke slowly, as if each word was carefully weighed and measured.

"Yes, but Linus was following Caro's." Kit told Joseph about the will and how Caro and Linus wanted to subvert it. "You can check it out with Wyndham Jones, the probate solicitor handling the estate." He went back to the beginning and told Joseph, an exemplary listener, about Joshua too. When he'd finished, Joseph thought for a while. Eventually, he said, "With regard to Hernandez, seems your account corroborates the information we already have."

"What will happen to him?"

"He'll be charged and receive a heavy prison sentence. In his blood, it seems," Joseph said, with a dry smile. "Already done time in France for the murder of a nightclub-owner."

Relieved he was going away for a long time, Raoul was a loose end, as far as Kit was concerned. Linus bothered him more.

"Now tell me about the gun," Joseph says. Focused. Fact-finding.

"I took it because I didn't want Linus grabbing it," Kit says. "I thought he'd kill Roz and me."

"Where is it?"

"There's a clearing in the woods. I can take you there." Less than twenty-four hours ago, Kit would have done anything to avoid the place where Joshua died. Now that it was over, the prospect didn't feel so bad. "Can I tell you something?"

A suspicious light entered Joseph's eyes; concerned, as if Kit was about to confess to something crucial he'd missed. "Go on."

"About Linus Verdi."

Joseph's solid jaw stiffened.

"I want it on record that, in self-defence, I injured him. I stabbed him in the eye."

"With what?"

"I don't remember exactly. It happened so fast. I snatched something sharp off the ground, a twig, maybe."

Joseph blinked rapidly. "You're prepared to sign a statement to that effect?"

"I am."

Joseph scraped back his chair, indicating that the meeting, for now, was over.

"It seems that you are to be a very wealthy man, Mr Trueblood."

"Only if I declare my true identity."

"Is that in doubt?" Joseph let out a deep chuckle.

"Depends."

"On what?"

"Stephanie Charteris. I need her to know that I'm not a ghost."

# Chapter 69

I sleep all the way back to Cheltenham in Mike Shenton's car. Can't tell you what it is other than it's black and comfortable, toasty warm inside, tidy, and goes like the clappers.

He nudges me awake when we pull into my street. I don't know what to say. 'Thank you' seems lame and doesn't do justice to his heroic action in rescuing me. "Would you like to come inside?" sends the wrong message, although what he might expect at ten-thirty in the morning (I know this from the clock on the dashboard) is, surely, debatable. I am dirty. I smell of sweat, earth and fear, and someone else's urine. We don't know each other and I am mentally pummelled. By life. By death. But I do like him.

Before I think of a suitable response, he gets out, strolls around to the front and opens the passenger door.

"Come on," he says. "Let's get you inside."

He suggests I go upstairs; take a shower and slip into bed, not a hint of innuendo. "I'll bring up a hot drink. Tea, okay?"

"Lovely." I drool at the prospect of hot water, shower gel and clean towels.

"Sugar?" he says.

"No, thanks. Oh, there's no milk," I remember with dismay.

"There's a shop down the road. I'll sort it."

And sort it he does. He is like a walking miracle and sunshine on a cloudy day.

Fluffy, clean and new, I should feel bizarre sitting up in bed with a strange man in my bedroom. As peculiar events go, this rates as nothing more than a blip on the 'things that are weird' spectrum.

"Mike," I begin, thinking I owe him an explanation, if only to satisfy the copper lurking inside him.

"We can talk later – only if you want to," he adds, kindness shining out of him. "Get some sleep. I won't be far away."


"Visitor for you," Mike announces.

I blink blearily. Kit, I think. "What time is it?"

"Gone two."

I sit up, straighten up; listen for Kit's prowling tread, senses alive. It isn't Kit. A herd of buffalo are on their way. A head peeps around the door.

"Roz?" Vick says.

"Vick," I say. "Shouldn't you be rehearsing, or something?"

"Tomorrow." She plumps down on my bed, a *pinch me, I must be dreaming* expression in her eyes.

And, daft mates that we are, we throw our arms around each other and cry like newborns.

\*\*\*

"Do you remember that bloke, what was he called...?"

"Greg," Vick chipped in with a giggle. "He would not leave me alone and..."

"I pretended to be your girlfriend."

The second we stopped blubbing, Vick asked if I wanted to talk about 'it'. Truth is, I don't. I want to hug this episode of my life to myself for as long as it takes me to think about and work out what it means for me. Vick, bless her, accepts, so we do what old friends do. We repeat tales of yore that we told each other a dozen times before. The room rocks with our laughter. Keen not to impose, Mike pops in and out with drinks and a steady stream of eats. Vick follows his every move with her eyes. After he closes the bedroom door for the second time, she says, "He's lovely. Great face."

"Um... yes." Her appreciation makes me feel oddly proprietorial.

"And a copper, too," she says, in almost reverent tones. Perhaps she thinks I need protecting. She could be right.

Vick twiddles an earring and grins.

"What?"

"Nothing," she says, hiking an eyebrow, meaning 'Everything'.

Later, when she hugs me goodbye, I get up and dress. The kitchen smells of basil and ripe, cooked tomatoes. Mike has his back to me. For a moment I think he is Kit.

He turns to me with a winsome smile. "Spaghetti, okay?"

"Lovely." I'm not hungry.

"Won't be ready for a while."

"Look, Mike," I say clumsily, "I'm grateful, but shouldn't you..."

"I don't want you to be grateful. God, Roz." He laughs good-naturedly, as though he can't believe I'm so dumb. I catch the sparkle in his eyes. He likes me and I like him. He isn't Kit, a voice squeaks inside my head.

I look around the kitchen; spot an open bottle of wine. "Drink?" I say.

"Why not?" Shenton grins.

I pour out two glasses, hand one to him. We chink and he looks into my eyes so deeply, I cannot help but feel his warmth.

"Are you flirting with me?"

"Do you want me to?" he says with a smile.

I don't know what to say because I don't know what I feel, so I give an awkward little smile back.

"Roz,' he says softly, "I understand how difficult this must be for you. Aside from everything you've been through, you can't just switch off from loving someone."

I meet his gaze. Words tumble from my mouth before I can gather them back.

"I loved a man called Tom Loxley, but Tom is gone." Putting it into words nearly does me in.

"And Kit?" His voice is mellow and caring. I don't think he is trying to trick me or avoid what I might say.

"I don't know him, Mike. I never will. He belongs to someone else."

"And you're cool with that?"

In truth, I cannot answer.

# Chapter 70

My mum calls, to ask how I am. I tell her I'm fine.

"You sound elated. Jittery. Is everything all right?"

"I'm glad to hear from you." Genuinely, I'm ecstatic. I thought I might never see or hear from her again.

"Patched things up?"

"Yes, and no."

"You're not making sense, Rosamund."

"We remain friends." I don't tell her the truth. A: she'd have heart failure and B: I wouldn't know how to encapsulate everything in a long-distance phone call.

"No such thing," she says in that spooky, witchy New Age way of hers. "You formed an intimate connection. It never dies. Me and your father...'

"Well, we are," I say stubbornly, not at all wishing to hear about her and my dad. With a terrible pang of dismay, I recognise that Kit and me are friends who are destined never to see each other again.

Predictably, when Reg calls, he doesn't mention Kit. Too busy extolling the advantages of life on the road. In Reg's world this translates to booze and fags, girls and more girls. I worry for that boy.

The police side of things rumbles on. Everything is slow and drawn out. Thank goodness I have Mike to talk me through the process and explain the arcane workings of the law.

And Kit...?

# Chapter 71

Kit sat in a hotel room, gazing out of the window and onto a garden lit with fairy lights and lanterns, and dared to dream about the future. First, he must deal with the past and the event from which he'd been running for most of his life. He reasoned that, if he did this and faced down his fears, only then could he move on.

*It started off all right. Uncle Geoff helped them make a bivouac, over which they spread canvas sheeting. They built a campfire. Everything was tinder-dry and the wood caught brilliantly, sending up spumes of flame into the night air. He tried hard not to show how thrilled he was, memories of the shed fire raw in his mind, not that Uncle Geoff said a word.*

*Uncle Geoff showed them how to make catkin tea that tasted disgusting. They cooked pieces of beef, which they pretended was buffalo. The best bit was the marshmallows, dark and crunchy on the outside and blisteringly soft and gooey on the inside. In his greed, Linus burnt his mouth and that pleased Kit enormously.*

*As the evening drew on, so did his anxiety. Uncle Geoff said that he would stay with them until ten o'clock, long after Joshua's* bedtime, tamp down the fire to make sure there were no stray flames and then tuck them each up in their specially insulated thermal sleeping bags. As each minute passed, Kit's fear increased. And Linus knew it. Kit read the feral gleam in his eyes.

When it was time for Uncle Geoff to leave, Joshua began to cry. "I don't like the dark," he snivelled.

"It's all right, Joshy," Uncle Geoff said, wrapping a meaty arm around him. "I've rigged up a lantern."

"But it doesn't work," Joshua wailed.

"I'll wind it up and by the time it goes out, you'll be fast asleep with the boys. And you've all got torches, haven't you?"

We grunted in unison. Joshua wasn't the only one who wanted to run back to the safety of his own room.

As soon as Uncle Geoff left, the name-calling started.

"Sticks and stones, Linus," Kit said in response, not really believing it. Words hurt way more. At least with a bruise it faded; even a deep cut like the wound to his temple eventually healed, not like verbal abuse that hung around in your head, slamming against your brain, for weeks, months and years afterwards. He hunkered down, shut his eyes tight, prayed that Linus would fall asleep. Fat chance.

"You little tyke," Linus scowled, sitting bolt upright. Next, he felt a crack, the business end of the torch flying over Joshua and smacking against his back. Joshua, the little shit, let out a girly giggle and Kit's hands itched to hit him, but he said nothing, sucked it up. Eventually, Linus would run out of steam.

But he didn't.

"Mummy says you'll have to pay for the shed you destroyed." Shame engulfed him. It was true. He didn't understand why *he'd done it, other than a compelling need to make something memorable and eye-catching happen. He'd loved the effect, the power of the flames, that there was a force bigger than his aunt and her wretched children. Staring into the blackened remains, the thrill swiftly turned to terror. It was the most stupid thing he'd done and there would be consequences.*

*"I know," he said flatly.*

*In the way a volcano rumbles before it finally erupts, he knew something bad was going down. It began with whisperings, grunts of laughter from Linus and more giggles from Joshua. He zoned out as best he could, but a loud rustling of nylon penetrated his hearing, followed by the sound of Joshua rolling over, the feel of the groundsheet shifting. A solid looming presence behind him, breathing, and the noise of a zip pulled down. The next he knew, a rush of heat that stretched from his neck down his back to his buttocks, swiftly followed by a horrible sensation of wetness that stunk.*

*Scrabbling out of his bag, he leapt up, caught Linus's features ghoulish and yellowing in the reduced lantern light. Half his face split into the widest grin imaginable as he tucked his cock back into his pants.*

*"You filthy little bastard," Kit cursed, launching himself, barrelling into Linus who, startled, trampled backwards over Joshua.*

*"Ow," Joshua screamed out.*

*Rage fuelling his muscles, he struck out again and again at Linus, raining blows, happily connecting with jaw, cheek, chest and stomach despite Linus being several inches taller. He didn't hold back. He couldn't. Not when his eyebrow tore, his bottom lip split and pain snatched at his ribs. Not when Joshy let out a howl of fear and pain as Linus trampled him once more, caught in the inevitable crossfire.*

*"Okay, okay," Linus said finally, breathless, flat on his back, palms up in submission, Kit standing over him, panting, every sinew straining to kick his head in. Only his father's ghostly voice and admonition to never hurt an opponent when down stopped him from following through and delivering a knock-out blow. Thwarted, he turned his attention to Joshua. "And you, you little prick, if you ever laugh at me again, I'll kill him first and then you. I'll fucking skin you."*

But he hadn't.

He'd forced Linus to give up his dry sleeping bag, pushing his smelly version into Linus's bloodied hands. Afterwards, he fell into a scratchy, shivering sleep, waking early when it was still dark. That's when he noticed Joshua was missing and woke Linus, who rolled over.

*"Probably gone crying back home to Mummy. He was pretty cut up after you bashed and threatened him."*

*"I did not bash him. You did with your big feet."*

*"Well, anyway, it took an age for him to drop off, thanks to you, dickhead."*

*Kit threw on a jacket and pressed his freezing feet into his boots and, switching on his torch, stumbled outside. A bitter wind blew through the trees, making them whine like banshees. Frost carpeted the forest and his breath smoked in the minus- zero temperature.*

*Joshua was frightened of the dark. Why would he go outside on his own? Because you threatened to kill him, a little voice of conscience whispered in his ear.*

*Stricken, he scoured the immediate perimeter, calling Joshua's name, his own voice echoing through the woods. With no answering cry, a shard of fear sliced through him. They would blame him. Linus would say that it was his fault and he had the bruises and cuts to prove it.*

*He speeded up, his cry more desperate. The woods went on for miles but, surely, Joshua, on his short legs, couldn't have gone far. Unless every kid's nightmare had come true and someone had taken him.*

*Wired for sound and movement, he searched for the next two hours, until his blistered feet could walk no further. And then, oh God....*

# Chapter 72

At Kit's request, we meet in Montpellier Gardens a few days after my return home. With sunshine drifting through the trees, we sit on a bench near the bandstand.

"How are you doing?" he asks.

"I'm okay. You?"

"Bit weird, but yeah."

"Have you seen Stephanie and Zoe?"

He shakes his head. My heart catches. Don't let this all be for nothing.

We talk about the police and who said what and what happens next. I don't tell Kit about owning up to hurting Linus, and Kit doesn't tell me what went on in the woods. The man is a no-go area for both of us. But I have a question that needs an answer.

"That night when you went camping with Joshua, the fight."

Kit takes my hand and reveals exactly what happened. Relief seeps out of me as I listen. I squeeze his hand when he finishes. Next, Kit tells me how much I mean to him. I jitter as he says that, without me, he could never find a way to escape his past. He talks of Joshua, his friend. He speaks of his parents. I learn of the life he had, the one before it went so dreadfully wrong. I also learn of the life he needs and for which he truly yearns.

I squeeze his hand once more. My eyes glisten. I think about our shared experience and the bond that is unbreakable between us. I definitely know I will always care for the man sitting next to me. Part of him loves and cares for me too – I recognise all this. But Kit belongs to Stephanie and Zoe. He always did. After all, they came first. And if I want him to be happy, I must set him free completely. We won't chat on the phone or meet for coffee or exchange birthday greetings. That part is over.

"It's a cliché," I say with a brave smile that nearly kills me. "But go to her. They need you and you need them."

"Thank you," he says, dropping a soft kiss on my cheek, the last I'll ever receive from him. It feels every bit a goodbye, a farewell. No adieu about it.

"Oh, and another thing," I say.

"Yeah?"

"There is nothing to forgive."

We part under warm sunshine. I walk one way, he another. Every step is bittersweet and takes me further away and closer to starting another chapter of my life.

At the entrance of the park, Mike is waiting. He slips an arm around my shoulder and pulls me close. I rest my head on his shoulder and take his hand. Together, we walk down the promenade and through town. I feel surprising lightness in my heart.

*In the end*

They meet on the common at Whitcliffe. April sunshine drills holes in the ground around him. He arrived over an hour ago to be sure that he wouldn't accidentally miss her. He feels like a man at the altar, worried that his bride will stand him up.

If she shows, he is frightened of what she will say. Terrified she will reject him. Joseph already broke the news and assured him that things would be fine. Kit isn't certain. He thinks Steph will view him like a ghost, or one of those men who return from fighting, damaged, changed and difficult to live with. He has no idea what the future holds or if they will share it together. He has no plan B.

He waits, as arranged, by the Toposcope. On a clear day you can see the River Teme and views of Ludlow town. She is late and he anxiously runs his fingers through his hair, straightens his jeans, checks for marks or grass stains.

And then she is there. Alone. Majestic. She holds her head high, walks toward him. Beaming. Alive. She looks more beautiful than ever. He can hardly bear it. Does she love him as much as he loves her? Or is she acting out of pity?

"I knew you were alive. I never doubted it," she says in that wonderful smoky voice he knows so well. Throwing her arms around him, she whispers, "I missed you so much."

He clings to her and his heart leaps. "Do you forgive me?"

She draws away, puzzled. "For what?"

"For lying and leaving you, Steph."

"You came back," she says, her big eyes shiny with tears. "That's all I care about."

For a moment, he thinks of Roz. He hopes she finds someone to love her too, and then he kisses the woman he loves most in all the world and promises that he will never let her go.

# Acknowledgements

This story is special to me in so many ways, not least because of several people involved in its publication. As ever, eternal thanks go to my agent, Broo Doherty. It was a truly magic moment when I first pitched the idea to you over a drink at Crimefest! However, as much as one's agent might enthuse, it takes a brave publisher to bring a book to fruition. For this, I'm enormously grateful to Charlotte Ledger at HarperImpulse for understanding what I wanted to achieve and for making the story so much better. I'm also indebted to Jo Godfrey Wood for her spectacular copyediting and for saving my blushes.

Paul Britton's 'The Jigsaw Man' was invaluable for information about children who kill. Finally, and most importantly, I couldn't have written the action scenes on the boat without John Goom's nautical knowledge. An experienced sailor, his enthusiasm gave me far better ideas than those I could have created on my own. It was also poignant for both of us because John is the father of our five children, and why this novel is dedicated to him.

Printed by RR Donnelley at Glasgow, UK